Jason Willow

Gareth Mottram

The Red Button Press

Hertfordshire
United Kingdom

i

The Red Button Press

Elsenham, Bishops Stortford, Hertfordshire, CM22 6EN

Copyright © Gareth C. Mottram 2009

The moral rights of the author have been asserted

First published 2007 (ISBN 978-0-9557471-0-6)
Second Edition (revised) published October 2009

British Library Cataloguing in Publication Data available

ISBN 978-0-9557471-1-3

Printed and bound by thinkink, Ipswich, England

Cover Artwork by Peter Callow

www.jasonwillow.com

Dedications

To Mum who gives everything and asks for nothing at all.

To my wife, Corrina, whose love and support still astounds me.

To James and Francesca, my raison d'être during dark times and my joy always.

To Charlotte, who reminds us all that life is sooo exciting.

And now to baby Dylan, who just does smiling.

Massive Thanks

To Corrina for believing and endless editing

To Nell for ploughing bravely through the first draft

To Pete for picturing perfectly

Prologue

'Get down!' Dad yelled and hurled Jason and Miranda to the floor.

Jason tucked into a roll and flowed to his knees pressing tight against a concrete pillar. Mum and Dad darted behind parked cars as the blacked-out van squealed to a halt and three armed men burst out.

Miranda leapt on Jason from her prone position and flattened him to the floor. 'Keep down, you idiot!'

Gunfire exploded through the multi-storey car park as bullets ripped concrete from the columns all around them. Jason slapped his sister's arm away and jerked his head up.

Dad crouched behind the next pillar, with a pistol somehow in his hand. One of the gunmen suddenly appeared, leaping across the bonnet of a 4x4, his black overcoat billowing out behind him like gigantic bat wings.

Dad shot his heart out with a single bullet. As the dead-eyed head smacked onto the floor, Dad surged to his feet, gun blazing. He thrust his empty hand out in front of him and stepped out of cover.

Miranda caught Jason in a headlock and pulled him flat again. 'Stay down, they're agents. There's nothing you can do.'

Jason fought against her expert hold. 'Dad needs us - it's three against one…'

Suddenly the shooting stopped. Silence slammed down around them.

'Not any more,' Miranda whispered and eased her grip.

Jason broke free and scrambled to his knees. Dad stood just a couple of metres away, scanning the cars with his gun still out.

'Where's Mum?' Jason asked.

'I'm so sorry…' Dad said, his voice quiet. He didn't look at them. 'She's gone.'

What was he talking about? Jason pulled himself to his feet – numbing panic pulsing into his head. Miranda stumbled passed him like a zombie and lurched to a halt next to Dad. She stared at the floor on the other side of a lurid yellow car then silently sank to her knees.

Jason was next to her a second later. Their mother lay there, unmoving, a single dark patch staining the cream blouse she had bought especially for the theatre tonight.

This couldn't be happening – not after they had survived for so long.

He forced himself closer and a hint of the perfume that had always been part of her reached him. He stretched out his shaking hand - her cheeks were still warm and soft. She couldn't be dead.

Police sirens faded in from somewhere. Jason looked up. A few stricken faces were staring at them – normal people with normal lives. One man held his mobile phone inches away from his mouth - frozen.

Dad dropped to one knee beside Jason and cupped Mum's cheek in one hand. He was absolutely silent but the tendons down his neck bulged almost out of his skin.

Jason's eyes began to burn from the inside and the car park blurred down to Miranda's silent tears dropping onto the concrete. Jason felt her slip one arm around him.

'We have to leave,' Dad said, his voice cracking. 'Kiss your mother – you need to say goodbye properly.'

Miranda hesitated for only a second then fell forward, clinging on to Mum's limp body. Jason couldn't move. Warm blood soaked into his jeans…

***

Jason's mother had been murdered almost a year ago now. The following day, he, Dad and Miranda had let their faces be caught on CCTV running for the Eurostar to Brussels. They had switched back through France, driving at night on tiny roads, and lost themselves working the farms and vineyards all around rural Spain.

Now they were back in Britain, flown in under the radar by private plane and en route for yet another change of life and identity. Dad always insisted they keep their real first names which was annoying as Jason didn't like his very much. Anyway, this time he was called Willow - Jason Willow.

He was fifteen now – more than old enough for Dad to finally explain why these agents had been hunting them all his life. Who keeps sending them... who exactly had ordered their deaths?

It was time the hunters became the hunted.

Chapter 1

'That man keeps staring at us Dad.' Jason whispered.

Miranda stopped trying to read her magazine and looked up at the Easter holiday crowds churning noisily around them.

'Dad…' Jason repeated

'Yes, son, I heard,' Dad said, gazing around the airport check-in area without seeming to take an interest in anything. 'Don't stare but tell me which man and where,' he mumbled.

Jason made a slight nod towards a tall, slim man standing at a magazine rack. 'In Smiths – long coat, big camera.'

There was something compelling about the man. Unshaven, greased back hair and sallow skinned, he should have come across as unsavoury at best, but something about the confident way he held himself made you want to watch him.

'That doesn't narrow it down very much,' Dad said.

Jason glanced over again. At least half a dozen scruffy men with expensive, big-lens cameras were milling around that area watching the arrivals board above them.

'Oops,' Jason said, 'I might possibly have been over-reacting.'

'Probably,' Dad smiled thinly, 'paparazzi are always on the lookout for the next shot. All the same, which one was it?'

'Black T-shirt and jeans – see him?'

Miranda turned to stare into the newsagents but the man drifted further into the store.

'Looks like you scared him away, Sis,' Jason said, 'he's probably worried you'd crack his lens.'

'Don't try being funny, Jason,' Miranda smiled sympathetically, 'it doesn't work for you.'

'Now, now children,' Dad said, 'be nice. You go into departures on your own and I'll meet you in the lounge after I've checked out our reporter chappie. Why don't you grab us a table for some brunch - okay? Get me something big with bacon, please.'

Dad ushered them away with their boarding passes as Miranda tried to walk and look backwards simultaneously.

'Definitely no photo opportunity for little old you,' Jason said, grinning.

'I bet he'd rather snap me than you, Adonis.'

'Maybe, but that's because I'm not a blonde bimbo wearing skin tight jeans and a pink fluffy jumper... again.'

'You're only jealous because I didn't let you borrow them.'

'Fair enough,' Jason said, looking over Miranda's shoulder. The photographer had disappeared and Dad had merged into the shuffling crowds. 'I feel a bit stupid now – pressing the panic button and everything.'

'You are stupid, but not for that,' Miranda said. 'Shush now.'

They joined the queue and passed through into departures.

'I think you should order Dad a Stella - help him chill out for our little holiday on the sun-drenched Isle of Mawn,' Jason said.

Edging their way through the Easter holidaymakers they spotted an eighties retro-bar with small trees growing out of chrome plant pots and neon lighting. Amazingly, there were still a couple of tables free - probably something to do with

Dad's unusual choice of time to have a meal - half past ten in the morning.

They collapsed into the red plastic seats and a spotty young waiter hurried over grinning inanely at Miranda. Jason chose the house special bacon burger for Dad and himself. Miranda of course ordered the ever-so-healthy slimmer's char-grilled chicken salad.

'It'll be good to see Grandfather again,' Miranda said, as the waiter disappeared.

'I'm not sure a week in sun-drenched Mawn with the old sod will quite match up to working our way around Portugal,' Jason said, relaxing back and pulling off his baseball cap.

Miranda caught his hand and whispered. 'Leave it on.'

Jason chewed at his lip in frustration but put the hat back on. After being on the run for fifteen years he still occasionally forgot the rules Dad had drilled into them. Good job his perfect big sister was always there to save the day.

He glanced around at the crowd with a twinge of envy at all the normal families who could travel through airports or railway stations whenever they liked without having to keep peaked hats on and faces turned down from the CCTV.

The spotty waiter weaved through the tables with their drinks. He dumped the Coke and lager on the table before fussing about undoing Miranda's mineral water and pouring it carefully into her glass over a double helping of lemon slices. Finally he left them, bumping into another table as he glanced back at her.

'Looks like you've picked up another love-sick puppy,' Jason said.

Miranda nodded but didn't flash her usual smile. 'I can't see him wanting to buy into our life though, can you?'

Jason took a slow sip of Coke. 'We might actually stay in one place this time – moving to Alan Brash's little empire and everything.'

'Maybe.' Miranda shrugged.

'And you're getting off school until September.'

'Yeah, great. I'll have to re-start the sixth form a year behind with a bunch of immature boys and cliquey girls.'

Jason raised an eyebrow. 'Oh my heart bleeds for you, Sis.'

Miranda licked the lemon juice from her fingers, a smile pulling at one side of her mouth. 'Hey - you might finally get a girlfriend at school without your big sister's utter gorgeousness intimidating them.'

'Yeah, yeah,' Jason mumbled, pulling his Coke back towards him again.

Miranda touched his arm. 'You will be careful there, won't you... just keep out of trouble.'

Jason looked across at her, waiting for the lecture about not using Dad's martial arts training on anybody. However, Miranda had stopped – she wasn't going into nagging session. Jason grunted. Miranda wasn't meant to be nice to him unless one of them was really upset about something.

They were quiet for a time, drinking their drinks and watching the stressed-out holidaymakers bustling around just at the edges of the café's sad brown floor tiles. Dad had been gone for maybe ten minutes – he always checked everything out really thoroughly – no matter how trivial.

Miranda broke the silence.

'This'll be the first time up in Scotland without Mum...' She stopped, swallowing back her next words.

Jason took a slow breath and he fixed his gaze on an electronic flight information board at the far side of departures. Miranda was scrabbling around in her bag and he passed over a napkin without looking at her. She never had anything useful like a tissue in any of her half a dozen handbags.

'Thanks,' Miranda said. He knew she was staring at him and that her eyes would be all sparkly with blinked-back tears. He didn't want to look back at her, not yet.

Luckily, he saw Dad slipping through the crowds to join them.

'I need a drink,' he said, shrugging his long raincoat on to the back of his chair.

'Did you find the photographer?' Jason asked.

'Yep – I spotted him and a couple of the others skulking about outside an emergency exit…' He frowned and wiped a thumb gently across Miranda's cheek but she smiled back reassuringly.

'Anyway,' Dad continued, 'being a good citizen, I shopped them to a security guard but he didn't seem bothered. Some reality TV star's flying in "secretly" with her new baby and they've been hanging around all day apparently.' Dad settled back into his chair. 'Now, where's my beer?'

Jason shook his head and slid Dad's lager over to him. If his hyper-paranoid father wasn't worried about the greasy photographer then why should he be?

Chapter 2

'There she is,' Dad said, 'our very own, real-life castle.'

Jason smiled. Eila Doone hadn't changed - it never would. Like something from one his favourite old horror films, the squat turrets and thick walls rose straight out of a misted loch.

They had been picked up an hour ago from the station in the small town of Strayfele – the end of the line in so many ways. Old Duncan was their chauffeur as he had been for all of Jason's life. He'd driven them into to a deep sea-loch valley where the small island of Mawn hunched down in an iron-grey lake surrounded by jagged, wind-ripped mountains.

As usual, they'd had to leave the first Land Rover in a ruined cottage to board an ancient ferry skippered by the equally ancient, white bearded, Frederick who made Old Duncan seem like a grinning loon.

Docking in Mawn's tiny harbour had been hard on Jason. Ever since he could remember, he, Miranda and Mum had crammed themselves inside the tiny waiting room there to shelter from the inevitable storms while Dad had played the hero, waiting outside and making pathetic faces through the window.

Now it was only the three of them, Dad wouldn't have to wait out in the rain any more.

'Snap out of it,' Miranda said, elbowing his ribs, 'we're here.'

Old Duncan pulled the island's battered green Land Rover Defender into the cow shed that served as the castle's garage. As he reached for the keys, a loud voice crackled from the cab radio.

'Are ye there, Duncan...? There's a man here for ye here at the station. He's wanting to stay at the castle.'

Short wave radio was the main means of communication with Mawn. Mobile phones had no signal in the mountains and laying a land-line had never been worth the cost.

'He could have shown himself when I picked you lot up from the train, couldn't he?' Old Duncan grumbled, banging the steering wheel.

'That'll be another sun-worshipper up for the weekend then,' Miranda said, staring up at the thick cloud. 'Another shamelessly bare body waddling in and out of the loch all day.'

'We should drown them all,' Duncan grunted.

The Willows clambered out as rain began to hammer down on the tin roof. Dad quickly pulled the bags out of the back while Old Duncan drummed his fingers on the steering wheel. Almost before Dad was clear, Old Duncan reversed out of the shed, winding down his window. 'Mr Darillian will see ye in the High Hall,' he shouted, 'I'm away back for this blasted late-comer.'

Darillian was Grandfather's surname. It used to be Jason's of course - about four lives ago, but they'd changed their surname each time they'd moved, together with bank accounts, passports and everything else that recorded who they were.

As the Land Rover roared away, Jason and Miranda stared up at the castle through the driving rain.

Eila Doone had always been a pause, a safe haven in which to hide whilst their next new life was put into place by the "fixer" from Dad's past - Alan Brash.

This was the only real home they'd ever known.

'Watch the bridge,' Dad shouted over the wind gusting in through the shed's empty windows, '- it'll be slippy.'

'Dad, you've made us walk along the edges of icy planks since we were five,' Miranda said without turning around, 'I think we can manage the...' Without any warning, she pushed Jason backwards and sprinted outside.

'Cheat,' Jason yelled and tore after her.

Miranda was too fast for him to make up for the head-start and she leapt onto the bridge first. It was no more than two metres wide, low walled and slick-stoned with rock-frothed waters churning below. Miranda streaked across it with Jason just a steamy breath behind.

On the tiny island, the second of two Himalayan Cedars was the traditional finishing post. The instant they were off the bridge, Jason flicked his right foot out and caught Miranda's left. She tumbled forward but tucked into a tight roll and came up running at Jason's side as he tried to pass her.

They swung semi-contact blows and trips at each other as they ran, each one blocked or dodged. Three metres from the finish, Miranda feigned a punch to Jason's head and simultaneously shot her foot out to trip him.

Jason fell, just managing a roll but to the side, away from the tree. By the time he flipped back to his feet, Miranda was waving to him with one of the lower branches, her breathing almost back to normal.

'You cheated,' Jason said, kicking a bit of mud up at her.

'I don't think your grandfather is very impressed, cheating or not,' Dad said, joining them under the branches. Rain ran from his hair onto the three cases he carried. He nodded towards the castle.

Jason knew exactly where to look. He swung his eyes up to a small window on the fourth floor – the High Hall. There, staring down at them through the rain-streaked glass, was the dark silhouette of their grandfather.

'Well you trained us, Dad,' Jason said, 'it's your fault if our Jakra isn't up to scratch.'

'I thought it might be,' Dad grumbled.

'It's all right, Daddy,' Miranda said, giving a joyful wave up to the window, 'Grandfather's smiling.'

'Yeah, right,' Jason groaned. After fighting dirty and nearly breaking his neck, Miranda was now going to put on her ultra-sweet, granddaughter act.

'Come on, let's say hello to the old… man,' Dad said. 'Remember…'

'Best behaviour,' Jason and Miranda chimed in unison. He'd been telling them that ever since he and mum had raced a pushchair each to the second cedar.

They each ducked their heads against the building storm and walked into the shadow of Eila Doone.

Ten-foot high, six-inch thick double doors studded with iron barred the entrance as they had done for about nine hundred years. Dad pushed them open easily enough though and they dashed inside. As Dad shut the doors behind them, the cold and silence of the castle closed in on them.

Eila Doone had given up very little of herself in becoming a hiker's hotel. Worn tapestries, pole arms, shields and claymores were still lashed to the walls from centuries gone by. The only sign that the ancient hall they stood in was now the reception area was a small desk in one corner. As usual it was unmanned.

Dad started humming "Home, home on the range" as they dumped their cases at the reception desk and started towards the main staircase. Brett Darillian, Grandfather, didn't like to be kept waiting.

The staircase split and they took the right hand fork into a much smaller stairway spiralling up through a turret. Cold, grey stone screwed around Jason as he trotted up steps worn smooth by centuries' of footfalls. Twice, the echoing walls broke open onto a narrow corridor and then sealed them in again before they approached the private fourth floor.

Jason smelled the fire in the High Hall long before he left the stairwell. It was one of the few family rooms Grandfather heated regularly. He stepped out onto the landing after Dad and Miranda and came face to face with the ogre himself.

'You should have recognized Miranda's feint, Jason – there was no power in it.' Brett Darillian stared steadily at his grandson through dark, double doors opened wide. He stood at the far end of the long hall, framed by the rain lashed window and with a twelve-seat, mahogany table stretched between him and his family. Tall, powerfully built and with cropped gray hair over a face chiselled from stone, Grandfather might have been part of the castle itself.

'We were only messing about,' Jason said, attempting a smile.

'There's no "messing about", not now ye're coming of age. One day, seeing the difference between a feint and a real blow might save your life.'

Miranda let the sage advice fly over her head as she strode past the table and threw her arms around the old man's neck.

Grandfather didn't flinch from his lordly stance behind the Lairds Seat as she draped herself over him. Jason winced – Grandfather must be as comforting to hug as a rock. Still, Miranda usually managed to crack the ice a little and today was to be no exception. Awkwardly, Grandfather patted one bear-like hand against her back then eased her away.

'That's enough girl - ye're no longer a bairn.'

'There's no age limit on cuddles, Grandfather,' Miranda said, smiling up at him sweetly.

Jason crossed the hall to greet him with a little more decorum. Men didn't hug each other in Grandfather's world. He shook hands with his grandfather, putting all his strength in returning the old man's cold, iron hard grip.

Grandfather gave a barely perceptible nod. 'You're getting somewhat stronger.'

'Hello, father,' Dad said. He'd remained between the open doors.

'Where are ye running to this time, Richard?'

No one spoke. This was the only thing Jason hated about Mawn – there was such contempt in Grandfather's eyes and it laced everything he said to Dad.

The two men stared at each other. Dad stood tall, not looking in the least bit intimidated but he dropped his eyes first, to give a sad smile to his children. 'Do you want to unpack while I have a chat with your grandfather?'

'Okay but no arguing, you two,' Miranda said, in a particularly air-head sort of way.

'As if…' Dad said, winking at them.

Jason grabbed his sister's arm and pulled her out, closing the double doors behind them.

'Your running away has cost too much, this time…' Jason heard Grandfather begin as he and Miranda pressed their ears to the thick wood.

'Father, will you lower your voice - the children…' Dad cut in.

'They're no longer children, Richard. You still haven't told them have you, even after having their mother shot in front of their eyes? They need to know – Jason will be coming into his…'

'Will you lower your voice or do we have to leave now?'

Surprisingly Grandfather did what Dad asked and his voice faded out of hearing.

'Bugger,' Jason whispered, and the two of them started back down the spiral stairs. 'What do we need to know? What am I coming into?'

'Your inheritance?' Miranda guessed. 'Perhaps Grandfather's going to leave sun-kissed Mawn to you when you grow up… which will be in about another thirty years I'd say.'

'Yeah, yeah,' Jason grinned. 'But really – d'you think it's just the same old argument?'

'Aye, laddie,' Miranda said, dropping into a terrible impression of Grandfather's Scottish accent. 'It's your duty to tell them everything, Richard – you can't expect *them* to run for the rest of their lives as well.'

Jason nodded. This was the reason they'd never moved to Mawn permanently – Dad had always told them that he'd protect them from the dangers of his old life and that included telling them virtually nothing about it until they were "grown up".

'Sometimes I wish Grandfather would just tell us – get it over and done with.'

'I wouldn't listen to him, and nor would you,' Miranda said, 'it would be like betraying Dad's trust. Anyway – what's he going to say that we haven't already come up with – Dad's an ex-spy, or MI5 or on some witness protection programme? Just let Dad tell us in his own time.'

'I suppose,' Jason grunted. 'I hate it when Grandfather has a go at him though. D'you think they'll end up sparring again?'

'I should think so but Dad can look after himself. Anyway, he needs someone good to train against. We don't really push him.'

'Speak for yourself, girlie,' Jason barged his sister out onto the second floor as they passed it. He ducked as she threw a punch at his head.

They clattered down the stone steps into the still deserted reception area. Their cases lay where they'd left them. Miranda wrinkled her nose. 'Sod the unpacking, let's go to the village.'

Jason groaned, looking out through narrow windows. 'But it's pouring down.'

'We're in Mawn - what do you expect?' Miranda said.

'Nothing will be open,' Jason mumbled, pressing his face against the cold glass and misting it up.

'You want to stay here and wait for them to finish arguing?' Miranda said, reaching for a bright yellow oilskin coat and hat hanging on the 'for guest use' hooks on one wall.

Jason shrugged but turned away from the window. 'Mmm, attractive,' he said, nodding appraisingly at her.

'Mmm, dry,' Miranda said.

Jason grabbed some waterproofs down for himself. 'That's a very practical, un-Barbie thing to say, Sis.'

She ignored him and pulled open the front doors then shrieked as a wall of freezing rain burst in.

Jason shoved her out and they both crossed the bridge then started up the hill leading to the village in the next dip. They trudged resolutely passed a small stable block. They were both excellent riders but taking out a couple of horses now would mean at least an hour's rubbing down and grooming afterwards.

About half way up the hill Jason heard the throaty growl of Grandfather's Land Rover. A moment later it struggled over the crest then came hurtling down towards them, veering from side to side on the rain-slicked track.

'Run for it,' Jason shouted, scrambling into the heather above the road. 'Quick, Old Duncan won't stop until he feels your head crunch.'

Miranda followed him, without the dramatics. 'He's got the latecomer with him, hasn't he?' she said, trying to peer through the rain streaked, misted up windscreen.

'Looks like it… easier to see if Duncan understood new technology like de-mister switches.'

'Oh goodie – someone apart from Grandfather for me to play with at dinner.' Miranda waved, smiling brightly with rain running down her face.

Old Duncan crashed the gears and roared passed without a sideways glance. They hadn't been able to make out the new guest at all.

Jason pushed his still-waving sister back down towards the track. 'He won't fancy you looking like that, whoever he is,' he said, nodding at her shapeless yellow oilskins and wide-brimmed hat flopping down over her straggly wet hair.

'Well I thought I just might change for dinner.'

'Into what - a half-decent sister maybe…?'

'…and you've said that one how many times now?' Miranda feigned a laugh and jumped back down onto the road.

Miranda fell quiet for a while as they walked. Jason chewed his lip - quiet meant Miranda was either worried about something or plotting. Finally she spoke.

'Will you be asking Laura back for dinner tonight?'

Plotting then, obviously.

Jason just grunted. He knew he should never have told his sister about fancying Laura McKenzie last year.

'Well?' Miranda nudged him.

Jason nudged her back, resigning himself for another attack of the cupid sister.

Sure enough, Miranda hit him with a relentless storm of advice as they walked. Even though he kept his head-down and only mumbled nonsense in reply, the chatting-up lesson didn't stop until they reached the village.

It was almost six o'clock and the place was deserted. The rain had eased off to a drizzle.

'Don't you just hate rush hour?' Miranda asked.

'Shall we see if The Star's open for once?' Jason mumbled, trying to push back his dripping hair into some sort of order beneath the hood.

'Oooh, now let me think...' Miranda said, 'there are so many other hot clubs we could try... oh go on then – the Star it is.'

Jason started forward, his heart starting to thump. The Northern Star was Mawn's one and only pub. It had a 'family room' where Les, the landlord, let the island's youth hang out, play pool, eat crisps and drink Iron Bru or Coke. If Laura was out anywhere this wet Saturday afternoon, it would be in there.

They pushed on past Mary Moore's general store/bakery/post office/chemist with its old bay windows then stopped.

'Typical,' Jason said, staring at a scribbled note, placed inside a plastic bag and hung by string from the Star's main door.

Open at 7 for the football

'I'm not hanging around for an hour,' Miranda said.

'Straight back to the castle, then,' Jason mumbled and began to walk. 'Who's master-plan was this?'

They were less than a mile out of the village when he realised they were being watched.

Chapter 3

A single silhouette waited on the hilltop before them, a long coat billowing out and a bushman's hat pulled low over its face. Ragged strips of cloud whipped across the darkening sky behind.

'Looks like a highwayman without his horse,' Jason said, glancing across at Miranda.

'I don't like this,' she said.

'Don't be daft – it's probably that new guest, looking to get a pint in before dinner.'

Miranda tugged him off the track and started marching off through the heather. 'Dinner's in half an hour – he'd hardly have time to drink it. Come on, we'll skirt around him.'

Jason glanced back up the hill. The stranger waved once and started to walk quickly down the track.

Jason could see him more clearly now - wide shouldered with the raincoat flapping open at the top to show a high necked, black jumper. His hands were thrust deep into his pockets, head still down so the hat brim covered his face.

'Move,' Miranda hissed and sped up.

'You're being paranoid,' Jason began, 'he's staying on the track. I tell you, maybe he fancies one of Les' grotty pies or…'

Suddenly, the man cut into the heather and broke into a run. He lifted up his face.

'It's the photographer from the airport,' Jason said.

'Oh hell,' Miranda hissed. 'back to the village - quick.'

Jason sprinted through the heather after her but could almost feel the photographer closing on him. He glanced back, the man was only thirty steps away now, seeming to fly over the hillside.

'Stop – both of you. I have a gun.' His voice was high and reedy but it cut through the wind like a fencing foil.

Jason ignored it and sped up as Miranda shot a look to check on him.

'Get down, Jason, he's going to shoot!' she screamed and leapt back into him.

They both crashed into the heather and rolled down the hill. Miranda pushed him away so they tumbled apart, making two targets instead of one.

By the time they'd both rolled into a crouch, the man stood just ten steps away, rock steady with both hands on a pistol, pointed straight at Jason.

'Just stay where you are.' The photographer's voice seemed to scratch inside Jason's head… some sort of East European or Russian accent but gratingly thin. He walked slowly towards Jason, dropping his gun to waist height.

Both Jason and Miranda, ten metres apart, knelt absolutely still. Dad had always told them you can't do anything against a gun or the next second you'll be dead. And yet…

Jason couldn't do much crouching down. He slowly stood up, not sure if he should put his hands in the air or not.

The photographer was almost on him, the wind whipping greasy strands of hair across pale skin. His dark, dark eyes held Jason's stare like the ends of two telescopic sights.

'What do you want?' Jason managed to say through the heart pounding in his head. His own voice sounded strange, breathless and echoing in his ears. The man had a gun – it was pointed right at him. One twitch of that trigger…

'Who are you?' Jason asked. 'What do you want?'

The photographer stopped a couple of feet away, still silent. His face was thin and hard as he looked Jason up and down then caught him in that dead-eyed stare again.

'You can call me Mr Black.'

'I don't care what your name is,' Jason said, 'what do you want with us?'

'I only want you, young Master Darillian, just you.'

So this was Dad's past catching up with them again. The man knew their real name - Darillian. He must be an agent. Jason had to keep the man talking, find out what he wanted, look for his chance.

'Dar… what? That's not my name? You've got the wrong person. My name's Jason Willow.'

Could Miranda get away? He could see her in the corner of his eye. If she started edging backwards… if he could just hold Black's full attention, maybe grab the gun…

Black smiled thinly. 'Oh I do not think I am mistaken, Jason. We have been looking for your father for such a long time and now, to find he has borne a son… I will be made a prince for bringing you to my master.'

Miranda shifted her weight and Black's eyes flicked to her and back again. Jason had to distract him.

'I still haven't a bloody clue what you're talking about.'

Black narrowed his eyes a little, then shook his head. 'I am afraid we have no time for your little games. You must both come with me. If there is trouble, I shoot your sister first.' He smiled and turned the gun on Miranda. 'Now – we walk to the harbour.'

Suddenly an engine roared and Grandfather's Land Rover flew over the hilltop a few hundred metres behind Black. It bounced madly back onto the road then a moment later, swung into the heather and raced towards them.

As Black glanced over his shoulder, Jason snapped his right foot out at Black's hand and sent the pistol spinning away into the heather. Black swore and dived after the gun.

Jason tripped him up and slammed his whole weight down on Black's spine, knees first. He slammed his open palm into the back of Black's head as hard as he could. Black's face smashed down with a crunch of nose-bone.

The Land Rover roared and whined as it tore through the heather towards them.

'This is for my mother,' Jason whispered and pulled back his hand for a neck chop. Before the blow landed, Black suddenly reached up with one arm, grabbed Jason's coat and threw him off as if he were a toddler.

Jason rolled and flipped to his feet but Black was on him instantly. His fist powered through Jason's desperate block and burst open his lip.

Jason staggered and crashed onto his back. Through flashing lights filling his vision he could just make out Black leaping for him. Desperately, he kicked up with both feet.

He connected – oh, how he connected. It was as if twin steel pistons had blasted Black away.

Jason struggled to his feet, spitting out blood and shaking his head to clear the swimming lights. His vision cleared enough to see Black lying eight feet away, arms wrapped around his chest. How had he kicked him that hard? A wave of trembling ran through Jaon and he bent over, almost retching. He and Miranda needed to get away. He turned to find her.

'Jason, watch out,' Miranda shouted, sprinting towards him.

From the edge of his misted vision, Jason saw Black flip to his feet and dash forward, whipping out a long bladed knife as he came.

Blaaaah. The Land Rover horn blared out long and loud but it was still thirty metres away. Jason's tried to straighten up but his legs buckled.

Black closed in and the silver blade licked out but Miranda flew in from nowhere, one foot outstretched to smashing into Black's shoulder. He span away, his blade missing Jason by inches. Miranda landed neatly then rushed over to finish him off.

'No Miranda,' Jason yelled, 'he's too…'

Black twisted in the heather as Miranda stamped down at him and his knife sliced deep into her leg. She cried out, stumbled and tried to roll away. Black rolled and punched down hard on her bloodied leg.

Miranda screamed.

For Jason, the world stalled into slow motion and a deafening wind rushed through his head. Black raised his knife over Miranda and plunged the blade down.

In that instant, Black's head snapped backwards as if a juggernaut had smashed into it. He whole body cart wheeled off Miranda and he landed metres away in a crumpled heap. Two thin shimmers flashed through the space where his head had been a half second earlier and disappeared into the heather.

But there was no one there. No one had touched him.

The world sped up again and sound rushed into Jason's head.

The Land Rover roared to a stop between Black and Miranda. Grandfather threw open the door, swung himself on to the bonnet then leapt towards Black.

'Stay down, boy.' Old Duncan shouted from the driver's seat.

There was a sickening crack from the other side of the Land Rover.

Old Duncan glanced out of his window, then switched the engine off.

In the sudden, intense quiet, Jason heard a heather-muffled pounding further up the hill. Dad was sprinting down from the copse, travelling faster than any human should be able to move. He powered over the heather in flying strides, his feet barely touching the ground. Suddenly he was with them. He took in Jason with a glance, leapt passed him and skidded to his knees next to Miranda.

Jason could only stare at him as he pulled out a knife from somewhere and sliced through the leg of Miranda's blood-soaked jeans in two quick cuts.

'You'll be fine, darling. I just need to stop the bleeding. Lie back, breath deep… be still.' He wasn't even out of breath.

Dad's knife slit the denim into a bandage and in seconds he'd tied it over the wound.

Jason's mind was freezing to a stop. He stared stupidly at Dad and Miranda. His sister had been a blade away from death.

Grandfather appeared around the Land Rover. 'He's dead.'

'I can't see anyone else, Mr Darillian,' Old Duncan wheezed. 'I dare say there will be a twitching curtain or two in the village, though.'

Jason looked up, his head still swimming with muddled thoughts and motes of light. Old Duncan had somehow got on to the Land Rover's roof. He was standing there, shotgun in hand, like some old-timer on a Western stagecoach.

'Ow,' Miranda groaned as Dad adjusted the denim bandage around her leg.

'You all right?' Jason asked, stumbling over to her. He didn't know what else to say.

'Oh I'm just bloody perfect,' Miranda said, lifting her head up and staring at him. 'Do you know how much these jeans cost me?'

Jason felt himself smile. Miranda was going to be all right. 'Um… thanks for… you know…'

'Saving your life? Don't worry about it - I'll find some way for you to pay me back.'

Dad touched her cheek with one hand smeared in her blood and winked at her. 'I think you probably will at that, sweetheart.' He stood up and pulled Jason tightly to him. 'Are you all right, Son?'

Jason hugged him back - a bit awkwardly. 'I'm fine, Dad but… what happened? It's that photographer who was watching us at the airport isn't it? Is… was he another agent?'

Grandfather cut in, his eyes narrowing to glints of obsidian and turning on Dad. 'You didn't bother to investigate why he was so interested in you?'

'He only glanced over at us,' Jason almost shouted. This wasn't Dad's fault.

'I checked,' Dad said calmly, 'he seemed to be part of a pack of paparazzi. And he wasn't on our plane.'

Grandfather stepped right up to Dad. 'You're a fool, Richard. You should haven't have taken any chances.'

'This is not... the old country, Father. Things are different here... they do not have the manpower to consistently cover the smaller airports.'

Grandfather flung out one hand over the Land Rover's bonnet. 'So what the hell is this corpse doing there? Wake up Richard - they're spreading like a cancer into the West. We must live here as if we still hunted in the Carpathians.'

'So I should have killed him – right in the middle of the airport? I'd have a dozen other photographers taking our pictures and airport security arresting us. We'd be all over the national press tomorrow and trapped in a police cell waiting for them to fetch us.'

Grandfather shook his head. 'Have you forgotten everything? There are ways... You're going to get the rest of your family killed, as well Richard.'

'Over my dead body,' Dad said.

Jason glanced up at him. Sometimes, when he was really focussed or angry, Dad's eyes turned to ice. They froze over now.

'Quite probably,' Grandfather said, taking a step back from Dad. He slammed his fist into one of the Land Rover doors. 'You're not enough to keep them safe - the boy needs to know how to defend himself properly, he needs to be trained in his Gift.'

'Stop now,' Dad said, 'or I swear you will never see your grandchildren again.'

Grandfather drew in a breath to answer but Miranda cut in.

'When you men have quite finished yelling at each other, I'd rather like to stop bleeding to death,' She struggled to sit up in order to glare properly at Dad and Grandfather with equal vehemence.

24

Dad stared at his father for a moment longer then turned his back on him. His eyes softened immediately. 'Sorry, darling. I'll put you in the back seat where you can stretch out and we'll stitch you up back at the castle.'

Dad gently lifted Miranda and helped her inside the Land Rover, trying not to jolt her. Miranda, amazingly, didn't complain or whimper.

'I'll take Robbie,' Grandfather grunted and he whistled once.

A snort came from the pines two hundred metres up the hill and Robbie, Grandfather's fastest stallion began to trot down towards them.

Willow chewed his lip. *If Dad had been riding why would he leave the horse there? Had he been running faster than a young stallion could gallop to rescue them?*

'Take them back to the castle, Duncan,' Grandfather said, 'then come back for the bodies.'

'Bodies?' Jason asked. 'Who else…'

'Mikhail's dead,' Grandfather spat. 'I set him to following the newcomer the moment he left the castle. It seems your "photographer" was rather handy with that knife of his.'

Robbie arrived, tossing his head and snorting at the smell of blood. Grandfather took his reins to calm him. 'Leave immediately, Richard - get the boy out of here.' He called back without turning around, his voice resigned. 'There's a chance this one wanted the glory of capturing Jason all for himself. If not…'

Grandfather hesitated, glancing back at Jason and Miranda. '… more will be on their way, a lot more.'

Grandfather swung up into Robbie's saddle. The big stallion pranced on the spot and as he turned, Jason saw a Japanese sword, a katana, strapped to the saddle. Grandfather gathered the reins and kicked Robbie into a gallop.

'Come on, Son.' Dad said, from the back seat next to Miranda.

Jason stared at him without moving – the last few minutes flashing through his head.   He and Miranda had almost been killed.

'Jason, come on,' Dad said, 'we have to leave. We'll talk all this through on the journey.'

Jason climbed into the Land Rover, carefully keeping his eyes away from the corpse sprawled in the heather just feet away.

Dad had better give them some answers this time.

Chapter 4

'What happens if that Black guy wasn't working alone?' Jason asked. 'Will Alan Brash relocate Grandfather as well now?'

He, Miranda and Dad were sitting alone in an old fashioned compartment of a rickety old train rattling its way down the west coast of Scotland.

They'd left their grandfather within an hour of the agent attack that morning. Old Duncan had sped along forest and mountain roads to drop them in a sleepy fishing town on the west coast where they'd just caught the last train. Flying, of course, was now out of the question so they had a complicated series of line changes ahead of them before they could pick up their car from Leeds-Bradford Airport.

Dad shook his head. 'Your Grandfather would never leave now – he'd rather stand and fight. Besides, he's kept himself hidden from Brash all these years – he trusts him even less than I do.'

'But what if they send a lot more agents up there?' Miranda said.

'Mawn's a good place to defend – maybe safer than running,' Dad said. 'Besides, from what you've told me it sounds as if Black was trying to grab all the credit for capturing you by himself.'

'Well, that's another thing,' Jason said, 'Black said something about finding out you'd had a son. But they must have known about me from the attack in the car park.'

'Maybe,' Dad agreed, 'but there's always a lot of in-fighting amongst the agents – vying for power and so on. They don't always share information throughout their organisation.'

'This organisation,' Jason started, 'don't you think we're "grown up" enough to know about them now? We were both nearly killed today and we still don't know why.'

Dad held his stare for a moment then glanced at Miranda.

'Jason's right Dad,' she said, 'even after Mum being… you know… we've haven't tried to rush you but now…'

Dad held up his hands. 'Okay… okay.' He tugged out the bag of mint humbugs he always seemed to have tucked away in one pocket or another and offered them around. Then he took a long breath then sat up straighter in the sagging bench seat.

'Once I tell you about this,' he began, casting a sharp glance at Jason, 'I don't want you thinking about doing anything… stupid.'

Jason shrugged. 'We just want to know, Dad.'

Dad searched his face for a moment longer then nodded. 'I'm not going to tell you everything – you don't need to know all of it, not yet,' Dad raised one pacifying hand as Jason slumped back. '… but you deserve to know more than you do now, so here it is.'

'Twenty two,' Dad brushed one hand back through his hair, 'no twenty three years ago now, I left an organisation that most of the world has never heard of. It's called the Watch. They're based deep in the Carpathian Mountains in the heart of the Balkans.'

'The Watch?' Jason asked. 'So what did you do, Dad – were you some sort of spy?'

28

Dad dropped his eyes for a moment then looked up, almost defiantly. 'The Watch hunt down and kill people, Jason - evil people who are killers themselves and who want to force their disgusting practices and beliefs on all of humanity. They call themselves the Brethren.'

'Like fanatics, you mean, religious fanatics… eradicate the unbelievers and all that?' Miranda asked.

'Sort of…' Dad began, 'you could call them a type of cult, I suppose. They instigate distrust and hatred between all the different religions and nations so we won't stand together when they're powerful enough to come out of the shadows.'

'So were you in MI5 or 6 or something,' Jason said, 'like Spooks on T.V.?'

Dad shook his head. 'No – I told you, hardly anyone knows that the Watch or the Brethren even exist – and that includes governments.'

'So who authorises this… this Watch to hunt down these people, Dad?' Miranda asked, her face intent.

Dad smiled thinly. 'No one does.'

'Then you're acting outside of any laws or controls or anything?' Miranda pressed.

Dad nodded. 'The Brethren have to be stopped quietly – there would be mass panic and witch hunts if people found out about what they do… how they damage people in ways you'd never believe. The Watch is there to protect us without causing worldwide chaos.'

'But governments work together to fight terrorists all the time – religious, racist, environmental… all sorts. We all know about them. What's so terrible about these Brethren that only a secret, unaccountable organisation should even know they exist?'

'That's something I'm not going to tell you yet.'

Miranda shook her head and looked at Jason. From years of pleading, tantrums, silences and arguing they both knew it would be useless to press their father for information he didn't want to give.'

'So why did you leave?' Jason asked finally.

Dad was obviously prepared for this question. He answered calmly. 'The things we had to do to stop the Brethren were unbearable. I just couldn't do it any more.'

'But if these people are as evil as you say…' Jason began.

'I don't want to go into that any more either,' Dad cut in. He brushed his floppy hair back with one hand. 'What I will tell you is that the Brethren never stop looking for anyone who stands against them even after we retire. There are relatively safe areas we could have lived, protected areas such as Alan Brash's town, but I thought if I could keep you two away from any part of that world, never meet any of its people or even know anything about it then you'd have a chance at a normal life.'

Dad ran a hand through his hair again, took a slow breath and carried on. 'The Brethren's agents have somehow always managed to track us down eventually, even with Brash's help to change our identities and move us all over the country but I always believed one day it would stop. Your mother's death was the end of all that - it made me realise I'm not enough to protect you. We need Alan Brash's organisation – the security it offers. I should have given in earlier…. perhaps if I hadn't been so bloody stubborn your mother would still be alive.'

'It wasn't your fault,' Miranda murmured. She shuffled over and rested her head on Dad's shoulder and closed her eyes. He put his arm around her and kissed her hair.

The train began to slow down for a station and automatically, the three of them sat back from their windows and pulled down their various hats.

The towns were getting bigger – thirty or so passengers edged forward out of the dusk to peer in through the glass.

Jason chewed his lip – any one of those outside could be the next agent to be hunting them down.

Low lights had come on in the corridor and an elderly lady in worn tweed shuffled past their compartment staring in at the three of them. She stopped, fumbled with the door handle then slid it open.

Dad stood up immediately to help her with her small, wheelie suitcase and hoist it up on the rack above the seats.

As he lifted it, the woman shot a hand out at his exposed heart.

Jason was half way out of his seat before she said 'Mind you don't strain yourself, dear.'

Jason made some half-hearted pretence of helping Dad with the case while steadfastly ignoring Miranda's smirking.

The old lady smiled a "thank-you" then tottered into the seat opposite as the train jerked forward.

Jason sank back down and turned to stare out into the oncoming dark.

He was getting paranoid.

* * *

By nine o'clock the next morning they were driving through the Yorkshire moors.

Two changes of train and a taxi ride had got them to Leeds airport just after midnight where they'd picked up their car. Of course, it had not been that straight forward. Jason and Miranda had hidden a half mile down the road from the open air, security fenced airport car park while Dad had disappeared into the dark. He'd appeared ten minutes later in their old Renault estate, picked them up and roared off. If any agents had access to airport surveillance tapes, they would not have seen a family of three leave the area.

Too shattered to drive through the night they'd crashed in a Travel Lodge.

Now, however, after a few hours night's sleep and a very unhealthy full English breakfast, they were all feeling marginally more human. Jason gazed out over the open moor rolling passed in bright, morning sunshine and found it difficult to believe that only a few hours ago, he and Miranda had been fighting for their lives in Mawn's darkening drizzle.

Jason had become expert at putting bad things to the back of his mind if there wasn't anything he could do about them. However, there was still so much he wanted to find out.

'What was Grandfather talking about when he said I needed to be trained in my gift or something?'

'That's another thing I'm not going to tell you about yet.' Dad said, concentrating on the winding road.

'Has it got anything to do with Black flying off Miranda without anyone touching him? A Jakra technique - something like the inch-punch the kung-fu masters can do…'

'Enough on that one, Jason,' Dad said. 'You'll need to know about it soon enough but it can wait until then. Change the subject.'

'But if it will help…' Jason began.

'Tell us about our new home.' Miranda cut in, shooting Jason a warning look.

'You'll see it for yourselves in a minute,' Dad said.

The Renault hauled them up a particularly steep hill and then dropped down into a wide, part-forested, river valley.'

'Ugh,' Miranda said, 'who dumped that town there?'

In the centre of the valley, ranks of grey, terraced streets marched in towards a sprawling factory centre like hunched-backed miners trudging towards the pit. A sun-sparkled river skirted the town keeping well clear of the grime.

'That will be Alan Brash's Drunken Abbot.' Dad said.

'I hope our house is in that nice bit,' Miranda said.

Jason grunted in agreement. Beyond the drab mass of the town, the regimented streets broke around two low hills. Tumbling down and around the twin hills were ramshackle wanderings of fairytale thatched cottages, parks and even a village green. Miles of glinting security fencing divided the two communities.

'That "pretty bit",' Dad said, 'is called Darkston Village and actually, Brash did offer us a little cottage in there. I was honoured – that's the original settlement, built around the same time as the abbey and he only houses his closest and most valuable employees there.'

'Abbey?' Jason asked. 'I can't see an abbey.'

'That's because it's hidden behind the hills.'

'And what's that huge grey building on top of one of them?' Jason asked again.

'Ahh, that one's for you, Son, you lucky devil. It's called Silent Hill - Alan Brash's private School "for the education and training of brewery children,"' Dad said.

'Brewery children – is that what all those factory buildings are in the town then – a brewery?' Miranda asked.

'Yep,' Dad said, 'a brewery and factories to make all the merchandise - Drunken Abbot nuts and pork crackling, engraved glasses, party products and so on. Everyone in the town and village owe their livelihood to Drunken Abbot Industries and Alan Brash controls them all.'

'There's a bit on Wikipedia about how successful Drunken Abbot ale is,' Miranda said.

'There's nothing about this valley on the net though,' Jason chipped in 'not even a satellite photo of the town on Google Maps.' The two of them spent half their lives staring into library and hotel lobby computer screens. They never had their own internet connection of course – that would be far too easy to trace.

'No, there wouldn't be,' Dad said, his jolly mood draining away. 'Alan Brash has the money and power to keep the whole place pretty isolated.'

Jason looked back at his new school as they dropped further down into the valley. The grey building loomed over the otherwise pretty village – an oppressive block of granite with scores of small, dark windows. 'Yeah, but back to this Silent Hill school,' Jason said. 'What's it like?'

'It looks like some sort of prison,' Miranda said. 'Glad I'm not going there in a couple of weeks.'

'Helping or not helping?' Jason asked his sister.

Dad glanced at him, a sympathetic smile tightening his lips. 'It is a bit rough but Brash assured me that the rules are strict and the prefects there have quite a lot of authority – they're the ones who really keep things in order apparently.'

'Mmm, as if prefects ever do anything,' Jason said, 'It'll be much easier if I just floor the first idiot who tries it on… they tend to leave you alone then.'

'Just try to stay out of trouble,' Dad said. 'Brash did warn me that there is some… friction between the town kids and the umm… posh lot from the village.'

'So I'll be with the posh lot then?' Jason asked.

'Well not really. I didn't want us living completely in Brash's pocket so he found us a place a couple of miles further up the river – a little hamlet called Darkston Wick. You'll be able to see it in a minute.'

'Great - some tiny little place is going to be dead – I bet I'm the only teenager living there!'

'Brash said he lays on a school bus,' Dad answered, 'so I think there must be more horrible "yoof" about the place.'

The road levelled out onto the valley floor, with a thick wood continuing to follow them on the right hand side. Perhaps a mile ahead the first Drunken Abbot houses rose out of the misty moor– their soulless, dark windows staring hopelessly out at freedom.

Suddenly the wood broke around a small road. Dad quickly slowed down and followed it into the trees.

'Damn – I nearly missed that turning the last time as well.'

'Hurrah – we're saved,' Miranda breathed. 'I'm sooo glad we're not going any closer to that disgusting town.'

Dad grinned across at her and put on his very bad, actor-luvvie voice. 'Oh, I know, darling – I knew that living too near to some industrial slum would quite simply kill you.'

Jason grunted and stared outside. Thick-trunked red oaks and slimmer ash trees crowded in on both sides of the narrow, twisting road, almost shutting out the morning sun entirely. The tree line broke for a moment on the right and a weed filled track flashed by. He twisted around to read a rotting wooden sign:

Darkston Woods – Picnic Area

Instantly the oak and ash closed in again to engulf them in a green filtered half-light.

'Uhh, Dad - exactly how cut off from civilisation is this village?' Jason asked.

'You'll see for yourself in a minute,' Dad said.

'Can't wait,' Jason mumbled.

Six or seven turns later, sunlight flooded back into the car as the trees peeled away. Squinting while his eyes adjusted to the returned sunlight, Jason leaned forward to get a first look at his new home.

Darkston Wick was just what Dad had called it – a river-crossing hamlet. Perhaps twenty thatched and slate roofed buildings faced each other on a street rambling alongside the river. A narrow bridge carried their road over the water and up into the heavily wooded valley side beyond.

'Oh it's so sweet,' Miranda crooned as they dropped down and passed the first whitewashed cottage.

Jason shook his head. It was a bright Sunday morning in the first week of the Easter holidays and there wasn't a soul to be seen. 'Does anyone actually live in this place?'

Dad smiled. 'We do… right here, in fact.'

Chapter 5

Dad drove through one of two matching gateways onto a horseshoe shaped driveway of raked white gravel and stopped. Five wide stone steps led up to double doors set deep in the shadows of a carved stone porch.

Jason swallowed hard and stepped out of the car. He had to shade his eyes to take in the sun gleaming from two floors of Georgian windows and spotless plaster work. 'No way can we afford this.'

Dad smiled. 'Actually, we can. The Old Mill is all ours - the magnanimous Alan Brash is renting it to us really cheaply.'

'Why really cheaply, Dad - what's wrong with it?' Jason asked.

'Nothing. We were just in the right place at the right time. Brash's only recently bought the place – the previous owners left suddenly apparently and he snapped it up just a couple of months ago.'

'There's a little shop across the street,' Miranda said. 'It looks like something out of Dickens with those old bay windows.'

'I bet everyone here is out of Dickens as well,' Jason mumbled.

'I know it's a bit quiet here but it's about as safe as we could ever hope for,' Dad said. 'There isn't another town within forty miles of Drunken Abbot and Brash has surveillance and a small army of private security patrolling all over the valley. If any Brethren agents ever stumble across this place they will be... dealt with before we even see them. We shouldn't have to move again.'

'Good,' Miranda said, 'about time we had a quiet life!'

'Yeah but not this quiet,' Jason said.

Dad ruffled his hair like he was five. 'Well, I'm sure you'll meet some friends here or at school, Son, and I can take you into Drunken Abbot anytime – they've got a cinema, I think.'

'Dad, I'm fifteen,' Jason said. 'I can probably make it into town all by myself.'

'Fair point but let's just wait to see how rough the place is, shall we?'

Jason grunted.

'Want to see inside?' Dad said. He walked up the steps and unlocked their new front door with a ridiculously large key.

'First choice on bedrooms,' Miranda shouted, pushing in front of Jason.

They burst into a huge entrance hall filled with chequered sunlight streaming through small-paned windows. Lustrous dark wood, worn smooth with age, gleamed from floors, walls and heavy old furniture and the dead eyes of foxes and stags stared down at them from stuffed heads hung high.

'It's like something out of Dracula,' Jason said, grinning.

'First choice, loser,' Miranda shouted, already halfway up a curving staircase.

Jason sprinted after her and they tore through seven bedrooms in a couple of minutes.

'Ok,' Jason said, breathless, 'they're all decent – you can choose.' It wasn't a huge sacrifice - all the rooms had huge beds, low beamed ceilings and real fireplaces.

They walked back down the stairs at a more leisurely pace. Jason tried to imagine how many generations must have grown up within these walls, all silently watched over by the ancient house.

They found Dad in an airy, flag-stoned kitchen. He was putting an old, black kettle onto a gas hob - for now, it seemed, shying away from tackling an iron Aga range which dominated one end of the room. They plonked themselves at a heavy oak table set in front of a huge, inglenook fireplace.

'This place is excellent, Dad. Miranda didn't even fight over rooms,' Jason announced.

Dad didn't respond - something outside had caught his eye.

Quickly Jason joined him at the kitchen window with Miranda a step behind. A beautiful, dark haired woman with perfect pale skin and dark eyes was staring in through their gates. She held Dad's look for a long moment, then turned and walked slowly on into the village.

'A neighbour, do you reckon?' Jason asked.

Dad continued to stare between the gateposts then reached for the kettle. 'I suppose so.'

'She could have waved or something,' Jason grumbled, 'you know – to be a bit more welcoming to us new folk.'

He stared out over the silent cottages. If the rest of the villagers were like that woman it was going to be a long, long Easter, trapped here in the village of the walking dead.

***

Jason shut the front door behind him and breathed in the fresh clean air. Dad had finally released him from endless moving-in chores saying that he and Miranda would sort out the kitchen.

He leapt down the stairs, crunched across the gravel drive and followed the path down one side of the house. It stopped at the edge of a little copse of ash trees to one side of the back garden. A manicured lawn ran down to the river to what Jason was really interested in – the three storey watermill rising out of the water.

'Just my luck,' Jason moaned as he trotted down the lawn. Every door and window on the watermill was boarded up. A small rowing boat caught his eye, however. It was moored against a narrow stone jetty that formed a breakwater around the mill.

He jumped in and started rowing across the Darkston River – thirty metres wide at this point and lazy apart from a fast running channel funnelled under the mill-wheel by the breakwater. Jason moored the boat to a tree stump on the far side and trotted up into the trees.

It was cool under the trees which rippled down the valley side in a series of low hillocks and bright clearings. This was the first chance he'd had to be alone to really think about what had happened on Mawn and what Dad had said about…

Crash!

Higher up the valley side, half obscured by thick trunks, something tumbled down through several branches of a huge oak and hit the ground with a solid 'thunk'. It lay perfectly still while twigs and leaves rained down around it.

For a moment Jason hesitated. What if this was another agent? But Dad had said the whole valley was safe – guarded by Alan Brash's private army and high tech' security cameras.

What the hell – he wasn't going to live the rest of his life being afraid.

Jason sprinted up the hill and stopped at the edge of a small clearing. The fallen thing was a boy, his face buried in the leaf mold and stocky shoulders heaving under a long mop of curly, dark brown hair. His black, "Meat Loaf Rocks" tee-shirt began to push up out of the mass of debris.

'Are you all right?' Jason ventured.

The boy started, snapped his face out of the ground and rolled over to face Jason. Small brown eyes squinted out of a heavy-boned face. Jason guessed the boy was about his own age, perhaps a year or so older.

'Ah, how very excellent – I am so happy to have had an audience for my little... accident.' the boy said, sinking back down.   His voice was quite deep, with a precise, slightly clipped accent.

Jason moved a bit closer, not knowing if he should try to help him up. 'Have you broken anything?'

'Thank you - no.   I have never felt better.' the boy grunted.   Jason stifled a grin – his accent sounded a bit like Count Dracula in a badly acted horror movie.

The boy sat up slowly and brushed the hair back from his face.   There was a trickle of blood from his forehead and the red smeared through the dirt all across his cheeks.   He stared up at Jason through the dark tangle of his fringe.

Jason edged closer.   'Umm, maybe you shouldn't move – in case your back is broken or something...'

The boy raised one eyebrow.   'I think that I may have noticed if my back was broken.   Who are you?'

'Jason, Jason Willow.   We've just moved into the village today.'

The boy nodded.   'A new neighbour then – good.   I am called Mouse.'

Mouse?   Jason thought, the boy didn't look much like a mouse with his bulging arms and shoulders.   Still, perhaps there was something mouse-like about him - his angular face, stocky body, short legs... and those little brown eyes.

'Mouse... right,' was about all Jason could manage.

Mouse grinned.   'It is because I am so gentle and shy...'

'Okay,' Jason said.

'... or perhaps it has something to do with my family name – Muskowicz... sounds a little like Mouse-kowicz to an English person ... do you think?'

'Um... a bit I suppose,' Jason agreed.

'I am happy with the name now - I became bored of breaking the mouths of each funny boy who thought it would offend me,' Mouse grinned again and wiped away the congealing blood from his forehead.

Jason reached into his pocket and pulled out one of the big cotton handkerchiefs Dad made them carry for "first aid".

'Umm, you shouldn't wipe the blood away, it won't be able to clot,' Jason mumbled. 'Just press this against…'

He began to bend down to pass Mouse the handkerchief and something like a steam train slammed into his shoulder. He flew backwards, sprawling to the ground in a heap.

Instinctively, Jason managed a clumsy roll to his feet and brought his fists up.

A girl skidded to a stop right where Jason had been standing over Mouse.

'I will send you back to your slum in an ambulance if you have hurt him,' she shouted, her large, dark eyes glaring at him.

Her voice was hard, defiant, with touches of the same Eastern European accent as Mouse. The words didn't really register with Jason, however. His focus was all on her lips – soft and full over perfect, white teeth. His fists dropped to his side. She was a younger version of the beautiful woman who had been watching the house earlier.

The girl's mouth tightened into a thin, line. 'What do you think you're staring at? Are you a dumb-wit? Why do you losers have to come out here to fight with us all of the time…?'

Jason struggled for something to say but his mouth refused to open. The girl looked a couple of years older than him and was tall with a figure to die for. She'd the same fair skin as Mouse but had big, dark eyes framed by a neat black shoulder bob. The Levis and white tee-shirt she wore might have been moulded to her.

Jason dropped his eyes. Was she Mouse's sister, doing her protective bit… or his girlfriend maybe?

'Ah, Louisa,' Mouse said, slowly easing himself up, 'be gentle with Jason – do you really think this long, thin boy could knock me down?' Standing at full height he barely came up to Louisa's neck.

'You know his name?' she asked.

'Of course. He is our new neighbour - we should be nice to him, yes?' Mouse brushed twigs and clumps of mud from his clothes, holding the girl's questioning stare.

'So why were you on the floor and bleeding?' she said at last.

Mouse leant back against the trunk. 'I... fell out of the tree – it happens sometimes.' He wiped a fresh trickle of blood from his forehead.

She moved closer to Mouse and pushed his hand out of the way to examine the cut. 'But he was reaching for you, threatening...'

'He was trying to give me a handkerchief for my terrible wound,' Mouse said.

The girl, 'Louisa' Mouse had called her, raised one eyebrow, shook her head and turned back to Jason. 'Boys,' she muttered as she wiped a little of Mouse's blood off her fingers onto the back of her Levis. She pursed her lips for a moment then smiled.

'My name is Louisa Russof,' she said. 'I am sorry for... hitting you. Sometimes the Drunken Abbot boys come out here looking to fight... I thought...'

'No, that's fine,' Jason cut in, 'it was an obvious mistake to make.' His voice sounded too high and squeaky - she must think he was about ten or something.

'Yes it was.' She turned back to Mouse and brought out a handkerchief of her own.

Jason was sure he glimpsed a smile pulling at her lips as she turned away. He stole another quick glance at her tight jeans but caught Mouse's hard, dark eyes staring at him over Louisa's shoulder as she fussed over his cuts.

Jason quickly looked away. 'So do you two live in the village?'

'Yes,' Mouse said, 'we share what you English would call a pretty "chocolate-box cottage".'

'Oh right,' Willow said. 'I have to put up with an older sister as well.'

'What makes you think Louisa is my sister? Mouse said.

Louisa handed the handkerchief to Mouse and turned around to face Jason. Her face was all innocent curiosity.

'Oh…' Jason stumbled, 'sorry, I just thought… when you said you lived in the pretty cottage… and you look a little bit the same. I should've realised… you're going out… or…'

Louisa smiled and said 'You are a very curious boy.'

Mouse pushed away from the tree and took a few steps forwards. He might have been a head shorter than Jason but he was about twice as broad.

'Do not worry, Jason Willow. Louisa and I are not "going out" or dating or being boyfriend and girlfriend…'

'Mouse.' Louisa stopped him with a gentle hand on his shoulder. 'I am sure… Jason is not at all interested in such things.' She shot Jason a glance from under her eyelashes and smiled.

'You think?' Mouse muttered and wandered back to the oak where he began fixedly searching through the branches that had crashed down with him.

'Uh look,' Jason started, 'sorry if I've said the wrong thing… I…'

Mouse dug out a sturdy branch and started to strip twigs and leaves from it. His mouth twitched into an exasperated smile. 'No harm is done, yes? However, it is probably best if you change the subject.'

'Mouse is a family friend,' Louisa explained, tousling Mouse's hair until he pulled away. 'He lives with my mother and me.'

'Oh, right, great' Jason said.

Louisa raised an eyebrow then turned back to Mouse. 'Come on,' she said, we should at least clean your wound of war with some antiseptic.' She started down the wooded valley side. 'Walk with us, Jason - tell us something of yourself . Where have you come from, for instance?'

Jason followed them. 'Oh… we've moved about a lot… Dad does supply teaching.' He gave his standard answer automatically. With their Eastern European accents, he was hoping Louisa and Mouse were connected with the Watch but he'd have to be certain before he started blabbing about his own past.

'A teacher?' Louisa asked. 'He's not going to teach at our school is he – at Silent Hill?'

Willow shook his head. 'I don't think so but I'm going there after Easter.' Suddenly the prospect didn't seem so bad.

Mouse coughed out a laugh. 'It is a lovely school – you will be very happy there.'

'I've heard it's a bit rough,' Jason said.

Mouse held up his branch – stripped of twigs and leaves it was fast turning into a staff. 'Why do you think I risk breaking my bones to find good wood like this? A little boy like me needs some protection from the gangs, yes?'

Louisa looked over her shoulder at Jason, raising her eyes. 'Mouse likes to hit people with sticks.'

'Only the bad guys, Louisa.' Mouse grunted. He flicked out his branch and smacked it into a trunk.

Louisa shook her head and smiled apologetically at Jason. He smiled back but quickly looked down feeling like some grinning lunatic. Why was he so rubbish with girls?

'Any top tips for surviving the "bad guys" at school?' he asked.

'Just keep out of the way of the Brash gang,' Mouse said, 'oh., and the Skins.'

'Who are…?' Willow began, but Louisa cut in.

'Can we talk about something else? I do not wish to think about that place until we have to go back there.'

'Oh, right… sure.' Jason said. Mouse just hit another tree with his branch.

'What is there to do around here?' Jason attempted. 'My dad said something about a cinema in Drunken Abbot.'

'Ah – making plans for a romantic evening already, yes?' Mouse said and glanced up from stripping the last pieces of bark from his branch long enough to wink at Jason.

'Mouse – you are so embarrassing,' Louisa said, gliding over to walk next to Jason, a grin tugging at the corners of her lips. 'Jason is just… what is the English word… chatting.'

Jason coughed. 'Um… yeah… I didn't mean….' was about all he could manage. Louisa let him suffer for a moment longer, then finally answered his question.

'Your father is correct - there is a cinema and also a bowling place in Drunken Abbot but it is not a nice town to visit.'

'Oh right,' Jason said. 'So what do you do over the holidays?'

Mouse answered. 'Outside, we row and swim in the river, walk in the valley and train in what you would call a martial art. Where we come from we are used to a simple life.'

'Where do you come from,' Jason asked.

Mouse and Louisa glanced at each other. Mouse nodded and Louisa said, 'We come from Romania. Mouse moved over here with us as his parents both... died at the same time as my father. Our families have always been very good friends.'

'Everyone is good friends where we come from,' Mouse said, 'it is like a "village thing".'

'Well, yes, quite so...' Louisa said, 'but we are like brother and sister.'

'Lucky me,' Mouse mumbled.

'So anyway,' Louisa carried on brightly, 'we have been here in England for nearly three years now.'

'And we are loving every minute of the time.' Mouse said.

'Don't you like it here, really? Why did you move so far away?' Jason asked.

'It is safer here... apparently.' Mouse said.

That left an awkward silence. Jason didn't want to ask private questions but if these two had come to Alan Brash for safety then surely they must have been involved in whatever past life Dad had left behind. They'd lost family as well. At last, he might have found someone who he could talk to.

Jason lost his train of thought. Louisa was walking very close to him and the uneven ground sometimes edged her close enough so her hand or shoulder lightly brushed his. Jason hoped his face wasn't blazing scarlet. He struggled unsuccessfully for something interesting to say - what if Louisa thought he was boring, or brain dead?

The trees broke onto the hard, cracked surface of a narrow road running up the steep valley side. They clumped onto the surface rutted and split by weeds and headed down to the river.

'This is the old coaching road,' Mouse said, 'The brewery built the other big road many years ago for the lorries full of their Drunken Abbot Ale. A good thing I think, they would have destroyed our little bridge.'

Jason nodded, following Mouse's gaze over the ancient bridge. At it's far end, a wooden beamed, four-storey building loomed over the river. A dark highwayman rode his rearing black stallion on a pitted and creaking sign whilst a dozen small dark windows silently peered down at the three of them.

'So,' Louisa said, leaning against the bridge's low stone wall and looking downriver, 'you must have moved into the Old Mill - it is the only empty house here.'

'Yeah, that's right. Have you been inside - it's fabulous,' They could see the watermill from here, steeped in afternoon shadow now.

Mouse and Louisa didn't say anything. He must have sounded like he was boasting.

'We don't own it or anything – Dad could never afford somewhere like that...' he quickly explained. 'A bloke called Alan Brash is renting it to us cheap... as a favour.'

Louisa looked straight into his eyes. 'Your father and Alan Brash – they are close friends, then?'

Jason hesitated. Should he tell them that Dad really didn't like Brash. If Brash had helped Louisa, her mother and Mouse to settle here from Romania, they might be big fans of his. Then again, if that was the case, why weren't they living in his exclusive Darkston village? He decided to take a chance.

'Not exactly close friends... or friends at all, really. They used to work together ages ago and Mr Brash has helped us move quite a few times but Dad never wanted us to move this close to him.'

'How could anyone not like the wonderful Mr Brash?' Mouse said.

'Just keep playing with your stick, Mouse,' Louisa said, shooting him a look.

Mouse shrugged and started poking around the cut on his forehead. He seemed to quite like the mess of congealed blood and forest floor that he had smudged over his fingers.

Louisa gave a satisfied nod and turned her dark eyes back on Jason. 'This is a good thing - we are not "exactly close friends" with Alan Brash either. Perhaps my mother should meet your father – they can… how do you say it… *bitch* about him together.'

Jason grinned. 'Sounds like a plan. You should all come around for lunch or something.'

'That would be nice,' Louisa said, 'but my mother has just decided we are going on holiday – this evening.'

'There was no planning,' Mouse said, 'she just came in for lunch and said we are going.' He smiled sweetly at Louisa. 'The Russof women are known for their madness.'

Louisa sniffed and turned her back on him. 'She was obviously upset about something – I will find out about it soon enough. Now, we should go to pack our suitcases.'

'Uh… okay. So I won't see you…' Jason began but Louisa was already walking away.

Mouse looked up at him and shook his head slowly. 'You have a saying in this country – a lamb to the slaughter – yes?'

'Uhh – yeah, I think so,' Jason said.

Mouse grinned. 'Enjoy your last days of freedom.' Then he turned and followed Louisa.

What was he talking about? Jason wondered as he tried not to stare at Louisa's skin tight jeans as she crossed the bridge and disappeared around the first cottage on the right.

Breathing out slowly, he climbed up to sit on the low stone wall, pulling both legs in and holding his knees.

Had he just made some new friends? He wasn't so sure about Mouse but he definitely wanted to see more of Louisa even if she made him feel like the he was the most un-cool teenager on the planet when he was around her. Perhaps she might come to see him as more than a friend given a bit of time. Mouse might have some problem with that, though.

At least with school starting in a week he wouldn't be going into the lion's den totally alone.

He needed to get back to the rowing boat and so he ambled back over the bridge towards the woods. It was hard to ignore the prickling feeling on the back of his neck as the Highwayman's blank, staring windows watched him walk away.

Across the river, the water-wheel churned away as it had probably been doing for centuries. What a fantastic house to live in, right in the middle of a tiny village lost in time. And now with Louisa in the picture... even if nothing happened between them, he had finally met someone else from Dad's past. This was the perfect opportunity to have a lifetime of questions answered... and to discover more about the agents who had murdered his mother.

Jason caught himself chewing his lip and stopped. Even if he did find out about the Brethren, what could he do about it – he was just a fifteen year old boy who was fairly handy at some obscure martial art?

He reached the little boat, untied it and settled in for the short row back. With every pull he found himself looking up to the huge oak halfway up the valley side where Mouse had fallen and he'd first caught sight of the lovely Louisa rushing out from the trees.

He stopped rowing.

When he'd rolled to his feet after being battered away from Mouse, Louisa was only just skidding to a halt at the oak tree.

She'd hurled him away from Mouse without being anywhere near him. It was just like when Black had been smashed away from Miranda up in Mawn.

The boat drifted passed the churning mill-wheel as the current ushered him downstream. Jason snatched up the oars again and fought the river's pull to get back to his new home.

Dad was hiding far more than just a secret past of hunting down some sort of cult. It was time he told them everything.

48

Chapter 6

'I hate Sunday nights,' Jason grumbled to himself, staring out of his bedroom window at the river meandering by.

Tomorrow he'd be going to Silent Hill school.

The Easter holidays had dripped by: Louisa and Mouse had not reappeared from their sudden holiday; the few other village kids he had spotted were all younger than him and not particularly friendly and Dad had point-blank refused to say any more about his past. To make matters worse, Dad had kept him in every morning in an attempt to catch up with almost a year's schoolwork – teachers!

Jason caught a glimpse of dark blue uniforms high in the woods. It was Brash security. There were dozens of patrol teams, Dad had explained the first time they'd spotted them on one of their evening "family walks". The teams of three were all armed with pistols and often at least one rifle. Dad had also pointed out a couple of the hidden security cameras which monitored the roads and tracks all around Darkston Wick and Drunken Abbot.

Jason watched the pair of security guards disappear back into the trees. Dad had explained that the third member of each patrol quietly trailed the lead pair to provide another viewpoint and backup crossfire if needed.

'Food, Son,' Dad shouted from downstairs.

'Coming,' Jason shouted back.

He pulled himself up from the window seat and groaned. He ached all over. With Silent Hill playing on his mind ever more, Jason had thrown himself into his training over the last few days. After the morning "school" sessions, he'd worked on countless stomach crunches, push and chin ups and Jakra patterns. He'd set up punch bags, climbing ropes and balance beams in the double garage and worked them hard every day. Finally, before any of them started to cook dinner in the evenings, he'd dragged Miranda and Dad into the garage for sparring sessions. He always lost spectacularly to Dad and Miranda beat him about half the time but he learned from every fall, kick, punch and bone-bruising throw.

He eased himself downstairs and into the kitchen.

Dad glanced up at him from dishing out goulash into big bowls. 'Cheer up, Son - Silent Hill might not be all that bad.'

'It's one long turf-war, Dad – two gangs virtually run the school.'

A smile flicked over Dad's lips. 'Those friends you met, Louisa and Mouse, told you this, I suppose.'

'Yes, Louisa can't even bear talk about it.' Jason helped himself to French bread and dunked it into his bowl.

Dad raised one eyebrow in his infuriating, teacher-like, 'aren't you missing something obvious?' type way. 'Don't you think they might have been exaggerating slightly, winding the new boy up a little?'

'No. Dad, they really hate the place.'

Dad raised his hands in surrender. 'I guess you'll just have to see for yourself tomorrow.'

'Anyway,' Miranda said, 'with all the training you've been doing you'll be able to handle yourself.' She smiled sweetly.

50

They finished eating quickly and Jason began to clear away the dishes. He put the kettle on for Dad's coffee and grabbed himself another Coke.

Dad gripped Jason's shoulder shoulder. 'Come on, let's take pudding onto the comfy chairs.'

Jason nodded, pouring the coffee as Dad went back to the table and sliced off three huge chunks from a home-made sponge cake he'd picked up from 'Mrs Miggins General Store' – the only shop in the village.

The three of them creaked along the floorboards into the drawing room at the end of the long, panelled corridor and Jason flopped into his favourite worn leather armchair by the side of the fire.

Dad turned on a standard lamp bringing a bookshelf to life with glints of gold leaf and warm leather bindings.

'There's one good thing about you going to school tomorrow,' Miranda said, draping herself over a leather Chesterfield sofa in the centre of everything, 'you'll get to see the lovely Louisa again.'

'Here we go,' Jason grumbled, 'I knew I shouldn't have told you about her and Mouse.'

'I'm sure Miranda could give you some really useful advice on how to charm this young lady…' Dad began, grinning broadly. Then he stopped as bright lights washed over the curtains from outside followed by tyres crunching over their gravel drive.

Glad of an excuse to avoid Miranda's "agony aunt" session, Jason jumped up to peer through a crack in the heavy velvet drapes.

The security porch light clicked on to show a massive black Bentley easing to a halt in front of the main doors. Its headlights faded out leaving the comparatively puny porch light bouncing back from the car's smoked glass windows.

Dad was suddenly beside him at the window. A blank expression slipped over his face. 'That's Alan Brash's car – one of them anyway. If he comes in… well, just be careful what you say. Switch some more lights on in here please.'

Dad pulled the curtains closed and walked calmly along the corridor to the entrance hall.

Jason turned, wide-eyed to Miranda. *The* Alan Brash was here. Despite all the times the man had helped them move lives, neither Jason or Miranda had ever met him.

Jason left the lights off. This side of the room was virtually in darkness with just the standard lamp glowing in the far corner. Miranda joined him and eased the curtains back open a little more so she could spy outside as well.

They were almost too late. A couple of dark silhouettes were already half way up the front steps. All Jason could make out was a tall man with a long, dark coat draped over broad shoulders and a woman with dark hair piled high on her head and a crimson cloak flowing out behind her.

Just before they entered the porch they both stopped and, as one, turned to stare directly at the drawing room window.

Jason and Miranda both jerked back from the curtains but Miranda stopped Jason from shutting them.

'They'll see the twitching,' she whispered then scuttled over to close the lounge door with just a crack to squint through.

A moment later, the old brass doorbell clanged about on its metal coil.

Jason dashed around the room switching on table lights and picking up a few fallen cake crumbs. He dashed over to join Miranda spying along the long corridor to the entrance hall.

Dad was brushing back his hair and straightening his shirt. Then he opened the door.

'Ah Richard,' a rich, almost theatrical voice said, 'sorry to call on you so late in the evening, old man.'

'Alan,' was all the greeting Dad gave in return. 'Is there a problem?'

'No, no, nothing like that. I just thought I should meet your boy before I bump into him at school... you'd prefer it that way wouldn't you?'

There was a moment's pause then Dad stepped back slightly. 'Yes, I suppose so. Come inside.'

Dad moved further back and Alan Brash entered.

The man seemed to fill the entrance hall. He must have been two metres tall and with the long overcoat rippling down from his broad shoulders he'd the commanding presence of a highwayman halting a mail coach… just without the horse.

One hand slipped out from the coat to shake Dad's before Brash turned back to the doorway with a rather flamboyant sweep of his coat-draped arm.

'I don't believe you've ever met my personal assistant - Miss Alicia Sirensong.'

Brash moved aside to let the woman in and blocked Jason's view. All he could see was Brash's light blond hair, shimmering down in soft waves to just reach his broad shoulders.

Jason caught a flash of crimson dress through Brash's legs and the top of Alicia Sirensong's dark hair. Her shining tresses were bound up high with delicate, silver tracery.

'Pleased to meet you,' Dad said, his voice a little husky.

'Hello, Richard. Alan has told me so much about you.' Alicia's voice was like honey - soft, warm and rich. Jason wanted her to speak some more.

Dad's voice took on a more guarded tone. 'Ahh – well try not to think too badly of me.'

Brash guffawed like an inflated, theatre impresario. 'Nothing of the kind, old man,' he said, slapping Dad on the shoulder, 'I have nothing but admiration for the work you did – you know that. Your early departure was a great loss to us.'

Brash whirled his coat from his shoulders and passed it to Dad in one smooth action. As he moved, Jason caught a glimpse of Alicia's pearl white face - green eyes flashed above high cheekbones and slightly parted red lips.

Then Brash began to turn down the corridor. 'You're in the drawing room, I believe,' he said, his voice resonating down the passage.

Jason and Miranda scuttled back their chairs.

'Yes,' Jason heard Dad say, 'go on through.'

Surprisingly light footsteps for such a big man came closer, followed by the unhurried click of high heels on the wooden floor. Jason tried to flop back in his chair, felt awkward and finally stood up just as Brash entered the room.

'Jason – we meet at last,' he said, a smile pulling back from strong white teeth with all the pleasure of a wolf sighting a trapped deer. His hard green eyes held Jason's.

'Mr Brash - pleased to meet you, at last' Jason replied.

Brash's smile changed a little – amusement perhaps – then he turned to Miranda. 'And you must be Miranda. What a vision of loveliness you are.'

Miranda smiled back. 'How nice of you to notice.'

Brash hesitated for a split second then laughed. He swaggered into the room to shake both their hands in a strong grip.

For a moment, Jason's mind was filled with the man. Not a clear image but more a sense of his presence. It was like the feeling you get when you know someone is behind you.

Brash let him go and stepped back. Jason's mind was still clearing when a cool, slim hand slipped into his and his every sense snapped into focus. Alicia Sirensong stood in front of him.

Jason felt every square centimetre of her skin against his hand, from the tips of her elegant fingers just touching his wrist to her soft, yielding palm pressing against his. He caught a trace of sweetly seductive perfume before it tantalizingly slipped away.

'Hello, Jason,' she said, 'I'm Alicia,' her voice wove around him, soft and warm.

'Hi,' he replied. He could not bring himself to look at her face. She'd set his cheeks on fire already. Alicia held him for a moment longer then, with a final, gentle squeeze, slipped her hand from his.

'Sit down, please.' Dad had edged past their guests to stand beside Jason. 'Would you like some tea, coffee... or something a little stronger?'

Brash took his gaze off Jason's flushed face to look at Dad. 'Alicia enjoys a decent whisky,' he said with an exaggerated wink.

Dad loved whisky as well. An expensive, single malt made in a small distillery near Mawn was always kept close at hand.

'I have a bottle in the kitchen,' Dad said, 'but it's only from the supermarket, I'm afraid.'

Jason glanced at Dad. Was he making sure Brash didn't have any clues to grandfather's home?

Brash smiled indulgently. 'At the risk of sounding rude, I have a rather nice single malt in the car… to help my longer journeys pass a little more quickly. Might I tempt you?'

'Fine,' Dad said.

Brash gave a faint nod and looked back at Jason. 'Jason, old chap, would you mind awfully just popping out to the car to dig out the whisky. Just let yourself into the back and you'll find the drinks cabinet easily enough.'

Jason nodded. 'Sure.'

'Hurry back,' Alicia breathed.

Jason glanced at her - surely she was taking the mickey. 'Missing you already,' he fired back.

She grinned warmly and winked. Jason grinned inanely and made for the door, Alicia Sirensong's fine porcelain face and vivid green eyes still burning into his brain.

He walked slowly along the corridor and into the hall, trying to make his footsteps sound measured and cool. He heard Alicia laugh at something, soft and rich, as he tugged open the front door and stepped out into the porch. He was grateful for the cool air on his face.

The motion-sensing porch light blinked into life, illuminating the steps but turning the rest of the world black. Dark against dark the Bentley waited. As his eyes adjusted, Jason could make out the two huge headlamps glinting at him from either side of a snarling silver grill. The car's powerful bulk crouched back into the darkness like a puma ready to pounce.

Whistling in admiration, Jason walked down the steps. He ran his fingertips along one wing, over the driver's door with its blacked out windows, and onto the double passenger doors behind.

He slipped his fingers around the cool silver handle and with a solid click, one door swung easily outwards. A soft, interior light glowed into life and the comforting smell of fine leather drifted out. The floor was carpeted in a deep maroon and a rich mahogany gleamed from all the doors and facings.

Jason placed one foot carefully inside and bowed his head a little to duck in under the roof. A hand shot out from nowhere and pulled him in.

Before he could even start to struggle he was yanked halfway into the driver's section with both arms pinned against his body by the two front seats. The back door clicked closed and the lights went out.

'You tryin' to steal from Mr Brash's car boy? I'll cut your ruddy hands off.'

Jason was helpless. One pincer-like hand gripped him around the back of the neck, pushing his face hard into the leather of the front passenger seat, whilst another held his body jammed between the seats.

'Whisky,' Jason gasped, struggling to breath. 'Mr Brash sent me to get his… whisky.'

The pressure eased on his neck a little and a moment later the lights faded up. Jason took in a deep breath, his lungs filling with polish. 'I live here…didn't you see me come…?' Jason twisted his head to see who held him and stopped breathing.

'…out,' he coughed.

A living corpse had him.

At least, it looked like a corpse. He was held down by a man with deathly pale skin stretched thinly over prominent skull bones. His black eyes were buried deep in their shadowed sockets and thin pale lips drew back over large, tombstone teeth. All this was dressed up in a grey chauffeur's cap and uniform.

'You tellin' the truth, boy?' Those thin, bloodless lips hardly moved as the man's East London accent rattled out like it was passing over dry bones.

'Yes… go in and ask Mr Brash yourself if you don't believe me,' Jason was starting to get annoyed. Accused of stealing, being bent over a car seat by some freak of a driver…

The man stared at him for a long moment then suddenly he was pulled effortlessly up by the shoulder and pushed back into the rear seats. With hardly a hum, a smoked glass screen slid up between the two compartments and the front light faded out. Jason was left staring at his own reflection.

'Psycho creep,' Jason muttered. He quickly found the drinks cabinet, grabbed an unopened whisky bottle from its mirrored interior and scrambled out of the car.

At the porch Jason looked back at the Bentley, brooding at the very edge of the circle of porch light. That skeletal chauffer must have seen him come out of the house – he'd just been having some twisted control kick.

He went in and shut the door, straightening his clothes and hair before hurrying along the corridor to the warm glow of the drawing room and the low murmur of voices.

'Hurrah,' Brash exclaimed as Jason stepped into the light clutching the whisky, 'the hero returns with the magical elixir.'

'Is everything all right, Son?' Dad asked, catching Jason's look.

'Ah - I bet you ran into Cadaveril didn't you, my boy?' Brash asked before Jason could answer. 'He's enough to give anybody a scare, the ugly old sod.'

Alicia looked up, her sparkling emerald eyes instantly drawing Jason's gaze. He certainly wasn't going to tell her he'd been helplessly pinned down between the Bentley's seats a minute ago. 'Uh… yes, sort of.'

'I see,' Dad said, taking the bottle from him and moving over to some crystal whisky glasses already laid out.

'Come sit with me, Jason,' Alicia said. She patted a cushion next to her on the central couch. The men had taken the high backed armchairs to either side of the fire and Miranda had pulled up a spare seat next to Dad.

Jason attempted a smile and joined Alicia. Dad had poured him some Coke into one of the heavy whisky glasses but he ignored it. What was Dad thinking - putting Coke in a whisky glass for him like he was a "big boy".

'How are you feeling about starting at Silent Hill?' Alicia asked, her lips taking a sip from the heavy crystal.

'All right... I've heard it can be a bit rough there though.'

'Nothing you can't handle, Jason, my boy,' Brash cut in, gently swirling the golden whiskey around his glass. 'You'll be able to get some Jakra practice in against some of our ne'r-do-wells. Just see it as a little extra training to help prepare you for what lies ahead.'

'What do you mean?' Jason asked.

'I think that's enough,' Dad cut in. He hadn't touched his drink.

Brash ignored him. 'You coming into your powers, of course.'

Dad stood up. 'You've no right to talk about this.'

Brash stared at Dad but held up one hand in mock-surrender.

'What powers are you talking about?' Jason forced his question into the icy silence.

Brash shrugged his shoulders and made a zipping motion across his lips. Jason glanced at Alicia for an answer. She'd straightened slightly in her seat but she kept quiet.

'This wasn't a good idea. You need to go now,' Dad said, finally. His voice was calm but Jason immediately recognized the relaxed stance he used just before sparring.

Brash held Dad's gaze. 'Jason needs to know what he is.'

'And he will be told in good time – by me. You need to go now,' Dad repeated.

Brash considered Dad for a moment then gave the slightest of nods. He leant forward as if to get up then suddenly launched his heavy-set frame into a twisting somersault straight over Jason's head and landed perfectly a couple of metres beyond the couch. Air rushed over Jason's face as he twisted around, open mouthed.

As Brash straightened up, Alicia hurled her empty whisky glass at him. Brash's hand shot out and the glass stopped dead - in mid air. He twitched his hand forward and the glass flew back into Alicia's grasp.

Jason was frozen to his seat, his mouth still wide open. A second, lesser breeze brushed passed him.

Brash winked at Jason. 'I really am getting too old for all this, you know.'

Alicia rose gracefully, picked up Brash's own glass from the table and passed it to him.

Brash smiled gratefully and drained the last half inch. 'I'm sorry, Richard, I really am, but I know you too well. I needed some way to make you start the conversation with your son.'

Jason remembered to close his mouth then turned to Dad. 'How did he do that? Can you do it... can I?'

Again, it was Brash who answered, flashing his perfect white teeth. 'That's just the tip of the iceberg, Jason, my boy. A bit of training and you'll be running up walls and levelling houses with the rest of us.'

Dad moved over the door and opened it wide. 'You never did consider the rules important did you Alan – any of them?'

Brash shrugged his heavy shoulders. 'Sometimes the rules need changing. Jason now knows there is more to this world than his physics lessons would have him believe. Either you tell him about the rest of it or I guarantee he will come to me to find out for himself.'

Dad continued to stare at Brash, his eyes cold. He didn't show a single sign of anger or annoyance, he never did when he was facing a threat. Jason swallowed. Dad's Jakra was devastating but pitted against the sort of things Brash had just done...

The air in the room almost shimmered with the chill between the two men but then Alicia Sirensong's warm voice flowed over the ice. 'You know your son's potential, Richard, the Gifts that are coming upon him now that he is... growing up. It is not safe to hide it from him any longer.'

Dad kept his eyes locked on Brash. 'See yourselves out.'

For a moment, no one moved then Miranda stood up and walked purposefully next to Dad. Jason got to his feet as well. Where was this going?

Brash held up his hands and smiled. With a glance to Alicia, they left and Dad closed the drawing room door quietly behind them.

The moment they heard the front door open and close, Jason started. 'How did he do that?'

Dad turned to Jason and his eyes seemed to darken to deepest jet.

'It's called the Gift – it's for killing demons.'

Chapter 7

The next morning saw Jason eating breakfast alone – Dad had left a note about going shopping and Miranda was still not up.

Jason put another couple of slices into the toaster and thought back to last night. Brash had said something about "knowing Dad too well and needing some way of making him talk about his past." He was right - once the pressure was off, Dad had given next to nothing away.

'Right,' Dad had said, 'demon spirits can really be summoned into this world and Jason, you'll come into some unbelievable powers now you're through adolescence. Now there is no way I am going to even start trying to explain it all at ten-thirty on the night before you start a new, god-awful school. It will take days and still you won't grasp the half of it. We are all going to bed… now.'

'You think I can sleep after this?' Jason tried.

'Blame that on Alan Brash.'

'Do I get some groovy powers as well,' Miranda asked, 'or is it just the golden boy here?'

'They only pass down to the first born of the same-sex until...' Dad stopped himself. 'Enough now... you're not going to draw me into this conversation. Go to bed.'

And so they'd left it at that. A lifetime of trying to question their father had taught them that he couldn't be forced to talk.

It didn't stop Jason fuming for half the night though – finally resolving that if Dad didn't tell him everything, and tell him soon, he really would go to see Brash for the answers.

Was that what Brash wanted – for Jason to betray his father's trust?

The toaster was taking ages. Jason read Dad's note again.

Sorry about not being here kids – didn't want to argue about not telling you everything this morning. Gone shopping..

Jason - don't forget the bus is at 8:00 - take the photo-pass that came last week – not sure where you put it. Good luck at school.

PS – finally got post from your grandfather this morning – everything's fine up on Mawn.

PPS - We'll talk this afternoon – I promise.

'Yeah – right,' Jason mumbled 'of course we'll talk this afternoon.'

He'd just been told that demons are real and he's up for some weird powers and his father is more interested in giving advice on what to have for breakfast. Still, Louisa and Mouse should be back from their holiday by now. Perhaps he'd take a chance and see if they really were part of it all.

Ten minutes later, with Miranda still flat out in bed, Jason heaved the front door open and slouched down the steps.

Beyond their gates, steam gently rose from the thatched roofs of a pair of mismatched old cottages leaning against each other for support. Small paned windows with lace netting peered sleepily back at him.

Jason crunched across the driveway gravel and out into the narrow, neatly paved High Street. Bathed in bright morning sunlight, the hamlet seemed lost in time. One shop and a score of houses, all tiny-windowed, jumbled up against each other with the Highwayman Inn looming over them all like some ancient patriarch. He didn't want to leave here for some rough, gang-run school in the middle of a scummy industrial town.

In a few dozen steps Jason reached Darkston Wick's only bus stop. It was set in front of the old general store owned by the equally old Mrs Miggins. There was no one else waiting there.

Jason checked his watch - five to eight. Shrugging his shoulders he plonked himself down on a little stone wall in front of the shop.

With nothing to distract him, the images from last night ran through his mind - Brash flipping his heavy body backwards over the sofa, landing effortlessly and freezing the whisky glass in mid-air. And then there was the breeze Jason had felt across his face when Brash did those things - what was that all about?

Some things had clicked into place last night between snatches of sleep. When he'd first met Louisa and Mouse for instance – he was sure now that he really had been pushed away from Mouse before Louisa got anywhere near to him… and he'd felt a similar brush of cool air then. She must have Brash's powers - this Gift, as Dad had called it.

Jason looked at his watch again - five past eight and still no one. He wondered if Dad had got the times wrong and the bus had already gone. He'd have to telephone the school – see if there was a taxi or something he could call. God, starting his new school by arriving late and everyone staring at him.

He was suddenly hit by an image of a vast assembly hall, filled with hard lads and mean-faced girls all turning to laugh at him as he blundered in through swinging double doors. Couldn't Dad even be bothered to find out the right bus times?

A door slowly opened halfway down the street and a boy and girl stepped out, their matching thatches of rusty, bushy brown hair bobbing as they moved.

Jason recognised them. He had seen the village children around a few times over the holidays – a group of two girls and three boys all aged perhaps between eleven and thirteen, all hardy and sun-browned presumably from a lifetime of roaming over the moors. He hadn't got to know them though – they'd always sidled off whenever he'd seen them and there was no way he was going to chase after them like some sort of loner desperate for friends.

Jason watched the two kids half-heartedly wave to someone inside before trudging down their garden paths. They looked like First World War soldiers in those old movies, leaving their families to be slaughtered in the trenches.

As if everyone had been waiting for someone else to crack first, more doors opened along the High Road and others appeared. They all shuffled along the road to finally plonk themselves on Mrs Miggins' wall. None of them talked.

Jason swallowed. How bad could Silent Hill be? And where the hell were Louisa and Mouse?

A heavy diesel engine coughed into life somewhere behind him. Jason twisted around but the noise was coming from somewhere in the trees on the road out to Drunken Abbot. All the others seemed to be doing their best to ignore it.

The engine roared louder and moments later the oldest, most clapped-out, double-decker bus Jason had ever seen smoked its way down out of the trees. It had once been some shade of green but most of the paint had peeled or been scratched off long ago. There were cracks in most of the filthy windows and black clouds of diesel exhaust billowed all around the vehicle as if it were coming out of hell itself.

Jason flicked his eyes back to the Highwayman – still no sign of Louisa or Mouse. The bus roared closer. Staring out of the wiper-cleared arc of the grimy windscreen was a long faced, greasy haired driver. As Jason watched, the man's eyes seemed to fire up with demented glee and he put his foot down.

The Darkston Wick children all pressed themselves back against Mrs. Miggins' wall as the bus sped past, missing their legs by barely a metre and clouding them in filthy black fumes.

Coughing, Jason stared in disbelief as with a scream of rubber, the old crate span around to come back for a second run at them. This time it jerked towards them, engine revving and belching out more thick black fumes.

The driver's face was pressed up against the window like some leering old letch. He seemed to be looking for someone in particular amongst the small crowd of coughing school children. As he pulled up next to them, he finally sat back in his seat, a thin smile playing on his lips.

The bus stopped and the doors snapped open with a hiss.

'Are they ill then, have they not turned up for their first day back, eh?' the man said, grinning with a face full of nicotine stained teeth. 'We'll have some fun on the way to school today, won't we children? And the new boy from the mill to play with as well... shame your lovely sister ain't here.'

Jason frowned. How did he know where he was living... and that he had a sister?

For a moment, no one made a move towards the blackened steel steps.

Jason took a deep, slow breath and took a step forward. He'd not be intimidated by this creep.

'What a fine and dandy morning this is,' a voice boomed from behind them and as one, the Darkston Wick children snapped their heads around.

Mouse, rock solid and smiling broadly, and Louisa, tall beautiful Louisa, stepped out of the swirling exhaust fumes.

Jason smiled a greeting then stepped up and thrust his bus pass at the driver like holding up a crucifix to a vampire before striding towards the back seat.

The others piled in afterwards, each flashing their passes before flopping onto the seats downstairs. Last to enter were Louisa and Mouse. The driver turned to stare out of the front window, his hand reaching for the door-close button. Mouse stopped on the stairs, half his leg still out of the door.

The driver's hand hovered over the button. Mouse waited a couple of seconds longer then continued up the steps. The doors immediately slammed shut and the engine revved up, enshrouding the outside world in swirling smoke. Neither Mouse nor Louisa hurried to take a seat. Jason caught the driver staring up at a tiny mirror, glaring back at his passengers. Louisa winked at Jason and slipped in between him and the window. Mouse grinned and joined them on the back bench seat.

The bus lurched forward.

Louisa leaned in to Jason a little, her hair just brushing his cheek. He caught a hint of her perfume – light and summery. She smiled at him conspiratorially. 'The driver is called Porter - he shut the door on Mouse... once.'

Jason grinned back at her, his stomach clenching with her leaning so close. 'He's a proper creep.'

'Alan Brash has many... creeps working for him' Louisa said, her eyes flashing. 'This one is always sneaking around the village pretending to be doing one job or another whilst he spies on us.'

Mouse tapped Jason's arm, breaking their secretive huddle. 'Do you like our lovely bus? Brash really looks after us, yes? In fact, I think they must have even cleaned it for us over the holidays.'

He patted the seat hard when he said this and dust mushroomed up and over them. He grinned. 'So – you are ready for Silent Hill, yes?'

Jason looked around. The children from Darkston Wick seemed perfectly unspectacular and they survived the school.

There was no reason he shouldn't do as well as them. Anyway, he'd more important things on his mind.

'I think I'll cope, thanks,' he said then lowered his voice although no one was likely to hear them over the engine noise. 'Talking of Alan Brash... he visited us last night. You wouldn't believe the things he did...'

Mouse and Louisa glanced at each other then back at him.

'I think you know that we would believe it,' Mouse said quietly.

'My mother talked with us on holiday,' Louisa said, 'she has seen your father in the Mill and she needed to get away to think. They knew each other well, you see, a long time ago in Romania.'

Jason nodded. 'So you *are* part of what Dad used to do... the Watch and the Brethren and all...'

'Quietly,' Louisa cut in and glanced down the bus. The Darkston Wick children didn't seem to be taking much notice of them as they stared miserably out of the windows or played with their MP3s and Nintendos.

'Sorry,' Jason said. 'I thought you were probably involved from what you said in the woods. It's just that Dad has never told us much about his past but now I've met you two...'

'We can not "tell you much", either,' Mouse said, shrugging.

'There is a tradition amongst us...' Louisa began

'There are many, many traditions... rules... laws...' Mouse mumbled.

Louisa ignored him. '... a tradition which states only a parent may decide when to first tell their child about... the work we do.'

Mouse cut in. 'Your father should have told you everything by now – he cannot have hoped you could live your life without knowing about it, especially now that you are clearly old enough to...'

'Mouse!' Louisa snapped.

Jason turned back around to face them. 'Old enough to what?'

Louisa stared straight into his eyes. It was almost as if he could feel her inside his head, pressing against his mind. She dropped her gaze, flashing a last look up at him before smiling tightly. 'I am sorry we cannot talk about this until...'

'Until my dad tells me first – I get it.' Jason said. 'That could be sometime never.'

Mouse shrugged.

'Well last night Brash told me about I am going to get some... super powers,' Jason said. 'He even gave us a little demonstration.'

Mouse and Louisa stared at one another for a moment. Finally Louisa turned back to Jason. 'He should not have done that.'

Mouse gave a harsh laugh. 'Alan Brash does what he likes.'

'Anyway,' Jason said, 'it means you can tell me a bit about the stuff he did... the Gift or something.'

'No it does not,' Louisa answered, 'not until your father has explained it to you.'

Jason shook his head. This was getting nowhere. 'Brash said I'd end up going to him for the answers.'

Louisa shook her head. 'That would be a stupid thing to do – he will try to... to own you.'

'For once, Louisa is right,' Mouse said. 'We only stay near him for protection until we are old enough to join the...' he glanced down the bus. A couple of the older Darkston Wick kids quickly turned back to look out of their windows. '... to help with the work that needs to be done.'

Louisa was watching the front of the bus. Porter, the driver, kept glancing at them in his mirror. 'This is not the place to talk of such things.'

'But...' Jason began.

Louisa placed a finger on his mouth. He froze, desperately hoping he wouldn't dribble under her smooth, cool touch.

'Come to our house after school – we will talk then but remember we cannot discuss anything your father has not explained to you already.' She slowly took her finger away, releasing him.

Jason hesitated for a moment then nodded and was quiet.

Mouse broke the silence with a grin. 'Did Brash have his assistant with him – Alicia Sirensong?'

'Did he ever…' Jason began, then glanced at Louisa.

'Sirensong,' Louisa said, '– such a stupid name. It should be warning to you about how Alan Brash controls people, how he thinks he owns people.'

'What?' Jason asked.

'Don't you see - he gave her that name. When people come to his valley wanting to forget their past life, he chooses stupid new names for some of them – like pet dogs. The others he just calls Smith.'

'Oh, I see.' Jason managed as Louisa turned her back on him to look out of the window.

The bus slowed down and Jason looked out as well. He'd been so engrossed in the conversation and Louisa's close proximity that he'd not registered driving into Drunken Abbot.

They were on a main road with small, grey houses falling back from it in a warren of narrow streets and shadowed alleys. On the high street, he could see a few run down shops, take-aways and newsagents scattered amongst many boarded-up buildings but the only businesses that seemed to be thriving were tiny pubs. There was one on at least half the corners where a dark terraced street slunk up to the decaying main road.

The pubs were all garishly decorated in vibrant shades of reds, greens or blues with liberal dashes of glossy black and gold. He read their names – "The Abbot and Altar", "The Abbot and Chalice" – in fact, they were all called the "Abbot and something".

The bus hissed to a halt in a quick series of air-brake jerks. Through the dirt-streaked windows Jason could make out a dozen or so youths, all in T shirts, dirty jeans and scuffed trainers. They shuffled forward through beer bottles and take-away rubbish dumped at the bus stop.

'Now you will have the pleasure of meeting some of the Skins,' Mouse mumbled and lounged back into the seat.

The doors opened and half a dozen skinheads pushed on first – one of them a girl. They ranged from perhaps twelve to older than Jason but they all had their noses, eyebrows, ears and even lips studded with a mixture of gold balls, skulls, daggers and guns. Tattoos including snakes and spiders crawled up their arms and necks.

Behind them, the other kids waited on the pavement, keeping well out of their way. The Skins piled in without showing their passes, pushing each other and swearing their way towards the stairs. Porter said nothing but his contemptuous sneer burned in the passenger-view mirror. Suddenly, the first skinhead stopped at the bottom of the stairwell - he'd spotted Jason.

The lead skinhead was big, stocky and maybe a little older than Jason - probably in year eleven. His lower lip was pierced through with a gold ball and his left eyebrow had three small daggers studded through it.

He started down the aisle, punching the metal headrests and hold-posts with his large, gold-coloured sovereign rings as he came. As he got closer, his lips split back over dirty teeth in a malicious smile and he flicked out a double studded tongue like a snake. The other Skins crowded in behind him. One of them, lanky but tightly muscled, had a spider web tattooed over half his left cheek.

The more normal Drunken Abbot kids getting on behind, scuttled onto the downstairs seats and turned to watch what would happen. The Darkston Wick kids kept perfectly still, trying not to catch the Skins' eyes as they banged their way passed. They need not have worried - the Skins' attention was all on Jason although all the boys kept glancing at Louisa.

Jason sat still, concentrating on breathing slow and deep. A fight in these close quarters would get messy.

'Hello, Hairy,' Mouse said to the lead skinhead. Jason winced - was that his real nickname or just one of Mouse's little witticisms? 'You have missed our company, yes?'

Hairy's small pig eyes narrowed. 'I ain't missed you, Mouse, don't be fick - you're too ugly for anyone to miss.' He turned to gawp at Louisa who stared coolly back. 'Got your sticks wiv ya, Mouse?' he asked, finally dropping Louisa's stare.

Mouse just smiled.

Hairy nodded and turned to Jason, leaning close to him as if peering at some grub found crawling along his mattress. His breath smelled - a mix of old beer, onions and decay. Jason stopped himself from swallowing hard.

'Wot you doin' on my bus, you skinny little rat?'

The skinhead girl snorted behind him. 'Hey, Mouse's mate would be a rat, wouldn't he?'

Jason moved his head to the side a little to get a breath of cleaner air and to smile sweetly at the female wit of the gang. She'd a thin little rat-tail of blonde hair, sticking out from the back of her head. Despite this, with fewer studs and a bit more hair she'd actually be really good looking. The boy with the spider-web face scowled and slung his arm across the girl's shoulders, mouthing some obscenity at Jason.

The bus jerked forward, wisps of black diesel fumes curling in.

'Well, rat-boy – you too scared to talk?' Hairy grunted, leaning even closer. 'Wot ya doing on my bus?'

Jason turned back to the big, ugly face in front of him. He was getting a bit sick of this foul smelling thug and there was no way he was going to look afraid in front of Louisa.

'I'm coming to your school to make some lovely new friends,' Jason said, straightening up so he was closer to Hairy's height.

Hairy's face split back into its dirty-toothed grin and he twisted around to face his posse. 'He talks posh, don't he?' Hairy nodded as he said this, giving them the right answer and so they nodded back, laughing. Only the girl with the rat-tail hair looked a little suspicious of Jason's apparent lack of fear.

Just then, the bus lurched and the skinheads half stumbled with it.

'You had better find a seat upstairs where it is safe, Hairy,' Mouse said, fiddling with something inside the thin leather jacket he was wearing over his black tee shirt. 'We would not want you all falling down and having your faces smashed in now, would we?'

Louisa sat up straighter and interlocked her fingers. She pushed out her index fingers to form an arrow pointing straight at Hairy's crotch. One quick flick of her foot at the target and the Skin would be in agony.

Hairy stared at Louisa's hands and nudged back into his gang. A muscle twitched in his cheek. 'Maybe we'll… make friends wiv ya' at school then, new boy,' he said, then turned away, pushing through the others and leading them up stairs.

The last Skin to go up was the rat-tail girl. She stared at Jason for a moment and he waved to her. She shook her head, cut one finger across her throat and followed her gang.

'Nice,' Jason said, forcing himself to relax back into the seat.

'Hairy and the baldies?' Mouse said. 'They're not so bad – it is Big Wig you need to watch out for. He is not so friendly.'

'Big Wig?' Jason snorted, his tension starting to drain away.

Mouse just winked.

Louisa shivered and wrinkled her nose as if she could smell something bad. 'He means Callum Mennis – the leader of the Skins. Do not call him Big Wig.'

'You said something about the gangs that time in the woods…' Jason said. 'Isn't there a Brash gang or something as well?'

'You actually listen to what we say?' Mouse said, raising one eyebrow.

'Only the interesting bits,' Jason said.

'So,' Mouse continued, 'there are indeed two gangs – the Brash and the Skins. It is like a fairy tale, yes - the Brash are rich, beautiful people from a pretty village but the Skins are poor and ugly, their families slave in the brewery and drink away their lives in these pubs we are passing.'

'Nice,' Jason said.

Mouse nodded. 'Luckily the Skins all live in the hovels of Drunken Abbot and are fenced off from the nice people.'

Jason stifled a grin. 'It must be quite a big fence to keep the whole town out.'

'Oh, yes,' Louisa answered, 'Brash is very strict about security. He says it is to protect the laboratories against spying but of course, we know it is to guard against... other dangers.'

Jason nodded. She must mean the Brethren rather than the Skins and brewery workers of Drunken Abbot.

He looked down the bus. The "normal" teenagers who had got on after the Skins, had all stayed on the lower deck. They looked fairly rough in their dirty, ripped jeans and crumpled T-shirts but they weren't threatening like the Skins. They were talking more loudly than the Darkston Wick children however, confident on their own turf and some of them openly stared back at the new boy. Were they guessing at his fate once he got into school?

'So, these town kids sitting here,' Jason whispered, 'they're not part of the Skins' gang then?'

Mouse answered. 'No – the Skins only want the best of the pickings... the strong or just the most vicious. The others are sometimes used as punch bags so they do their best to be invisible most of the time.'

Jason nodded and looked out of the window. It wouldn't be difficult to disappear in the dilapidated buildings and rat-runs of Drunken Abbot.

'They are not all bad people, of course,' Louisa said, snapping his attention back to her. She paused for a moment, then looked straight into his eyes. 'For an example - you seem to have caught the eye of that nice girl, Lindsey Davenport.'

Trapped in her gaze like that, there wasn't another girl that existed for Jason. He swallowed hard and stammered 'The skinny, rat-tail girl? I think she wants my throat cut.'

Louisa held him for a few more delicious moments then smiled. 'Be careful of her, Jason, she is clever.'

'Okay,' Jason said. Was Louisa bothered that he might like another girl? Feeling his face start to burn at the thought, Jason looked out of the window again.

They trundled along the main road, passing more rows of indistinguishable grey terraced houses – many of them boarded up like the shops.

'Why are there so many pubs?' Jason asked.

'I think you would need to drink if you lived in this place, yes?' Mouse asked.

'Brash sells Drunken Abbot Ale and whisky very cheaply to his workers,' Louisa explained, looking out of her window. Her voice sounded flat, bordering on hopeless.

Mouse carried on. 'Brash is very clever - he pays very little but gives them their homes and feeds their... what is your word... addictions - yes? This makes it very difficult for anyone to leave the town where they might spread rumours and secrets that might bring... unwanted attention.'

'Have you ever tasted it?' Louisa said, suddenly facing Jason. 'Drunken Abbot Ale I mean... or the whisky?'

'Uhh, no, I've had plenty of lager and cider and stuff though,' Jason said then immediately felt like a pathetic schoolboy trying to impress a girl about how big a drinker he was.

'Do not ever try it,' she said. 'We do not know what Brash has found to make the drink become so addictive but it happens very quickly.'

'So there are no magic potions that you people use then?' Jason asked, trying to keep his voice light whilst digging for a little information about the world of demon hunting.

Louisa hesitated a moment then spoke quietly. 'No, we have no potions or magic spells to change princes into frogs.'

They stopped twice more to pick up Drunken Abbot kids. Each time it was the same - a bunch of skinheads pushing and swearing their way upstairs followed by more normal children, often running from across the street to catch the bus at the last minute presumably to avoid waiting with the Skins.

All the normal pupils stayed downstairs, happy to stand once all the seats were filled rather than venture onto the upper deck.

Hating to admit it to himself, Jason didn't blame them.

'Is there much trouble with the Skins at school?' Jason asked.

Mouse grinned. 'Only the fighting.'

'Don't the teachers do anything about it?'

Mouse shrugged. 'They don't care as long as it is outside the buildings. They are scared to come out into the grounds, I think.'

Louisa scoffed. 'It is more likely Alan Brash has told them to let the gangs get on with their fighting. It is good training for the Brash gang – he chooses the best ones for his private army of security guards.'

'This is true. The Brash gang are like the Securitate or the KGB of the school,' Mouse grunted, 'his secret police.'

'And now you will see where they live,' Louisa said, nodding out of the windows.

They had arrived at the fence.

Razor wire stretched six metres high between towering, bright steel poles and ran continuously across streets blockaded by concrete posts and behind derelict and boarded up houses. The wire was electrified too, according to the yellow streaked lightening signs and there were floodlights and motorised cameras on top of the foot-thick poles.

The bus turned down a narrow street and everyone started reaching inside their coats and trouser pockets to pull out dark blue pass holders.

'Get your pass out,' Mouse said. 'These security people are not very patient.'

The bus shuddered to a halt some way before a glistening, sheet-steel gate hung between twin watchtowers. Two metres in front of the gate a double row of thick, steel bollards jutted up out of the road.

Jason tugged out his photo pass just as the bus door hissed open and four dark blue uniformed security guards stepped on board. They each wore a belt hung with a long police baton, handcuffs, spray can and bulging pouches. They wore dark blue helmets, complete with smoked visors pushed up for the moment, and some sort of tiny web-cam and microphone stuck on the side.

'Brash likes his security, doesn't he?' Jason whispered.

Mouse kicked his foot. 'Just keep quiet.'

Two of the guards went upstairs and two moved slowly along the lower deck checking everyone's photo pass in small card readers.

'The readers blue-tooth to a database,' Mouse whispered. 'If the pictures don't match they shoot you,'.

Jason stared at him, eyes wide. He couldn't tell if Mouse was joking or not.

The foremost guard reached Jason and stopped, the tiny helmet camera lens staring at him like a dead glass eye. The bus was silent. Jason heard a tinny voice inside the guard's helmet.

'You're new.' the guard said.

'I am.'

Mouse knocked his foot and so he added 'My name is Jason Willow,' and held his pass higher.

The guard took the pass and fed it into his machine. Jason held his breath. Dad had sent one of his old passport photographs to have the pass made – his hair was a bit longer now and his spots had cleared up.

The guard frowned at the photo but then turned around at some shouting from the upper deck.

'I just bloody forgot it, all right. Leave me…'

A moment later, a skinhead crashed down the metal steps and sprawled across the floor. He struggled to stand but a black boot lashed out from the stairwell straight into his stomach. The boy doubled over and another guard from outside stepped in, grabbed him around the neck and dragged him off the bus.

Nobody moved. Jason's interrogator turned back to him. He didn't seem in the least perturbed by the violence as he handed the pass back.

'Get a new photograph authorised… soon.'

And that was that. In moments, the guards were out of the bus and the door hissed shut. The shining bollards slid down into the road and the steel gate rolled to one side to allow them into Darkston village

***

The bus rattled through a community that couldn't have been more different from the decaying streets of Drunken Abbot. It was a perfectly landscaped picture of paved lanes winding between thatched cottages and breaking into small parks and a village square. The whole place rambled down the sunny south sides of two gentle hills.

On top of one of those hills brooded an ominous black marble gatehouse and on the other, the grey monolith of Silent Hill school.

'How can Brash get away with treating people like this?' Jason asked. 'Half of them in a slum and the other in some chocolate box heaven with crazy armed guards to keep them apart?'

Mouse grunted. 'Brash has many loyal, well paid friends in high places – they are like a big family, yes? This is how he can have his own little empire in this valley and keep it all secret.'

Louisa stared out of the window. 'This is where Brash gives his important people their beautiful homes, luxury food delivered to their door and, best of all, free Drunken Abbot Ale.'

'What, totally free, as much as they like?' Jason asked.

'Of course,' Louisa said, keeping to a whisper that did nothing to hide her vitriol, 'these are Brash's most valuable tools – his chemists, accountants, lawyers and managers as well as those relocated from... abroad. They know too much to ever leave his service and so he ties them to him in many ways.'

She turned to face him, leaning closer and dropping her voice. 'This is what Brash does – he gives people everything they want until he does not need them any more . You must have nothing to do with him, Jason.'

Jason struggled to concentrate. He could feel Louisa's warm breath on his neck as she spoke. She was wearing that light, summery perfume again, sending tendrils of delicate sweetness weaving through his head.

Mouse nudged him, a little harder than was necessary to get his attention. 'His people will try to tie you to him as well – the first will probably be the Brash gang. They will offer you protection, training and… other rewards.'

Jason nodded, sitting back and closing his eyes. Here he was, on his way to a nightmare school in the middle of a high security fantasy village and being told not to trust a middle aged businessman who last night had performed a ten foot back flip and stopped a glass in mid air and who seemed to be the only person who wanted to tell him about demons that were being summoned into our world and show him how to use the miraculous powers he was about to develop.

This wasn't normal.

'We're here,' Louisa cut across his thoughts.

Jason looked up and Silent Hill school filled the windscreen in front of him.

Chapter 8

Row upon row of small dark windows stared blindly out from a massive, grey granite wall. The regimented glass only broke ranks once - for a small, iron bound door which opened into a dimly lit tunnel.

Jason followed Louisa and Mouse as they got up and shuffled down the bus behind the other students. No one spoke – it was as if they were being herded towards the gallows. Thankfully the Skins upstairs seemed in no hurry to leave either and had not even appeared yet.

Jason stepped off the bus onto flagstones worn smooth by centuries of shambling feet. The yard was immense, stretching for two hundred metres or more across the face of the building. In the centre was a granite dais rising in three square blocks to a platform four metres up. On top there stood a black-wood gallows.

Jason shivered. Standing still in the cold shadow of Silent Hill, he could smell the stone and almost feel the thousands of tons of granite leaning forward, overwhelming him with its weight of centuries.

'Perhaps a small flower basket would brighten it up a little, yes?' Mouse suggested, slapping him on the shoulder.

The spell broken, noise flooded back into Jason's head. Pupils were everywhere - sitting on the gallows' steps, milling in front of the walls and door and skulking off into some woods which fell away down the hillside on the far edge of the yard.

The new arrivals began to trudge towards the single doorway, the Darkston Wick children hurrying away as the Skins finally piled off the bus behind them. Thankfully, the gang members headed straight for the left hand corner of the school and disappeared from view.

As they approached the dark doorway, the looming granite and press of pupils seemed to fill Jason's head.

'Are you alright?' Louisa said, touching his arm. He forced himself to focus on her lovely face and block out the school. He didn't want her to leave him on his own here – not yet anyway. He just needed a little time to adjust, that was all.

'You do get used to it,' she said, smiling as Jason forced a nonchalant shrug. 'It is supposed to make you feel bad – Silent Hill was built a thousand years ago as a House of Correction for those disobeying the sacred laws of the Darkston Abbey monks. If the inmates spoke, they were flogged or worse.'

'Lovely,' Jason croaked, 'that helps.'

Mouse shoved between two groups of younger pupils. 'Come on, we should get inside before the fun begins out here, I think. Jason would perhaps wish to avoid that on his first day.'

He forged ahead towards the passage. The door which was thrown back against the wall was almost a foot thick, banded with iron and with a barred watch hole two thirds up. Jason pushed away the image of it being slammed shut and trapping him inside.

'What does he mean – "before the fun begins"?' Jason asked Louisa.

She glanced across at the left hand corner and Jason followed her gaze. A couple of Skins had appeared and were lounging against the wall, smoking and watching the crowd. She shook her head and pulled Jason into the tunnel after Mouse.

'He means the swearing and stone throwing when the Brash arrive... perhaps a small fight as it is the first day of term.'

'Better and better.' Willow mumbled.

The passage ran for perhaps fifty metres or so and opened into bright sunlight at the far end. It was badly lit by old fluorescent tubes, half of them broken and most of the others flickering intermittently. Doors opened off on both sides about every five metres or so and half way along there were opposing flights of stone steps rising up into more gloom.

Jason felt buried alive here, passing under countless tons of granite and struggling to breathe in the musty air of a passageway not touched by sunlight for hundreds of years. Countless harsh voices and the buzzing of the fluorescents echoed around the walls, growing louder by the second.

'Come on, almost there,' Louisa whispered in his ear and her voice cut through his new-found claustrophobia. Jason focussed on the growing arch of glaring sunlight ahead and moments later they stepped outside.

They were in a work-yard, one corner blazing bright with sunlight, the rest in deep, cold shadow. Five huge boulders of chisel-scarred granite stood around the yard with a number of half-fashioned blocks lying by each one. Four grey storeys of tiny dark windows rose up on all sides to completely enclose the yard. An identical tunnel to theirs ran out of the work-yard through each of the other walls but apart from these, the only escape from the yard was one small black door set deep in the shadows.

Jason swallowed hard. All the passages had heavy, iron strapped doors on the inside as well – the work-yard could be entirely sealed off from the outside world.

Louisa tugged him through clusters of students to the nearest boulder. It was taller than him with chisel cuts gouged deep into its surface. Jason traced a deep cut with one finger, feeling the cold stone pulling at his skin. How many centuries ago had some ragged prisoner, bound in silence, scored that cut in the cold shadows of this yard? Jason shivered.

'It is cold now but wait until midday,' Mouse said, clasping Jason on the shoulder, 'it becomes an oven in here with the sun overhead. This was the monks' rock garden, yes?'

Jason didn't laugh. Mouse shrugged and carried on anyway. 'The Brash and Skins keep out of here most of the time and so the normal kids keep in. This is a safe place.'

Jason looked around. Mouse was right. Dozens of 'normal' kids clustered around in groups, straddled the half-carved blocks and leaned against the walls. A bunch of younger kids were helping each other climb out of the shade onto the top of one of the smaller boulders. There were certainly no Skins around and Jason didn't know what the Brash gang members looked like.

'Keep out of quiet corridors and toilets, go straight to lessons and come here at breaks is my wonderful advice to you,' Mouse said. 'Now, I am going to see if any of my many, many friends have survived Easter without me.' He slapped Jason on the back and wandered off towards a small group of boys lounging against the next boulder. They grunted and nodded as he approached.

'How are you feeling?' Louisa asked.

'I've had better days,' Jason said and Louisa smiled, flashing perfect white teeth behind her soft, red lips.

'Listen, Louisa, it sounds a bit sad but thanks for you know… sort of being my friend. Things could have been pretty bad moving to a new house and school and all that and…'

Louisa touched a finger to his lips and he froze mid-sentence. She left it there – cool and still. She must use hand cream that matched her perfume as once again, Jason's head was filled with the light evening scents of a summer garden. He hoped he didn't dribble.

'No thanks are needed, Jason, none at all. We are "all in the same boat", as you English say.' She slowly took her finger away, which was probably a good thing because it was all Jason could do to stop himself from kissing it.

Louisa glanced around. 'I know you have questions after Alan Brash's visit last night. We will talk after school – at home, where we are private.'

Jason just stared at her, managing to mumble 'Okay, great.' whilst trying to untwist his stomach and clear his mind. A cold dread of being left alone here shivered up through him but he forced a smile.

'I also should find my friends,' Louisa continued. 'You will be safe here. The year ten form classes are all through the West passage, on the ground floor.' She pointed towards one of the identical passageways. 'We will see you at break time… if you survive that long.' She winked at him and then turned to walk away towards a group of good looking girls all dressed in tight jeans and sleeveless, brightly coloured tops.

Jason watched her go. Did she fancy him… even a little bit? He'd worked out she was in year 12 but what difference did a couple of years make?

Four hand bells suddenly clanged out simultaneously, each reverberating down one of the passageways. Everyone started moving so Jason headed for the tunnel Louisa had indicated and tried to ignore the fact he was surrounded by a couple of hundred kids who all seemed to know each other. He wasn't exactly new to starting new schools.

He gripped his small sports bag which held his pencil case, calculator and a couple of rough books. He wondered if he should have bothered bringing it – most of the pupils slouching off into their various passageways carried nothing whatsoever.

He heard some swearing from behind him and saw the Skins barging their way out of what must have been the East Passage. Trying hard not to look like he was rushing away from them, he reached his tunnel and disappeared into the flickering fluorescent gloom.

***

'Very good, Jason – whatever school you joined us from is obviously very hot on Pythagoras. Now, everyone get on with the worksheet - you have fifteen minutes to finish.'

Jason sank down into his wooden desk. Why was it always so embarrassing when teachers praised you?

He was coming towards the end of his first lesson at Silent Hill – double maths – and was starting to get his bearings. Things here were very simple. There were three form classes in each year group and you were taught in your very mixed ability form class for every subject. There were no options to be taken until the sixth form so everyone was taught the same thing whilst sitting in the same seating plan with the same kids for every lesson. Simple.

Jason had already worked out that he was probably the brightest in his class with the possible exception of the girl he'd been placed with – Violet Gray.

Violet ventured a quick smile at him then quickly buried her head in her worksheet. She was a third of the way down the page already. Jason watched her work for a moment; her slightly pointed nose followed each rattled-out line of trigonometry as her left hand absently pushed back her long straight mousy hair over skinny shoulders. She'd barely whispered more than a few dozen words to him so far but she was pleasant enough he guessed and far better that he'd been seated next to her than with some of the others in his class.

He'd been put in form 10A with Alan Pastor as form tutor. When he'd finally found the right form class, he'd been unsettled to see four Skins sitting at the back of the room. One of them was the boy with the web tattoo on his face from Jason's bus but he hadn't seen the others before - two fairly well built, tall boys and a whip thin girl with a number 1 crew cut and small, hard eyes.

The form class also housed what he guessed must be five members of the Brash gang – three boys and two girls. They were all impeccably dressed in designer labels and immaculately groomed. All five seemed to watch him with a sort of superior curiosity.

No one had made an effort to talk to him but neither had there been any trouble in form or in his maths lesson, not even from the Skins. There seemed to be some sort of understanding in the school buildings and all the kids did more or less what the teachers told them to... apart from work particularly hard.

Mr Pastor had given him a printed timetable, put him next to Violet Gray and told her to show him around for the rest of the day.

Violet was obviously neither a Brash nor a Skin; in fact she didn't seem to be anyone at all really. Painfully quiet, she answered his questions with yeses and no's and occasionally offered the odd bit of information: 'If you're not in class by the second bell it's a half hour detention', 'Call all the teachers sir or miss', 'Those are the quickest stairs to the yard for break.'

Feeling very ungrateful, Jason nevertheless hoped that Violet would not follow Mr Pastor's instructions to the letter and stick with him all through break and lunch as well.

Jason checked his watch – just a couple of minutes to go until the end of maths with a formidable Scottish teacher called Mrs Strachen. He looked around the room for about the thousandth time. The classrooms were all long and narrow – he guessed they were made from five or six cells knocked together. The only natural light came from tiny windows built high up the walls centuries before. The same dodgy fluorescent tubes as in the entrance passageways were set in the low ceilings which added to the feeling of incarceration.

At last the bell went for break and everyone packed up and headed for the door. Violet burst into a sudden rush, almost a panic, stuffing her books and pens away. She dropped a pencil and Jason picked it up for her.

'Thanks' she said quietly, then fumbled to fasten her bag.

'No problem,' Jason said. She reminded him of some flighty, skinny legged fawn rattled by a cracking twig in Bambi. He packed away more slowly. Around them, the 'normals' shot past and out of the door. Violet leapt up and started after the pack.

'Uhh, thanks for your help this morning,' Jason said to her back. 'See you next lesson.'

She stopped and turned to him, her brown eyes big and round in her thin face. 'Come on, hurry up,' She said and glanced behind him where the Skins and the Brash were scraping their chairs back. Her mouth set in a determined line. 'I'll take you to the yard.'

Jason was not going to look as if he was running scared. He stood up and stretched. Just as he lowered his arms, the spider-web Skin pushed between them and went for the door at the same time as one of the Brash boys. The Brash boy elbowed in front so the Skin shoved him through. The Brash boy span around in the corridor, fists coming up but before he could do anything, the Skin was grabbed by the neck from outside and slammed against the opposite wall.

He twisted around swearing, and then froze. A huge lad stood in front of him, his arms crossed. The fight instantly drained from the Skin and he stood up straight, back against the wall and stared at the floor.

'You're scum, Richard bloody Baldwin – don't you touch decent people again – you understand?' the big lad said and cuffed Baldwin hard across the head.

The Skin – evidently named Richard Baldwin - didn't react at all but just stood, head bowed and fists clenched.

Suddenly Baldwin's tormentor span around to stare at Jason who had moved to watch through the doorway.

'You want some of this?' he asked, a sneer tugging at one corner of his mouth.

From the corner of his eye, Jason saw Mrs Strachen deliberately turn away from the door and begin wiping the board.

He let his bag slip from his hands. No way was he going to let some lout try to intimidate him.

'He's with me – he's new,' Violet almost shouted from behind Jason. She picked up his bag, thrust it into his hand and shoved him down the corridor.

'That's one of the Brash prefects,' she whispered, still nudging him forward.

Jason glanced back. The prefect was still staring at him. He was well dressed in an open shirt and blue blazer, much like the Brash boys in his class, but he also wore an ebony badge of the Drunken Abbot logo - a freakishly jovial monk's head with its exaggerated features etched in ivory. Squinting out above fat, laughing cheeks were eyes cast in tiny glinting rubies. Jason thought the logo had the look of a sinister clown from some old-time touring circus.

'Come on,' pleaded Violet and tugged him down the stairwell.

They ended up in the South Passage which was packed full of kids. The pupils split into two streams - Brash and Skins heading out of the building, presumably to their respective turfs, and the normal kids scurrying deeper inside to the work-yard. Jason followed Violet into the "normal" kids stream. It didn't seem right to be forced into the work-yard because the gangs ruled on the outside. Still, too early to make any heroic challenges just yet.

They stopped in the lee of one of the boulders. Sunlight had edged its way down the west wall but half the yard was still deep in shadow. Jason looked around the grey flagstone landscape. Everyone else was in pairs or groups, talking and stuffing snacks in their mouths. It seemed half of them kept looking over at him and Violet. Didn't they have many new kids in this place? Did they think he and Violet were... an item?

'I'd better go.' Violet whispered, fiddling with the straps of her bag. 'Keep away from the Brash prefects – they're the ones wearing...'

'The little monk badges – I noticed,' Jason cut in.

Violet nodded. 'I'm just trying to keep you out of trouble.' She stared up at him, her gray/blue eyes hard. 'We've got science next, west passage, second floor. Think you can find your way there on your own?'

'Yeah, I think I'll manage,' Jason dropped his gaze. He was being a prat. He looked back up at her. 'Listen, Violet... thanks for your help...'

Violet's eyes softened and she gave a tight smile 'You need it,' she mumbled and walked off with a cursory wave.

'Why are you talking to Violet Gray?' Willow jumped as Mouse, appeared from behind the boulder.

'She's in my form, - Pastor appointed her as my nanny.'

Mouse watched Violet disappear into the crowd. 'You know she is Alan Brash's ward, yes?'

'No.'

'Well, now you do. Watch what things you say to her.'

'She's all right,' Willow said, 'she saved me from one of your evil prefects. Everyone seems terrified of them.'

'How strange, I wonder why that is?' Mouse said, his eyes widening in mock surprise. 'Could it perhaps be that they can do anything they please to a pupil who is... misbehaving?'

'What, anything?'

'More than less, as long as no one dies – that would lose Brash a future brewery worker or security guard.'

'Don't the skin-heads fight back – gang up on the prefects or something?'

'You saw their pretty badges? That means they are part of Drunken Abbot Industries. Their friends are those nice guards on the bus this morning, yes?'

Jason nodded.

'Also, the prefects will all work for Brash security next year. They will have guns and batons of their own at that time... it would not be sensible to make them your enemy, I think.'

'Yeah, okay, I see your point but what about the parents? Don't they get involved with their kids being knocked about by prefects?'

Mouse laughed. 'Every parent here has a job and a home tied to Alan Brash... just keep away from the prefects - there is no one to stop them.'

'Great - so I have to run away from the Skins and the Brash, especially the Brash prefects... anyone else?'

'Also, our caretakers are not very nice...' Mouse said, 'and then if you went into Drunken Abbot at night, to not become dead you should...'

Just then, Louisa stepped out from the West Passage and Jason's attention was pulled over to her. She looked radiant, the sun kissing her face and turning her white blouse to shining incandescence. Her hair gently lifted behind her in the tunnel breeze as she surveyed the yard. She spotted Mouse and Jason and glided over.

'I see you have found something more interesting than my wise advice,' Mouse mumbled to the back of Jason's head. 'This, as you English say, will all end in tears.'

'Mmm?' Jason said, not really registering what Mouse had said. Then Louisa reached him.

'I think I need private lessons from your father, Jason – you said he teaches chemistry, didn't you?'

'Yes, yes he does,' Jason said, trying not to grin. Louisa, alone at his house for private lessons – what could be better?

'Good. I have just had isotopes and they make no sense to me at all.'

'Dad will be able to show you – he explains everything with daft pictures,' Jason said.

'Perfect – well that is a date then,' Louisa winked at him. 'You seem to have survived your first morning quite well – no cuts or bruises.'

'It's not so bad here,' Jason said, his mind still racing at the prospect of Louisa coming over to the Old Mill on her own.

Louisa nodded but she was distracted by a boy striding towards them. He was about her age, tall, well built with black hair tied back in a short ponytail. He was munching on some sort of cereal bar.

'Mmm, the light has suddenly become too bright for me here.' Mouse mumbled and wandered away to join his friends grouped nearby.

'Hey, Louisa, who's your little friend?' the pony-tail asked in a rich, confident voice.

Louisa looked up at the boy, holding his gaze for a little too long Jason thought, before answering.

'This is Jason Willow, he has just moved into Darkston Wick. Jason, this is Darius – he is in my class.'

I wouldn't have said that Jason thought. He nodded a greeting, not wanting to appear any more friendly than he felt.

'I hope you can run fast, Jason, you're a bit skinny to stand and fight the bad boys we have around here.' Darius grinned. His teeth were perfectly straight and white.

'Well I'm sure I can always hide behind a mighty hillock such as you,' Jason said.

Louisa raised an eyebrow. Darius's forehead creased in concentration. 'Better learn to run…' he said finally, then put a large hand on Louisa's shoulder, 'I'm likely to be a little too busy for you to hide behind.'

Louisa smiled at him and Jason felt sick. Surely she didn't like this idiot.

'Listen, Louisa,' Darius said, 'Can you just go over that palindromic equation stuff with me before maths? Old Strachen said she was going to give us a test today, didn't she?'

Louisa gave an exaggerated sigh. 'Quickly then, we have only five minutes before the bell.' She smiled back at Jason. 'Remember – stay inside the building.'

Why did she have to say that? He could look after himself.

A few minutes later the bells started clanging and Jason trudged off to science.

***

Double science passed uneventfully. Just as in maths, most of the class were behind Jason in the topics they'd covered, even with his taking a year out of school after his mother's murder. Violet however, was ahead of him by quite some way.

On the way out of the classroom, he came face to face with the prefect from outside maths.

'He hasn't done anything wrong.' Violet said, stepping up beside Jason. The rest of the class, including Baldwin scurried off to drain away down the nearest stairwell.

'Shove off, Gray,' the prefect rumbled, 'Willow you stay exactly where you are.'

'You can't just take him – he's been assigned to me for the day,' Violet said, stepping further forward.

'Violet,' Jason hissed, 'I can look after myself.'

'Shut it Willow,' said the prefect then turned to Violet. 'You do know, little orphan, that Mr Brash has personally told us that you're to be treated no differently from any of the other scum infecting our corridors.'

'Rubbish' Violet almost shouted, but she took a half step back. 'Now think hard... he didn't actually say that, did he?'

'More or less. Now don't worry about your boyfriend, here. He hasn't done anything wrong... yet. I just need a little chat with him.'

'Everyone knows what your "little chats" involve...' Violet began but Jason cut in.

'Violet, it's fine. Thanks and all that, but you're showing me up.'

Violet flashed a glance along the now deserted corridors then stared at Jason. 'Showing you up? Duh... there's no one else here.'

Jason shook his head in exasperation. 'I know, but...'

'Fine,' Violet said and stalked off down the stairs.

'Right,' Willow turned back to the prefect, 'what do you want?'

The prefect waited for Violet to disappear down the stairwell then looked down at Jason.

'You're new, Willow, so I gave you a chance outside maths. Learn quick – don't interfere with anything the prefects do. Just keep your head down, do what we tell you and sod off out of our way.'

'Is that it?'

The prefect stared at him. 'For now.'

Jason turned to leave but another prefect had silently arrived at the top of the stairwell.

'He's to use the east stairs, Greg,' the new arrival said, his voice filling the deserted corridor, 'these are busy.'

'Yeah, I know,' replied Jason's escort. 'This way, Willow.' He pointed to the left and with a shrug, Jason started walking.

Greg followed him. The building had the same layout on all four floors - four corridors forming a square around the work yard outside. Each corridor had a narrow spiral staircase dropping down into one of the entrance passages below.

They reached the east stairs and Greg grunted that he should go down first. The science labs were on the fourth floor and the big prefect's footsteps echoed ominously behind Jason as they dropped down passed each of the other corridors. They were all deserted now – cleared for the lunch break.

Finally Jason stepped down into the flickering gloom of the East Passage. Anxious to be away from Greg, he immediately turned towards the yard and found himself staring at Louisa. She stood a step back in the yard's sunlight, staring down into the dark passageway. Darius was standing close to her, looking annoyed about something.

'Ah, Jason my boy, what a coincidence. How is your first day going?'

Jason span around. Alan Brash was standing about two feet away holding a briefcase and a pile of files. He was in a light grey suit, perfectly cut to his impressive frame.

'Oh, uh, fine, Mr Brash, thank you.'

Greg faded back upstairs at a nod from Brash.

'Good, good,' Brash smiled and then struggled to shift the files under one arm whilst holding his briefcase.

Jason didn't really have much choice. 'Can I help you with those, Mr Brash?'

'Ah, I was hoping you would say that - your father has brought you up well.'

He swung the files into Jason's arms. 'Governors' business I'm afraid - even the Chairman gets homework in this place. Just bring them over to my car would you, Jason?'

Brash began to walk towards the outside.

Jason flashed a look back at Louisa. She was biting her lip and even Darius was looking vaguely concerned. It was lunchtime – only the gangs would be out there.

'This way, Jason – you're allowed out of the building at lunch you know.' Brash called over his shoulder.

Again, Jason had no choice. Quickly, he caught up with Brash and fell in step beside him.

'Not afraid of a few youths with wild spirits are you, Jason - not a lad with your… talents?'

The section of block-paved drive Jason could see outside was dazzling in the sunlight and completely deserted. 'Mr Brash,' he began, 'those things you did last night – Dad has never shown me anything like that. He hadn't told me anything about the Gift or demons or… anything really.'

'I know,' Brash said, stopping just short of the sunlight at the end of the passage. 'Remember I've known your father a long time and I can understand his wanting to hide things from you – he went through some terrible times, we all did.'

'Yes, but he won't even explain properly about the agents who killed my mother. What do they want, where are they coming from? And what about these… powers you said…'

Brash held up his free hand, his eyes holding Jason's. 'Let's give your old man a chance to come through, shall we… it's meant to be his responsibility to tell you everything and begin your training. I don't want you to rush into finding out things from… other sources?' He winked at Jason then glanced at his watch. 'Sorry, but I'd better get on – I've a lunch meeting at the brewery.'

They both stepped out into brilliant sunshine forcing Jason to squint. A wide drive ran along this side of the school and a wood dropped down the hill on the far side. Another superb black Bentley waited for Brash in the shade of a large oak. Jason recognised it as the sporty Continental model.

A bottle smashed somewhere to the right. Jason peered through the dazzling sunlight to see half a dozen Skins materialise out of the wood. They stared back at him, lighting up cigarettes and lounging against the trees.

Brash smiled thinly. 'Lovely lot – the studded and tattooed faces of the future… if we're not careful.' He put one hand on Jason's shoulder, gripping him firmly. 'As slovenly as they are, Jason, do remember they can be dangerous. They won't follow any sort of rules… should you happen to wind up in a fight with any of them, for instance. Still, perhaps that wouldn't be such a bad thing.'

'What do you mean?' Jason asked. More Skins were slipping out from the trees to join the others now – a mixture of heights and builds but all studded and tattooed with hard muscled arms hanging out of dirty T-shirts and vest tops.

'Your forthcoming Gifts are not some all-powerful magic, Jason, there are no wizardly spells to save the day and there will be limits to the power, even for you. Most of what we can do is exercised through physical skills – strength, speed, suppleness, coordination and martial techniques.'

'You mean Jakra, don't you? Dad's been teaching Miranda and me that all our lives.'

'Good, good… at least he did that much for you. However, training against people who don't want to seriously damage you is no substitute for a real fight where anything can happen - where there are no rules. To survive in our world you must win quickly and move on. Our friends in the trees over there could be considered as… practice.'

'Oh – I see,' Jason said, his stomach tightening. 'What about the others… the Brash gang? Are they "practice" as well?'

'Ah now then, they're a different class of vicious youth,' Brash said, making no move towards his car as still more Skins sloped out of the trees. There were perhaps thirty of them now, gathering like hyenas closing on a cub guarded by just one lion.

Brash looked down at Jason. 'You would do well to get to know the Brash boys and girls I'd say, they could teach you a thing or two, not to mention safety in numbers and all that. Now I really must leave for this meeting.'

He began to cross the road. Jason glanced back at the Skins then hurried to catch up with Brash who was almost at the Bentley. He wondered if Cadaveril was sitting behind the blacked out windows?

The boot opened as Brash reached it and Jason put the files inside. Brash shut the boot with a heavy clunk. 'Sixty in five and a half seconds, you know?' He said, running one finger along the gleaming paintwork to the driver's door. 'I like to drive this one myself.'

'It's brilliant, Mr Brash,' Jason said, ignoring the Skins for a moment to gaze down the aggressive lines of the Bentley.

Brash nodded. 'We are special people, Jason, you and I… even your father. If you accept and keep your place in our world the rewards can be… substantial.'

Brash glanced over to the East Passage as he spoke but Jason couldn't see anything in the comparative gloom.

'Remember – choose your friends carefully here in Silent Hill. Off you go now - I shall see you soon, no doubt.'

Jason nodded. 'Bye.' Trying not to seem hurried, he turned back into the shadow of Silent Hill.

On his left, the Skins had slunk closer and now began slouching away from the trees in a ragged line. He forced himself to walk at a steady pace - there was no way he was going to run for the passage in front of them.

A movement to the right caught his eye. Two boys appeared around the front corner of the school. They were tall and smartly dressed in designer jeans, trainers and polo shirts – Brash gang members. More followed – boys and girls, all clean and well dressed.

Jason glanced back at the Bentley. It just sat there, its blacked out windows reflecting the still branches overhead. Alan Brash must be inside, watching him.

Jason continued to walk towards the passage.

It was only twenty steps away but the Skins were going to get there first, their loping strides covering the ground surprisingly quickly.

Fifteen steps. The Brash gang were closing in too, picking up speed, their eyes flicking from him to the Skins and back again. No one said anything to break the silence as over fifty youths converged in the heat of the morning.

The Skins slipped into place to block off the cool safety of the passage.

A cold bead of sweat trickled down Jason's back but he looked straight ahead at the arch of fluorescent flecked darkness and carried on walking. The Brash closed in on the right, their leather soled footfalls almost silent.

'Going somewhere, wimp?' Richard Baldwin, stepped out from the mess of Skins.

Jason totally ignored him and tried to walk straight past but Baldwin shoved out a hand and pushed him in the chest. He was strong and Jason was forced a half-step backwards. Baldwin grinned and the blue spider web tattoo crinkled on his cheek.

Silence pressed in on Jason. The two gangs had formed a rough semi- circle behind him – the Skins on his left, the Brash on his right. They'd left a gap between the them through which he could still see Mr Brash's Bentley.

Baldwin pushed him backwards into the ring of excited faces. 'You too scared to answer me, chicken?'

No sense in running from this but if he took out Baldwin would the rest of the Skins mob him? And what would the Brash do – just stand and watch?

'I said…' Baldwin began, hitting his shoulder again. Jason twisted with the blow and it grazed past him. Baldwin over-balanced and stumbled forward.

'Slippery little worm in't ya?' Baldwin sneered, recovering his balance and coming up close, chest out, chin up and hands out wide. 'Come on then, worm, take a poke at me.'

Baldwin shoved Jason with both hands. Jason let the blow land and stepped back a few paces – he needed the space between them if this wasn't going to turn into a wrestling match. He checked to see if any of the other Skins were closing in but they just leered at him with eyes hungry for violence. The crowd was eerily quiet – where was the usual 'fight' chant and jeering?

'We don't like chicken-shit, stuck-up kids around here.' Baldwin pushed him again and Jason faked a stumble to the right, circling around closer to the passage. It would give him half a chance at breaking through if the rest of the Skins joined in.

'And here was I thinking we were getting on so well,' Jason said, his voice calm and just loud enough for everyone to hear.

Baldwin tried to push him again but Jason blocked with one hand and stepped further around to the side.

Now he was ready.

Suddenly a hand lashed around Jason's throat from behind and yanked him back into the Brash gang.

Jason grabbed the arm half strangling him but it felt like a steel bar locked into place.

'Calm down,' a voice whispered in his ear, 'we're on your side.'

Jason relaxed slightly – there were too many of them surrounding him to fight now. The stranglehold lessened.

A girl stepped passed him and pushed Baldwin back into his own kind.

The Skins erupted in a storm of foul-mouthed protest and started forward but a Brash boy moved into the ring – tall, slim and tightly muscled under a blue blazer. He had floppy blonde hair framing a handsome face and the ruby eyes of a prefect's badge glinted from his lapel.

A huge Skin at the front held up a hand and his gang stopped dead. He must have been their leader – well over two metres tall, he was massively muscled, broken-nosed and with a scar running out of his cropped hair straight through a black skull tattooed on his right cheek.

'Thank you, Grizz,' said Floppy Hair. He stepped further into the ring. 'Forgive the interruption but it would be such a shame to waste this opportunity don't you think?' His voice was light, confident and just a little too far back. He sounded like a younger version of Alan Brash.

The girl who'd pushed Baldwin, moved to stand just behind the speaker, pushing her lustrous red hair back over her shoulders. She twisted around to nod at whoever held Jason and the arm immediately slipped away from his neck. The ruby red eyes of another prefect's badge sparkled at him before she turned back to face the Skins.

Jason twisted around and a big, black haired youth held up his hands and whispered. 'No hard feelings – just following orders.'

'I shall be happy to make the arrangements, Grizz old boy,' Floppy Hair said. 'if that suits Callum, of course.'

The mountain of tattooed muscle hesitated for a moment then grunted. With the show apparently over, Skins and Brash broke into chatter and started dispersing into small groups as if nothing had ever happened.

Floppy Hair turned to Jason and held out his hand. 'Quite a first day for you, young Jason. I'm Edward Braithwaite but everybody calls me Eddie.'

Bemused, Jason shook hands.

'And this ravishing young thing is Erin Brock,' Eddie continued, 'my second in command.' The red head flashed Jason a smile.

'Don't worry – you'll get your chance to teach the little baldy scumbag a lesson.' Eddie said, flicking his head back at Baldwin who was disappearing into the trees surrounded by his mates. 'I'll catch you tomorrow to explain the arrangements.'

Eddie slapped Jason on the shoulder then he and Erin began to stroll back towards the front of the school, immediately falling into quiet conversation

And Jason was suddenly alone - his adrenaline still pumping from the almost-fight. What was going on? Why had the Brash stepped in right when he was going to floor Baldwin? It must have looked like they'd sent in a girl to save the wimpy new-boy.

Chewing his lip in frustration, he turned to finally walk into the passage but stopped dead. His nightmare was complete - Louisa was watching from the shadows and standing far too close to her was Darius.

'Are you alright, Jason?' Louisa asked, stepping into the light.

'Why didn't you floor the tosser?' Darius asked, shaking his big head.

Behind him, Jason heard the Bentley growl into life – Brash was driving away. No doubt he'd be thinking Baldwin had him running scared as well.

Without a word, Jason strode into the gloomy passage. This had to be sorted out.

Chapter 9

Jason sat on the bus, staring through the diesel fumes as the shabby grey buildings of Drunken Abbot rolled passed.

News of his near-fight with Richard Baldwin had flashed around the whole school like wildfire and half his form class had been chasing him for news.

'Was Callum there?'

'D'you think you could have taken him out?'

'When are the prefects setting the fight?'

Even Violet Gray had put her oar in. 'It must have been horrible - surrounded by all those vicious idiots. What a horrible first day for you...'

Baldwin hadn't turned up for English that afternoon. Jason had seethed his way through two chapters of "Of Mice and Men", ignoring the stares and whispers of his classmates. At the end of the lesson, there seemed to be Brash gang members and their prefects all over the corridors and in front of the school so nothing more than sneers came from the Skins as he walked between scattered groups of them on his way to the bus.

Louisa and Mouse had been waiting for him on the back seat. He couldn't meet their eyes – he didn't want to see Louisa's pity or Mouse's disappointment at him not fighting back against Baldwin. If that Erin girl had just waited another couple of seconds before jumping in, he'd have floored Baldwin.

Luckily, Mouse and Louisa didn't seem to want to talk about the fight - not on a bus filled with curious eyes and ears. At least when the Skins had got on they'd done nothing more than stomp upstairs, raggedly humming the Death March in time to their thumping footsteps.

Gradually, stop by stop, the bus spewed the Skins and Drunken Abbot kids back out onto to their filthy streets. The bus broke out of the last line of terraces into the open moorland of the valley floor and Jason started to breathe easier. Determined to clear his name, he drew in a breath to speak.

Mouse started before he could say a thing. 'You have walked right in to their trap, I think. I told you to keep away from the gangs.'

'What?' Jason asked.

'You were talking with the wonderful Fast Eddie after your little show at lunch today, yes? You and the spider-web boy will be fighting soon... for their entertainment and betting'

'What are you on about?' Jason asked, glancing passed Mouse to Louisa. She was just watching him - reserving judgement probably. 'It's not entertainment. Baldwin jumped me... started pushing me around. I was just about to hit him when that Erin girl stepped in.'

'But why were you there – on the Skin's... what do they call it... turf?'

Louisa cut in. 'Alan Brash led him there – I saw it.'

Mouse frowned. 'Ah, so he has started to pull you in already. You have agreed to be his gang's little gladiator, yes - in a day or two, you will be fighting in the Pit for them?'

Jason shook his head. 'Look - Brash just asked me to carry some stuff to his car for him and then I got cornered.'

Mouse just grunted.

'Anyway - what's the Pit?' Jason asked to break the silence.

Mouse didn't reply so Louisa explained. 'The gangs have their fights hidden away in the woods by the school – in a hollow which they call the Pit. They charge money for students to watch and they bet with each other on who will win - first blood, a knockout and so on. If you do well, the gang who put you forward might let you join them.'

Mouse cut in. 'Fast Eddie didn't explain this to you during your little talk?'

'No, he didn't say anything like that…' Jason thought back and his eyes widened as he remembered. 'He did say something about "explaining the arrangements" but I haven't even seen him today so it'll probably all fizzle out.'

'No,' Mouse said, leaning back into the seat. 'I do not think so. He is just building up the… tension. You will be their gladiator and if you do well, you can join their gang.'

'I don't want to be in any sad gang.'

'Then do not fight for them,' Mouse said.

'What,' said Jason, 'after the whole school knows about Baldwin pushing me around? It'll only get worse. He won't stop and everyone will think I'm scared of the little…'

'Then fight.' said Mouse, shrugging. 'Fight and join their gang and be controlled by Alan Brash.'

Jason stared at him. What could he do? He looked to Louisa for help but she just stared back at him. *Did she think he wanted to join the Brash or worse, did she think he was scared to fight Baldwin?*

The bus hissed to a stop. They were in Darkston Wick, outside Mrs Miggins' store. The doors spasmed open and they followed the others off the bus and Mouse walked off without even a grunt goodbye.

'You will have to take this decision yourself.' Louisa said, ignoring the leering Porter and jumping down lightly.

Jason shrugged and started to turn for home.

'This way,' Louisa said.

Jason looked blankly at her.

'You were coming to our house to talk after school – have you forgotten?' she added.

Jason nodded. He'd forgotten.

The bus doors jerked shut behind them and Porter roared away in a cloud of diesel fumes.

'Good first day, son?'

Jason span around to see Dad wandering across the road towards them.

'Yeah, thanks… fine,' Jason said. 'I'm just going to Louisa's and Mouse's for a bit.'

Dad gave a tight smile. 'Ah – sorry, not today – we need to talk.'

'What,' Jason began, but Dad cut across him to speak to Louisa.

'Sorry to steal Jason away but I owe him some… explanations. Come on, Son.'

Louisa smiled. 'Of course, Mr Da…' she stopped herself, then continued. '… Mr Willow. Jason and I will have plenty of time for chatting on other days.' She held up one hand and gave a little finger-wave before walking away.

'Right… uhh… see you tomorrow, then.' Jason said, just managing to stop himself returning the wave.

Perfect timing, Dad he thought and followed his father back to the Old Mill.

***

'So how was Silent Hell?' Dad asked as they walked back along the ancient street towards the Old Mill.

'Great - I was nearly in a fight - a skinhead called Baldwin. If he starts on me tomorrow I'm going to kill him…'

'There is a chance of that,' Dad said, catching and holding his eyes.

Jason took a slow breath. 'So what – you think I should just walk away?'

'What if you punch this lad too hard... what if you really do kill him...?'

'As if that's going to happen - you've been training me and Miranda for years, you know I can control myself.'

Dad glanced down.   'Things are changing... you're changing. Now you're through adolescence...'

Jason felt his cheeks start to burn. He coughed and decided flippancy might be the best cover. 'Yes, so what difference does it make if I've done my time with spots, squeaky voices, sticky sheets...'

'What's that about sheets?' came Miranda's distracted voice from their porch. She was leaning forward, looking over their heads.

'Nothing,' Jason said quickly. 'Why are you skulking around up there?'

Miranda trotted down the stairs wearing a sullen pout. 'Dad made me promise to stay here so as not to embarrass you in front of the lovely Louisa.'

'I owe you one, Dad' Jason mumbled.

'Humph,' Miranda snorted, 'as if I would... after all the girlie advice I give you...'

'Anyway,' Dad cut her short, 'just bring the backpack down Miranda and both of you follow me... quietly.'

Miranda and Jason exchanged glances, then Miranda nipped back up to the porch, grabbed a small haversack and they followed Dad around the side of the house.

'What's going on,' Jason mouthed to her.

Miranda shrugged then they stopped just behind Dad as he stood in the shadows scanning the steep woods across the river.

'Come on, quickly,' he whispered, taking the haversack from Miranda and slipping it on his back.

They ran down the side of the gently sloping lawn into the cold shade of the watermill with its boarded up doors and windows. Dad led them along the near side, running his hand over the wooden slats rising row upon row above them and then stopped at the corner to peer into the woods once again.

'Okay,' he whispered after a minute or so and dashed out onto the narrow wooden walkway which stretched from the garden to a stone cob that funnelled the sluggish river water into a churning frenzy beneath the waterwheel itself. The small rowing boat Jason had used on his first day was moored on the calm, far side of the cob.

Hoping no one was watching them play ninja-spies in the garden, Jason followed his father with Miranda behind him.

Dad stopped before they reached to boat, right in front of the waterwheel and pointed.

The waterwheel turned in a sort of square tunnel under the mill building. There was over a metre gap between the wheel and either side of this tunnel and a stone ledge ran along each side.

Willow crouched down on the walkway for a better look. He could just make out that the ledge ran past the far rim of the wheel and ended at a narrow ladder. It was dark in there but it would be an easy climb, as long as the wheel didn't catch him on the back of the head, knock him out and pull him down into the freezing waters to be mashed and drowned.

Dad stepped across the metre of water and braced himself against the mill, settling one foot on the ledge. Then he scuttled inside.

'What the...' Jason mouthed to Miranda but she just pointed after Dad then flapped her arms like chicken wings at him.

Jason shook his head, sat down and reached out a leg. This close, the churning wheel seemed a lot bigger and louder. Its wide wooden blades sliced into roiling white water with an incessant slap, slap, slap. A heavy mist filled the wheel-tunnel and ice cold gobbets splashed up and soaked into his T-shirt as his foot touched the ledge.

Best not to think too much about it. He focussed on the ledge, took a deep breath then slowly shifted his weight forward reaching for the wall above the ledge. Got it. A bit wet but solid enough. He pulled himself onto the ledge and hugged the wall.

The wheel churned inexorably on just five feet behind his head. Dad was only a few feet into the near-dark. He took Jason's wrist and guided his fingers onto an iron ring set deep into the stone.

Jason squinted and found more of them - they must have been there for workmen to tie themselves on to or something. Gripping each rusting ring, he followed Dad along the ledge towards the axle, his trainers slipping with every other step on the slick stone.

Miranda joined them and found the rings on her own. They each stepped carefully over the revolving axle and edged towards the ladder just a few feet away.

Suddenly Jason's foot slipped and plunged into the icy water. Immediately the current clutched at him, dragging his leg down hard towards the wheel-blades. He yanked his foot out, gripping on to two slick rings for dear life just as Dad grabbed one arm and Miranda gripped his other.

'I'm fine,' he shouted over the roaring water, then remembered they were supposed to be being silent ninja types.

He took a couple of deep breaths to calm down and then followed Dad to the ladder.

Moments later, Jason hauled himself up onto the floor of a small chamber next to Dad and watched a smug and very dry Miranda pop up after them.

Dad nodded and they crawled through a half-height doorway onto the dry wooden floor of the main mill room.

'Are you all right, Son,' Dad asked.

'Just fine and dandy,' Jason said, pulling off his soaking trainer and tipping out the water. 'I take it we can talk now?'

Dad smiled. 'Here we can. Sorry about all the secret squirrel stuff, it's just that…'

'Alan Brash has got everywhere bugged?' Jason asked, looking around at the many small wheels, cogs, levers, chains and grain shutes that filled the surprisingly big room. All the machinery, including a thick wooden shaft rose which rose up to pass through the ceiling, was silent and still. Jason wondered what lever he could pull to get it all going.

'I'm afraid so,' Dad said. 'He's got every room in the mill on a microphone and the front of the house on video. I wanted a place we could talk in private.'

'Why not a nice little drive into the moors, then?' Jason said, now wringing out his sock.

'It's an idea but open ground is vulnerable to long distance listening devices,' Dad said.

'Not that you're paranoid about the evil Alan Brash,' Miranda said, smiling.

Dad nodded. 'Fair enough but I've had all Easter to search this place and I know this building's clean... and as we haven't undone any of the boarded up doors or windows, hopefully Brash won't suspect we've found a little safe house right here under his nose.'

'Great,' Jason said, limping around the room with one trainer on, one off.

Slashes of sunlight cut through the boarded windows and doors to illuminate a ceiling of long white planks stretching over him. In its centre were two open trap doors – one large, one small. A rope dropped down to a winch through the larger opening and a sturdy ladder ran up through the other.

Dad cut into is thoughts. 'So what do you want to know?'

Jason stopped gazing around and plonked himself down on a huge cog. 'When do I get my super powers?'.

Dad smiled. 'You've already got them.'

Miranda's eyes went wide. 'What – can he do those things Alan Brash did last night?'

'Yes, that and much more,' Dad answered her then turned back to Jason. 'All you need is some training to unlock and control them properly – otherwise there's no telling what damage you could do.'

Jason's heart leapt. 'When are you going to show me how to do it?' He hadn't realised just how excited he was about the prospect of having some sort of "super powers".

'I'm not, Jason,' Dad said, 'not the way you think. The only thing I'll teach you to do is how to suppress your Gift. I want to train you to stay normal.'

'What? Why? You don't trust me do you? You think I'm...'

'I do trust you, both of you, I always have, in everything. Please don't doubt ever that. It is just... oh there's so much you need to know. Learning to use the Gift, joining the Watch – it's not a question of being some sort of superhero in a comic book. It's real life – people die horribly all around you, You're forced to kill... and once you get involved you can never truly escape from it. Once you know more about it, then maybe you'll understand.'

'So tell me.'

'So tell *us*,' Miranda said, sitting down next to Jason. 'You're not going to put it off again are you?'

He heard Dad take in a slow breath. 'No, sweetheart, not this time.' He pulled off the backpack, opened it and handed them both a bottle of Coke. Then he sat down against one wall and began.

'Things happen that most people never see, never know about. Good things, bad things. There are demons trying to come through into our world – malevolent, powerful spirits trapped in another dimension which we call the Abyss. The cult I told you about on the train - The Brethren – have some people who can summon the demons – break through the barriers and free them from the pit. It's difficult and very dangerous, but a few are brought through each year.'

'But what exactly are they?' Jason asked, still not quite believing they were talking seriously about demons.

'We don't know, not really. They're no more than spirits when they first come through, like a stream of black mist that forms into a half-visible ghost. Once in our world they can't survive long unless they possess a living creature, a human when they can, but anything fairly big will do – wolves are a favourite. The demon feeds on its host's life, burns them up from the inside. It has to constantly replenish blood and flesh to keep the body alive or move on to the next victim.'

Jason shuddered. 'But why would the Brethren want to call up demons in the first place?'

'Because whoever summons the demon can control it…
as long as they guard against being possessed themselves.
Once inside another living creature, demons can make their
host incredibly strong and resilient to harm. The more
powerful ones can conjure fire and darkness and worst of all,
they can all infect others.'

'Infect?' Jason asked.

'By biting usually – they inject a tiny quantity of their
essence into the victim's blood.'

'So if you're bitten, you're possessed by the demon as
well?' Miranda asked.

Dad shook his head. 'Not quite. We call them
"Touched". They do become stronger and heal from damage
and the demon can see and hear through their eyes and ears
but they're not actually possessed. The strongest demon can
control dozens of humans or scores of animals.'

Jason bit down on the two dozen questions that bubbled
out of his mind and chose one. 'So the Brethren control the
demons and the demons control these infected people…'

'Touched.' Miranda corrected, swigging back some Coke
as if they were discussing some great movie plot.

'…these Touched people but what for? What are they all
trying to do, what do they want?'

Dad shook his head. 'Something else we don't really
know. It's been going on for centuries - the first records of
what we think may be the start of it all was in the time of the
Ottoman Empire but we still don't know what the Brethren
want.'

'Well it's got to be world domination, hasn't it?' Miranda
said.

Dad smiled. 'We know two things that they do. Firstly
they infiltrate powerful organisations, either with normal
Brethren agents or sometimes with the Touched. Centuries
ago, they wormed their way into noble families and religions,
then they also moved into rich merchant houses and in modern
days – governments, multi-national businesses and security
organisations. They possess, Touch and kill to make

themselves richer and more influential but we don't know why.'

'But why isn't anybody stopping them?' Jason asked.

'That's where the Watch come in. We have soldiers, spies, accountants and lawyers but Gifted families like ours have always been at the heart of it. We hunt down the demons, their summoners and the hundreds of agents who fight, spy and scheme for the Brethren.'

'And when you find them…?' Miranda asked, all trace of humour gone from her voice.

'We kill everyone and utterly destroy the demon and whatever poor sod it happens to be inside.'

Jason was open mouthed. He wasn't sure he could believe all of this, even after seeing what Brash did last night. 'Dad, I don't understand why people don't know about all of this? Why aren't governments and armies hunting down the demons?'

'Because neither side wants to tell the secret. The Brethren obviously don't want more people trying to stop their summoning and infiltrations but the catch is that the Watch need it to be kept quiet as well.'

'What? Why? Surely…' Jason began but Dad stopped him.

'Because of mass panic, over reaction. Mankind can't cope with the existence of the supernatural. Anyone, anyone at all who seemed just a little bit different or showed any sign of unexplained powers is hunted down and killed. And that means our side as well as theirs.'

'Okay, I can see what you mean, but surely governments could sort it all out if you told them… you know, quietly with the S.A.S and secret services and all that.'

Dad just raised an eyebrow. 'Governments keep a secret like this - I don't think so. There have been times, over the centuries, when the Watch were desperate and were forced to call for help. They have always ended in disaster - the witch-hunts in England, the Spanish Inquisition. Some Brethren were caught, but so were many of the Gifted from the Watch. Then of course, there were the thousands of innocent people not connected in any way with the struggle who were tortured, burned and drowned.'

'So the Watch is on its own?' Jason asked.

Dad nodded. 'More or less. We still have a loose... relationship with elements of some religions but we don't really trust each other.'

'Wait,' Jason said, shaking his head, 'my brain hurts. Let me get this straight – our side is called the Watch and we hunt down the Brethren who summon demons; the demons possess humans or animals and the possessed can infect other people to make them into some sort of super slaves,' Jason snorted. 'It sounds like a really bad horror movie, Dad.'

Dad stood up and stretched. 'Where do you think all those vampire and werewolf legends come from?'

'What – you mean Dracula and his furry-faced buddies were demons?' Jason asked.

Dad shrugged. 'The Brethren have always hidden behind folklore and superstition.'

Miranda stood up as well and handed Dad her empty Coke bottle for the rucksack. 'You said you knew two things the Brethren did. Get their people into government and business and things and...'

Dad nodded as he slipped the rucksack back on. 'They try to track down Gifted people before the Watch finds them.'

'Why – to kill them, stop them joining the Watch?' Miranda asked, glancing at Jason.

'No – they don't kill them if they can help it. They take them away.'

'And do what with them?'

Dad shrugged. 'They turn them... sometimes we have to face Brethren Gifted.'

'So I need to be able to protect myself – I need to learn how to use these powers.'

Dad shook his head. 'You need to be able to hide. Using the Gift leaves a trace that Touched can pick up on...'

'Yeah but we're safe here,' Jason said, 'and Brash wasn't afraid to do his stuff last night.'

'Even so,' Dad said, 'blending in to the ordinary is the only way to stay safe.'

'It hasn't worked though, has it?' Jason said, standing up. They've caught up with us how many times now and... and blending in didn't help Mum, did it?'

They went silent and Miranda glared at Jason before shaking her head and moving over to stare through the cracks between the window boards.

Jason wasn't going to let it stop there. 'And what if I want to join the Watch, hunt down the people who sent Mum's killers? You're not even giving me that choice.'

Dad took a slow breath. 'Everyone from your grandfather to Brash and the Watch Council will be desperate for you to join – you could be really powerful. I don't want to be any part of that pressure – I don't want you to have anything to do with it.'

'But why, I know it's dangerous but...'

'Because it's a sickening world, an horrific life,' Dad cut in. The demons often possess the young as they have less will power to resist and those are the ones you have to kill. I... I just couldn't do it any more and you shouldn't be expected to start.'

Dad stopped for a minute, calming down.

'It must have been horrible,' Miranda said from the window.

Dad nodded. 'It was unimaginable... and I started to make mistakes, to hesitate at crucial moments and that put everyone in danger. They didn't need me anyway... there were others who were just as powerful and far more willing to do the job, too willing in my opinion – Alan Brash for instance. So I walked away. I wasn't the first or the last. Gifted and their families have been drifting away from the Watch for centuries, there are others that can be found and trained to...'

'Dad,' Miranda cut in, edging back from the window, 'there are a couple of Brash security watching the house.'

Dad moved to the side of the window and slowly peered through one of the cracks. 'Mmm. Probably wondering where we are – no pick up from the mikes inside the house and they didn't see us leave with the front video.'

'What do we do?' Miranda asked.

'I don't want them to know we can get in here or they'll cover it in surveillance as well. Come on, we'll get out on their blind side. Quickly now.'

Dad climbed the ladder to the second floor which was cluttered with moulding sacks and broken chests and then up a smaller ladder into the overhanging attic. Even as Jason and Miranda followed him up, Dad was hauling up the long rope with the hook on. He dropped it down through the overhang trap door into the garden and checked its strength. The mill completely blocked them from the security guard's view.

'Slide down, stop before you get to the hook.'

'Yeah – thanks for the advice,' Willow said. He grabbed the rope and slid down out of the attic.

Miranda was right behind him and nearly landed on his head. She dropped lightly to the floor and looked up. 'If they check from the front they'll see the rope.'

Dad was already sliding down. 'Glad you're thinking ahead.' He moved them a little away and flicked one hand up towards the inside of the attic. Something shimmered through the air and the rope dropped down in a coil at their feet.

'How…' Jason began.

'Don't ask,' Dad said, pulling off the rucksack and handing them back their coke bottles. 'Now stroll out onto the lawn as if you've been lounging about here in the shade all along.

As Jason and Miranda followed his instructions, Dad gathered up the rope and hid it in the trees that ran down one side of their garden. Then he joined them on the lawn, still drenched in afternoon sunlight.

'They're leaving,' Miranda mumbled, not looking across the river to the woods.

'I thought they might,' Dad said. 'Now remember the house is bugged so no more about the Watch for now.' He roughly hugged Jason around the shoulders before he could object. 'We'll talk about how to avoid fights at school instead, okay Son?'

Jason chewed his lip. He'd forgotten about Silent Hill and Richard Baldwin.

Chapter 10

By the time he crawled out of bed the following morning, Jason was already running late. He dived into the shower, snatched a banana and his school books and dashed out of the silent house and into a bright, sunny morning.

Dad and Miranda had already left for Whitby. Dad was looking for some supply teaching work from September and Miranda was obviously desperate to catch up with some vital shopping for shoes and make-up.

Jason had been mulling everything over for half the night before finally drifting off to sleep. There were real demons out there and he had special powers to hunt them and their summoners down. The hunted would become the hunter and he could avenge his mother's murder.

All he needed was someone to show him how to use his abilities, his Gift as Dad called it.

Louisa could help him there. She was Gifted – he was sure of it now. That first meeting in the woods, she'd pushed him from a distance. They could talk about it now that Dad had explained so much - perhaps it would bring them Louisa closer together. Maybe she could even train him to use his

Gifts, if Dad wouldn't change his mind. That would mean they'd have to see an awful lot of each other, of course.

He hurried out through the gates to see Mouse and Louisa already standing with the others at the bus stop. He reached them just as their bus came hurtling down out of the woods.

Jason only had time to marvel at Louisa in tight jeans and a fresh, white blouse and to say "Hi" before the dilapidated old bus thundered passed them.

'That man is what you would call a loser, I think.' Mouse said as they all stepped back to avoid being run over.

The three of them took the back seat as usual. Jason waited for the bus engine to fire up before speaking.

'I think I need help.'

'This is very true,' Mouse chipped in, grinning.

'Help to keep out of the fight with the web-face boy?' Miranda asked.

'Uhh… no – I'm not going to walk away from that.'

Miranda shrugged and turned to look out of the window. Mouse just shook his head in a "you've got to make your own mistakes" type way.

Jason tried again. 'Dad explained loads to Miranda and me yesterday but he still won't help me learn my Gifts. Would…'

'This is not the place,' Louisa said, resting a hand on his knee to stop him. 'We will talk after school, yes? If your father doesn't take you away again, of course.' She held him spellbound with touch and gaze a moment longer and then turned back to the window.

Mouse was watching them. He didn't look angry or even jealous. He just looked resigned and something else – sympathetic perhaps. With the briefest of nods, he turned to watch the moors bump by out of his window.

Jason sank back against the seat and remembered to breathe. This could be where it all started between Louisa and him.

Even the shadow of Drunken Abbot's first terraces falling over them didn't darken his mood.

116

'Jason Jason, wake up.'

Jason snapped out of his day dream. For about the hundredth time, his mind had been on the bus ride that morning, staring into Louisa's eyes with her hand on his knee.

'Well, what's the answer, lad?'

Oh hell, what lesson was this?

'Two reasons why the German people were so willing to follow Hitler's ideas,' whispered Violet, sitting next to him as always.

'Uhh - resentment over World War 1 reparations and the resulting economic hardship, sir?'

Mr Holmes looked at him in silence. Jason smiled, sweetly.

'Do you think Violet will be sitting next to you in your examinations, Jason?'

'Probably, sir,' Jason moaned.

Violet elbowed him and slid her chair further away. A secretive little smile slipped over her lips though.

Mr Holmes glanced at Violet and then back at Jason. 'Just try to stay in the same universe as us, Jason, all right? Now,' he said, turning his round-spectacled gaze back onto the whole class, 'The reasons Jason gave are correct and when you have a charismatic orator such as Adolf Hitler to capitalise on such strong feelings...'

Holmes droned on. He was quite a good teacher really, making lots of cause and effect connections but he didn't get down and dirty enough for Jason's tastes... what must it have been like to be one of the thousands of angry Germans, whipped into a frenzy at the Nuremberg Rally, filling with a hatred so strong for anyone Adolf Hitler pointed the finger at? What if you were a Jew, passing by the stadium, hearing the massively amplified, resonating voice, the roar and chant of the party-faithful? What would you feel was coming down on you?

Finally, one mind-map and four review questions later, the bell went for lunch.

'Are you all right?' Violet asked him as they packed away their books. 'You've been really quiet all morning. Is it about yesterday – the fight with that Baldwin creep?'

Violet's eyes strayed towards the door. "That Baldwin creep" was just going out, not even glancing back. He'd steered clear of Jason so far today.

'Oh, that was nothing – don't worry about me so much,' Jason said, glancing across at Violet. She was all right really, a bit fretful sometimes but she'd a good heart and an offbeat sense of humour when she loosened up. He was getting used to her being around.

'Listen... you know I was only joking, moaning about you sitting next to me in the exams and all that don't you?' Jason said.

Violet got up quickly but glanced back over her shoulder. 'I know,' she said, her crooked little smile appearing again for an instant before she walked off.

Jason smiled and packed his books away. His day had gone much better than expected so far. Baldwin was keeping out of his face and the other Skins in the class seemed to be too wary or at least, under orders, not to start anything.

'Wait your turn!' Violet's thin voice brought his head up.

Just at the door way, a Drunken Abbot kid called Mick was trying to shove Violet out of his way. He was a big, act-hard ape who Jason had already worked out desperately wanted to join the Skins.

'Leave her alone,' Jason snapped, dropping his bag and pushing his chair back.

He needn't have bothered. Violet was back on balance in an instant and deftly snap-kicked the side of Mick's knee.

'Aggh.' he yelled, catching hold of the door frame for support.

'Don't worry about me so much.' Violet said, winking at Jason and flouncing away.

'Prat,' Jason said, picking up his bag and pushing past Mick.

'Shut it, Jason, or I'll set Baldwin on you again.'

Jason span around but caught sight of a Brash prefect three doors along. 'Any time.' was all he could manage, before storming off down the corridor.

It didn't take him long to forget his anger however. It was lunchtime and before he'd even walked half way across the yard to the refectory, Louisa found him.

'Listen, I have to hurry away, I have maths revision, but could we meet on the bridge this evening, after dinner, about half past six?'

Could he ever?

'Sure, no problem,' Jason stammered, wishing there was something for him to lean against to make him look just that bit more cool and relaxed about it.

Louisa smiled and dashed off. Darius, "Master of the Universe", was waiting for her at the West Passage but even that didn't bother Jason too much. Tonight was the night - alone at last with Louisa.

The two lessons in the afternoon, English and Technology, dragged on forever. Jason tried to take his mind off his date that evening by teasing Violet how her kicking like a donkey was the only way she could get a boy to fall for her. She took it well and only ripped out and screwed up one page of his homework.

Then at last, he was on the bus home. Louisa wasn't talkative and stared out of the window the whole time. Mouse had simply said "bad day" as soon has he'd sat down and that was it until they reached Darkston Wick.

'See you later,' Jason said as they stepped off the bus. He must have had a stupid grin on his face because Mouse just shook his head in despair.

'Half past six,' Louisa said with a small smile. Mouse grunted his goodbye.

Moody git, Jason thought, but then felt guilty. Mouse was actually being pretty good about him drooling all over Louisa. If he and Louisa did end up going out with each other he'd be really careful not to flaunt it in front of Mouse. What more could he do?

**

At twenty past six, Jason was fed, washed, tooth-scrubbed and sitting on the bridge wall. This was it - he and Louisa were the same, both Gifted - what a bond that gave them. She was so gorgeous, he couldn't believe he was sitting here waiting for…

He caught his breath. Louisa rounded the corner, saw him and smiled. She was still in her tight jeans but had changed into a red T shirt that clung to every inch of her… and she was on her own. *Should he get up? No, just sit here and look cool.* He smiled back but stopped himself from waving.

'You look like a grinning madman,' Louisa said as she walked out of the shadow of the Highwayman Inn. Her eyes sparkled mischievously.

'Thanks. You look really nice too,' Jason answered.

'Ahh, how very nice of you to notice.' She winked. 'Come on, let's walk.'

Jason stood up and caught the merest trace of Louisa's light, summery perfume. They set off up the hill and into the woods with his head swimming.

'What have you done with Mouse?' Jason asked, hoping he didn't sound too obvious.

'Oh, I am sorry – are you missing him? We can always go back to fetch…' Louisa stopped and turned back towards the village.

'No… no that's fine. Just wondering, that's all,' Jason said, daring to touch her shoulder lightly to turn her back up the hillside.

Louisa shrugged, a smile tugging at one corner of her mouth and carried on walking into the woods. Jason hurried after her. He couldn't stop staring – her long legs, the movement of her hips as she walked, the curve of her waist, straight dark hair gleaming in a pony tail down her back and the perfect, lightly tanned skin of her neck.

They reached the huge oak tree where Jason had first seen Mouse, flat on his face after falling. Jason tried to clear his mind as Louisa leant back against the trunk, one leg bending slightly. She just watched him without saying anything, her dark eyes steady on his. Was he meant to kiss her now? No, not yet. Talk first.

'We're the same aren't we?' he asked.

Louisa looked him up and down. 'There are some differences, I think...'

'You know what I mean. When you pushed me away from Mouse that time... you used the... uh... Gift.'

Louisa slipped down the tree to sit on an exposed, mossy root. 'How much did your father tell you last night, about the Gifted and... so on?'

Jason sat down cross-legged opposite her. 'He explained a bit about the Watch and the Brethren, how both sides want everything kept secret and told us about... demons, the Touched and possession and all that.'

'I see,' Louisa said.

'But he doesn't want me to learn anything about how to use my Gifts,' Jason continued trying not to blurt everything out like an over-excited toddler. 'He says using them could attract the Brethren Agents and he wants to keep me totally out of the whole thing. He's not giving me the choice to decide for myself if I want to help, you know, become part of the Watch.'

Louisa nodded. She was serious now, not flirting. Somehow that made Jason less nervous. He felt less like he should try to be cool and witty. It was almost like talking to Miranda.

'Do you believe everything your father has told you so far?' Louisa asked.

'Yes, of course. Dad doesn't lie to us but... well it does sound like a bad horror movie – the Carpathian mountains, demon cults, possessed innocents.'

'It is not *like a movie,*' Louisa cut him short. She took in a slow breath. 'Not when you are there... not when your father is killed trying to redeem a young boy...' her words drained away.

'I'm sorry,' Jason stammered. He didn't know what she meant by 'redeem' but now wasn't the time to ask.

'You should not think badly of your father. I have tried to forget that life as well... living in a walled village, protected by armed guards, my mother and father disappearing for days or weeks at a time to 'work' and then coming back exhausted, often injured and their eyes still filled with horror.'

Louisa paused for a moment, dropping her gaze and absently digging with a twig into the rich, dark loam of the forest floor. 'One day, only my mother came back - I remember ripped clothing, bloody slashes all over her body. She could hardly stand. She told me my father had been killed... both of Mouse's parents as well and many more. Shortly afterwards, we left for England. We brought Mouse with us and we were... relocated here by Alan Brash. Soon after that I started to develop my gifts – my childhood, such as it had been, was over.'

They didn't say anything for a short while. Jason knew how she must have felt, losing one of her parents. He didn't want to think about that. Mum's murder was still too close. He guessed Louisa didn't want to dwell on her loss either.

Finally, he broke the silence.

'Have you learned how to use your powers? What sort of things can you do?'

Louisa smiled a little then, shaking her head. 'Boys and their toys. I am afraid I am not very powerful... did your father explain about the Gift passing down from mother to daughter, father to son, becoming stronger each time... about the Triple Six and so on?'

'No – he said Miranda wouldn't have any powers but that's about it.'

'Then I shouldn't really say any more.'

'It can't do any harm, can it?' Jason said. 'I mean, I already know about the Gift – that's the main thing.'

Louisa thought for a moment then nodded. 'There are three Orders, you might call them stages, of power. Each generation of the same family goes up a step in the order, so if your father was level one, you would become level two.'

'So I'll have stronger magic than my Dad?'

'It is not magic,' Louisa said, 'there are non of your Harry Potter spells and potions.'

'Yeah – sorry, I know that.'

'Good. Louisa shook her head. 'Now can your small brain cope with any more today?'

'Go on, try me.'

She nodded. 'It takes six generations to pass through each Order. Then the step from step 6 in the first order to step 1 in the second order is a very large leap of power and ability. Do you understand?'

'Yeah – I think I can cope. So the highest you can be is…'

'… third order, sixth generation – we'd call that person a 6,6,6 – a triple six. Such a person is more powerfully Gifted than I can ever imagine.'

'Great – 666 - all very demonic. So what happens after with a triple six's kids… nobody gets any powers?'

'The Gift switches gender, from a Gifted mother to her first born male child or from a Gifted father to his first born, female child.'

'Why?'

Louisa shook her head. 'We don't know. Perhaps it is to prevent any one family from becoming too powerful.'

'Ok. So what… order thing are you?'

Irritation flashed across Louisa's face for a second and then it softened.

'You do not know… it is fine. We do not discuss our generations or bloodlines. If the Brethren knew who were the most powerfully Gifted they could concentrate all their forces on hunting them down.'

'Oh – sorry I…'

Louisa suddenly held up her hand. 'Quiet.'

Somewhere, close by, a twig snapped. Jason and Louisa slowly stood up and peered around the great oak she'd been leaning against to look back down the hill.

A thinly bearded man, tall and gaunt, was trudging up the hill towards them. Even though he was probably only in his fifties, he walked with a thick stick, limping on his right leg. The loose grey trousers and shabby open shirt hanging off him added a decade or so to his appearance.

The man was only ten metres away and making a lot of noise as he hobbled along. Why hadn't they heard anything before he got so close? Jason stepped forward a little, just in front of Louisa. She immediately moved to stand next to him again.

'Ah – I am sorry to have disturbed you. It has been a long time since I was courting.'

His accent was foreign, similar to Mouse and Louisa's – Eastern European or Russian or something. The man didn't look dangerous, but then again, neither did the agent in Mawn.

Jason glanced around - this whole area was meant to be patrolled by Alan Brash's highly trained security forces and littered with hidden cameras.

He whispered to Louisa, not taking his eyes from the man. 'I think we should go... now.'

The man stopped just then, leaning heavily on his stick and catching his breath.

'Please do not be afraid - I know you are warned about talking to strangers in the woods but I am not a stranger, not really. My name is Marakoff.'

'We really have to go,' Jason said. 'Come on.' he whispered to Louisa.

'Excuse us Mr... Marakoff,' Louisa said, giving Jason an annoyed look.

Marakoff smiled, lifting his face to reveal green eyes twinkling with unexpected life in the leaf-dappled sunlight. He raised his stick-free hand in farewell.

'Ah, it is better to be safe than sorry, yes? I expect we will meet again, however.'

The two of them nodded and backed away. Marakoff waved again and limped off in the opposite direction. Very soon he was out of sight, lost amongst the trees.

'You are very cautious, Jason' Louisa said as they began jogging down the forested valley side.

Jason kept moving, Louisa easily keeping pace with him. Between breaths, he told her a shortened account of the attack on Mawn. By the time he'd finished they'd circled around towards the old forest road leading back towards the bridge.

'You are right to be so careful...' Louisa said, 'but this time I think there is no need. This man, Marakoff - I suspect he may have slipped passed Brash's guards and cameras, but he is one of us, I think.

'What do you mean, one of us? And how could he have just slipped past all the security?' Jason asked.

'It is not important just now. Look, we are here.'

They stepped onto the road a few metres from the bridge. Jason stared back into the woods, the leafy avenues dimming in the evening twilight. What if this Marakoff had followed them? Suddenly Jason felt Louisa's soft lips brush his cheek.

'I have to go, Jason – I should tell my mother about our Mr Marakoff. I have enjoyed our talk together... thank you.'

Louisa started towards the bridge.

'Wait, I'll walk you home... that bloke...'

Louisa looked back at him over her shoulder and winked. 'I will be fine, thank you. See you very soon.' Then she was across the bridge and turning out of sight.

Jason shook his head. *Girls! What did that kiss and her flirty little wink mean? What did Louisa really think of him?*

And why did she seem to think that guy, Marakoff, was okay?

Enough for one day. His head buzzing, Jason ambled across the bridge towards home.

***

Two minutes after Jason walked into the Old Mill, the phone rang. It was Louisa – could she come over, with Mouse and her mother?

Dad was in the kitchen, putting the kettle on as usual and Miranda was testing out some chocolate cake at the table.

'Sure, see you in a minute,' Jason said and put the phone down.

'You'd better fill the kettle a bit more, Dad,' Jason called through to the kitchen from the phone table in the hall, 'Louisa's coming over with Mouse and… her mother.'

Dad hesitated for a moment, took a slow breath then nodded, still with his back to Jason. He calmly filled the kettle with more water and dug out some more side-plates. Then he turned to face them.

'It's only fair to tell you two that I knew Louisa's mother a long time ago – her name is Ilena. She's the woman we saw looking in on our first day here.'

Miranda had forgotten her cake completely and was looking at Dad like some hungry cat about to pounce on a carelessly twittering bird.

'Why haven't either of you "old friends" called around to see each other yet?'

Dad's face was impassive. 'It's been over twenty years since we last spoke. Ilena and I worked together for a long time and we were very close once. After I… left that life, the last I heard was that Ilena had married a mutual friend. It was a bit of a shock finding out she was here.'

Miranda frowned. 'Wouldn't Alan Brash have known you two were… friends. Didn't he say anything to you?'

Dad's eyes flashed. 'Oh he would have know but Alan likes to play his own little games.'

'Louisa says they don't like Brash much either,' Jason said.

'Mmm,' Dad said, 'I can imagine. Brash was always very fond of Ilena, though.'

Miranda smiled. 'Things must have been interesting back then, when you and this Ilena were 'very close' and

Brash fancied her... and who's this mutual friend she married?'

'It doesn't matter right now,' Dad said. 'Now go tidy up the drawing room a bit while I make a fresh pot.'

'He was killed,' Jason whispered as he and Miranda crossed the hall towards the long corridor, 'Louisa's dad. That's why they moved here.'

Miranda nodded but didn't reply.

The drawing room wasn't too bad, probably because Miranda had been assigned house-keeping duties as she wasn't re-starting school until September. They were half way through stacking up the two-day old Sunday papers when the doorbell clanged.

Jason peered along the corridor, through the hall and into the kitchen. Dad was making no move to answer the door but was keeping extremely busy stacking cups and plates on to a tray.

'I'll get it then, shall I?' Jason called, already halfway to the door.

Dad didn't reply. Jason ran his fingers through his hair, turned the iron door ring and heaved the heavy oak open.

'Hi, come in.'

'Thank you, Jason,' said a woman who was Louisa's spitting image with perhaps a couple more decades or so of sophistication added on. Ilena Russof stood as tall and elegant as her daughter, wearing close fitting black trousers and a floaty white blouse. She smiled but it was a little too tight to be relaxed and her eyes darted around the hall, taking everything in.

Jason stuck out an awkward hand towards the drawing room. 'Hi... pleased to meet you. Come in and have a seat. Dad's just making some tea.'

Mrs Russof seemed to steel herself before stepping inside. She started down the long corridor without looking left into the kitchen.

'Such a bright and cheerful hallway,' Mouse muttered, looking around the dead animal heads rapidly falling into shadow with the setting of the sun.

'Come on,' Louisa whispered to Jason, taking his arm and following her mother towards the drawing room, 'this will be… interesting.'

With Louisa's hand draped lightly around his arm, Jason's mind instantly froze in panic. Then Miranda appeared at the drawing room door. Her eyes flicked over Louisa walking arm in arm with her brother then settled on Mrs Russof.

Mrs Russof slowed to a halt. 'You must be Miranda,' she said, 'how lovely you are. Your mother must have been beautiful, indeed.'

Miranda dropped her gaze. 'Thank you,' she said quietly, 'she was. Please take a seat.'

Mrs Russof nodded and took one of the high backed chairs by the fireplace. Louisa slipped her arm out of Jason's and took the other while, bringing up the rear, Mouse plonked himself down on the sofa.

Jason stayed by the door, unnecessarily holding it open as, down the hallway, Dad came out of the kitchen with his tea tray.

Mrs Russof seemed to stiffen with each footstep. Finally she stood up out of her chair, just as Dad entered the room.

'Hello, Richard,' she said. Her eyes flicked over Dad, taking in every detail then fixed on his face. A small smile wavered on her lips.

Dad stared straight at her, holding her gaze, his face unreadable, the heavily laden tray rock steady in his hands. 'It's good to see you safe, Ilena. I am so sorry about Ivan - he was a good man, a good friend. You must have been…'

'… angry.' Mrs Russof walked a few steps towards Dad, her smile a bit firmer.

Dad stared back into her eyes. 'I'm sorry I wasn't there… perhaps I…'

'You're not to blame, Richard… no one is.' She stopped an arm's length away, looking up at him. Dad was perfectly still.

'If our teams had been assigned together…' Dad began, keeping his voice flat.

'There is no telling if you would even have been on that mission and besides...' she glanced back at Louisa, '... a lot of other things might have been different if you had stayed.'

She reached out and lightly touched Dad's cheek then turned to face the three teenagers.

'I'd like you to meet my daughter, Louisa, and Mihail – ahh - Michael Muskowicz, a close family friend who now lives with us.'

Dad nodded and attempted a smile. He seemed unable or unwilling to speak for the moment.

Mrs Russof carried on. 'And now I think we should all talk... perhaps over this lovely tea Richard has prepared.' She turned back to Dad who nodded.

Mrs Russof sat back down on her chair and Jason and Miranda sandwiched Mouse on the sofa after pulling up a spare chair for Dad. As Dad poured the tea and offered biscuits around, Mrs Russof began to talk.

'I must apologise Richard. I really did mean to wait until you were ready to meet with us but Louisa gave me some news this evening. A man named Marakoff is here – from her description it is the same Marakoff who...'

'... worked closely with my father – the ghost?' Dad cut in.

'Yes. Louisa said he walks with a heavy limp – perhaps he is here to be relocated by Brash.'

'I doubt it,' Dad said, 'none of my father's team would go anywhere near Alan Brash.'

'So why do you think he is here? Because of you perhaps...?' Mrs Russof asked.

'There's not a lot of point guessing, is there?' Dad said a little sharply. 'He'll find us when he wants to talk.'

Mrs Russof nodded once and sipped at her tea. Louisa flashed Jason a look and raised her eyebrows.

'So,' Dad said after a few moments of silence, 'how is life under Alan Brash's... tender care?

Mrs Russof sipped her tea before answering. 'He no longer has the Council to... moderate his behaviour. He tries to control everything in his valley.'

'It was much worse in Darkston Village,' Louisa said.

'Which is why,' Mrs Russof added, 'I demanded that we be allowed to move here after just a few months. We were being... protected too closely.'

Dad nodded. 'What's he up to? Do you know how many of us he has gathered here? I thought his job was to help scatter the majority of them over the country, help them disappear into a normal life. Instead he seems to be forming one huge enclave of his own.'

Mrs Russof nodded. 'I do not know the exact numbers, Richard, but there are many Watch families living in Darkston village and Brash has perhaps a hundred or more of them guarding and training in his abbey – including some Gifted.'

'So they've hardly left the Watch at all?' Dad said.

'Those who I talked to before moving out of the village all seemed happy to be there.' Mrs Russof shrugged her slim shoulders. 'They're safe and Brash provides everything they need – a home, work, entertainment, high wages.'

'They should not have left the Watch,' Mouse suddenly said. He was staring into his tea cup, his face set. 'There are many things I do not trust about Alan Brash but he is right to prepare as many soldiers and Gifted as he can. In two years, when I am old enough, I will return to Romania, to the Watch. We all should do this - they need our help. The fight there is worse than anyone living can remember.'

'I am going back there too,' Louisa said. 'I am not powerfully Gifted but I will do what I can.'

'Nice that you have the choice,' Jason mumbled.

Dad cast him a warning glance.

Mouse looked up from his cup at Jason. 'You should be trained - there is no doubt of this. The Watch cannot afford to be without someone of your power,' He turned to Dad, his eyes defiant. 'My parents died because there were too few powerfully Gifted with them on their last raid...'

'Mihail - that is enough.' Mrs Russof stared hard at him. 'You have no right to...'

'It's all right, Ilena,' Dad cut in, returning Mouse's stare coolly. 'I know it must all seem black and white to you,

130

Michael - train, kill all the Brethren, Touched and possessed. But you must know that the Touched have no free will and the possessed... from the tiniest corner of their mind, they can see themselves killing their own families, tearing the bodies apart, eating their flesh, drinking their blood. Would you still want to cut the head off a child to get to the demon inside?'

'So you are saying we should not fight them?' Louisa asked, shaking her head, 'just let them multiply - in the end have us all just as food?'

'No,' Dad said, as calm as ever, ' but I am saying it's not a fight I would want anyone to be forced into.'

Jason straightened up. 'But we should be given the choice. They killed Mum right in front of me, Dad – they would have killed Miranda as well. I've been running from them all my life – I want to stand and fight... they deserve to pay. I want you to teach me how to use my... my Gift.'

'You know I won't do that,' Dad said quietly.

'Then Alan Brash will.' Jason answered quietly.

No one spoke for long moments. Dad held Jason's eyes until Jason turned away in exasperation.

The Mrs Russof broke the silence. 'I agree that you should have the choice, Jason and the Watch are desperate for Gifted of your potential strength.' She glanced at Dad then continued. 'But Alan Brash should not be the one to train you. He is highly Gifted but many of us believed he... enjoyed his work too much. With him, the end result was the only thing that mattered. People were just tools for him to use. We do not know why he was stopped from hunting and sent here to relocate families but it would have been for something very serious. The Watch cannot easily afford to lose someone of his power.'

Mouse was staring into his tea cup again. 'That leaves you, Mr Willow. We know of your power – you should train him... unless you would let him face the Brethren knowing nothing.'

'Enough.' Mrs Russof stood up. 'We had better go Richard. I am sorry. Mihail... all of us have no right to question your decisions like this.'

Dad shrugged and stood up as well. 'Why not? I do - every single day.'

Louisa ushered Mouse off the sofa and out into the corridor. Jason followed the two of them leaving Dad staring through one of the windows. Miranda hugged him from behind, her chin resting on his shoulder.

Mrs Russof stayed in the drawing room with him for a moment, just a step behind his resolute back. She said something Jason couldn't hear, Dad nodded once, then she joined them in the hallway.

Jason glanced at Louisa. *So she was going to go back to the Watch, to hunt demons. What would she think of him if he didn't even learn how to use his Gifts?*

They reached the hallway and Jason opened the door. 'I want to train, you know,' Jason said, 'I want to learn how to use my Gifts but Dad...'

Mrs Russof held her hand up. 'Jason - you have no idea at all what your father has been through... what terrible, terrible things hunters have to do. Neither have you two,' she said, glancing coldly at Mouse and Louisa. 'You should not blame him for wanting you to stay away from... our world.'

She smiled then, sadly and touched Jason's cheek with cool fingertips. 'In the end he knows you will make your own choices, but always listen to what your father has to say – listen really well. He is only trying to do what he thinks is best for you.'

Jason nodded guardedly, but Mrs Russof seemed to accept it. She led Mouse and Louisa out into the hazy dusk. Louisa looked back at him once, her eyes searching his and then she turned and walked away.

Jason closed the door and turned to watch his father still staring out of the drawing room window with Miranda wrapped around his back. He needed someone to train him and it didn't look as if Dad was going to change his mind any time soon.

Chapter 11

Fight fever spread quickly at Silent Hill. Jason noticed the whispers and glances directed at him the moment he stepped off the bus into the glaring sunlight of the massive forecourt.

Skins, Brash and normals all kept looking at him - the Brash members pushing up Ray Ban and Armani sunglasses into their shining, floppy hair and the Skins sneering and running one finger across their tattooed throats. The normal kids, those not in either gang, stared with everything from admiration down to pity.

'I am guessing today is when you become Fast Eddie's little gladiator,' Mouse said disinterestedly.

The three of them had hardly spoken on the bus in. Mouse had mumbled something about 'not supposed to talk about it,' and '...your father's decision,' before pretending to study for some maths test or other.

'Good,' Jason said, his eyes scanning the crowds unsuccessfully for Baldwin who hadn't been on their bus this morning, 'I need to get some practice in if I'm to join the Watch.'

Louisa looked at him and her lips pursed in thought. *She wasn't expecting that,* Jason thought.

'I thought your father wasn't going to allow it,' Mouse said, as they moved through the crowds to the relative calm of the entrance passage.

'My father can't control my life forever – I'll do what needs to be done.'

Mouse only grunted but Louisa bent close to whisper in his ear. 'This is not the way to learn, not with Alan Brash or his creatures.'

I haven't got much choice, have I? Jason thought but Louisa was already walking away, Mouse following in her wake.

'Thanks for your help,' Jason mumbled to himself.

So the fight was planned for today. It would have been nice if Fast Eddie had let him know yesterday, or even spoken to him for that matter. Perhaps the Brash leader was washing his hands of him as well.

Baldwin was in form class and actually made it to the first two lessons. He constantly stared at Jason, whispering with his three fellow Skins.

Jason ignored it all. He felt calm - content to let the fever rise around him whilst he sat back with a cool head. He'd been at the centre of a dozen or more proper fights before - when you constantly moved to new schools there was a lot of "settling in" to the pecking order to be done. He'd won them all – life-long Jakra training against opponents as strong and talented as Dad and Miranda gave him a huge advantage over hot-headed bullies relying only on their size and aggressive intimidation.

He was confident he'd put on a good show today for Louisa.

Violet was not so sanguine about it all, however. In maths, just before break, she touched his arm and whispered to him. 'Listen, do you want me to tell a teacher about this? If I told them then it wouldn't look like you were trying to avoid the fight.'

Jason smiled across at her, as he finished off his last simultaneous equation. They'd only known each other two and a bit days but she was definitely growing on him. Behind her quiet voice and skinny figure Jason there was a tough streak of determination and she always said what she felt. Best of all, was her cutting sense of humour.

'Thanks, Violet but I'm not sure you understand - I have to fight Baldwin. It would look really bad if I didn't see it through.'

She raised on eyebrow, holding his eyes with her grey-blue ones. 'I'm not a stupid as you look, Jason. I understand far better than you what's going on. You really don't want to get sucked in to all of this gang stuff.'

'And what do you know about this "gang stuff"?'

'Hasn't anyone told you who I am yet? I'm Alan Brash's ward.'

Jason dropped his gaze. 'Oh yeah, my mate Mouse did say something about that...'

'So maybe you should listen to me for once.'

'But where's the fun in that?' Jason tried.

He was met with a stoney glare. 'You do know all this gang fighting is just a sad selection process for Brash's little private army don't you...?'

'And the problem with that is...?' Jason answered.

'You don't know what he's like.'

'I've a lot of people trying to tell me, though.'

Violet didn't answer so he carried on, a little less abrasively. 'Look – all schools are the same - if I don't flatten Baldwin now I'll have every little punk of a bully trying to push me around – whether they're in a gang or not. I'm doing this for me, not for anyone else, all right?'

Violet stared at him, her normally bone-white skin flushing with a touch of red. 'You think so?' she said finally and started to pack away her dozen pencils.

Jason passed one he had borrowed back to her. 'Look, sorry. I know you're only trying to help. Don't worry about a thing, all right?' he said, a lot more softly and touching her on the shoulder. '...and don't tell any teachers.'

Violet just ignored him, focussing on the inner depths of her bag.

The bell went for break and Jason felt a small twist in his stomach. This could be it. He stood up and stepped towards the door.

'Jason...' Violet almost whispered. He turned back to her as the rest of the class started clearing out of the room.

'Be careful.'

'Thank...' Jason began, then suddenly crashed sideways into her desk.

He pushed himself back up and span around, fists up. Baldwin stood laughing a couple of feet away.

'Just thought I'd help you two get closer...' He sneered and snaked his studded tongue in and out of his mouth.

'Watch my tables, boys.' Mrs Strachen, their middle aged, battle-axe of a maths teacher snapped, looking over her shoulder from wiping the blackboard. 'I know you may be in a hurry to escape maths but leave the room in one piece.'

Jason didn't take his eyes off Baldwin. 'See you soon,' he whispered, and walked past.

'Oooh, I'm scared,' Baldwin sniggered and his three skin-headed friends laughed with him.

In the dining hall, things were heating up nicely. As Jason entered, there were a few cheers from various Brash dotted around the place. Perhaps they had decided to adopt him after all.

There was a good deal of hissing from the Skins dominating one corner of the hall and even a low chant of 'die, die, die' before a couple of teachers walked in.

Jason sat down and pulled a packet of crisps from his bag. This was all good hype - when he took Baldwin down in front of the wound-up crowds, Louisa would see what he was really made of.

Mouse came into the hall, looked around and spotted him. He gave a tight smile and walked over. As he sat down he pinched a handful of Jason's crisps. 'Listen, we are friends, yes? This fight is not the way to prove anything or even to train. I mean what I said – the Brash will just use you as a gladiator, to make their betting money on. And all this will help Alan Brash suck you into his abbey training and you will be his pawn forever. Perhaps there is a way to get you out of this before it all starts. If...'

'I don't want to get out of it, Mouse,' Jason said, keeping his voice down. What was Mouse trying to do – make him look like some snivelling coward running away from a fight?

'You're being very stupid, I think. Louisa doesn't...' Mouse began then stopped and looked behind him.

Fast Eddie was standing there, a frown creasing his perfect skin.

'You never were our greatest fan were you, Mouse, old chum?' he said. 'Time for you to leave... I think.'

Mouse returned the stare for a moment then deliberately turned back to Jason.

'Are you coming with me?' he said.

Jason shook his head. 'I'll see you later.'

Mouse hesitated for a moment then nodded and left without a backward glance.

Eddie sat down next to Jason. Half the heads in the refectory twitched around and the other half huddled in excited whispering.

'You've got the whole school talking, young Jason,' Eddie smiled, perfect white teeth lighting up his handsome face. 'Your uhh... friend, Mousey, hasn't given you second thoughts has he?'

'Just the opposite,' Jason said.

'Good – excellent, in fact. One does wonder at his motives of course... he has always avoided the Pit himself and he probably won't be best pleased when the lovely Louisa will see you make your triumphant debut today. He does rather fancy her, doesn't he? Not that I can blame him of course, being so close to her all day... and night.'

Jason didn't like what he was hearing – it was too close to his own thoughts. Still, he wasn't going to show his weak spots.

'He just doesn't like the idea of me... being like some prize-fighter or something.'

'Really – is that what he says?' Eddie smiled, pinching one of Jason's dwindling supply of crisps with a nod. He lowered his voice. 'I find that surprising as he must know this is just training for taking on... a more serious enemy.'

Jason scanned the room. They were still being watched but no one sat close enough to risk cramping the leader of the Brash or be accused of eavesdropping on his conversation.

'Do all the kids here know about...' Jason began.

Eddie raised a finger to stop him. 'No – none of the Drunken Abbot scum and only those from the village who have come from... abroad shall we say.'

'Right.'

Eddie flashed him another white toothed smile. 'Seriously Jason – do well today and it could lead to the best training you could ever wish for... and I don't just mean fisticuffs.'

Eddie laid one hand casually on the table top and pointed one finger at a salt cellar... which suddenly shot off the edge of the table and smashed against the back of a Skin on the next table. Salt exploded all over the year-eleven who span around then froze half way out of his seat.

'Oops,' Eddie said. 'So sorry, I dropped it.'

The Skin swore under his breath and stormed out of the canteen, three or four smaller hairless ones clambering out after him.

Eddie smiled. 'That'll make them mad. Do you know, Jason, we haven't had a proper Pit-fight for almost a month, with Easter getting in the way and so on. We really do need to see a severely squashed Skin.'

'Not a problem...' Jason said, 'As long as a teacher doesn't get in the way.'

Eddie tapped his golden monk badge, the ruby eyes glinting. 'The prefects run the fights old boy - which means the teachers keep away... as if any of the drunken sots were brave enough to venture outside the school building anyway.'

'Drunken sots?' Jason asked, distracted from thoughts of the fight for a moment. 'They don't seem drunk to me.'

Eddie shrugged. 'Of course not – but you can hear the wheel spins at three thirty as they dash off to the village inns for a spot of ale.'

'Really?'

'It's the only way to keep them teaching in this place,' Eddie winked. 'Anyway, the point is, don't worry about being interrupted in your… work this lunch time.'

Jason nodded. His stomach twisted again - things certainly were different at Silent Hill. He'd a sudden feeling of being alone - friendless and slipping down a path he couldn't get off. He shook himself. Rubbish - this was what he wanted, what he needed to do.

'Lunch time then is it? Where is this… pit?'

'It's a lovely venue.' Eddie smiled again. 'I've been in there a good few times myself during my meteoric rise to the top - a bit slippy underfoot but that's all part of the fun.'

'Mmm. So where is it?'

'Don't worry. I'll send someone to fetch you from the yard after fourth lesson – it's a little unseemly if I bring you in myself, you understand.'

'Uhh, right.'

'Excellent, young Jason. Today could be the first day of a very different life for you.' Eddie stood up, smoothed his immaculate Armani shirt, winked at Jason and left.

Students were still watching him, more boldly now that Fast Eddie had left the building. Louisa had not come in all break - probably doing maths homework with darling Darius.

Jason chewed his lip. He needed this fight to go well.

* * *

Two minutes into lunch break Jason strode out into the yard and leant against one of the chisel-scarred boulders.

The noise quickly grew as pupils flooded out of the tunnels and milled around the yard. Most of them seemed to be staring at him and whispering. He did his best to look laid back, ignoring everybody and picking at his fingernails. *Where was the escort Fast Eddie was sending to take him to the Pit.*

At last, there was a general drifting of bodies towards the south passage. It led out to neutral territory where the woods surrounding most of the school dropped steeply down to finally thin out into one of the many small parks landscaped across Darkston Village.

Jason's stomach began to clench. *Where was his escort? He'd have to go out and try to find the fight himself in a minute or the whole school would think he was too scared to move from the yard.*

'Not a friend in the world, huh?'

Erin Brock, the tall red head who had stepped in to stop his fight with Baldwin, was suddenly at his shoulder.

'Feels like it,' Jason mumbled, working on taking slow, deep breaths without anyone noticing. 'Let's get on with it?'

Erin smiled, showing small, white teeth which were a little crossed at the bottom. 'Right you are – nice to see you're so keen.'

'I don't like the waiting,' Jason said, straightening up from his supposedly cool, leaning-on-the-rock pose.

Erin winked. 'It's good for winding up the crowd though – a little feverish anticipation does wonders for the betting.' She winked and led him towards the south passage.

The press of pupils in the yard edged out of their way. A few took one glance at them and rushed ahead - no doubt to announce Jason's approach to their friends.

Erin set a steady pace through the crowds, chatting as if they weren't even there. 'You've caused quite a stir with us sort of backing you.'

Jason didn't reply. Erin glanced across at him and her smile faded a little. 'You'll smash this Baldwin kid, you know – I've seen him in the Pit a couple of times before and he's mainly mouth… although he did win both times come to think of it.'

'Not helping,' Jason mumbled.

'Just remember to ignore the crowd this first time and don't show off with any fancy stuff.'

'Suits me,' Jason said, forced to raise his voice as they entered the tunnel and excited chatter echoed all around them. The far end was all blazing white sunlight.

'Good,' Erin said, her smile returning. 'Now remember that the Skins in the front row are likely to try a few tricks, so keep away from them. They won't be too out of order as we're behind you but... just so you know.'

Pupils had stopped to line the last half of the passage. Jason just stared straight ahead, not wanting to talk any more. Some of the kids shouted 'good luck' and 'smash' im' type comments but many more let him know that he was going to get slaughtered.

'Drunken Abbot scum,' Erin told him, '- wannabe skinheads most of them.' One thin faced boy with a double nose stud stepped in their path to cuss Jason. Erin slapped him out of the way so hard that he flew back into the wall and slid down it. She didn't even break stride.

They came out of the tunnel and into the light. The whole area was filled with clusters of staring, chattering pupils. Jason wasn't hearing them anymore – it was like he had one of those "listen-to-the-sea" shells pressed against each ear. He wanted this over with. If only his bloody stomach would loosen up. It always clenched up before a proper fight until he got hit a few times and then he usually became ice-cold angry and forgot to be nervous. There had never been this sort of build up in any of his other schools however – this was like stepping into the Coliseum in ancient Rome.

Erin led him through the crowds to the edge of the woods. Ten metres down the wooded hill the Skins waited for him.

At least twenty of them were lined up between the trees forming a human corridor. They all stared at him, totally silent.

'We have to go through them or it'll look bad,' Erin whispered. 'Watch their feet.' Without missing a step they strode between the first two Skins.

The jeering leapt out at them - foul language, pointing fingers darting out, hate filled faces pushing forward. Steel tipped boots kicked out for Jason, threatening to cripple him before he even set foot in the Pit. He blocked them with his own feet but they were slowing him down. If they stopped in the middle of this they wouldn't have a chance.

Erin flicked out two extendable steel batons from her sleeves and then, like some demented Morris dancer, she smacked four knees and ankles in little more than a second. The Skins all shoved back, swearing loudly.

'Your friend Mouse is not the only one who plays with sticks.' Erin grinned, casually striking another knee without even looking.

The Skins all pulled far back while still swearing and gesticulating. Erin spun her sticks happily, looking for an excuse to hit something else as the two of them ambled through the foul-mouthed gang. Just as they were stepping out of the human corridor, one big Skin with a snakehead tattoo on his cheek lent forward and spat at Jason. Jason dodged most of it and flicked out two fingers to strike the lad's nose.

The Skin roared and stepped forward, blood already welling out of his nose. Erin whacked him on the head with one steel tip and he crumpled. Furious shouts erupted from the Skins and they surged in around them. The next moment though, Brash members appeared from nowhere and formed a tight circle around Erin and Jason.

'Warming up nicely,' Erin laughed as she grabbed Jason and dashed out of the Brash-Skin face-off.

And then Jason caught his first view of the 'Pit.'

It was like a three sided amphitheatre in the hillside, perhaps fifteen metres across at the bottom with steeply sloping sides rising up the hill and a low lip leading down. The sides heaved with pupils.

'Fight, fight, fight...' it started quietly at first, everyone - Skins, Brash and normals - joining in and staring at him with violence-hungry eyes.

Without realising it, Jason had stopped. Erin touched his elbow and they pushed down through the crowd.

There was a definite hierarchy here – non-gang members higher up the slopes, gang members lower down sitting 'ringside'. The Skins were on the left half, being joined now by the dispersing human corridor who pushed through to find their places. The Brash, smartly dressed, some sipping from silver hip flasks as if they were at Ascot races, stood smiling and joking on the right.

Jason and Erin got through the ringside crowd unscathed and stepped onto the Pit floor. It was a mix of scrappy grass tufts and dry dirt. There was a massive tree stump in the centre of the hollow, smoothly sawn off about a metre above the ground. The noontime sun streamed through the break in the leafy canopy overhead and spot-lit the stump.

Jason looked around him, trying to appear calm. There must have been five hundred or more faces staring down at him from the slopes, chanting louder and louder, pushing, hanging out of trees - all of them baying for pain and blood.

Baldwin was nowhere in sight. Had he chickened out?

Very self-consciously, standing at the edge of the hollow, Jason began to loosen up - swinging his arms, turning his wrists, his neck, stretching and flicking out his legs. The noise got louder. Jeers and laughter rose over the chanting now, fingers pointing, the back rows of Skins mimicking his actions like demented monkeys. Jason felt heat flare up his cheeks but he carried on – settling in to his warm-up routine, trying to clear his mind.

Then the taunting broke into a cacophony of cheers from the Skins and boos from the Brash. Jason eased up from a split stretch to see Baldwin rising above over the lip of the hollow.

A huge Skin, broken-nosed and bare-chested with a black skull tattooed on his right cheek was walking up the hill carrying Baldwin on his shoulders. It was Grizz – the Skin who had held his gang in check during Jason and Baldwin's initial confrontation.

The two of them lurched to a halt in the hollow and soaked up the cheers. Grizz's heavy muscles rippled as

143

Baldwin perched on his shoulders and punched his fists into the air.

'Oooh, the big guns are out,' Erin said, winking down to Jason who had resumed his stretching. 'You remember Grizz... as in Grizzly Bear? He's Callum Mennis's second in command. Big bugger and bloody strong... I wish I hadn't asked to be your escort now.'

Jason swallowed as Grizz started a circuit of the hollow with Baldwin sneering down from on-high and whooping with presumptuous victory. The Skins loved it and the shouting and screaming began to be underscored with a chant of 'Grizz... Grizz... Grizz...'

Jason shook out his wrists again and glanced at Erin. 'Where's my shoulder ride?' He had to shout to make himself heard over the crowd.

'In your dreams,' Erin said, without taking her eyes off the two Skins.

Grizz and Baldwin rounded towards them. Standing where they were, close to the edge of the hollow, the human bear would be forced to walk around... or through them to complete his circuit of the hollow.

Erin's twin batons slipped into her hands again. *Was this how it would begin – some impromptu tag team fight?*

Then Erin tossed her weapons away to another Brash girl in the crowd on their right.

'What're you doing?' Jason hissed as Grizz and Baldwin stomped towards them.

'No weapons allowed in a bare knuckle fight,' she said calmly, glancing across at him and shrugging.

'Bugger - hope you're some use without them,' Jason managed.

'Sadly, today I'm just here to pick up your pieces.' Erin grinned.

As the two Skins approached, Jason and Erin squared up to them. Jason steadied his breathing and settled on the balls of his feet. If they tried to bulldoze right through then...

144

Grizz stopped a step away, lumbering to a halt like a fall of boulders. Above him, Baldwin's web-stained face loomed down seemingly from the tree tops.

The crowd stilled, waiting to see what would happen. Baldwin's lip curled in contempt and he began to chant, jabbing one hand down rhythmically inches above Jason's head.

'You're gonna diiiiie - and you know you are.

'You're gonna diiiiie - and you know you are.'

The Skins to his left began to join in, drowning out what seemed half-hearted jeering from the Brash to his right.

'Bugger this,' Jason mumbled. Without a hint of what he was going to do, he suddenly stepped back a pace and leapt into the air, flinging his right foot in an arc-kick and slapping Baldwin's jabbing hand away.

Jason landed in a crouch and whirled his right foot around to stop an inch behind Grizz's knee. Had he hit him, both Skins would have come crashing down... as long as Grizz's tree-stump of a leg buckled of course.

There was absolute silence. Jason looked up at the mountain of muscle looming over him and wondered if he'd made a mistake.

Grizz's rock-troll face was unmoved by his display of skill but Jason was glad to see Baldwin trying to flex his hand without anyone noticing.

Erin leapt into the silence. 'Anybody want to see a fight?' she shouted and sprang onto the central stump. Her long red hair flamed in the sun and sunlight seemed to burst from her.

The crowd erupted into cheers, the Brash loudest of all this time.

Jason, still crouching, rolled back from Grizz's mighty legs and flipped to his feet. He was almost beginning to enjoy himself.

He strolled over to wait at Erin's right hand below the stump and scanned the crowd. He stifled a satisfied smile - standing a good way up the hill was Louisa. She had her back against a tree and was watching him silently. Mouse was next to her, arms folded and his face set like stone. Then Darius stepped into view on Louisa's other side, brushing his shiny blond hair back from that pretty-boy face. Jason looked away.

The crowd began to quieten down again.

'Right, here comes Callum Mennis, leader of the Skins.' Erin whispered down to him from the corner of her mouth. 'No fancy, Bruce Lee stuff with this one or he'll kill you... he's not as friendly as Grizz.'

Jason looked around to see who she was talking about.

From the midst of the Skins stepped out the meanest looking youth Jason had ever seen. He was only as tall as Jason but tightly muscled and perfectly poised. Wearing ripped jeans and only a sleeveless black leather top, Callum Mennis was completely hairless. His face, eyebrows, head and chest were all smooth and glistening. Half his torso was tattooed with all manner of tortured souls, triumphant demons and red-eyed snakes. A scar ran from his right ear down most of his neck.

Baldwin quickly slid down from Grizz's shoulders and the two of them took their places behind Callum.

Erin stepped down from the stump as the crowd fell quiet and still. Complete silence descended all around the hollow now - no one daring to show any disrespect.

A stirring in the Brash crowd caught Jason's eye and Fast Eddie stepped out from the sea of designer jackets and sunglasses. He was the tall, floppy blond haired, immaculately dressed antithesis of Callum Mennis' raw malevolence.

'Kind of gives you hope for the world doesn't he?' Erin whispered to Jason with her eyes fixed on the leader of the Brash gang.

Callum Mennis and Fast Eddie met in the centre of the hollow and stepped up onto the stump at the same time. They faced each other with just a foot or so between them. Eddie, a head taller than Callum, reached up to slip off his Ray Bans and pocketed them before nodding once. Callum lifted his chin, his small, mean eyes like obsidian chips. Without a word, they turned their backs on each other to face their respective gangs.

Callum began, his voice, hard and clipped. 'Fight-time. A new boy, Jason Willow, has pissed off one of ours and now he's gonna pay his dues.'

The Skins all straightened up, threw a fist in the air and cried 'FIGHT-TIME.'

Fast Eddie took over, his voice rich, cultured and in total contrast to Callum's. 'Fight-time. Young Jason here is not one of ours... but as he is taking on one of theirs we offer him protection in and out of the Pit.'

The Brash all clapped three times then shouted in rhythm 'FIGHT-TIME.'

Fast Eddie and Callum stepped down without looking at each other and walked back to their gangs. Released from this bizarre ceremony, the crowd burst into roars and whoops.

'Kick-off,' Erin shouted to Jason over the bedlam. 'You'll be fine – just remember to hit him harder than he hits you.'

Jason nodded as Erin trotted off to join Fast Eddie, front and centre of their gang.

Jason stepped further in to the hollow, closer to the stump. Opposite him, Baldwin did the same, the huge Grizz slapping him hard on the back and grunting 'kill him' above the crowd's hysteria.

As Grizz strode back to join Callum in the Skin's front row, Baldwin stared at Jason and ran a finger slowly across his own throat.

Jason just raised his eyebrows. He'd calmed now, his stomach was still slightly clenched but with excitement as much as trepidation. He took a ready stance, his left leg a little forward and his fists relaxed but up at face height.

The crowd started up again. 'Fight, fight, fight..'

Baldwin sneered. 'Your kungy fuey won't help you in here, you prat.'

'How's your hand?' Jason shouted above the chanting.

Baldwin rushed forward and punched with a right. Jason blocked easily, latched onto Baldwin's wrist, twisted and propelled him straight into the crowd.

Laughter broke out through the chanting.

Baldwin span around. He was furious but there was no rushing this time. He stalked up to Jason with murder in his eyes and started punching.

Jason blocked each blow with his eyes levelled on Baldwin's chest so he could see every limb. Baldwin tried a vicious kick but Jason swept it aside almost before it left the ground and pushed him away while he was off balance.

Baldwin stumbled sideways, almost falling, and the laughing grew louder from the Brash and the normals higher up the slopes. Jason glanced up to the top of the hollow to see how Louisa was enjoying the show. She wasn't even watching; she was whispering something in Darius' ear.

Smack. Baldwin's furious punch hammered into Jason's cheek and sent him sprawling in the dirt. Head ringing, Jason automatically tucked into a roll to get him away but Baldwin was right on him. A steel capped boot caught Jason in the stomach and he crashed into the front row of Skins.

Immediately hands and fists jabbed at him. Jason pushed himself up but someone kicked his hand away and he crashed down again. Baldwin was on him instantly, another boot cracking into his ribs sending a red wash across his eyes and bile halfway up his throat as he sprawled face first into the dirt.

Anger and fear surged up in Jason and desperately, he swung his arm up in an arc at Baldwin's knees.

It felt as if a wave of ice shot through his arm and balled in his fist. The strike should have unbalanced Baldwin at best, but Baldwin's legs were hammered out from under him and he flipped backwards to slam down on his back.

Gasping for breath, Jason scrambled away from the Skins' clutching fingers and clambered to his feet. His head still swam and his ribs shot hot spikes into him but he could stand. Groggily he stumbled over to stare down at Baldwin's prostrate body.

What had he done to the boy?

Suddenly Baldwin grabbed his leg. Without thinking, Jason lashed out a back-fist at his temple. Baldwin went down again, instantly pole-axed. Jason stepped in to flick-kick him in the chin, but stopped an inch before making contact. There was no need. Baldwin wasn't getting up anytime soon.

Dizzy, his vision blurred and ribs aching, Jason stepped back and raised one fist.

The crowd erupted, jumping up and down and chanting his name – everyone that is, apart from the Skins, who began pushing their way out of the hollow in silence. Grizz, as Baldwin's escort, was presumably the one meant to pick up the pieces. However, he just spat on Baldwin and left with the rest of his gang. Baldwin groaned on the floor and curled up in a ball.

Jason felt suddenly drained as if he'd spent too much of himself. His mind seemed to become encased in a sight-blurring, sound-muffling jelly which vibrated with each throb of pain from his ribs. A mass of jumbled faces began to flood down the banks into the hollow and converge on him. Desperately he searched passed them to look for someone to get him out of there. Where were Louisa and Mouse – had they already left? Had Louisa even stayed to see him win?

A moment later, Fast Eddie was standing next to him, flanked by Erin and about thirty Brash.

'Well done, old boy – a fine show.'

Baldwin, curled up amongst scores of milling feet now, struggled to stand then stumbled quickly away.

Eddie glanced at him, his nose wrinkling as if there was a bad smell. 'One less baldy-boy to worry about, I think. Something tells me they'll cut him loose after that little performance. Good work - Mr Brash said you were one to watch.'

Jason gingerly touched his bleeding lip – it felt huge. 'Thanks - I was just trying to hit him harder than he hit me.'

Standing by Eddie's side, Erin grinned broadly at him but she stayed quiet. Her leader was doing the talking.

'Good tactic. However, flipping him into a somersault while you're lying flat on the ground was a little obvious. We should have mentioned that you don't want to show everyone here all your... skills.'

'I don't know how I did that,' Jason whispered.

Eddie smiled. 'Oh really? Well now, we could help you there.'

Jason didn't answer - he just attempted a smile and rubbed his ribs again.

Fast Eddie shrugged, his eyes narrowing for just a fraction of a second. 'I dare say Mousey and his delightful non-girlfriend have been warning you about me and my nasty gang. They've told you we'll steal your soul, have they?'

Jason kept his mouth shut and looked at the floor. Eddie laughed amenably. 'I'd want to stay in the lovely Louisa's good books too if I were you, Jason, but do remember that there are other equally lovely girls that Silent Hill has to offer to the... right boy.'

Jason shrugged. *Was Eddie taking the mick?*

'A shame they didn't stay until the end... make sure you were okay and so on.' Eddie said. 'Anyway old chap, fantastic job today but don't get too... complacent. You need to learn what you're really capable of in case you antagonise someone a little more scary than Dick Baldwin next time.'

'Uhh... right – I'll think about that. Thanks,' Jason nodded then had a mental picture of himself as some nodding-head dog in the back of a beaten up old car and held his head still. He glanced at Erin. 'and thanks for, you know, your help and all that.'

Erin winked at him.

'Plenty more where that came from,' Fast Eddie said, breaking into his characteristic broad smile. 'You know where we are.

Then he slipped an arm around Erin and led his gang up out of the hollow, shooing away the few remaining gawking normals.

Jason spat out some more blood and started back towards Silent Hill on his own.

***

Baldwin wasn't on the bus home that afternoon although that wasn't anything unusual. The Skins could catch any one of a dozen or so other buses that expelled the Drunken Abbot 'scum' swiftly through the beautiful cottages and landscaped streets of Darkston village and out beyond the fences into the town's grey terraces.

However, Louisa wasn't there either.

'She has revision classes.' Mouse said, obviously noticing Jason's disappointed face.

'Right.' Jason said, plonking himself down with Mouse on the back bench seat

'The wonderful Fast Eddie was pleased with your performance today, yes?' Mouse said.

'At least he stayed to see if I was okay.'

'We waited until the Skin wasn't moving any more and then left you to finish kicking him.' Mouse said casually.

'I didn't kick him – I stopped.'

'You are too kind, I think.' Mouse said. He pulled his bag up from the floor. 'We may not see a lot of you for a while – we have the examination study leave and you perhaps need some time to play with your new friends, yes?'

Mouse held Jason's eye for a moment more. 'Choose them carefully,' he mumbled before shifting away along the seat and pulling out a book to read.

Willow stared at the back of Mouse's head for a moment then turned to stare out of the opposite window. *What was the use in arguing?*

When Jason arrived home, the house was silent so he went to check the garden.

Dad and Ilena Russof were there, sitting at the garden table which overlooked the river and the woods beyond. The remains of what must have been a very long lunch and an empty bottle of Cava were laid out before them.

Ilena stood up the moment Jason stepped through the kitchen's back door. She looked fantastic - today in fitted black trousers and a deep red blouse, her dark hair tied up with a few wispy strands blowing in the soft breeze from the river.

Dad took one look at Jason's bruised face and dishevelled clothes and put his wine glass down. 'You've been fighting.'

'I should leave,' Ilena cut in. 'I will telephone you tomorrow, Richard.' With a half smile to Dad and a concerned glance over Jason, she walked out of sight around the side of the house.

Jason would rather face the music than lie to his father. He waited until Ilena had gone then moved over to the table.

'Yes – I had a fight, Dad… with one of the skinhead gang like I told you.'

'Why?'

'Because he's a prat and kept getting at me.'

'And did you hurt him badly?'

'He'll live.'

'That's lucky,' Dad said, throwing the remains of his wine out onto the lawn. 'I told you - you're coming into your Gifts - you can kill with one blow if you're not in control, smash bones, permanently damage brains…'

'Then teach me how to use it properly.'

'I will…' Dad said, 'I've already said that I'll teach you how to suppress your Gifts, keep the powers locked away. We'll start this evening.'

'I don't want to suppress it. What happens when the next Brethren agent comes along to try to kill us?'

'We've been through this… the best defence is anonymity - look at Ilena and her family...'

'Louisa has been taught how to use her gifts - she pushed me over from ten feet away the first day I met her'

'She was brought up in the Watch and besides, she's only a first generation Gifted. If you learned your Gifts you would be able to "push" houses over – with the accompanying zephyr drawing in any agents for miles around.'

'The agents always find us anyway – with mum and on Mawn…'

'That won't happen again.'

'How do you know?'

Dad had no answer. Jason didn't want to stop. 'And what if I don't want to hide? What if I want to join the Watch?'

Dad stared at him, then asked quietly 'Why in God's name would you want to do that?'

'Oh, now let me think,' Jason said, 'maybe because the Brethren sent men to kill my mother and maybe because if the Watch lose there will be Brethren agents and Touched and demons everywhere. Even here. No one will be safe ever again.'

Dad brushed his fingers through his hair. 'Listen Son, do you think your mother would have wanted you to risk your life time and again to avenge her or would she have wanted you to have as normal, happy and safe a life as you possibly could?'

Jason just stared at him.

Dad carried on, his voice soft. 'And I told you the fight between the Brethren and the Watch always ebbs and flows, no side can ever really win. The Watch are just on a low at the moment - they'll recover, they always do.'

'So why are Louisa and Mouse going back to join them if there's nothing to worry about? They've lost half their family there, both Mouse's parents – they want to make the Brethren pay as well.'

'Is that another reason you're thinking of doing this - to follow Louisa Russof?' Dad said quietly.

How did he know that? Jason's anger flared. 'No – I'm thinking of joining the Watch because I'm not a coward.'

Jason hated himself the moment he'd said it. Dad however, was completely calm.

'Whatever you think of me, of my reasons for trying to leave that world behind, you need to understand… if you do join them, it will never stop. The things you will have to do will… change you forever. You don't have to throw your life away, Son.'

'Not much of a life to throw away is it?' Jason said and stormed into the kitchen, slamming the door behind him.

***

Mouse did little more than grunt a greeting to him on the bus the following morning and Louisa wasn't there again. It was probably a good thing or doubtless she'd have moaned at him about having the fight as well.

Once in Silent Hill however, it seemed everyone else appreciated his efforts in the Pit yesterday. The moment he walked into registration, most of his form started clapping and cheering. Obviously the two big Skin boys and the whip thin girl just scowled at him. Baldwin himself was nowhere to be seen.

Jason nodded to the class, half raising one hand but quickly found his place next to Violet as Mr Pastor started taking the register.

Violet had not clapped - she'd slapped on her stern face and Jason guessed the 'voice of disapproval' would come out of it any time now.

The moment the register and notices were called, Violet started.

'When's the next fight, then? With you being so friendly with Fast Eddie, I assume you're joining the Brash... should I watch what I say now in case it goes straight back to my guardian?'

'Do they report everything back to him?' Jason asked.

'Yes – obviously... duh, they're called "the Brash" aren't they?'

Jason shook his head. 'I guess.'

Violet raised her eyes. 'Anyway, don't try to change the subject. Are you going to be a little Brashy boy then? Are you...'

'Violet - shut up,' Jason said, not unkindly. 'The truth is I don't know if I want to join them or not. My dad and sister are dead set against having anything to do with Alan Brash.'

'They're obviously a lot brighter than you, then.' Violet mumbled.

'I can't see what you've got against him - a super-rich guardian living in some huge abbey.'

Violet clapped her hands in mock joy. 'Lucky me.'

She pulled her invariably bulging bag onto the table and started rummaging through it for no apparent reason.

'Look,' Jason began, 'I don't know about the gang but if some idiot tries to push me around I'll push them back. There's nothing wrong with that is there?'

Violet slowed down her rummaging and faced him. She looked shy again, like when they'd first met. Her gray-blue eyes didn't quite manage to meet his and she quickly angled her head so that long, mousey hair covered half her face.

'I suppose not... it's just... well I liked the fact that you were one of the few people around here who weren't playing *his* games and... well, you might get really badly hurt in the Pit. They'll keep putting you up against stronger and stronger Skins and then...it'll go further' Violet's voice faded away without finishing for once.

'Go further – how?'

'Never mind,' Violet said, 'I just don't want you dripping your blood all over my stuff, that's all.'

At that moment, the prefects rang their hand-bells for lessons.

As he followed Violet to the door, the Skins tried to push in front of her. Instinctively, Jason shot his hand out to stop them. Amazingly, they stopped and even pulled back a step.

Violet flashed Jason an unreadable look and disappeared into the corridor. As he followed her out he heard a muttered 'bloody hero!' from one of the Skins but he ignored it. Prefects were everywhere and Mr Pastor was still in the room - there would be plenty of opportunity to follow it up later.

It was Friday, the end of Jason's first week at Silent Hill. His first two lessons went well enough - French and Geography. Violet stopped preaching and prattled on about the forthcoming exams and some television talent show she was going to watch on Saturday night – she had her own suite of rooms at the abbey apparently, complete with a huge HD TV and surround sound.

It was good to have her inane chatter back. Almost too soon the bells were rung for break and it was time to face the rest of the school.

The corridors were buzzing louder than usual as he found his way from Geography into the packed yard. Everyone kept glancing at him as he made his way to one of the rocks and wondered if a Brash messenger would turn up with an invite to join them. He didn't know what he'd say if they did, but hopefully it would be Erin Brock again – what a mix of gorgeous looks and hard fighter.

No Brash came for him, however. Jason was starting to become annoyed, feeling like he was some animal in a cage for everyone to gawp at, when Mouse came strolling towards him, a bag of crisps in hand.

Mouse just looked at him for a time, finishing his mouthful. They stank - cheese and onion flavour.

'So what – you're talking to me again, now are you?' Jason asked.

'Not with my mouth full – Ilena is very quick to correct bad manners.' Mouse said.

'I haven't joined the Brash if that's what you've come to find out. They haven't asked me.'

'Ah – but they are about to do so, I think,' Mouse said, nodding backwards slightly. 'This is what I came to warn you about.'

Jason looked behind Mouse. People were drifting around them – probably trying to eavesdrop for any news of the fight. He noticed a group of three girls in particular - all very good looking in short floaty skirts and pristine white blouses with several buttons open. Two were blonde, one with her hair long and wavy and the other with hers straight and cut above her shoulders. The third girl had Louisa's look – tall, curvy figure and dark hair in a neat bob. All three girls caught him staring at them and the dark haired one smiled at him.

'They're very... tasty, yes?' Mouse said, without looking around. 'You see how nicely they're dressed.'

Jason shrugged. 'They look all right.'

'It means that they are Brash girls,' Mouse explained, slowly. 'Large amounts of pain will happen for anyone who is not in the gang if they... try anything with them.' Mouse smiled tightly. 'Of course, it is also true that your good friend, Fast Eddie, likes to reward his favourite gladiators... as long as they keep winning.'

Jason glanced back at the threesome. 'So you reckon Eddie sent those girls to tempt me into joining up?'

Mouse nodded.

'Don't you think it's at all possible that they might actually fancy me?' Jason asked.

Mouse looked him up and down. 'No,' he said and then walked away.

Jason watched him barge through the yard and into the shadows of the east passage.

A whiff of sweet perfume made him turn around and suddenly he was face to face with the three Brash girls.

'Hello, Jason.' said the long-haired blonde.

'Hi,' Jason said, his throat going instantly dry.

'My name is Farah, and my friends here are Tanya and Beth.' Farah's voice was light and airy. She had big blue eyes and her cheeks sparkled with some sort of lightly glittered blusher.

'Hi, uhh, I'm Jason.' said Jason.

'We know.' said Tanya, the dark haired one. She smiled which made her eyes narrow and glint mischievously. She reminded him very much of Louisa... when she was in a good mood, that is. Jason felt his heart pounding up though his chest and into his throat.

On the other side of Farah, Beth brushed back one side of her glistening blonde hair and ran one finger down her cheek to play around the corner of her mouth. Her head was angled down slightly so she looked up at him from under prettily plucked eyebrows.

'We saw you fight yesterday... we thought you were very good.'

Farah cut in. 'I liked it best when your shirt ripped open a bit... Mmm.'

Jason's cheeks caught fire.

'Were you hurt very badly?' Tanya asked and reached out slowly to gently touch his left ribs where Baldwin had kicked him. Jason winced slightly. All the girls were standing very close to him now.

'Oh, I'm sorry,' Tanya said, stepping back a little and covering her mouth in shock. With her lower face covered, her dark eyes look even bigger.

'It's fine... really,' Jason stammered.

'We think you need someone to... nurse you back to health,' Farah said, holding his wide-eyed stare.

'It must have been very frightening in the Pit.' said Beth, her eyes still looking up at him coyly.

'Uhh... that would be great but you're... you're Brash girls, aren't you? Aren't you supposed to only uhh... hang around with Brash boys?'

'Oh, not all the time - especially when there is something a little more tasty on offer,' Farah said.

Tanya raised her eyebrows. 'We can... hang around with anyone we please, Jason - being in the Brash doesn't mean anyone "owns" us.'

'And besides,' Farah said, flicking back her wavy hair, 'Eddie is very pleased with you right now. He wouldn't mind at all if we kept you company for a while.'

'So... would you like...' Beth began, clasping her hands in front of her and glancing up from under her trembling fringe, 'would you like...?'

'For heaven's sake, Beth,' Farah cut in. 'What little miss innocent here is trying to say is would you like one of us to... show you around the village? We could have a lot of fun.'

Tanya smiled. 'You're new and having a bit of a tough time so we'd like to show you that not everyone in Silent Hill is horrible. That's all.'

'And outsiders aren't allowed to wander around the village without someone who lives there, you see?' added Beth, gaining some confidence, it seemed.

Jason's mouth dropped open. No one had ever asked him out on a date before and now here were three gorgeous girls...

'So choose,' Farah said, smiling and smoothing down her blouse.

Jason ran his fingers back through his hair. *This can't be happening - not to me.*

Suddenly the bells rang out from the three passages - the end of break. Farah raised an eyebrow - he had to choose, now. 'Tanya… please,' he stammered, '… but you're all so…'

Farah shrugged. 'We know. Maybe next time. Enjoy yourselves.'

She slung her arm around Beth who gave a little nod farewell before they disappeared into the crowds already draining away into the four passages.

That left just Tanya standing in front of him.

'Good choice,' she said.

'Thanks… I mean…'

Tanya touched his arm. 'We can't talk here, the prefects will have us.'

Jason glanced around. The yard was almost empty already – how had that happened?

'Listen,' Tanya continued, 'today, after school – let's go for a walk and have a pizza or something. Fridays are always fun in the village.'

'Yeah… yes. Great. That would be… great.'

Tanya smiled, her eyes glinting again. Smoothly, without any hint of rushing, she leant forward and kissed his cheek. 'I'll meet you by the gates, then,' she said, turning on one shiny black heel and clipping away across the yard.

Speechless, Jason just watched her go then sprinted towards the south passage before the prefects caught him.

Things were looking up.

Chapter 12

The rest of Friday seemed to take an age to get through. Jason got a few cat-calls in the yard and corridors mainly about the fight but some alluding to his new "girlfriend".

Violet was unnaturally quiet in their last lesson. She seemed almost sad for some reason and didn't even bother messing through her bag much.

After a couple of attempts at asking, Jason gave up on finding out what he'd done wrong this time and tried to concentrate on his work..

At last the waiting was over. The prefects' bells actually made him jump at the end of the lesson. It was time for his date.

He was impervious to the stares and whispers as he strode through the corridors. He was finally getting a life after years of shying away from making friends, let alone girlfriends. And for the first time, he'd a clear future open to him if he wanted to take it – learn to use his Gift and join the Watch.

His confidence wavered just a little as he strode down the West tunnel towards the main school gates. What if this was all some big wind up and Tanya wasn't there?

However, when he broke out into the sunshine, she was waiting for him. She was leaning against the wall close to the open gates in her short skirt and that fine white blouse which the bright light rendered virtually transparent. Farah and Beth were with her, chatting away, but Tanya spotted him immediately and smiled.

Jason forced himself to keep a steady pace towards her and smiled back. Tanya held his eyes briefly then said something to her friends. They turned around, Farah blew a kiss to him and then she and Beth walked off before he got there.

'Hello.' Tanya said as he reached her.

'Hi,' Jason said. His stomach was churning but he ignored it. He was supposed to be enjoying himself but it wasn't easy when the whole school was watching them.

'You alright?' she asked.

'Yes, fine... thanks. I'm just... glad school's over.'

'Me too – this afternoon seemed to take forever for some reason.' She smiled again and held out one hand. 'Shall we go?'

Taken by surprise Jason just stared at her beautifully manicured, light pink fingernails. Suddenly he realised what she wanted him to do and grabbed her hand. Tanya eased away from wall and stood next to him, her cool fingers curling around his hot ones.

She didn't start to walk, however. She just stared at him, seeming like she was deciding something. 'You're going to be a wreck until we get this over with, aren't you?'

'No I'm not...,' Jason started then slowed down. 'Get what over with?' Any small amount of cool he might have had was slipping away fast.

'This...' Tanya said softly. She brought both hands up and slipped them around the back of his neck, leant forward and kissed him for one long, delicious moment.

As she pulled away, Jason's head was already spinning. *This sort of thing really didn't happen to him.*

'Better now?' she asked.

His eyes focused on Tanya's face, on the soft lips that had just been on his. 'Umm, not quite' he said, 'maybe one more would do it...'

Tanya grinned and shook her head. 'Mmm – definitely losing your jitters. Come on.'

She took his hand again and led him up to the front gates. A convoy of dirty buses packed with Drunken Abbot kids was pulling out passed ambling groups of well-dressed village pupils.

Paddy Chubb, Silent Hill's 'caretaker' was manning the gates this afternoon, with two of his three assistants. Although he'd only been at Silent Hill for a week, Jason had glimpsed Mr Chubb many times out of the classroom windows. He and his assistants didn't seem to do any normal caretaking type work like picking up litter or fixing things. They just patrolled around the school grounds and manned the gates.

Paddy must have been well into his forties, a tall man, well built and tattooed on both, permanently bare, forearms. He'd a flat face and eyes that seemed to pop out and look around the side. His assistant, Morton, was tall and skinny but in a wiry muscled sort of way. He'd lank, dark hair to his shoulders whereas Paddy shaved his head almost bald.

Tanya grinned at Paddy. 'I have a guest Paddy - we're off for pizza… and things.'

Paddy grinned back. 'I bet you are Tanya, darlin'.' He had an East London accent and sounded like a ham-actor in some early evening soap. He took out some sort of high-tech palm top computer and a stylus which looked completely out of place in his big, rough-skinned hands.

'Now, then – wot's 'is name?'

'Jason – Jason Willow,' Tanya said, glancing up at Jason and smiling. Jason grinned back but it faded quickly as he noticed Morton staring at him with something like a snarl contorting his mouth.

'Jason... W-i-l-l-o-w,' Paddy said, writing Jason's name onto the palm top and tapping the screen a few times, 'mind you see 'im signed out yourself at the outside gates before ten or security will come lookin' for 'im and you don't want that, do you.'

'Oh, I'll get him home to bed on time, don't worry,' Tanya said, pulling Jason a little closer.

Morton shifted, clenching his fists and making the sinewy muscles in his bare forearms flex. Paddy shot him a glance then grinned at Tanya.

'You do that my girl – remember you 'av responsibilities living where you do. Get him out well before curfew – those security boys aren't nice people to mess wiv'.' Paddy's eyes flitted across to Morton again then back to them.

Tanya just waved and pulled Jason out of the gates. 'Ugh - he's such a creep.' Tanya whispered.

'Who? Chubb? He seemed alright,' Jason answered, glancing back. Chubb was busy signing out another couple of guests but Morton was scowling after them.

'No of course not – Chubby's a sweetheart. I mean Morton. He's asked me out about eight hundred times.'

'I can't blame him for that,' Jason mumbled, casting a glance at her.

Tanya stopped and faced him. 'Ahh - you're really quite sweet, aren't you?'

Jason couldn't stop his stupid grin in time and Tanya laughed and slipped her arms around his neck again, rising on tip-toes as she moved to kiss him.

BANG, BANG, BANG.

They pulled away from each other and span around. Hammering on the upstairs windows of a Drunken Abbot bus were half a dozen Skins. Hairy was among them, his face pressed up against the window and his studded tongue licking the glass in long, slimy streaks. The others all started making a whole variety of disgusting, suggestive movements.

'Prats,' Jason said, returning a suggestive movement or two of his own as the bus pulled away. 'I can see why those losers are fenced out of here.'

163

Tanya dropped her head and looked down. A moment later, she took in a deep breath and turned back to him with a slightly faltering smile on her lips.

'Are you okay?' Jason asked. 'Just forget about them – they're not worth thinking about until they need dealing with.'

She nodded, but her eyes started to glisten.

Jason tentatively took her hand and she squeezed his fingers.

'I'm sorry,' Tanya said, 'I'm just being stupid. You're right - we can pretend they don't exist here most of the time - they don't often manage to get in to the village.'

'You mean the Skins break into the village sometimes? Even with all the fences and cameras…?

Tanya nodded. Watching the bus disappear below, they set off down the school hill.

'Sometimes. I don't know how they get in… but they always come looking for a fight… with anybody.'

'Don't worry - if anything happens tonight, you just run and I'll hold them off.'

Jason meant it as a joke but Tanya slipped her arms around his neck again and she kissed him - longer this time and more fully. He breathed in a hint of her sweet perfume and edged his hands around her waist to return her kiss. When, long moments later, she pulled gently away, her eyes were shining.

'Come on, my knight in shining armour.' She smiled at him and tugged him along by the hand.

He could not believe he'd said that corny line, even as a joke. Still, the result was pretty good.

They were half way down the school hill. Darkston village spread out before him, beautifully landscaped down the gentle slopes and back up a second hill to the monumental black abbey gatehouse less than a mile away. For once, not rushing through the village in a filthy-windowed bus, Jason had a chance to take in the scene of old thatched cottages rambling along terraces punctuated with large, houses with red tiled roofs and tree shaded gardens. He could see at least half a dozen immaculately kept parks and greens with old fashioned lamp posts every twenty metres or so.

Then he started to chew his bottom lip. From up here he could clearly see Drunken Abbot pressing up around the village despite heavy screening by trees and hedges. The great steel fence glinted between the greenery, holding the grey, dilapidated buildings at bay.

'It's just like somebody's plonked toy town in the middle of a city slum,' Jason said.

'Come on then, Noddy, catch me,' Tanya laughed and dashed off.

The next hour or so was one of the happiest Jason could ever remember. Tanya took him on a grand tour of Darkston which was interspersed with lots of teasing, chasing and kissing. At each new turn everything was just perfect - no litter, every building freshly painted, every garden manicured. Any other time, it may have seemed a bit too perfect - like the set from the Stepford Wives film or The Prisoner series, but right now, it fitted right in with his mood.

The villagers they passed all played their part in the chocolate-box village scenario as well. Everyone seemed to know everyone else. People stopped for a chat, smiled and waved to each other. The tea rooms - one in each park and also in the main parade of shops - were filled with women of all ages and young children. With school over for the weekend, the town's teenagers had all piled into a couple of squeaky-clean burger joints like something out of 1950s America.

He was with the perfect girl in the perfect town and nothing should have disturbed his joy. He tried hard to ignore it but every so often the illusion was disturbed – here a glimpse of the perimeter fence, there a steel watchtower looming over a perfectly thatched roof. Security guards watched them pass from the tops of those towers but worst of all were the scores of security cameras.

Jason had quickly realized the reason for the big, old fashioned lamp posts set at such regular intervals - they each housed a turning, zoom lens camera. More often than not the cameras whirred around to follow the two of them as they passed. The feeling of someone in a darkened security room watching his every move sent a chill down Jason's spine.

Tanya had quickly picked up on his unease. As they wandered through the cobbled streets she frequently pulled him into quiet corners, small alleys and tree groves that were screened from the sweep of the camera's glinting black lenses.

After an hour or so, Jason noticed Tanya begin to glance at her watch. Finally, at about five o'clock, she announced she was starving.

'Let's eat something then,' Jason suggested. 'Burger maybe?'

'No - pizza.' she announced. Then after a second's thought, she said 'There won't be so many kids there and it's a little more romantic than a cheese burger and fries don't you think?'

Jason smiled. 'Do we get candles and soft music?'

Tanya sidled up to him and toyed with collar of his polo shirt. 'We don't need it... Romeo.' She kissed him quickly, then grabbed his hand and pulled him along.

'Come on, I know just the place.'

***

"Just the place" turned out to be Little Italy - a small Italian restaurant with an umbrella-sheltered terrace where you could watch the world go by... and they could watch you.

Tanya chose a table near to the pavement. After much debate, they ordered a large Quatro Staggioni to share and a jug of Doctor Pepper.

Vaguely Jason wondered when to let Dad know he was going to be late home. Just how he was going to get back to Darkston Wick was also something he should have thought about. He decided he'd call from one of the old fashioned red phone boxes scattered around the village – perhaps Dad would pick him up. Still, all that could wait for later – he didn't want to seem like a little boy phoning his daddy.

He reached for Tanya's hand under the table. She gave his fingers a quick squeeze but then gently pulled her hand away and took a sip of Dr Pepper. *Was she nervous being on display with him for half of the Village to gawp at? She chose the place.*

'Are you all right?' he asked. 'You've gone a bit quiet.'

Tanya attempted a smile that didn't quite ring true. 'Oh I'm just hungry... where's this pizza?' Instead of looking back into the restaurant for the food however, Tanya's eyes flitted along the pavement.

Jason decided chatting might help. 'Tanya, I don't know anything about you... apart from you're gorgeous.'

She flashed a small smile at him but it quickly faded. He carried on anyway. 'So what's your surname? What do your folks do? Where do you live? All that sort of stuff.'

Tanya finally focussed on him to answer. 'Well, my name is Tanya Elli Baxter, my father is a chemical analyst in the brewery and mum works part time in a lingerie shop just around the corner.'

Jason gave an evil grin at the mention of lingerie. Tanya didn't notice however - she glanced down the street again as she reeled off more facts.

'We moved to the village about four years ago when Mr Brash head-hunted Dad from Manchester. It was a great deal, we got a gorgeous house really cheaply as part of his salary or something.'

Just then a camera whirred to focus on them from across the street. A few moments later it panned away.

'Doesn't all this security bother you though?' Jason asked.

'You get used to it after a while – learn where the hidden cameras are and talk quietly around the ones with microphones and all that.'

'It sounds like a nightmare.' Jason said.

'Well we need to keep the brewery secrets... secret, don't we? There are loads of companies who want to find out what makes our beer so popular and that could put everyone here out of a job.'

'I suppose so.' Jason said.

'Besides,' Tanya continued, glancing at the nearest camera, 'it also helps to keep the village safe from the Drunken Abbot lot.'

Jason nodded. *Did she know there was anything more to it than that? Would she feel happier knowing that all the security was to keep out something far worse than town thugs and industrial spies?*

The pizza arrived and Jason started to cut Tanya a slice.

'Oh no, this is the last thing I wanted,' Tanya interrupted, stiffly.

'It's what we ordered…' Jason began but his voice trailed off as he followed Tanya's gaze down the street.

The creepy assistant caretaker, Morton and another nineteen or twenty year old lad were crossing the road towards them. Morton had swapped his dark blue work uniform for jeans and black, sleeveless vest. Both of them had their mean little eyes fixed on Tanya.

'Who's Morton's little friend,' Jason asked, stopping cutting the pizza but keeping hold of the wide bladed knife.

'That's Billy,' Tanya whispered, 'another caretaker. He's just as rank as Morton.'

The two caretakers swaggered over and stopped right in front of their table. A low, flower-planted wall was all that stood between them.

Morton put one foot on the wall, crushing a bright yellow pansy and leant forward. He grinned, white, level teeth failing to hold back rancid tobacco-breath.

'What you doing with this wimpy kid, Tanya? You could be with me.'

'Go away Morton – you know I'm not interested.' Tanya said, drawing back in her seat.

From the corner of his eye Jason saw other diners were turning around. He kept his focus on Morton and Billy.

'You know, I think I'll stay - I like the view.' Morton ran his eyes over Tanya's blouse.

'Yeah,' chipped in his mate, Billy, 'I like the view as well.'

Jason had had enough. 'Bugger off, Morton - Tanya doesn't want you anywhere near her and nor do I. Go get a life.'

Morton and Billy both turned towards him. Morton clenched his fists, showing his sinewy forearms again. He leaned further forward, crushing more flowers underfoot. His breath really did stink. 'Shut your mouth you skinny little…'

Jason didn't give him time to finish. Snake quick, he slapped the pizza knife across Morton's throat. Morton jumped back, his hands flying to his neck – they came away slimed in red.

'You slashed me… I'm dying.' Morton pressed his hands back to his throat while Billy frantically tried to pull them away to see the damage. People on the other tables were half out of their seats and staring; one man stood up and started folding a napkin into some sort of bandage.

Tanya stared at Jason open mouthed, shaking her head slowly.

Jason smiled, held up the pizza knife and mouthed 'flat edge – it's pizza sauce.'

Tanya took a moment to realise what he was saying then burst into a laugh. Jason grinned back.

The manager and two waiters rushed out to see what the noise was and Jason coolly asked 'Could we have another knife please, this one has touched something… unpleasant?'

Morton realized there was no pain and no blood gushing out anywhere and stopped shouting. He pushed Billy's hands away and pulled out a bit of melted cheese from his lank, greasy hair.

One by one, people at the tables grasped what had happened and returned to their meals with more than a few sniggers. The man with the napkin sat down, quickly laying the cloth back across his lap. The manager ushered the waiters back inside, handing one of them Jason's pizza knife. He stayed on the terrace however, watching.

Morton stared at Jason. 'You'll pay for that, you little prick.'

Jason looked back coolly. In a quiet voice he said 'Just think if I'd decided to turn the blade a little, Morton... think very hard about it.'

Morton's face screwed up but he didn't come any closer.

The manager started to walk down the steps to the pavement. 'Get out of here, Morton Locker, or security will be paying you a call this evening... I'm sure your father wouldn't thank you for that now, would he?'

Morton stared balefully at the manager for a moment then spat and slouched off.

The new pizza knife arrived and Jason began serving again.

'Wow, how did you do that,' Tanya asked, 'it was almost like Fast Eddie?'

Jason kept his eyes down, concentrating on the pizza. 'Uh – my dad. It's part of a martial art thing he teaches me and my sister – he calls it flick fighting... it's all about just touching pressure points and stuff.'

'Whatever it's called, it certainly got rid of that creep.'

'Well you'd better keep me around to protect you,' Jason said, cringing inside the moment he said it. This girl was turning his brain to mush.

Tanya rubbed one foot up and down his leg under the tablecloth. 'You do make me feel all sort of safe... although...'

'Although...?' Jason asked

'Well if you were in the Brash that probably wouldn't have happened at all.'

'But you are in the Brash and they still bothered us,' Jason answered.

'I'm not really,' Tanya paused for a moment, 'I'm just sort of associated with them. I don't do any training or anything.'

Jason put his cutlery down – he didn't feel particularly hungry any more. 'Are you just here to persuade me to join the Brash or something?'

Tanya glanced at the security camera. 'I'm supposed to talk to you about it, yes.'

'And that's the only reason you came out with me?'

'To start with but... well you're really nice and we're sort of hitting it off aren't we?' She slid one hand over the table to rest on his.

Jason grunted but didn't move his hand away. This wasn't exactly a surprise and at least Tanya was being honest with him.

'Well, I don't know if I want to get involved in this whole gang thing,' Jason said. 'I mean, Eddie seems like a nice guy and I really want to get some training but I don't want somebody telling me who to fight in the Pit so they can win a few bets and ordering me around all the time.'

'Oh but Eddie lets us do whatever we want mostly and you get loads of respect from everyone.' Tanya looked up at him while taking a sip of Dr Pepper. She'd beautiful eyes, big and dark.

'How much does Alan Brash have to do with the gang?' Jason asked.

Tanya shrugged. 'That's the whole point isn't it? Being in the Brash is one of the best ways to get a good job from him. You're sort of proving your loyalty and showing off whatever skills you have to offer. The fighters are after security jobs patrolling the village and valley and the best ones like Eddie and Erin, will get into the abbey itself. All the Pit stuff is a bit of a test really – you know, to see if they would be any good in a dangerous situation.'

Jason nodded. She hadn't mentioned anything about the Watch. It would make sense he supposed, that even in the Brash gang itself, few or no people knew about that world until after Mr Brash had recruited them as adults... perhaps not even then.

'What about you – what do you get out of being "associated" with the Brash? Jason asked.

Tanya smiled. 'I want a decent job in Brash Enterprises and live here in the village of course. Look - my dad's not got a very... influential position and I'm not the world's brightest girl which means I could end up with a factory-floor job in Drunken Abbot or having to try to pick up some high flyer who will probably dump me after a year or so. In the gang I've got a good chance of being noticed for some cosy office job - marketing or P.R or something.'

Jason brushed his hand through his hair and relented. 'I'll give you a reference about how persuasive you can be.'

Tanya smiled. 'Well there you are – I'm another reason for you to join... we'd get to see a lot more of each other.'

'But we can do that anyway, can't we? Didn't you say Eddie "let" you do what you wanted most of the time?'

Tanya gave a tight smile. 'He does but... they prefer us to mix with people they know, people that are going places.'

'People in the gang, you mean,' Jason said.

Tanya gave an apologetic smile. 'I wish you'd just say you'd join us.' Her eyes were wide, almost pleading.

Jason tried to return the smile. This was getting far too heavy.

'Well let's just enjoy ourselves for now, while you're sort of allowed to see me and I'll think about it.'

'You get protection as well,' Tanya blurted out. 'Callum and Eddie don't let the gangs fight each other outside the Pit so...'

'The Skins don't scare me, Tanya. I don't need to join any gang for protection, okay.'

Tanya looked at him for a moment then nodded. She leant over and gently kissed his cheek.

It felt like a kiss goodbye.

***

They finished their meal and Jason paid, leaving a good tip. He wanted to keep on the right side of the manager and staff after the trouble with Morton - hopefully he and Tanya would be back here soon. It was lucky Dad had given him and Miranda fifty pounds each to always be kept with them for

172

emergencies. There was still more than enough left for a taxi ride home if Dad wouldn't come to pick him up.

It had gone half past six when they hit the pavement again. The pubs were open now - all of them traditional inns, mostly thatched and with small, neat beer gardens. The clientele were all relaxed and chatting away happily. The early evening air was deliciously warm and scented by the flower baskets hanging from every lamp post and most of the people sat at the tables and on the grass outside enjoying the late sunlight.

Nearly everyone held a pint or a half of Drunken Abbot ale, including the women. It was always served in the Laughing Abbot logo glasses with the slogan 'One taste and you're mine.' underneath in illuminated script. Dad, who normally let him have a glass of wine or half a pint during a big dinner, had forbidden Jason to even taste the ale. He said it was dangerous – it tasted fabulous and somehow lifted you, but the thought of it increasingly niggled at you until you had your next glass, almost like a mild craving. Dad had told them it had taken him three days to get passed those feelings after just one pint and he'd never touched the stuff since. No wonder the new "brew" had swept all over the country in the past year or so and was earning Alan Brash a fortune.

They walked towards the far side of the village. Tanya said she knew a little park there where they wouldn't have dozens of adults watching their every move. She'd gone quiet again, almost nervous. When he took her hand, hers was hot and she kept squeezing his gently but wouldn't look at him for more than a moment.

Suddenly she stopped. 'Jason, I don't know if we should go to this…'

A camera whirred above them and a moment later, Tanya's mobile rang - some unintelligible dance anthem. She stopped speaking and pulled away a little to slip it out of her jeans pocket.

'Oh, hi… mum. Yes… yes everything is fine. No… no trouble that… uh came to anything. We're heading off to the park, now. Yes… yes I'll leave before then.'

She glanced across at him with a weak smile and walked a little away, turning her back on him. He could still hear her though. 'Yes, yes… all right, I know that. Look, I… don't think we need to…'

Tanya shut up. For long moments she just listened and then said a quiet 'Okay, all right.' and flipped her phone closed.

She drew in a deep breath, wiped her face quickly and turned back around. Her eyes were shiny. 'Sorry about that… my mum… full of the usual… advice and dire warnings about being alone with boys… you know.' She didn't look at him.

Jason slipped his arm around her shoulders. Something was really bothering her but she obviously didn't want to talk about it. All he could do was play along. 'Parents – they're so embarrassing.'

Tanya nodded. She was stiff and tense under his arm and after a few steps he took it away. She glanced up at him apologetically.

'It would be different if you would just agree to join us… I mean, my mum knows all the boys in the Brash are decent and wouldn't do anything they shouldn't… and…'

'You can be a good guy without joining the smart-set, you know,' Jason said, a little too harshly. Was recruiting him into the Brash the only reason she was with him after all?

She looked across at him again - holding his eyes for a moment.

'I know you can.' Then she started to walk faster. Jason let her get a step ahead of him and watched her. She no longer swayed sensuously with every step. Now she was stiff with tension.

This was stupid. It's not as if he'd even decided he wouldn't join the gang – he might have to if Dad really wouldn't teach him how to use his Gift – Alan Brash might make it a condition of training him.

Tanya stopped at a corner and turned to wait for him. 'We're here - Abbeywell Park,' she said. She sounded as if she were turning up to a funeral.

Despite himself, Jason smiled at the awesome imagination of whoever had named the places in this town. The park centred on a large well, in the lee of the abbey gatehouse hill – hence Abbeywell Park. The evening sun was low now, sinking behind the hill and releasing the gatehouse's shadows to creep across the manicured lawns and flower beds, draining them of colour and warmth. In a short while, the central well with its columned and roofed plinth would be in darkness too.

'Come on... let's sit down,' Tanya said, without turning around. Shrugging, Jason followed her through a small side-gate into the park and across the grass towards the well.

The place was deserted. It must have been a good three acres in area, taking up an entire corner of Darkston village. A small wood of tall evergreens grew all along its edge - probably to hide the steel fences and the dark town beyond.

Tanya sat on the edge of the well plinth, facing the park entrance, her back set against the trees. The street lamps were coming on, casting glowing pools of yellow over the gentle hills of Darkston.

Jason sat down next to her. It was time to talk properly. 'What's wrong?' he asked.

'Nothing.'

'Yes there is. We were having a great time and then, ever since the pizza place, you've gone all... sort of... cold and "don't touch me".'

'No I haven't,' she said, crossing her arms and looking away.

Jason raised one eyebrow and half a smile.

'I... like you,' Tanya said, quietly.

Jason frowned. 'But that's a good thing, isn't it? Especially as I like you too.'

'No, I mean I really like you.'

Jason swallowed. He needed to keep things light. 'Don't sound so surprised - I'm really nice. In a minute or two, I'll even look good as well,' he nodded towards the gatehouse shadow which was only a metre or so away from them now.

Tanya stared at the dark and shivered.

Jason slid up close and put his arm around her. She tensed for a moment then sank into him.

'Look, you're freezing. Let's go to find somewhere with a bit of sunlight left.'

'No we can't.. I mean... oh, Jason, I want you to know... I didn't think it would be like this... it's been really nice, just you and me...'

She looked up at him for the first time in ages. Her eyes were shining again and a single tear spilled down her cheek.

'I'm glad I make you so happy,' Jason smiled, brushing the tear from her soft skin with one gentle finger. She lifted her face to him, lips parted and slightly trembling. Slowly, tenderly, he kissed her.

Tanya crossed one leg over his and they stayed like that for ages, bodies touching, holding each other tightly and kissing.

The cold shadow crept over them. Tanya shivered and pulled away. 'Let's go,' she said, 'quickly. I'm not going to do this.'

Clink. Iron on iron - a gate latch?

Jason jumped and stared around.

In the glow of main gate lamps, Hairy stood watching them. He was flanked by two other, even larger Skins.

Jason tried to stand but Tanya wouldn't let him go.

'Don't worry,' he said, gently taking her hands where they gripped him and easing them free.

He stood up. More Skins were coming out of the trees near the little side gate he and Tanya had used... three, four, five of them. There was no Grizz yet, or Callum Mennis.

'Evening, lover-boy,' Hairy shouted across the park, his voice harsh in the shadows, 'what's she feel like then, eh? I wouldn't mind having a little cuddle myself... once we've finished with you.' He pushed the gate back and it clanked shut.

Four of the five skins from the trees were slowly closing in - one of them stayed to guard the side gate. There was nowhere to run. Surely the cameras would pick this up and they would send some security.

Jason shouted back, trying hard to keep his voice steady. 'Tanya's a Brash girl, Hairy - let her go or all of you'll be dead meat when Eddie hears of this.'

Hairy mused for a moment then pushed himself lazily away from the gates and made a mocking bow towards them.

'Off you go then, gorgeous – wouldn't want to break the code now, would I? But you'd better hope you can explain to Fast Eddie what you were doing out here all alone with this wimp.'

One of Hairy's companions, shorter than Jason but thick set and with a nose stud in each nostril, opened the main gate a couple of inches.

The four Skins from the trees reached the plinth. Two of them leant against one corner sniggering and leering at Tanya. The other two circled around the back.

'Come on - I'll walk with you to the gates,' Jason said, glancing down at her and forcing a hopefully reassuring smile.

Tanya's eyes were wide, her lips a tight line. 'I don't want to leave you… if I stay they might not…'

'Oh we will.' laughed one of the Skins at the plinth corner. He'd a mean ferret-like face and black eyes. 'Stay or go, darlin', we will have our fun with your little boyfriend, whatever. It just means you'll get all upset and splashed in his blood if you stay.'

Jason ignored the ferret-face. 'Come on. It'll be okay,' he said and held out his hand.

Tanya hesitated then took it and he led her towards the main gates. The four skins from the plinth spread out and followed a short way behind them.

Half way to the gates, Tanya suddenly stopped and threw her arms around Jason. With her lips close to his ear, she whispered 'I'll phone Eddie for help as soon as I'm out – I'll get this stopped.'

Jason squeezed her and nodded. They were right on the edge of town - by the time any of the Brash got here it would all be over. That's if they bothered to come of course - after all, he wasn't in their gang.

'Aaah - how sweet,' Hairy shouted out again, his voice seeming to fill the night. 'Hurry up, lover-boy – I thought you'd be eager to kick some more Skin arse.'

Jason gently pulled Tanya forward, staring at Hairy but whispering to her from the side of his mouth. 'Don't watch, all right? Just get as far away as you can... they may forget their manners when I do a bit of damage to them.'

They reached the main gates. Hairy's big, rugged face was a shadowed, evil yellow under the lamplight. He and his two mates tightened ranks in front of the gate.

Tanya dropped Jason's hand and pointed at Hairy. 'You can't do this – Jason is about to join the Brash...'

'Save your mouth for what it's good at, darlin',' Hairy cut her short. 'No one's told us the wimp's joined up so he aint got no protection. Now sod off, my boys are gettin' twitchy an' I might not be able to hold 'em off you for much longer.'

She opened her mouth to argue but Jason laid his hand on her shoulder. 'Go Tanya, get out of here.' His voice cracked just a little. 'It won't do any good.'

With a last, desolate look up at him, Tanya nodded. She had to squeeze between Hairy and one of the others to get through the gates. Jason wanted to smash the leering grins off their faces as Tanya was forced to rub up passed them, but it was too important that she get away safely before anything started.

Then she was out and Hairy shut the gate with an ominous clang that echoed through the night.

He just caught a glimpse of Tanya running down a side street, her hand already pulling out her mobile, before the Skins closed around him in a circle. Attacked from all sides he'd have no chance.

'Not so hard now, are you hero?' Hairy said.

'You and I are going to need a bit more space than this to fight, Hairy,' Jason said as calmly as he could manage. 'It is one on one, I take it... I mean, you Skins wouldn't want a reputation for being cowards, would you? I mean, all of you against me would look like you were scared or something, don't you think?'

Jason spoke slowly, breathing deeply. He glanced around the circle as he talked, noting the weakest looking one – a spiky blonde haired lad of about his own build.

'Different rules out her here, wimp - you've offended the honour of the gang so we're all going to teach you some manners.'

There was no sense in letting them start when they were ready. Break out of the circle, run like crazy and lose them in the dark woods. Easy.

Jason dropped his defiant stare. 'Look... I didn't mean to offend the whole gang – it was just ...' he began, in a small, pleading voice then leapt for the spiky blonde.

He grabbed his neck, spun him into the circle and catapulted himself out into the shadows of the open grass.

There was a half second's confusion and Jason pelted for the trees.

He was fast, but one of the Skins was faster. Ferret-face caught up ten metres from the tree line and tripped him. Jason fell, rolled straight back up to his feet but they were already on him.

Fists and boots flew at him out of the darkness. He'd no chance of blocking so he just lashed out in all directions. He hit a few, felt noses crunch under his fists but their punches and kicks rained in on him. His whole body was being beaten and the Skins were leaping over themselves to punch his head and face. Any moment now he'd be knocked to the ground.

'Scum' he screamed and threw his arms out to push his way clear. A surge of ice-cold energy shot down each arm and out though his palms. Two skins flew back from the circle in different directions and Jason burst into a panicked, half-blind run for the deep dark of the trees again.

His legs wouldn't work properly - they were too heavy, weak and throbbing with pain. His head was spinning and blood ran into his eyes and mouth. He couldn't move fast enough - the Skins would be on him again any second now.

He could still feel their fists in his ribs and face, their boots biting into his shins.

The first tree rose up before him, black and massive. He dodged passed it and stumbled further into the woods. At least they couldn't all hit him at once in here.

Two shadows materialised before him, others detached themselves from the trees to either side. *Oh hell - they were everywhere.*

Jason had no choice - he just ran at the nearest silhouette.

He smashed into a chest which twisted to take the force from his charge. Two steel-strong arms slapped around him and held him fast with his face pressed up against a silk-smooth shirt.

Jason gasped in a breath for one final attack and smelled aftershave.

'Steady old boy, we're the good guys.'

Jason's knees gave way. He felt himself being passed back to other hands, then lowered to the ground to flop against a tree.

The shadows flitted away and he was suddenly alone.

It was cool here. He hurt everywhere, everything was blurred, his ears rang and his head throbbed out all thought. Somewhere back towards the park there was shouting, cries of pain, swearing, and dull thuds and smacks.

He didn't know how long it went on for. The next thing that really registered was a soft cloth touching his face, dabbing his nose. A delicate, sweet perfume filled the one nostril that wasn't full of drying blood.

'Oh God, I'm so sorry, Jason. I never wanted this to happen. They took so long to get here... I phoned straight away... the scum wouldn't stop hitting you...'

'Tanya?' Jason tried sitting up a bit straighter but stopped at a jabbing in his chest. The silhouette of a girl was leaning over him, soft hair just brushing his cheek as she leaned in close.

'Yes, yes, it's me. Please say you're all right...'

Jason couldn't stop himself - he coughed up a laugh and hot, metallic blood trickled into his mouth from lips that felt three inches thick.

'I've felt better.' His words didn't sound right – short-tongued and slurred. He forced open his eyes against his swelling cheeks.

A blurred Tanya was inches from his face. She kissed his mouth, as softly as she could, her lips trembling, salty tears running down to sting his cuts.

'Ouch,' he said and she quickly pulled away.

'Oh, I'm so stupid… sorry.'

Jason reached out his less agonized arm and rested it on Tanya's knee. 'Sh'okay. What happened?'

'Eddie and a some of the others came in the van. They ran down through the trees and surprised the Skins when they saw them chasing you in here.'

'Wish they'd got here a bit quicker,' Jason coughed, his head ringing with the motion.

'Now there's gratitude for someone who bled all over my second best Armani shirt.'

Jason lifted his head slowly - it hurt, everywhere hurt.

Faint moonbeams lanced through the branches above to reveal Fast Eddie dabbing a handkerchief over the glimmer of a white shirt. Even a glint of his perfect smile somehow managed to catch the faint light.

'Whersh everyone elsh?' Jason asked. It seemed important.

'Skin hunting. I left them chasing the cowards back out through whatever little rat-hole they used to get in here. It'll probably go on half the night and I need my beauty sleep.'

'Thanksh for…'

'No problem – all good exercise,' Eddie cut in. 'Now, don't talk anymore or I might have to laugh.' That smile flashed again.

Jason nodded. Tanya dabbed at his face some more and brushed his blood-matted hair back from his eyes. If he'd had the strength he'd have stopped her fussing over him… at least in front of Eddie.

'You did well out there Jason – you would have had no chance in that circle. Your er... running push was pretty effective, too - you really sent those skins flying. I think one of them might have broken an arm in the fall... but we made sure of it, just in case.'

Jason nodded but something immediately didn't ring true. Hadn't Tanya said Eddie arrived when the Skins were already chasing him into the trees? How did he see Jason break out of the circle by the gate? He must have it wrong, he couldn't think straight with his brain pounding out of his skull.

'Of course with the proper training, someone of your... talents could have taken them all out,' Eddie continued. 'Then there would have been no need to abandon young Tanya here, and run away.'

Jason snapped his head up. Ouch. He'd not abandoned Tanya - he'd got her safely out of danger... and then what else could he do but run from those sort of odds?

Fast Eddie seemed to read his mind. 'Now don't take offence, I know you didn't have much choice this time but the thing is, we could teach you...' he glanced at Tanya, 'so much, Jason. To be honest, I think you're going to need it. After tonight, you'll be a hot target... and that means the big boys will take notice.'

'There are bigger boysh?' Jason asked, wincing as a couple of lip cuts cracked open again. Tanya winced with him.

Fast Eddie laughed. 'Oh yeah but we'll talk more when you can speak properly. Come on Tanya, let's get the Elephant Man here into the van.'

Tanya took one arm, Eddie the other and they hoisted him to his feet. Eddie's help was a lot less delicate than Tanya's. It was almost completely dark now, even once they'd hobbled out of the trees. The entire park had turned into a mass of shadows clawing their way out of the earth.

Eddie steered them towards a small gate at the top end of the park and then into a low-lit side street. A big, black Mercedes van with heavily tinted windows waited for them. The three of them climbed into the cab, Tanya helping Jason

182

in and drawing breath with him at every jolt. As he sank gratefully into the leather seats Jason risked the pain of twisting around to check in the back. It was empty but as the courtesy lights faded out, he saw the van had been converted to seat about another dozen people - complete with a black fridge and television screen for their travelling comfort.

Fast Eddie turned the key and the engine growled into life. He flicked on the lights and pulled out onto the brightly lit street running past the park. Jason tried to think through the throbbing in his brain - why had Eddie bothered carefully hiding the van in an alley if the Brash had been rushing to his rescue?

Tanya kept looking over at Jason, her eyes shining each time they passed through the yellowed light of a street lamp. He leaned further back so she couldn't see his face so clearly and closed his eyes.

He felt wretched - he ached all over, sharp spikes stuck in him whenever he moved and he'd not only abandoned his sort-of-girlfriend but he'd run like a rabbit before half the Skins.

He'd be the laughing stock of the school on Monday morning. He'd never live this down and have to leave the school, just when he was starting to settle in.

There was one way to get out of this of course – if he fought all of tonight's Skins, one by one, in the Pit he could clear his name.

Of course, the Pit might only be part of it. Hairy had said something about "different rules out here". If he wasn't even safe in Darkston village, fenced off from the Skins by razor wire, cameras, armed guards and watchtowers, how vulnerable would he be in Darkston Wick – less than an hour's walk through woods and meadow from the edge of Drunken Abbot. And what had Eddie meant by the "big boys would take an interest in him now"?

If he was going to survive this he needed some friends who would stick by him and now, more than ever, he needed to learn how to use his Gift. That was exactly what Eddie seemed to be offering.

Jason opened his eyes and sat up straighter - ignoring the burning blades jabbing in to his back and ribs. No one was saying anything. Tanya had even stopped her fussing over him although she still kept glancing across.

Jason just looked outside - he was in no state for deep and meaningful conversation right now.

Nightfall had changed Darkston. The picturesque houses were dark, the quaint overhanging thatch roofs casting windows and walls deep into shadow. Little alleys between houses, quaint in the daytime, were dark beyond the reach of the streetlights.

Pub life had changed as well. In the two inns they'd passed so far, the gardens and tables stood dark and deserted, the only signs of life were silhouettes, distorted in the lace-draped windows, slowly, steadily drinking back their ale.

Eddie flipped open a tiny mobile and said 'Taxi' into it.

'Hello Barbara... yes it's Eddie. Listen, I need a car from West 3 to Darkston Wick... yes, I know it's late. Better get someone to ride shotgun as well, I've a feeling things might be a little stirred up tonight... Okay, cheers old girl - be there in five.'

Eddie snapped his phone shut and slipped it away.

'Sorry I can't drive you all the way home myself... the van is a tad conspicuous and we're not very welcome out there after dark.'

Jason started to nod but quickly stopped himself. His head was about fourteen times too heavy to move anymore. 'Thatsh fine. You've done enough... thanksh again.'

'How're you feeling?' Eddie asked, glancing across at him.

'Not exactly shparkling.'

'Mmm. They aren't very nice, our baldy friends, are they? Things can get a little out of hand away from school... and we're only playing in the kiddy-league here.'

Tanya put her hand on Jason's thigh. 'You can't go through this again Jason, not on your own... you just can't.' She stared at him, trying to draw his gaze. Jason just looked out of the front window, watching the street lights drift by, catching the glint of a camera lens following the van.

'Mmm,' he grunted.

'Seriously Jason,' Fast Eddie said, 'Tanya's got a point. Next time we may not happen to be around to help out. Let's not prat about here… you're, um… talented and you need to know how to build on those talents…' Eddie glanced across at Tanya again. From his caginess it was obvious Tanya didn't know anything about the Gift. Eddie carried on.

'But no matter how good you get, you also need to even up the odds a little. Nobody can take on all the bad guys by themselves. For your own safety…'

Jason couldn't take much more. 'All right – I've thought about it and I want to join you. I want to pay the Shkinsh back, shtarting with every one who was in that park tonight.'

There was silence for a moment. Tanya hesitantly slipped her hand into his.

Jason caught Eddie's thin smile in the rear view mirror. 'About bloody time,' Eddie said. 'Now let's get you home.'

***

Getting home was no simple affair.

Fast Eddie drew up to a small gate in the fence and turned his headlights off. A huge, dimly lit garage opened up on their right and he slipped the van straight into it. The electric garage door was coming down even as Eddie switched off the engine.

Fluorescent light flickered into life and Eddie stepped out onto the dusty concrete floor. Jason limped out after him, forcing down memories of the concrete floored, fluorescent-lit multi-storey car park where his mum had been murdered.

Two Brash Security were waiting for them. They were in their midnight blue uniforms, radios, handcuffs and police batons swinging from their belts. Something bulged under both of their jackets on the left hand side - a pistol of some sort, Jason guessed. Little would surprise him about Alan Brash's little empire now.

'Taxi ready, gentlemen?' Eddie asked.

'Top of Pew Street. Go out the normal way.' one of the guards replied.

'Wait for me here, Tanya,' Eddie said, 'this is no place for pretty young things.'

Tanya nodded. 'See you Monday,' she whispered to Jason and gently kissed his cheek.

Jason nodded.

The security guards led them over to a small door at the far end of the garage. One of them switched off all but a single, low red light as the other tapped a pin number into a keypad. Eddie swung open the steel-cored door on silent hinges and he and Jason stepped out into Drunken Abbot.

Behind them, a five metre wall topped with razor wire rose up in shadow to seal them off from the village.

'Sorry about all this cloak and dagger stuff, old boy.' Eddie whispered, flashing a smile as he scanned the dingy street. 'It's just if any of the Skins are still around they might be watching the gates for you. It's best they don't know how you're travelling over their turf.

Jason grunted – he'd be quite happy to meet a couple of them now.

Eddie led them off in silence along two or three narrow and dirty alleyways. He moved easily through the dark cover of derelict buildings and broken streetlights as if he'd done this journey a hundred times before.

At last, when it felt as if his bruised bones were rubbing through the cartilage and sparking off each other, Jason saw his taxi home. It was an old, pea-green Audi battered with scratches and dents. Even the unlit 'TAXI' sign on its roof had been smashed.

'No expensh spared,' Jason grumbled, splitting open his lip again.

'None whatsoever, but it does blend in better out here.' Eddie said, opening the back door.

No interior light came on but Jason could make out two huge, crop-haired meat-heads sitting in the front. Neither one turned around as he eased himself onto the rear seat. The front passenger was holding the top of a baseball bat which disappeared into the darkened foot-well.

'Keep your head down, sunshine,' Eddie said, 'and remember not to go too far from home until we officially take you under our tender wing.' Then he quietly clicked the door closed.

The driver rolled down his window and Eddie bent down to speak through it, handing in a couple of folded banknotes as he did so. 'The Old Mill in the Wick, please George.'

The man grunted and the Audi's engine stuttered into life.

'You're safe now, young Jason,' Eddie said, grinning through the driver's window, 'George and his mate here are old hands at this.'

The "taxi" sped away before Jason could reply and George closed the window and locked the doors. The Audi rattled through a number of maze-like back-streets and alleys before finally pulling into a main street and accelerating up to sixty. Despite Eddie's words, nothing felt particularly 'safe' about this ride home.

Jason sank lower in his worn fabric seat. They sped along the wide street without slowing down for junctions. Irregular streetlights – those not yet smashed - flashed by in a harsh yellow blur. Dark buildings loomed up and fell away with hardly a window lit. They passed pub after pub, all with dark silhouettes drinking behind filthy frosted windows.

Not everyone was inside, however. Lounging against pub walls and on street corners were groups of youths - many of them Skins. They all watched the cab speed by with malevolent eyes. Jason sank lower still. *What if the cab crashed or got a flat tyre. He'd have to step out into those streets and find his own way home.*

There were men walking the streets as well, hard looking men. Again, many of them were skinheads in white T-shirts or leather vests like Callum Mennis. They were all heavily tattooed - tormented demons, skulls and writhing women for the most part, glowing lurid blue-green under the street lamps. Their eyes all followed the cab but they didn't slow their trek to the next pub.

Jason tried moving his stiff arms and legs. Everywhere hurt, but at least his mind was clearing a little more now. Had he done the right thing? He'd just agreed to join the Brash. Dad would do his "*I'm disappointed with you but you need to make your own mistakes*" bit. Mouse and Louisa would probably never speak to him again.

Well... whatever. He wasn't going to run any more, from anyone or anything. And joining the Brash meant he'd get training and a chance at having his revenge on the Skins. It would also open the door for him learning about his Gift if Dad carried on being so stubborn.

Smash.

Glass - a bottle or something, shattered on the cab's roof. The man riding shotgun pulled up his bat but George accelerated away leaving more bottles crashing harmlessly behind them. Jason twisted painfully around - a dozen or so skinhead men had run out into the road - shouting and flashing the finger after the taxi. A last bottle came hurtling towards them but they were on the edge of town. The Audi roared out onto the moors and left Drunken Abbot behind.

It was suddenly quiet again with nothing but dark fields stretching away to the black mass of the valley sides. The driver slowed down and the whole car seemed to breathe out slowly. Jason opened his window a little and fresh, cool air streamed in.

Soon they turned into the little forest road towards Darkston Wick. Jason only closed his eyes for a moment but suddenly they were pulling into the gravel drive of the Old Mill and Dad was yanking open the house door. As he rushed down to the taxi, three silhouettes took his place at the top of the steps with the hall lamp shining like a beacon behind them.

He was safe, he was home.

Chapter 13

'Jason, are you all right? Can you walk?' Dad had snatched open the cab door and was half inside. His hair was all messed up as if he'd been raking his fingers through it for hours. Miranda peered over his shoulder.

'I'm fine, don't fuss,' Jason mumbled.

Ilena Russof appeared at the driver's window. She pulled out some money and offered it to him. George took it, even though Fast Eddie had paid him already. Jason bit his lip, glancing at the men's weapons in the shadows, and decided not to say anything. When he joined the Brash he'd get a refund for Ilena from these two crooks.

'Perhaps you should let him get out, Richard,' Ilena said. Her voice was soft and compassionate, its slight accent making her sound almost husky when speaking this quietly.

Dad pulled himself out of the cab. 'Yes, yes of course. Come on, Son. Do you need help?'

'I'm not bloody dead yet,' Jason said and edged himself out of the cab, every cut seeming to tear open again as his bruised and aching muscles flexed to move him.

Dad's mouth dropped open as Jason straightened in the lamp light. Then he closed it and his whole face set like stone around eyes suddenly hardened to onyx. Ice mode.

'Who did this to you?'

Ilena quickly put a hand on Dad's shoulder and turned him half towards her. 'We should just take him inside for now, Richard - clean him up a little. It looks worse than it is… mostly dried blood.'

Dad stood rigid for a moment, staring at his battered son. Then he turned on his heel and strode back into the house. With an encouraging smile at Jason, Ilena stepped quickly to catch up with Dad, talking softly to the side of his set face.

'We thought you were… in real trouble.' Miranda said then stormed back up the steps.

'I was…' Jason grunted to her back.

'Better luck next time, kid.' George grunted through his window as he pocketed the money and pulled away.

As the headlights disappeared down the High Street, the mystery third silhouette he had seen stepped out of the shadows. It was the man he and Louisa had met in the woods – Marakoff.

His limp was more pronounced on the stone steps and he leant heavily on his walking stick. It looked like he was wearing the same loose grey-green shirt and trousers he'd had on two days ago.

'I did say that we would meet again, yes?' Marakoff smiled and gestured towards the front door.

Jason started walking up the steps

'Your father has been very worried about you,' Marakoff continued in his stilted, Dracula accent as he limped up next to him. 'It was hours ago that he telephoned your Mr Brash to see if he and his cameras knew where you were. It seemed there was no sight of you in the village.'

Jason frowned but didn't reply immediately. He and Tanya must have walked passed dozens of cameras that evening – there should have been loads of footage of them. How embarrassing though – Dad panicking and calling Alan Brash for help.

'Nobody needed to push the panic button,' he mumbled. 'Anyway, who are you, why are you here?'

Marakoff smiled. 'Ah – I am an old friend of your grandfather – we worked together for a number of years before he retired.'

Marakoff's walking stick clicked to a stop at the top of the slate steps. Dad and Ilena where waiting just inside the hall, Ilena touching Dad's arm and still whispering earnestly to him. Miranda was nowhere to be seen.

Jason raised his voice a little to Marakoff. 'Why didn't Dad come looking for me himself if he was so worried.'

Marakoff glanced at Dad then turned his steady grey eyes on Jason. 'A good hunter must know his ground and would never rush in blindly, you understand? Alan Brash has almost every square metre of Darkston village covered by camera… how much quicker would he be to find you than all of us running up and down every one of those little streets?'

A mean image flashed through Jason's mind - one of Marakoff hobbling around the fluorescent yellowed streets of Darkston, searching through bushes for him with his walking stick.

Dad shut the front door as they stepped into the hall and was in his face again. He wasn't in ice-mode anymore though - how had Ilena managed that so quickly?

'What happened, Jason? Brash's people eventually found you on camera; they said you'd been in a fight but you were in a taxi home… why didn't you phone?'

Jason felt his cheeks begin to burn. 'Why the hell did you have to call Mr Brash? How stupid does that make me look?'

'Just tell me what happened.' Dad's voice was calm and low but his eyes were hardening again.

'Nothing much. I was walking with my… friend, Tanya and I was jumped by a bunch of skin heads and beaten up. Tanya phoned a guy called Eddie and his mates and they helped me because I was being thrashed. Aren't you glad you didn't teach me any Gift stuff - I might have hurt those poor Skins instead of it being me ending up like this?'

Dad pulled back like he'd been slapped. 'You... you had your Jakra...'

'Against a dozen or more, Dad... I don't think so. Jakra's not enough.'

'Son... I know how you feel but...'

'So your whole body is throbbing and stabbing knives into you as well, is it? You feel like a bloody coward for running away, do you - leaving the girl you're with and having to be rescued by her mates?'

'Jason, if you had been able to use the Gift against those youths you could have killed them - literally killed them - dead. How do you think you'd feel if that happened – you'd be a murderer?'

Jason's eyes were starting to burn and prickle inside his head. Flashes of the beatings, the kicks and punches filled his mind.

'And if they'd killed me... or Tanya? Dad you weren't there, you're never there. It's just like in Mawn - I've got to learn to look after myself.'

Jason made for the stairs, hot tears welling up. Dad grabbed his shoulder, stopped him.

'Jason...' he started.

Jason froze, half of him burning to slap Dad's hand away and the other half wanting to bury his face in his father's shirt.

'Get off me. I'm going to train with these kids at school and then decide for myself about... learning how to use my Gifts and hunting bloody demons or whatever.'

'Training with what "kids at school"?' Dad asked. 'Brash's little gang of well-dressed thugs?'

'Yes it's with the Brash,' Jason almost shouted, 'I'm not going to run away any more. The Skin's are going to pay for tonight.'

Ilena gently put her hand over Dad's and eased it away from Jason's shoulder. Jason stared at her – this had nothing to do with her.

Marakoff stepped to the other side of Dad. 'Jason – you are angry. All three of us here have been beaten, many times. You need to recognise when winning is impossible or simply

192

just too high a risk and then you get out, you need to run. There is no shame in escaping so you can continue the fight another time – you understand this, I hope?'

Jason grunted. 'And leaving your girlfriend to look after herself is just fine, I suppose?'

'Was she in danger? Were these… skin heads intending to harm her or were they just hunting you?' Marakoff asked.

'Well… no… she's sort of protected from them… they let her leave the park but…'

Marakoff clumped a little closer and leaned on one banister. 'Then she was safe and you were… outnumbered. Time to run, yes?'

Jason stared at him – what did this crippled stranger know about how it felt to run from scum like Hairy? What right had he to even be in on this conversation?

'You don't know what you're talking about,' Jason began, 'I don't even know who you are.'

'I think my brother's had enough for one night.' Miranda's voice cut across the hallway. 'Maybe we should just let him go and clean himself up and sleep. Dad and I can interrogate him tomorrow.'

Dad took in a slow breath then held up his hands in submission and headed off towards the sitting room.

Ilena gave a sympathetic smile and followed him with Marakoff who raised a hand in farewell.

Willow glanced at his sister. 'Thanks,' he said.

Miranda nodded. 'You owe me,' she grunted and followed the grown-ups.

***

'So what do you know about this Brash gang?' Dad asked.

'Enough,' Jason said, sitting down to breakfast the following morning. 'The kids train up in the gang and then go to work for Mr Brash after leaving school… but then so does everyone in this place.'

'Have you joined them already?' Dad said.

Jason dropped his gaze and reached for his toast. As nonchalantly as he could manage he answered before taking a bite.

'No but told them last night that I will.'

'So you're going to train with this gang and then go to work with Alan Brash?' Miranda said.

'Not necessarily,' Willow said. 'I'm going to train in Jakra with them, let their leader sort out some fights so I can take on the cowards who jumped me one by one and then I'll see what happens.'

Dad poured them all some more tea. 'Listen Son, Alan Brash is a very clever manipulator. When he hunted in the Watch he'd use anyone, in any way to achieve his goals. He was successful but his methods didn't count the cost of human life.'

'He can't be all that bad – he's still working for the Watch, isn't he?' Jason said.

'Well, yes… but he was ordered to leave active hunting and was sent far away to relocate the injured or bereaved.'

'So they trust him – why can't you?'

'Because he controls and uses everyone he can. Look at this place – a relocator is supposed to help Watch members disappear into normal society but he's gathered them to him and built up a powerful little army of Gifted well trained, well armed soldiers. We don't know what he's up to'

'So why aren't the Watch bothered about it?'

'Because he still has many powerful friends on the Council there and because his brewery makes a fortune for them - money they need for weapons, vehicles, surveillance technology – all things to hunt the Brethren across the world.'

'Well that all sounds good – he's helping them.' Jason said.

'In many ways, yes, but my point is that he wants to draw you into it all. He's always wanted us to move into the valley – every time the agents were getting close I had to ask for his help to relocate and he put more pressure on me to 'come under his protection'. Finally, after your mother was… well, I thought it would be best. Now he's got you right where he wants you.'

'You're not getting it, Dad, are you?' Jason said. 'Maybe I want to be part of it – learn my… my super powers and join the Watch.'

Dad took a slow breath and nodded. 'No I do get it and to be honest, I can't really stop you. However, I'm asking you not to get mixed up with Brash… at least until we can work out just what he is up to.'

'And just how are you going to do that?' Miranda asked. For once, she'd been listening quietly to the conversation - almost, Jason thought, as if she were trying to decide who to back – him or Dad.

Dad nodded. 'Fair question. Sergei Marakoff can help with that. He's what we call a ghost - a spy and assassin for the Watch. He and your Grandfather worked very closely with each other.'

'What's he doing here?' Miranda said.

'Your grandfather asked him to come when we moved into the valley. He doesn't trust Brash either and wants to know we'll be safe.'

'Ahh, I knew Grandpa loves us really.' Miranda purred.

'So how is this Marakoff guy going to find out what evil stuff Mr Brash is supposedly getting up to?' Jason asked.

'Marakoff has told the Watch Council that he wants to retire here,' Dad said, 'and they've informed Brash that he'll be arriving in the next few weeks for relocation.'

'So then he can just spy his way around the abbey and village whenever he wants – very clever.' Miranda said.

'I'm sure he'll find out loads with all the cameras, security guards and his… walking problem.' Jason said, finishing the last of his tea and getting up. 'I'm going out.'

'Jason,' Dad said, putting his cup down, 'join this gang if you have to, practise your Jakra but for now, keep away from Alan Brash and learning your Gifts. Wait until we know more about him and… give yourself time to think.'

'Okay, Dad – for now but no promises, all right?'

'No promises,' Dad said and went to refill the kettle.

✱✱✱

The following Monday saw the start of a month of intensive training with the Brash gang.

His first week quickly blurred into a daily round of squeezing Jakra into lunch hours and after school sessions before going home in time to eat and sleep.

The Brash gang-hut was actually a fully equipped training hall, complete with mats, punch bags, wooden weapons from knives up to quarterstaffs and body protection for serious sparring. There was even a set of four power-shower cubicles and lockers for spare clothes.

Most of the training was led by Fast Eddie and Erin Brock. The two of them trained in Alan Brash's abbey at the weekends and then in turn, instructed the Brash members at lunch times, after school and whenever they felt like skipping lessons.

Training was hard and punishing. If you lost concentration, Eddie or Erin wouldn't hold back with the blows, throws or locks you had allowed through your defences.

Fast Eddie deserved his name. Jason had never seen anybody move so quickly, one move flowing into another. His hands were a blur as they punched you three times before you could breathe or slapped on a lock and flipped you onto your back in some greased lightening body throw. Jason learned quickly however, his lifetime of training and his determination helped soak up Eddie and Erin's instruction.

The Brash version of Jakra emphasised limb breaking, incapacitating and even killing. Every style of punch, knife-hand, kick, throw and lock was designed for maximum damage against a stronger opponent. Dad's techniques had also been focussed on incapacitating but only to allow you time to escape from a situation quickly. Consequently, Jason found he could block a lot of his sparring partners' moves and floor them but he'd a lot to learn about finishing off an opponent so that they would not get up again... possibly ever. It all had the feel of going far beyond even the Pit fights in Silent Hill. This training was for life and death situations and Jason kept reminding himself this is exactly what he needed.

By the end of that first week Jason was dimly aware that he was changing.

His training filled his mind and normal, non-Brash life faded into a hazy background. He still kept up with his lessons but moved away from Violet to sit with the only two other Brash members in his class - dark haired twins, Jack and Jayne Ryehouse. Neither was Gifted but they both trained hard in the hope of getting in to Brash Security when they left school. Jayne, who was almost as stocky as her brother, was the better fighter of the two but they worked exceptionally well as a pair, seeming to know each other's moves and defending and attacking almost as one body. Working together, they beat Jason more often than not in those first few days.

He felt a bad about dropping his friendship with Violet but he didn't want to hear any of her arguments against his joining the Brash. Twice, she moved over to talk to him when he was on his own between lessons or strutting through the tunnels to the clubhouse. Both times he made some excuse and walked on. She stopped trying after that.

As for Mouse and Louisa, examination study leave had begun and that meant they were hardly in school at all. No doubt Dad had told Ilena about him joining the Brash and so neither of them would want to see him anyway. What did he care?

At home, there was a sort of quiet acceptance. The Brash organised a taxi home for him each night so he could stay to train. He usually arrived back at the Old Mill after eight o'clock, wolfed down whatever Dad had left for him in the kitchen and exhausted, hit his bedroom. Miranda and Dad were always there when he got back, even attempting to sit with him while he ate for the first few days. Conversation was stilted – he was doing something Dad didn't want him to but was powerless to stop – what more was there to be said.

Miranda gave up on him by day three and ate in front of the television. Dad stayed as Jason's withdrawal didn't seem to concern him too much – not now he'd his two friends to "play with" - Ilena Russof and Marakoff. Marakoff it seemed, had moved into the attic rooms – they didn't want Brash to know he was here yet while he snooped around the valley.

In the second week, the revenge fights began. First Jason took out Hairy – the big Skin from the bus. After that, Fast Eddie said it would give them better odds in the Pit-side betting if he tweaked things a little. The next fight he matched Jason against two of the park-attack Skins at the same time.

Jason got hurt in that one. Dad had trained him and Miranda in fighting two opponents and he'd had some multiple Brash opponents in training the previous week but this was something else. One of the Skins managed to get behind him as he was smashing the other to the floor. Jason took a hard kick in his back and went down. It took a desperate snap-kick from the ground to crack his second assailant's knee and then a leg sweep to bring him down, lock him up and make him scream for a while before letting him submit. Erin had to help Jason out of the Pit as the crowd ranted and screamed for more blood.

In the third week, the fights really began to heat up. Particularly satisfying was fighting the ferret-faced Skin who had run Jason down in the park. The Skin had been given a baseball bat to even up the odds a little. Another was against a huge but slow monster who Jason dimly remembered laying into him with massive punches as he'd been struggling to get into the trees. Jason dealt out a lot of pain in both bouts with only minor damage to his own hardening body.

Now the kids at Silent Hill moved out of his way in the corridors. Everybody looked at him, their glances coming in two flavours - fear or admiration. The Brash whooped him or slapped his shoulder whenever they passed, the Skins muttered and swore under their breath and there were still a few that held his gaze defiantly... that would change, they would all learn eventually.

It wasn't all training and fighting in the Brash hut - there was always the very pleasant distraction of the girls. Tanya became very friendly although there were no more after-school pizza trips on offer during his intensive training. After each fight she was always around to strip off his shirt and massage his back however, while the rest of the gang celebrated with cans of lager and pounding rock music. None of them went to lessons during a post-fight afternoon and no teachers ever came to dig them out of their hut.

One month after the ambush in the park, Jason was stronger, faster and more lethal than he'd ever been in his life.

***

On the Monday of the fifth week since joining the Brash, the last one before summer half term, Violet cornered him.

'Have you had enough yet?'

Jason looked around to see who was watching. Violet had caught him coming out of the west passage en route to the Brash hut which most normals and obviously Skins avoided. Apart from a few of his gang, there was no one around.

'Hi Violet, how are you?' Jason asked, leading her a little away from the hut. Now he looked, she appeared even more harried than normal.

'Fine and dandy, thanks. Have you had enough of it yet?'

'Enough of... the fighting?' Jason ventured.

'Yep.'

'No, not really.' Jason said, resigning himself to a lecture. 'There's still three Skins I need to get even with and...'

'You haven't seen the half of it yet.' Violet said, quietly.

'The half of what?'

'The fighting doesn't end at the Pit you know... that's just practice. They take you out onto the streets – into Drunken Abbot mainly, but sometimes here, in the village late at night... after curfew.'

'Violet, I want to keep training, I need real fights to...' Jason began.

'You've never been here in Darkston after curfew have you?'

'No, but then I guess that's sort of the point of a curfew, isn't it?'

'Well obviously... but have you ever wondered why a sweet little village like ours needs a curfew... it's a little unusual don't you think.'

Jason ran his fingers back through his hair. What was Violet getting at? 'Something to do with stopping gang fights...?' he asked.

Violet shook her head slowly. 'Just the opposite – curfew's when the real fighting starts. It keeps everyone else out of the way – makes sure they don't see anything. People get killed, Jason... as in dead.'

'What...?' Jason began.

'Ah, there you are my little gladiator,' a rich voice rang through the still summer air.

Jason turned around to see Fast Eddie step out of the Brash hut a few dozen metres away.

Violet grabbed his arm. 'I'm trying to help you. Leave the Brash, don't get any more involved with my guardian... he's not a nice man. He plays God. He'll use you for whatever...'

'Jason,' Eddie shouted, walking towards them now, 'shoe away your little admirer, we need to talk.'

Jason looked down at Violet. 'You'd better go.'

She shook her head and for the first time, Jason saw her looking scared.

'Look,' he said, touching her lightly on the arm, 'we can talk about this later, okay?'

'I don't think I'll get the chance again.' Violet said quietly, just as Eddie drew up close.

200

'Take a walk, Violet,' Eddie said, 'you know Mr Brash doesn't want you hanging around us.'

'I'm sure you'll let him know all about my crimes, Edward.' Violet said, already starting to walk back towards the passage entrance.

'Already have, sweetie.' Eddie said, blowing a kiss to her back.

'She's all right, you know,' Jason said. 'She's not doing anything wrong,'

Eddie turned to him. 'She's a spoiled little brat who's never shown the proper gratitude to Mr Brash for taking her in.'

Jason watched Violet disappear into the tunnel. She'd never seemed the least bit spoiled to him. Still, what was the point in arguing?

Eddie patted Jason's cheek playfully to bring his attention back. 'You know Jason - I think you deserve a little reward after taking out so many of the baldies.'

Jason shrugged. He looked forward to the Pit fights now - the harder the odds, the better. However, he was constantly aching and hurting in some part of his body from the fights and the never-ending training. A reward would be good.

'Surely you're not going to cut me in on the betting profits, Eddie?' Jason asked.

Eddie smiled, broad and charming. 'I like you - but not that much, old boy. No, the reward is I'm moving you up to the next level. Meet me at the gates after training this evening.'

Chapter 14

Training went on late into the evening with a couple of breaks for food and stretching. It wasn't until almost ten o'clock that Jason was freed from the hut.

Eddie's black van was waiting for him at the school gates - nothing more than a silhouette in the fast fading light.

'Jump in,' Eddie called as his blacked out window hummed down smoothly.

Jason got in the passenger side. 'I'm not late am I – they said you knew it was a late session?'

'No, no old boy – we needed to wait for the dark.' Eddie grinned across at him then pulled away from the school. 'Now then, about tonight's little adventure… you have seen who's in the back of course? I hope you'd never get into a van without first knowing everyone who's in there.'

Jason turned around to see who was with them. Erin Brock and a Brash member called Oliver Stone. They both leaned forward into the dim streetlight pulsing in through the windscreen and waved.

'Not a clue, eh lad?' Oliver grunted in his deep voice.

'Jason, Jason, Jason,' Eddie chided, 'you have so much to learn if you're ever going to survive. What if they'd been a couple of agents with a gun to my head? You would be splattered all over this expensively tinted windscreen by now.'

Jason shrugged apologetically at the other two passengers. He didn't know Oliver very well. He was another year 13 like Eddie and Erin – only a little taller than Jason but very stocky with long straight brown hair and a big, somewhat pitted face like an old rock star. Jason had only seen him sparring once. It was against three good year 11s and Oliver had crushed them. Eddie had introduced them just after that but explained that Oliver spent a lot of time training in the abbey. He was going to join Brash security in August after his "A" levels.

'Hi,' Jason said and turned back around, swallowing quietly. Never mind gun-toting agents being in the back, he was in a van with the three best fighters in the Brash gang.

'Quite august company for a new boy, wouldn't you agree?'

Jason nodded. 'Yes. What's going on?'

'Well,' Eddie said, driving them passed the "Little Italy" pizza parlour now, 'we need some fresh challenges to push you a little further – show you something of what you might face in the real world.'

'Great…' was about all Jason could manage.

'So we are going on a mission, dear boy. You see, there is a certain… gentleman who has been denigrating our generous Mr Brash and, in fact, the whole order of things in Drunken Abbot. He's just trying to stir up trouble really, mess about with the status quo as it were. The thing is, he's starting to gather a little following of other losers and we can't have that, can we?'

'I guess not,' Jason mumbled.

'So we're going to make a little surgical strike into the rotting heart of Drunken Abbot to see if we can't take out this malignant little tumour.'

'Oh.' said Jason. 'And why do you need me for this?'

Eddie smiled thinly and looked across at him. 'We don't exactly "need" you, old boy, but as I said earlier, it's an ideal opportunity to bring you on a bit. Mr Brash is very pleased with you so far - your Jakra is coming on very well indeed. He wants to accelerate your training - begin developing other skills in you now.'

'You're talking about the Gift? I haven't decided if I'll learn...'

Eddie's left hand flashed up for silence. 'You owe it to yourself to learn everything you can do – one day your life, or that of someone close to you, may depend on it.'

'I know all that and believe me, I want to learn them but my Dad is dead set against it... I kind of promised him I'd hold off... at least for a little while.'

'And what happens if the Brethren find us here tomorrow?' Eddie asked.

'But we're protected here.'

Eddie shook his head. 'And maybe you should be doing your bit to keep it that way.'

'I...' Jason began but Eddie cut him off.

'Anyway, it's not an issue just yet. Tonight there's lots of other things you need to work on... a bit of stealth, watching out for your team, fighting multiple opponents... all good stuff.'

Jason nodded. 'This is all part of training to be in the Watch, isn't it?'

Eddie glanced across. 'It's all part of training to stay alive, actually. You and yours are a bit of a hot target as you well know and if the Brethren ever managed to track you down here... well, living out in the Wick as you are...'

'I thought the whole valley was protected?'

'Enough now,' Eddie said, 'we're about to head into enemy territory.'

He switched off the headlights as they pulled up in front of a small steel gate, just wide enough for the van to pass through. There were three nondescript garages to either side of them. A security man, dressed in the usual dark blue uniform and helmet stepped out from a brick watch-box to one side of the gate and strolled over.

'Hello Eddie - out on the town again, then?' the guard said as Eddie rolled down the window. The guard had small, hard looking eyes but he seemed to be genuinely glad to see Eddie.

'Can't keep a good man down, Mark. Any movement out there?'

'Pretty quiet... but I guess that's about to change.'

Eddie smiled. 'Now that is a definite possibility. Usual swap, if you please.'

'Certainly. Give 'em what for, the scumbags deserve it.'

Mark unlocked one of the garages, pushed the door upwards and disappeared inside.

'Time to leave the lap of luxury, I'm afraid.' Eddie said, opening his door and stepping out. Jason followed him as Oliver and Erin jumped out of the back. Like Eddie, Oliver and Erin were in loose fit jeans and dark tee shirts. Out of her fine blouses and skirts, Erin appeared lithe and hard and Oliver just looked huge. Even with his month of intensive training and fights Jason thought both of them were way out of his league.

An engine sputtered into clanking life and a moment later a rusting blue van reversed out of the garage. It was scratched and filthy and both small rear windows were cracked. It pulled up next to them and Mark jumped out, leaving the engine running.

'Lovely,' Eddie grinned at Jason as he jumped up into the driver's seat. 'Still, it does blend in a little better than the Merc,' Erin indicated Jason should take the passenger's side and she and Oliver climbed into the back again through the two rusting rear doors.

Mark winked at them as he settled in to Eddie's pristine van and eased it into the now empty garage. A moment later there was an low whirr and the small steel gates into Drunken Abbot rolled back.

Eddie drove through and the gate immediately began shutting again behind them.

They pulled away into the dark streets of Drunken Abbot and left civilisation behind.

'Right,' Eddie began, his usual jaunty camaraderie dropping from his voice, 'a couple of things to remember out here. Firstly – this is not any sort of organised training session. If you get cornered there is no one to stop them beating you to a pulp and maybe worse. Mr Brash cracks down heavily on guns and actual killing, but that is no guarantee of anything. The people we are going to play with tonight sometimes tool up with knives or bats – especially if they've got wind of some trouble coming their way. Players on both sides have… not come back from nights like these.'

Jason looked at him but didn't say anything. He wasn't ready for this; it seemed like he'd stumbled into some sort of Quentin Tarrantino movie.

Eddie was driving slowly, navigating by their one working headlight and the occasional intact streetlamp. Jason heard an metallic clinking in the back. He twisted around to see Erin and Oliver keeping watch out of the small, cracked rear windows whilst checking and strapping indistinct glinting objects about themselves.

Jason breathed in slowly, trying to calm himself. That agent on Mawn would have killed him and Miranda. There was a good chance he would face being murdered again by agents hunting him down even if he didn't decide to join the Watch. He needed to do this, to face real danger and do it now. Like Eddie said – "what happens if the Brethren find them tomorrow?". This was just the next step up from fighting in the Pit.

Eddie glanced across at him. 'Don't work yourself up about this – with a bit of luck, most of them will be half-cut on the ale by now. It'll only get really sticky if we're recognised by one of the Skins from school… then we can expect a mob to be whipped up from the local pubs in a matter of minutes. The three of us and now, to some extent your good self, would be quite a catch for these low-lives – we do keep beating up their kids, after all.

Jason's throat was dry. Outside, the van's shaky headlight beam crawled over dark doors and windows. Eddie was keeping to the back streets but every so often Jason glimpsed a corner pub with its small, yellow-lit windows playing host to menacing silhouettes like some shadow-puppet nightmare.

Suddenly a pub door burst open and three men stumbled out. They were all in jeans, trainers and dirty T-shirts. Two of them held bottles and the little laughing monk logo reflected brightly in Eddie's headlight. The men squinted around in a daze but Eddie quickly turned down another alleyway so the men were lost from sight.

'Mmm, adventurous ones… by this time they've normally settled into their favourite boozer for the rest of the evening,' he said, peering out through the windscreen.

The van's headlight seemed unable to push back the gloom for more than a few metres. They were in a narrow passage running between the backs of two long terraces. Small, black windows stared blindly down at them as the van crunched over rubbish and nudged passed overflowing metal dustbins.

'Why would anyone want to live here?' Jason mumbled, almost to himself but Eddie heard him.

'Mr Brash shipped most of them in when he first took over the spring water plant here and began turning it into a brewery. He brought them in from the cities of the North and Midlands - homeless, petty criminals, the losers with no family or friends to… help them out.'

'Or miss them,' Erin said, sliding forward along the bench seat to join them. 'Mr Brash gives them everything they want – a house, simple work, food tokens, cheap ale – if they left they'd have to walk out of the valley with no money, no home and a growing thirst for ale they can't afford on the outside.'

Walk out of the valley? Jason scanned the street and alleyways around him. Erin was right – there were no cars, moving or parked. It dawned on Jason that he'd only ever seen a few cars in the town over the weeks he'd travelled to and from Silent Hill. There were a half dozen burnt out wrecks on the school route and from the rust on them it looked like they'd been there for years. Brash really had arranged things so no one ever left Drunken Abbot.

'Why bother shipping in a whole town of workers in the first place?' Jason asked, glad to be distracted from the thought of stopping and getting out of the van. 'Why not just use machines?'

Erin smiled but she didn't look at him. Her eyes were meticulously searching every alley and doorway they passed.

'Skilled craftsmen lovingly brew and cask Drunken Abbot Ale by hand from the finest Yorkshire spring water and our merchandise is all hand-assembled.' Erin said, as if quoting from some brochure.

'And besides, we need people to practice on,' Eddie said, shrugging. 'Now, history lesson over for today - we're here.'

Eddie pulled into another side street, shut off the headlight and free-wheeled silently into the deepest shadows.

This was it – they were going to walk into some pub and pick a fight. Jason breathed in slowly, trying to stay calm. 'What do you want me to do?'

'Simple really,' Eddie said, switching off the engine, 'Your only job is to stop anyone from reaching Erin. You're going to be her protector or, as the Watch would put it, her shield, for the night.'

Jason twisted slightly to see Erin. Her face was very close. 'So I just watch your back?'

Erin's eyes were in deep shadow now but Jason could feel them staring at him. 'As simple as that. Stick to me like glue and keep the buggers off me,' her voice had a catch to it, almost a tremor. Jason nodded. He wouldn't let her down, whatever hell hole Eddie led them in to.

'Don't worry about a thing, old boy,' Eddie said. 'The plan is we walk into the Abbot and Lashing pub where a gentleman by the name of Jack Delaney is always to be found by this time of the evening. He's the chappie who's been stirring up more trouble than usual - moaning on about not enough ale money and the odd unexplained disappearance or two.'

'Disappearance or two?' Jason asked.

Eddie's voice hardened. 'Nothing unusual in that - remember where these people came from – sometimes they cut loose, drift on. Now stay focussed on the plan.'

'Right, sorry,' Jason said. He pushed one hand back through his hair. *People drifting on - hadn't Erin just been explaining why no one ever left Drunken Abbot?*

'Now then,' Eddie cut into his thoughts, 'We'll just give Jack a bit of a slapping in front of his mates and walk out - the trouble makers in this town need to know Mr Brash is watching and listening and nowhere is beyond his reach.'

'What about his mates,' Jason asked, 'won't they join in?' .

'Yes, possibly some of Jack's drunken pals will take exception to his… warning, in which case Erin and I will likely have to do lots of damage to people and pub. That's when you and Oliver make sure no one sneaks up behind us to interrupt our work. Then we leave, very quickly, before the word gets around to other pubs.'

Eddie was silent for a moment, his face just a silhouette in the darkened van. 'Remember, Jason, this is not a game. If it kicks off, don't hold back with the Jakra or they will slaughter us. No fancy sparring here – break them in one strike or two then move on to the next. Above all, protect Erin - Oliver will be too busy watching my back to help out.'

'They'll know we're up for trouble as soon as we walk in, won't they?' Jason asked.

'Not necessarily. They'll know we're not locals – everyone knows everyone in their street here, but that's okay. Men and occasionally women, from our lovely village sometimes step out into the town to sample a little of the rough life. Some of the pubs put on special… entertainment for the posh folks.'

Eddie smiled and slapped Jason's leg. 'We'll give them a little entertainment of our own, eh?'

Jason attempted a grin but Eddie was already looking into the back of the van.

'Clear?' he asked.

'Clear, Eddie.' Oliver replied, his voice low and serious. Erin slid back over to him.

'Let's do it,' Eddie said, switching the cab light to permanent off before he eased his door open.

Jason shuddered as he reached for the handle. Somehow, being in the van let him believe he was safe, just an observer watching the dangerous town pass by on three hundred and sixty degree television. Now he had to get out and be a part of it.

'Snap to, Jason,' Eddie hissed, quietly sliding his door shut.

Jason took one more deep, calming breath and stepped out into the dark.

The alley was narrow with no lights at all. About 50 metres back the way they'd come was a larger street, lit in patches by its few remaining, non-smashed streetlamps. Eddie and Oliver Stone crossed to the other side of the alley, pulling slightly ahead. Oliver was tying back his long hair into a pony tail. Jason started to cross after them.

'No, Jason - stay by me, remember.' Erin whispered, laying a cool hand on his arm.

He moved back to Erin's side. She curled one fist in his T-shirt.

'Get it into your head - you're my shield from now until we get out of here, okay? Stay a step behind me wherever I go and give it everything you've got to watch my back while I dish out some damage in front. D'you understand?'

Jason nodded clearing a lump in his throat - quietly. 'Yes… I won't let you down.'

'I know,' Erin said, releasing his T-shirt and pinching his cheek gently. 'Your Jakra is really good – let's hope it's enough to keep them off me.'

Jason tried to smile but Erin was already moving.

Ahead, Eddie had reached the edge of the alley and was watching the main street from the shadows. Oliver's muscular bulk was a step behind him, tucked in tight against the wall. Erin flattened herself against the opposite wall and trotted silently towards the street. Jason slipped in behind her, sure the whole town must be able to hear his heart pounding. He didn't want to go out into the light.

As they drew up, Eddie stepped out into the street, confident and relaxed. Oliver followed and a moment later, Erin walked out behind them. Jason hesitated. He felt as if he were glued to the wall. A drop of cold sweat trickled down the small of his back.

Erin was moving away from him - he should be at her shoulder. Gritting his teeth, he dashed after her just as she glanced behind.

'For God's sake, stick to me like glue - I've got to know you're there.'

Jason just stared at her. Erin looked paler that usual, her mouth and eyes pulled tight.

'Sorry… sorry. Just getting my head together.'

'Jesus,' Erin hissed under her breath and quickened her step to catch up with Eddie.

The street seemed ten times as wide as it had when he'd been riding in the van. The lights were so bright - Jason could almost feel eyes watching them although there wasn't a soul to be seen.

Straight in front of them was the pub.

The Abbot and Lashing had its name etched in peeling gold leaf over a dirty green background. The motif was a monk tied to a whipping post. Through the nicotine-yellowed windows, Jason could see at least a dozen silhouettes moving, drinking, smoking. Heavy rock music pounded out, the black double doors pulsing with menace in time to the beat.

Eddie and Oliver were there already. Eddie glanced back then pushed in through the doors, Oliver at his heels. Erin slowed down a little, letting the doors swing shut again.

'We won't go in with Eddie - we act as if we don't know them. You're some rich underage saddo trying to take his older girlfriend to the pub, alright?'

Jason nodded and Erin carried on. 'The scum will think it's suspicious - two sets of strangers coming in so close to each other, but they won't be sure and it will split their attention. Don't look at Eddie when we get inside.'

'Right.' was all Jason could say. His heart was hammering hard enough to break out of his ribs and cold sweat ran all down his spine.

'Eddie will face down this Jack Delaney character if he's there. I only step in if anyone else joins in.'

Erin placed one pale white hand on the doors and glanced back at him. 'You ready for this?'

Jason swallowed. 'Piece of cake.' he lied.

Erin's lips got tighter. 'Just keep them off me.' She turned her back on him and turned the handle.

***

Rock music, heat and cigarette smoke hit Jason the instant he stepped into the Abbot and Lashing. He concentrated on staying a step behind Erin while trying to get his bearings in the smoke-hazed, low red light of the pub.

There were people everywhere - mainly men in jeans and T-shirts. A dark bar lay directly in front of him and stained round tables filled the floor space. Four women, heavily made up and dressed in short skirts and tight tops, sat at the table nearest the door.

Jason caught sight of Eddie and Oliver, already settled in with their backs to him at the far right of the bar. He forced his eyes to brush over them and followed Erin as she edged between the tables and made directly for the centre of the bar. The music – Jason recognised something about images in a rear view mirror by Meat Loaf - thumped out from an old fashioned jukebox in one corner but that was the only sound. Every eye was on the two of them, flicking over to Eddie and Oliver and back again.

Erin ignored it all. She found a space at the bar and caught the eye of one of the two barmen – a middle aged, short man with a solid beer belly and greasy hair brushed over a bald patch. The other bartender stared at them with open contempt. He was a tall, young man with an emaciated appearance - bare arms of bad skin stretched over sinewy muscle, chicken neck, drawn face, pulled down eyelids.

Beer-belly sauntered up. He looked Erin up and down, his eyes lingering on the front of her T-shirt which was stretched tightly across her firm body. He smiled coldly, surprisingly white teeth flashing in the bar's red spotlights. He ignored Jason and spoke to Erin's chest.

'He's too young to be in 'ere.'

Erin shrugged. 'Who's to check? I'm baby-sitting and I need a drink. Pint of Abbot and a coke for my little brother.' She'd obviously decided to change the plan for some reason.

Beer Belly stared at her for a long moment then nodded. 'The Thirst got you, eh?' he laughed and reached up for a glass embossed with the Drunken Abbot logo. 'You know,' he said as he caressed the long handled pump and then eased it down, 'if you're short of cash to pay for this, I'm sure we can work some sort of... deal.'

Erin didn't flinch. 'We'll see – I've got enough for a couple.'

Beer-belly shrugged and slipped the still swirling pint over to Erin. 'We'll see.' He mumbled, glancing over the pile of coins Erin put on the bar whilst sorting Jason's Coke. Finally he waddled off.

Jason breathed again. Trying to appear relaxed, he hoisted himself up on a slashed barstool and took a sip of his coke as he looked around.

Some conversation had started up again although there were still plenty of narrowed glances being levelled at the strangers. A grating cackle from one of the four women cut through the rock music. All four of them seemed much the worse for drink, some of their eye make-up had run and there was more lipstick around their glass rims than on their mouths.

Most of the men had that semi-glazed look - taking a little too long to focus on anything but the glass in their hand.

There was one table of three men however, who looked anything but drunk. They sat just below a window against the far wall and although they'd half full pints in front of them, none of them were drinking now. One caught Jason watching them and mumbled something. The other two looked up to stare back at the boy at the bar.

'Turn away, stupid - that's Delaney.' Erin whispered.

Jason tore his eyes away and turned back at Erin. She was knocking back the dark ale greedily as if she'd not drunk for a week. 'I thought that stuff was bad for you – really addictive?'

'You're not my mother,' she snapped, putting down her already half-finished pint. Then she smiled, thinly. 'All part of the addicted sister cover story.'

Jason nodded, unconvinced. 'What happened to you being my girlfriend?'

Erin took another drink. 'It looked like baldy fancied me and he'd be nicer if I was a sister hooked on the ale and dragging out her little brother for a bit of protection. More of a chance to... Anyway, drink your...' Erin trailed off as Eddie's voice rang out across the pub.

'Not slagging off Mr Brash tonight then, Jack?'

The pub went silent apart from the jukebox finishing off 'Girls Just Wanna Have Fun'.

Jason looked over at Eddie. He guessed it was all right to do so now as everyone else was staring that way - apart from Erin who was watching the watchers.

Two of the three men around the table sat up straighter but the third, sitting in between them, slouched back and resumed supping his pint. The drinker had thick curly black hair, a hard but handsome face and a heavily muscled physique under a clean white T-shirt. The man stared at Eddie - arrogant, lazy almost. Eddie was leaning against the bar, a pint sitting untouched by his side. Oliver stood to his left. Like Erin, he was watching everyone including the bar staff. Eddie carried on.

214

'So what's the problem, Jack? Have you run out of lies about the man who houses, feeds and clothes every single person here – the man who puts money in your pocket so you can drink with your mates every night?'

Jack still didn't say anything. One hand slipped down under the table.

Eddie straightened up, making a show of loosening his shoulders and neck. 'You know, Jack, there are some people who don't like to hear loud mouthed, ungrateful drunks making up rubbish about Mr Brash, stirring up trouble… even if that drunk is kissed-off about being passed over for a supervisor's job.'

Eddie started to walk slowly towards Jack Delaney's table and Jack's two mates pushed their chairs back. Dotted around the floor and tables, two or three other men began to shift, clench and unclench their fists or slip hands into pockets. They would be the first ones to leap in. Oliver stepped away from the bar, staying a pace behind Eddie. Erin just watched, toying with a heavy glass ashtray with one delicate finger.

Jason glanced around, his heart had started thumping again. Beer Belly and Chicken Neck, the fat and skinny barmen, edged quietly over to where Eddie and Oliver had been then leant on the bar. *Were they after a better view?*

'Of course,' Eddie continued, now just two tables away from Delaney, 'those same people know Jack Delaney was passed over because he's too busy chatting up other men's wives and girlfriends to lead a team to their monthly bonuses.'

Eddie stopped with just one table seating two middle aged, cropped haired men between him and Delaney. 'Girls Just Wanna Have Fun' finally finished and the jukebox whirred to find the next disc. No one spoke, no one drank. Everyone stared.

Jack put down his pint and sneered, one corner of his lip curling. 'Who the hell are you, boy – Brash's trouble-shooter? Shut your pretty mouth and sod off before I make up my mind how many pieces to leave you in.'

Eddie held Jack's stare while behind him, Oliver scanned the room. Erin continued stroking the ash tray - no one else moved.

Eddie slowly brought his hands together and cracked his knuckles. 'It's not my mouth I've come to shut, Jack.'

It all happened at once.

Delaney shot to his feet, grabbing the table with his two mates and hurling it forward. Two fat men leapt for Eddie from behind and a small, pig-eyed man pulled a baseball bat from nowhere and swung for Oliver.

Eddie shot out one hand and the flying table leapt off his palm to hurtle back at Delaney. Erin's fingers snapped shut around the heavy ash tray and she span it straight into the head of one of the fat blokes running for Eddie, felling him instantly. Oliver caught the other fat bloke's wrist, locked his arm and span him into the swinging baseball bat.

The whole pub erupted, surging up around the two strangers like some human volcano. Men of all shapes and sizes seemed to fly off Eddie's punches, to crash into walls and tables. There was no doubt he was Gifted. Behind him, Oliver took on all-comers like some great swaying oak, breaking whatever arms and legs dared come in reach of him or Eddie.

However, there must have been twenty or more men on their feet and shoving each other to close in around the two of them.

Erin stepped forward and Jason jumped up after her. Instantly he lost sight of Eddie as he and Erin quietly closed with the mass of heaving bodies and flying furniture. Methodically, unnoticed by any but her victims, Erin skirted the heaving crowd sending jabs to the neck and snap-kicks to the backs of knees. Men dropped and fell away before her as she thinned the drunken, baying mob struggling to reach Eddie and Oliver.

Feeling useless as he bobbed around behind her, Jason suddenly realised something. Snap attacks didn't usually have enough force to take grown men out in one blow… Erin must be Gifted as well.

She'd dropped perhaps five men before three or four others realised what was happening and turned on her. Erin blocked every punch and kick thrown at her and sent men flying or dropping to the floor with heavy side kicks and palm strikes. Suddenly she stepped too far into the crowd and a big bloke in red reached for her from behind. Jason leapt forward, grabbed his wrist, locked it and snapped the bone.

The man screamed and backed away.

It felt good.

More came at them as the rest of the crowd realised there were two fights going on. The room filled with shouts and screams as Erin and Jason edged further in. Jason moved faster than he'd ever done in his life. His every move was deadly, aimed to break limbs and joints with no mercy but even so, Erin was taking out two or three for every one that Jason fought off. Only metres in front of him, bodies kept flying away from Eddie and Oliver as if caught in a reverse cyclone.

It should have been over quickly but the drinkers kept on getting up. Noses broken, eyes puffed shut, coughing up blood, the drunken sots still came on. It seemed they knew no fear, no pain. Only broken limbs stopped them.

Suddenly a couple of lights were smashed and they were enveloped in semi-darkness. The fighting intensified. Jason snap-kicked the knee of one man, blocked, threw and stamped another one and just caught a punch aimed for the back of Erin's head from a third. They were almost up to Eddie and Oliver when something smashed into Jason's shin and he fell to one knee.

The crowd closed in over him and Erin... it was just like Abbeywell Park, hammered on all sides by punching, grabbing, kicking hands and feet. Jason struggled back to his feet, lashing out in all directions and searched for Erin.

A baseball bat was swinging down for the back of her head.

He saw it in slow motion, just like the agent's knife dropping down at Miranda on Mawn. Screaming a warning, he dived forward and pushed Erin away.

The bat whistled missed her head by an inch but smacked into her shoulder. She dropped as if her legs were water. Beer-belly stepped out of the crowd to loom over the two of them. His white-toothed grin split wide as he kissed the bat and pulled it up for a second strike.

'Eddie', Jason screamed, slapping away grasping hands and swinging fists he leapt over Erin and lashed out a high kick at Beer-belly but someone grabbed him around the neck and yanked him back. Beer-belly leapt back and his kick missed as the neck-lock cut off Jason's air.

Unable to breathe, Jason cracked the ribs behind him with two elbow strikes but the arm only spasmed tighter around his throat.

Beer-belly winked at him, stepped forward again and raised the bat high over Erin who was fighting to get to her knees. The instant the bat began to swing down, Beer-belly flew back into the crowd scattering bodies and tables like skittles.

Eddie burst through the mob, punching faces to every side of him. He was on full power – his fists were a blur and every person he hit was launched backwards to take down another two or three. Oliver followed him, walking backwards and now armed with a couple of table legs which he swung like synchronized windmills to demolish anyone who stepped in range.

Jason slipped his hips to the left and swung down with his right fist, crushing the testicles of the man who still held his throat. The man dropped, screaming and Jason leapt over to Erin as Eddie and Oliver reached her. Suddenly there was space around them. The half dozen attackers still standing were finally backing away.

Oliver slipped one table leg into his belt and lifted Erin to her feet as if she were weighed nothing. She could stand but only with her good arm gripped around his shoulder.

Eddie glanced at Jason. 'Get the door.'

The black doors stood firmly closed on the far side of smashed and upturned tables and several groaning bodies covered with blood and broken glass. Two younger men, both skinheads and both bleeding profusely from their noses stood in the way. Jason brought his fists up and moved towards the door but the skinheads backed off before he'd taken his second step. Jason walked between them to the door and reached for the handle.

'When Jack comes out of hospital - ask him to show a little more respect for Mr Brash, would you?' Eddie announced to no one in particular. 'Otherwise, we might have to get serious.'

Jason glanced past Eddie and shivered. Jack Delaney hung upside down, his legs and groin shoved through a shattered window and the rest of him swinging limply against the wall. Eddie motioned Oliver and Erin passed him and followed them, taking the rear guard.

'Have fun out there, arsehole,' crowed a voice - thin and high. Chicken Neck, the second barman, smiled at them from behind the bar. He waved an old fashioned black Bakelite telephone in the air and laughed.

'I'll pop back to thank you for that very soon,' Eddie said and turned to go.

Chicken Neck whipped up his free hand from behind the bar. There was a metallic glint as he threw something at Eddie.

'Knife!' Jason yelled and leapt forward to knock Eddie out of the way.

There was no need. Eddie span back around, caught Jason and flicked a finger to one side. The spinning knife thudded into the wall panelling by his head, quivering silently.

Eddie winked at the stunned barman. 'You need a little more practise.'

Oliver, now at the door, pulled it open and stepped out. 'Bugger,' he said.

Eddie nudged Jason towards the door and they backed out of the pub.

'Mmm, bugger indeed,' Eddie said.

A hundred metres up the street, a mob was stumbling out of the next pub along. Every one of them seemed to be carrying a bat, knife or chain. They spotted the four strangers coming out of the Abbot and Lashing and surged towards them, baying like hounds first catching the scent of fox.

'The van, I think.' Eddie said, pushing Oliver and Erin into a sprint across the street.

For a moment, Jason was transfixed. He just stood and stared at the mob screaming towards him. A bottle arced through the air and smashed just a step away. He tore after the others who were already disappearing into the alley.

They were still thirty metres from the van's shadowed hulk when the screaming mob surged into the alleyway behind them.

Eddie pushed something metallic into Jason's hand. 'The keys. Help Oliver with her, then get the van started.'

Suddenly, Erin's arm was around Jason's neck and they set off at a run.

Jason kept looking back as best he could without tripping up. Eddie just stood there, a darker shadow in front of the black mass of the onrushing mob. Then he dropped to his knees and drew his hands slowly apart like he was swimming breaststroke.

The entire front row of the mob were jerked down flat as if they'd tripped over something. Those behind tumbled over them and for a moment, confusion reigned.

Eddie rose and started to walk backwards, keeping both hands pointing outwards. The Drunken Abbot men scrambled over the fallen front runners only to trip over again.

'Open it.' Oliver hissed as he slowed the three of them to a stop with Jason still staring back at Eddie.

Jason reached out with the keys to unlock the back doors and dropped them in the dark. 'Oh hell.' He stepped forward to feel for them and heard the clink of his foot kicking the keys further away.

'Bugger,' Oliver swore, dropping to all fours and scrabbling around for the keys. Jason did the same as Erin slumped against the locked back door.

'Can't hear an engine, gentlemen,' Eddie shouted, from not very far away. 'I can only keep this up for a few more seconds...' His voice was thinner than his normally rich timbre. He was straining.

No keys. They could see nothing in the pitch black shadow.

Suddenly there was a glare of light as Erin flashed a torch beam over the ground.

'Going,' Eddie said from ten steps away, '...going...'

'There,' Oliver snapped and reached behind a tyre to pull out the keys.

'Gone,' Eddie groaned and his arms flopped to his sides. Fifteen metres beyond him, the mob began picking themselves up. A tide of obscenities rose up with them and they surged forward, baying for blood.

Somehow Oliver was in the van and starting the engine. Jason grabbed Erin's good arm and threw it over his shoulder. Tearing his eyes away from the onrushing mob of shadows, he started to drag her around to the passenger side.

'The back doors, idiot,' she hissed through gritted teeth.

Jason yanked open one door and almost threw her inside.

Eddie sprinted towards him. The closest of the mob were just steps behind him.

'Get in,' he yelled. 'Leave the door open.'

Jason leapt in and hurled himself to one side as Eddie dived in head first behind him.

'Go.' Eddie yelled and Oliver hit the accelerator just as the first hands locked on to the open doors.

Jason kicked the grasping fingers away, reached out over the tarmac blurring beneath him and yanked both doors shut.

He fell back on the cool metal floor as they screeched out of the alleyway and into the streetlight beyond.

***

Oliver didn't slow down but hurtled along another of the main streets which ran right through Drunken Abbot.

Shuttered shop fronts, side streets and yellow lit pubs whipped past as Jason pulled himself up against one of the bench seats.

Erin eased herself up opposite him, swearing under her breath each time they hit a bump. Eddie had already climbed into the front next to Oliver. No one spoke.

After a minute or so, Jason roused himself. Stinging cuts and throbbing swellings began to override his diminishing adrenaline. He twisted painfully towards Erin – her face alternately cast in a yellow, fluorescent sheen then brushed back into shadow. She looked awful – her eyes and mouth drawn tight in pain.

'How's your shoulder... I'm so sorry - I just couldn't stop them all. There were too many. All I could do was try to push you out of the way when that bat came down. I wasn't good enough to...'

'Shut up, Jason,' Erin said. She stared straight ahead. 'You did what you could.'

'Yes, but...'

'But nothing – stop looking for some sort of absolution,' she spat. 'Oliver – for God's sake slow down or this heap will blow up and I don't want to walk home.'

Eddie grunted his agreement and Oliver eased up a little. Jason stopped talking.

'I'm bloody knackered,' Eddie said from the front.

Jason could see half of Eddie's face in the rear view mirror. In the now slower flashes of streetlight, his gang leader looked deathly pale, as if drained of life.

Jason swallowed and asked. 'Is that what using the Gift does to you...? I mean...'

Eddie snorted. 'Only if you use it too much, old boy... things did get a little more hairy than I expected back there. Young Erin and I had to pull out a few more stops than is strictly advisable. We'll feel like death for a couple of days, but then we'll be back to our usual, bouncy selves.

'Unless my shoulder is actually broken,' Erin said. 'That might stop me being quite so bloody bouncy.'

Jason chewed his lip and looked out of the window. 'Jakra isn't enough is it?' he asked none of them in particular. 'If that bat had hit Erin's head...'

Nobody said anything. Just the occasional wince and intake of breath from Erin as the van jolted or rounded a corner. In a short while they would be out of Drunken Abbot, away from the harsh, fluorescent yellow glare and into the cool moorland dark.

Jason stared out of the window. How could the others be so calm? All of them might have been killed tonight. He'd been next to useless – even with all his training and pit fighting over the past few weeks, one or all of them could easily have be lying with their heads crushed in the Abbot and Lashing or that alleyway now. It was the Gift that had kept them alive.

'I want to learn,' Jason said, 'I want to learn how to use my Gift. This isn't going to happen again.'

'Are you certain you're ready to go against your father's wishes? Eddie asked, now leaning his head against the side window and seeming half asleep. 'You're not going to change your mind once you talk it over with him?'

'He won't stop me - it's my life. Erin... all of us could have been killed tonight. My sister and I were almost...' Jason trailed off. 'I've decided - I need something more than just my Jakra.'

There was silence for a long while. Jason thought Eddie might have drifted off but then, out of the dark, he spoke.

'Good decision – now pipe down and let me sleep.'

***

It was nearly midnight when Oliver pulled into the Old Mill's drive. There were no silhouettes in porch-light this time, no-one waiting at the door full of concern and frustrated anger. Jason had been getting home later and later since joining the Brash and it seemed Dad had given up worrying.

Perhaps he didn't care if Jason came home at all now. He'd left the outside lights on though... very good of him.

The van crunched to a halt on the gravel right outside the front door but Oliver kept the engine running. It looked like they weren't planning on popping in for a cup of tea.

Jason turned to Erin. She still sat rigidly with her face tense and white in the moonlight.

'Erin, I'm really sorry...'

'I know.' She glanced at Eddie who's head had lolled back in his seat . 'Still, it looks like mission accomplished so don't worry about it, eh?'

Oliver twisted around. 'Jump out, Jason. We all need to get some sleep.'

'Of course, sorry.' Jason fumbled for the door release 'Thanks for getting us out of there, Oliver.'

Oliver snorted a laugh. 'I only drove, kid - thank Eddie for holding off the mob.'

Jason finally found the door handle. The last time he'd touched it, less than half an hour ago, there had been dozens of crazed men just outside screaming for their blood. He pulled the lever with an effort and stepped out into the still night of Darkston Wick.

Jason shut the door and Erin nodded to him with a tight smile through the dirty rear windows before Oliver roared away, wheels spinning in the gravel. In moments the van's red lights had disappeared up into the trees.

Jason breathed in deeply, letting his head fall back to look at the stars. He ached and stung in a hundred different places. He was just fifteen but tonight he could have been killed - his life over before it had really begun.

He eased himself up the stone steps, opened the doors and stepped into the dimly lit hall.

'About time – d'you know how late it is?' Miranda's voice wrapped around him.

At the far end of the corridor, the sitting room door was wide open and shimmering firelight spilled out. Resigned, Jason started down the corridor. Unlike Dad, Miranda would follow him to his room if he tried to ignore her.

He stepped into the room. Dad was in one of the fireside armchairs and Miranda lounged on the couch. At the sight of him, her eyes sprang wide open but the next moment her mouth pulled into its angry tight line.

'What happened to you? Did you find a war?' she asked, finally. Dad just stared at him, appraising the damage.

'Training got a bit heavy,' Jason said.

'Training?' she asked. 'Training shouldn't do that to you. They're a bunch of perverted sadists if that's how they teach you to fight. And it's almost midnight... have you any idea how worried Dad is about you and what you're doing... where you are every night... if...'

'Who are you,' Jason cut in, '...my mother?'

Miranda's head went back as if she'd been slapped. Then she took in a slow breath and stared at him. 'You know, you're turning into someone quite crap.'

'Alright – that's enough,' Dad said, quietly. He held an almost empty mug of cocoa. 'Is anything broken?'

'No,' Jason said, 'but it could have been.'

'What are you on about?' Miranda asked.

Jason looked away. His throat was all tight and he didn't want to get into this now. 'I'm going to bed.' He croaked and quickly turned to stride down the corridor.

He heard the creak of someone standing up in the sitting room.

'Let him go, Miranda... he needs to work this out for himself.'

His stomach clenching, Jason ran upstairs to his room.

Chapter 15

For the rest of the weekend Jason managed to largely dodge both Dad and Miranda by taking long runs in the woods and rowing up and down the river. Although he could tell Miranda was itching to either nag or talk to him, both she and Dad gave him space.

On Monday morning he avoided any chance of deep and meaningful conversations over breakfast by getting up late and just grabbing a banana before darting out of the front door.

There were no interrogations at the bus stop either as Mouse and Louisa were on study leave. Grateful for the peace, Jason sank onto the back seat alone and watched the countryside waft by through the diesel fumes

They lurched into Drunken Abbot and started picking up the Skins and normals. At the second stop, Hairy, Richard Baldwin, Deano and Rat Tail got on, pushing in front of the other town kids as usual. They'd taken to largely ignoring Jason ever since he'd joined the Brash and was massacring Skins in the pit. This morning seemed no different. The boys didn't even glance at the back seats at all as they trudged upstairs, eyes down. Jason allowed himself a small smile. He was out of their league now.

Rat Tail was last to start up the stairs. Suddenly she stopped and the normals behind froze so as not to jostle her. She turned to look at Jason, her eyes narrowing, her lips tightly set. She seemed to be wrestling with some decision then she spat out what she wanted to say. 'Enjoy yourself on Friday did ya?'

Jason just looked at her calmly.

'My old man was in the Abbot and Lashing, you know. He's a crap dad, knocks me and my mum about an' everything but at least the sod brings home the food vouchers with his beer money at the end of the week.'

Jason continued to watch her impassively. *What little plan were the Skins up to now? Whatever it was, they would come off worst.*

Rat Tail spat on the bus floor. 'Not any more though, eh? Not after what you and your big friends done to him. He won't be back at the brewery for a month and no work means half-vouchers and no ale money. You don't know what he's like if he don't get his ale every night.'

The kids behind her were trying to edge into the bus but Porter, the driver, seemed in no rush to set off just yet. He was enjoying the show, peering around the back of the drivers cab with his little black eyes shining.

'Leave it, Rat,' Hairy's voice sounded from upstairs. 'He'll get what's coming to him soon enough.'

Rat Tail spat again. 'Hope you're proud of yourself, big man,' she hissed at Jason, 'me and my little sister are gonna suffer for this.' She stamped out of view up the twisting stairwell.

The doors hissed shut, nipping at the last normal to get on as the bus jerked forward.

***

There was a reception committee of sorts when Jason stepped off the bus in Silent Hill. Skins and normals were hanging around in groups just watching the busses disgorge their loads and as Jason appeared Rat Tail shouted out of the top window. 'Here's the hero who broke some faces at the Lashing.'

Jason glanced back up at her and she gave him the finger. When he turned back, the disparate groups of pupils started shifting in towards him.

As if they were waiting for this, four Brash prefects appeared out of the north passage and began ringing their hand bells. Jason looked at his watch – there should have been another ten minutes before registration.

Slowly, reluctantly, the groups turned away and shuffled towards the school as the Brash prefects strode through the clusters shaking their brass bells in various ears.

'What the hell did you do on Friday night?' Violet was somehow standing next to him as the bus pulled away. 'Half of Drunken Abbot is gunning for you.'

'I don't know if I should be talking about it...' Jason began but Violet cut him short.

'It doesn't matter. Listen...' she said then one of the prefects glanced back from herding the rest of the school into the passage.

'You too, Grey – you're nothing special. Get in there.'

Violet grabbed Jason's arm and started walking him slowly towards the school. 'We haven't any time. Brash is going to try to take you out of school, bring you to the abbey. Get out of it if you can but if...'

The deep purr of a powerful, perfectly tuned engine rolled over them. Alan Brash's large black Bentley, gleaming in the bright sunlight, swung in through the school gates.

'Oh bugger,' Violet said, 'now I'll be for it.' She stared up at Jason. 'Things are getting weird at the abbey, really weird. Don't get involved, all right? And don't tell him I said anything...'

'Violet – I want to be trained...'

'You should be in classes, young lady.' The Bentley eased up next to them and Brash stepped out of the rear door.

Violet stared at him defiantly.

'Now.' Brash said, quietly, holding her gaze.

With a last glance at Jason, Violet almost stomped her way back into the tunnel. Jason nodded to Brash politely and began to follow her.

'Hold on, Jason my boy,' Brash called after him.

Jason turned around slowly.

Brash let loose his bright smile. 'Your little excursion into town on Friday has stirred up a lot more... interest than we might have expected. It won't do anyone any good if you stay in school today.'

Jason nodded. 'Are you sending me home?'

'If that's where you want to go,' Brash answered. 'Alternatively you can keep your word to Edward and poor injured Erin and begin your real training.'

'What – right now?'

'Unless you've changed your mind or Violet has said something to make you think again...'

'Violet?' Jason made a show of looking puzzled that he hoped wasn't overdone. He couldn't pull out now – not without breaking his promise or admitting Violet had been trying to dissuade him. 'She was telling me off for fighting like normal... why - is there something she could have said to change my mind?'

Brash studied him for a long moment then smiled again. 'Violet isn't very keen on our training methods. Come on, get in... you're the type of young man who likes to make up his own mind, aren't you?'

'Fine.' Jason walked over to the car.

The Bentley looked a lot less menacing in the morning sunlight than it had that Sunday night when Brash had visited. As he got in he saw the darkened glass screen was up between the front and back seats. He wondered if the skeletal Cadaveril was behind it.

They glided out of the school gates with Beethoven's Moonlight Sonata fading in from hidden surround-sound speakers. Jason caught a hint of polished wood and leather in the gently circulating cool air while outside the windows the hot summer's day whispered by.

Brash poured himself a cut glass goblet of some white wine and Jason a whisky tumbler of iced water from a discreet chiller cabinet. Two flat screen monitors and umpteen silver switches and knobs filled a mahogany panel next to the cabinet but despite all the gadgets, nothing, anywhere in the whole car, rattled.

Jason took a sip of his water, not looking at Brash. He wanted to learn his Gifts but this was all happening too fast.

'I know you're worried about this, Jason,' Brash said, swirling his wine, 'your father doesn't want you to accept your powers or become involved with the Watch but the truth is, you're already a part of it all. You have the potential to be massively powerful and because of that you will always be a magnet for the Brethren. If they could possess you…'

Brash shook his head and tasted his wine. 'Wherever you run, they will always find you eventually – you must realise that by now. You need to be able to protect yourself and your loved ones and for that, you need your Gift.'

Jason took a slow, deep breath. It should be his father in front of him, offering to teaching him the Gift, seeing him through all of this.

'Dad would hate me being here with you.'

Brash nodded gently and sank back into the sumptuous leather to take another sip of his wine. He smiled sadly over the sparkling crystal.

'Undoubtedly.' The smile faded. 'The reason your father is being so… stubborn about this is because he loves you. He doesn't want you to go through what he has suffered.'

'What made my father leave the Watch?' Jason asked.

Brash cupped his glass in both hands and stared into the depths. 'Our world is a living nightmare at times. We are faced with visions of hell, day after day, week after week. You can't know what it's really like to hunt down and kill a demon-possessed human being until you've actually done it yourself. We may be called upon to murder anyone from an old tramp plucked from the street, a powerful politician or perhaps even a child younger than you. Your father, and others, could not accept the Touched and Possessed were no longer innocent men, women and children but vicious, intelligent, powerful monsters intent on enslaving humanity.'

'So... Dad really had to kill children, possessed children?' Jason asked, feeling his stomach clench.

Brash lifted his eyes from gently swirling his wine. 'We all did, Jason. We had to do whatever it took to win... we still do.'

'But in the films... can't you... I mean... can't you just get the demon out?'

Mr Brash nodded slowly. 'Yes... and no. It can be done by a Gifted who is powerful enough – we call it redeeming. But the Redeemer risks being possessed himself through the direct contact, mind to mind, with the demon spirit. It is far safer and quicker to destroy the host and so force the demon into the open. Then we can trap it, hold the unprotected spirit and let the sunlight do its work.'

'What does sunlight do to them?'

Brash drained his glass and returned it to a red velvet cushioned slot in the drinks cabinet. 'Demon spirits can't withstand bright sunlight outside a host body for more than a few moments. Even inside a strong host, a demon can only be in direct sunlight for a few minutes... then they burst apart – gone forever.'

The Bentley smoothly dropped down a gear as the road began to rise steeply. Jason glanced outside. The cottages gave way to a beautifully landscaped hillside with low fountains and ponds and bright flowers of every colour and size.

The dark driver's screen blocked out the front view but as they eased to a stop the immense black marble gatehouse rose up on either side of the car. Etched into the gleaming façade, directly over the arched gateway, were two words:

DARKSTON ABBEY

'Home, sweet home,' Brash said, barely louder than a whisper.

Massive steel gates swung open and two security guards waved their boss through the tonnes of polished stone.

***

Arches. Gigantic, gothic window arches two and three floors high. Darkston Abbey was magnificent - a sprawling mass of shining black marble totally dominated by its dark tower lancing up through the church's vaulted roof and lunging for the sky.

The whole abbey was sheltered by the heavily wooded slopes of a small valley which dropped down to emerald lawns where the Darkston River meandered peacefully past the ancient buildings.

'It's not much but I'm happy here.' Brash said.

'It's incredible...' Jason managed.

The Bentley glided down a wide sweeping driveway which ran from the hill-top gatehouse to the valley floor and crunched into a huge gravelled quadrangle. On Jason's left, to the north, was the church entrance - grand steps leading up to immense double doors with a dozen metres of magnificent stained glass above. On his right was a large, three storey building with a double set of stone steps curving up to the front doors. Directly in front of him was a long building with a bank of perhaps fifteen tall arched double doorways – all closed.

The Bentley crunched to a halt in front of one of the arches and the double doors slowly opened out towards them. Mr Brash took Jason's glass and stowed it with his in the console cupboard and brushed off some non-existent fluff from his suit.

'This building is the West Range.' he explained. 'It used to serve as storage bays for the monk's crops, ale and wines but now I use it to house slightly more exciting things...'

The double doors eased to a halt, fully open now, and the Bentley growled forward.

Jason couldn't see much as they left the bright sunlight for the dim interior. The doors closed silently behind them as he stared out of the windows into diffuse, musty light. Giving up, he reached for the door handle just as the locks clicked open.

He hadn't realized that he'd been locked in for the entire journey. A little unnerved, Jason opened the door and stepped out on to a marble floor and gasped. They were in the most spectacular garage imaginable. Dozens of small lights faded up to reveal a vaulted ceiling spreading out to either side of him to form well over a dozen bays. In each bay, tiny spotlights illuminated gleaming, prestige cars. Jason knew a few - a silver Aston Martin Vanquish, a black Jaguar e-type, two large Mercedes, a dark blue Range Rover Vogue, a red Ferrari something-or-other, a yellow Lamborghini and, at the far end, a massive, black limousine.

'Do you like cars, Jason?' Brash asked.

'I like these ones,' Jason replied, shifting a little to get a better view.

Brash laughed - a short but rich laugh that echoed around the chambers. 'Good – perhaps I'll let you play in some of them when you're a little older.'

The Bentley's driver-door clicked open and the driver stepped out.

It was Cadaveril.

Jason shivered. In the dark of night outside the Old Mill the chauffer had looked like a living skeleton as he'd pinned Jason to the seats of the Bentley with almost demonic strength. The subtle garage lighting didn't help Jason shake the image. Cadaveril's eyes were half lidded over in deep cavernous eye sockets and his high cheekbones seemed to be pushing through pale skin that was too tightly drawn around his hairless skull. His body and limbs were stick-thin and made to look worse by the dark suit hanging off him and the crisp white shirt buttoned tightly over his ribs.

'You have met Cadaveril, of course,' Brash said.

Jason nodded briefly. The chauffer just looked at him from beneath those heavily veined eyelids.

'A man of few words, Cadaveril.' Mr Brash smiled. 'But very useful... he's been with me for more years than either of us care to remember...'

Jason looked away from the walking corpse and caught a smile flashing across Mr Brash's face.

'Now then, time for a whistle-stop tour of the old place, followed by a spot of brunch I think. You should get your bearings, Jason, as you'll be spending a lot of time here with us... I hope.'

Jason nodded. He glanced back at Cadaveril but he'd gone. Jason just caught him disappearing into the shadows of one of the bays. The chauffeur hadn't made a sound. A chill shivered down Jason's spine - he really didn't want to meet that man on any more dark nights.

'Before we set off,' Brash said, producing one of the ruby-eyed, golden monk badges the prefects wore from his pocket, 'do make sure you keep my little podgy face on you at all times while you're in the abbey – it'll let my people know you're on our side.'

Brash pinned the badge onto Jason's polo shirt then led the way to another bay and opened a small, very thick door. A wave of heat and light hit Jason as they stepped out onto a dazzlingly bright, sunlit lawn.

'The Cloister.' Brash announced. 'Sort of a crossroads really for all those monks silently moving from six or seven church services a day to the dormitories, refectory or the fields for a little hard labour. Rather a nice sun trap, don't you think.'

Jason turned slowly about. The pristine grass was totally enclosed by buildings and the sun glinted off black marble in a thousand different places sending shards of broken light over them. A covered walkway all around the grass offered some relief from the sun. The church and tower on his left, immense and glorious, dwarfed the other Cloister buildings but Jason's attention was caught by a plain wooden cross standing in the very centre of the grass.

The cross was perhaps three metres high, the wood stained dark in many places. Dangling from it's arms were a pair of rough iron manacles.

Brash followed Jason's gaze.

'Ah yes... the cross of repentance. The monks of Darkston were a fairly strict lot... they were into making an example of any of the brotherhood who transgressed their rules – perhaps they were late for service or shirked a bit of work or... well just about anything really. Still, better a day or two hanging around here than being sent over to Silent Hill - the House of Correction.'

Jason looked at him and Brash smiled. 'Unbelievable isn't it, that our lovely school used to be a sort of monastic punishment prison... to teach errant monks and villagers the correct way to behave.'

Brash stepped out from the covered walkway and on to the pristine grass. Jason followed him, staring at the cross as they drew nearer. The manacles hung deathly still in the sheltered cloister and inside each bracelet were tiny black spikes. He was sweating already... what must it have been like to be chained there in the full heat of the sun staring into the cool shadows of the walkway with those spikes biting into your flesh?

Brash continued his lecture. 'Very famous, the Silent Hill House of Correction was. The monks there did some of the nastier work for various nobility of the day... the sort of stuff the Tower of London couldn't handle. That's one reason why Darkston survived the Reformation and so forth.'

'One reason? Why else didn't Henry VIII tear this place down then?' Jason asked.

'Glad to see you know your history, young man. Well, for a start, the Darkston monks weren't exactly Catholic and for another they knew how to defend themselves and had a few hundred slavish town and village dependents hanging around who would fight to the death for them. It also helped that they were stinking rich of course and bought their way into favour.'

Mercifully they passed into the shade of the cloister walk and entered a three-story building through heavily studded oak doors. Inside it was blessedly cool, if a little too bright - the black marble façade of the exterior walls had given way to brilliant white inside. A sea of cool blue shag pile carpet swept his gaze around a large reception area with marble step-benches rising up one side. A narrow corridor ran away to a small door at the far end of the building.

A dark suited, severely beautiful woman with scraped back blonde hair stood up behind a desk opposite the stone benches. Brash waved her back down and led the way down the corridor past closed doors on the right. Everything was quiet and still, even their footsteps sank silently down into the deep carpet.

'This is the chapter house,' Brash said. 'Once a day the monks read a chapter of their good book back there on the benches and then used it as a sort of business centre. I've followed their example... after putting in a few basic comforts.'

'How come they were so rich – the monks I mean?' Jason asked.

'Well, their order brought a large amount of wealth over with them from eastern Europe, then there was the farming and brewing of course and their... correction services. The Darkston monks developed the mining unrecognisably and provided work for the local villagers and townsfolk... provided all the work in fact, owned all the houses... they'd their own little kingdom really.'

Brash looked down at Jason and winked. 'Quite a good plan, I'd say.'

They reached the small door at the end of the corridor and Brash opened it out on to a small garden with benches set around the edges. Gleaming stained glass windows soared up the church wall on their left but the rest of the shady area was enclosed by single storey buildings.

'A little cooler here for my staff to take a break,' Brash said, striding across the grass towards a door directly opposite. They entered a bright, white marble corridor.

On the right was a 'T' junction with another long corridor lit by shafts of sunlight streaming through dozens of small windows set high along one wall. On the left, towards the church, was an arch- covered stairway leading up to sturdy double doors inlaid with golden Greek crosses.

'This place is like a maze,' Jason said.

Brash frowned slightly. 'You need to get your bearings quickly if you're going to survive here. Think carefully – all you've done is walk in a straight line across the cloister, through the chapter house and across the shady garden.'

'Sorry...' Jason began but Brash waved a nonchalant hand.

'It's fine. You probably just need a little brain food inside you,' he said and turned left towards the golden crossed doors.

Jason hurried to keep up as Brash trotted lightly up to the double black mahogany doors and stopped. He placed his hand on the marble to one side and a small section of stone slid silently down revealing a deep, black recess illuminated from within by a faint, green light. Brash pointed one finger inside and jabbed it as if pressing buttons. Jason heard a slight scraping as if bars were sliding within the mahogany doors and they clicked open a fraction.

'I'll think you'll like my church,' he said and pushed the doors open wide.

A rush of cool air flowed over Jason and he was bathed in light. An immense stained glass window blazed incandescent with sunlight to illuminate a twenty seat, carved ebony dining table. Sparkling crystal and silver tableware glinted along its entire length.

'Go through,' Brash said.

Jason stepped past him and into the dining room... which was the high altar of Darkston Abbey church. The immense building opened up on his left – two hundred feet of black marble arches and alcoves, shimmering stained glass and shadowed ceiling vaults.

The church had a cross shaped floor plan and a man appeared from the left hand arm. Totally white haired, he wore a black tail coat and trousers, crisp white shirt and a thin, black tie. His shining black shoes sent sharp clicks echoing around the church as he walked smartly towards them. He must have been over sixty but he carried himself easily and his round, friendly face lit up with a small smile when he caught Jason's eye.

'Good afternoon, young sir. Welcome to Darkston Abbey,' the man said, his heels clacking on the bare stone as he walked up a set of three wide steps to the high altar area.

'Thank you,' Jason managed, finding himself smiling back.

Brash joined him in the dining area. 'Good afternoon, Myers. An early lunch is needed – just a cold platter, I think. Is Miss Sirensong around?'

'Indeed, sir. She has been awaiting your return... hungrily.'

Myers winked at Jason, who grinned. He'd vivid memories of the gorgeous, dark haired, Alicia Sirensong whom Brash had brought with him to the Old Mill when he came to visit.

Brash smiled. 'Really – well we had better feed her as well, then. Let her know we are here, won't you?'

'I'd imaginé she already knows, sir. Would you care to introduce me to the young gentleman?' Myers replied and raised his eyes to the ceiling at Brash's momentary lapse of good manners. Jason grinned again. It looked as if Myers treated the mighty Alan Brash like a favourite, but occasionally errant, nephew.

'Oops,' Brash said, putting a hand on Jason's shoulder. 'Jason, this is Myers, who on paper is my butler but in fact runs the whole place. Myers, this is Jason Willow who will be training with us.'

'I am very pleased to meet you, Jason.'

'Hi,' Jason said.

'Will Jason be needing rooms?' Myers asked.

Brash hesitated and Jason glanced up at him. Was Brash expecting him to stay here?

'Have somewhere prepared in the student quarters for him to freshen up after training but I suspect he won't be staying over... this time.'

'Very good, sir,' Myers nodded, turned smartly on his heel and left them.

'Rooms – am I... do you want me to stay... here?' Jason asked.

'Only if you want to... we'll see how you get on in your training. It helps enormously to keep you focussed on learning your Gift if you stay in the same environment.'

Jason nodded non-committally. As much as he'd thought about learning his Gift, he hadn't reckoned on staying away from home. Dad had never allowed him or Miranda on school trips or sleepovers – always saying they needed to stay close to each other.

Brash pulled out a heavy chair for him at the dining table and they sat with their backs to the windows, looking down the magnificent aisle.

'Best seats in the house,' Brash said.

Jason nodded absently and tried to take it all in. Darkly gleaming choir stalls rose up in three banks against each wall and ended at an extravagantly carved, roofed seat which looked like something out of a dark fantasy film. Then the gleaming nave ran between many arched alcoves to the immense main doors and stained glass window that he'd seen from the outside when he'd first arrived at the abbey.

'Stunning.' Jason breathed.

'Why thank you.'

Jason started at the sexy female voice that caressed the back of his neck. He twisted around to see Alicia Sirensong watching them from the doorway. *How did everyone move so quietly in this place?*

Brash's personal assistant had been breathtaking the first time he'd seen her but now, as she glided towards him through the split-spectrum sunlight from the stained glass windows, she was nothing short of a goddess. Her lustrous dark hair cascaded over the simple white dress she wore. The fabric hugged her curvaceous figure down to a belt of thin black rope then flowed around her long legs to reveal elegant strappy high heels flashing into view with each graceful step.

'Alicia – how lovely you look today... don't you think so, Jason?' Brash said, standing up to greet the lady. Jason felt his face burn as he lurched up from his own chair.

'Yes... very..,' he spluttered, then attempted a recovery. 'Hello Miss Sirensong.'

Alicia crested the steps and stopped to gaze at the two males before her. Finally, she smiled, a full smile showing perfect, white teeth and slightly creasing the corners of her bright emerald eyes.

'Why thank you both – what charmers. It is lovely to see you again, Jason, but please call me Alicia... Miss Sirensong makes me feel so old,' her voice was soft and low, calming him despite the very bad thoughts he was trying to suppress about her.

Brash pulled out the chair to his right and Alicia walked sinuously around the table, her fingers tracing the tops of the chairs.

Brash and Jason sat down once Alicia was settled and almost immediately, Myers reappeared from the south transept. This time he was accompanied by two suited footmen carrying silver platters. The meal was laid out quickly – plates of cold hams, cheeses, breads, pickles and fruit, together with chilled water in iced crystal. Jason began to carefully load up his plate, terrified of dropping something and appearing gauche in front of Alicia.

'So you have decided to train with us at last, have you Jason?' Alicia asked, deftly spearing some meat with a serving fork.

'Yes, yes I have. I can't wait to learn how to use my Gift... oh,' Jason shut up, glancing over at the departing footmen and then up at Brash. Quietly, he asked '... I'm sorry, I didn't mean to... does everyone here know about the Gift and... things...'

Brash raised his eyebrows. 'We're a bit stuffed now if they didn't, aren't we...?' He left his words hanging for a moment, putting down his cutlery and reaching for some water. Then he winked. 'Actually, everyone who lives and works in the abbey itself knows about the whole of... our world. Do remember though, outside – even in Darkston Village, few people know anything apart from this is the head quarters of Drunken Abbot Industries. Nobody knows what we really do here.'

Jason nodded, then thought he'd take Brash's answer as an opening. 'What exactly are you doing here, Mr Brash? I mean, I know you're training people in Jakra and their Gift, but why? Dad said it was just the injured that came here... to be relocated somewhere safe?'

Brash nodded. 'Well, you know, Jason, the struggle doesn't just stop when you leave the Carpathians ... the injured or mentally broken Gifted can sometimes be brought back into the fight – rehabilitated if you like. And of course, many have Gifted youngsters who come back with them or they start new families here. The entire future of the Watch depends on safe enclaves like this to provide the next generation of hunters.'

'So you're training everyone here to join or rejoin the Watch?'

Brash smiled. 'They will be hunting down the Brethren one way or another, that's for sure.'

'And what do you think about joining the Watch?' Alicia asked, looking at him over the rim of her silver-rimmed goblet, her emerald eyes sparkling above the sun-shot crystal.

Jason tore his eyes from hers to clear his mind. He reached for his water and almost knocked over the glass. 'I still don't really understand what I'd be getting into... what the hunting is all about.'

'It might be easier to understand what you would be hunting before worrying about how,' Brash cut in. 'For that we need to flit through about six hundred years of history.' He swept his hand over the platters laid out before them.

'Help yourself Jason, this may take some time.'

Jason nodded and began to top up his plate as Brash began to talk.

'It began, as far as we can tell, towards the end of the Fourteenth Century. In the heart of the Southern Carpathian Mountains there arose a cult known simply as the Brethren. They were, in fact, an order of dark monks who had discovered what we now call the Rift. This is a sort of weakening in the barrier between this world and a many-layered dimension where demons are supposed to be sealed away from humanity. We call that the abyss.

Jason cut in. 'Sorry, but what exactly are demons? I mean, I've seen the films but...'

'No one knows for sure – the souls of evil human perhaps, the embodiments of evil acts, fallen angels, beings from one of the infinite planes of existence, dark gods, aliens? Now back to my thrilling history lesson, if you don't mind?' Brash raised an eyebrow and Jason nodded, mumbling an apology.

'So the Brethren worked out how to summon demons through the Rift. Only a few people were capable of summoning however, and as no one can control more than a single demon, we estimate there have never been more than a few dozen on this side. However, right from the beginning the Brethren always made best use of their summonings by attempting to possess the powerful - provincial nobility, army generals and religious leaders, that sort of thing. It worked and the Brethren began to gain power and influence in what we now call Romania.'

'After about a century of the Brethren's slow rise to power, the Watch was born. It started as a sort of pseudo-Christian faith that began to track down people who were rumoured to have special powers – powers to make things move, to perform impossible feats of strength, to become almost invulnerable to weapons or fire. Now in those days, of course, the choices for such people were fairly limited – hope nobody notices, run away and hide or be burned as a witch. The Watch however saw these powers as gifts from God which could be used to fight evil. So they began gathering these Gifted and their families together and hiding them away in remote locations to protect them against the witch hunters. Eventually, Gifted people started seeking out the Watch on their own, to join the one church who accepted them rather than burning them to a crisp.'

Alicia picked up the story in her velvet tones as Brash took a sip from his water, 'The Watch grew quickly. Family and friends of the Gifted often came with them and they helped protect the settlements. They began to travel out across Europe, setting up other small enclaves from which to track down more Gifted. They followed any rumours of people with strange powers and caught up with the families of those burned as witches and warlocks in case a Gifted parent or child had survived. To be seen to be on the right side of God, some of the Watch enclaves would portray themselves as witch finders, often in a life or death race to reach the Gifted before other churches.'

Brash coughed. 'This is my story, I believe, Alicia.'

Alicia raised her eyes with an indulgent smile then nodded for Brash to continue.

'So more and more Gifted were tracked down or found their own way to the Watch enclaves and they all learned from each other just what they could do with their gift from God. It wasn't long before they crossed paths with the Brethren – probably following stories of leaders who seemed to have inhuman strength and other "magical powers". Of course, they quickly realised these people weren't Gifted, but possessed, and so the fight began.

Hunted by the Watch, the Brethren were forced back into the Carpathians and turned to ever greater strategies of stealth, corruption and secrecy. Slowly the "normal" world forgot about them - blurring history into legend and legend into myth.'

'But you said the Brethren were getting stronger and beginning to win.' Jason said.

'For many reasons, Jason.' Brash said, topping up all their glasses with water and skewering himself some more cold meat. 'The balance of power between the Watch and the

Brethren has always gone in cycles over the centuries. Only certain people in the Brethren can actually summon demons – Summoners we call them, oddly enough. Similarly, only some people in the Watch are Gifted. As one side finds or draws in more of these special people then they become more dominant. What gives the Brethren an advantage is that one person possessed by a high order demon can empower and control perhaps a score or more humans by infecting them with their own corrupted blood – we call that Touching.'

'Dad told me a bit about that,' Jason said, 'the Touched people get stronger or something.'

Brash nodded. 'The victim then becomes like a… mini-possessed – they develop abnormal strength and some ability to heal its wounds.'

'How strong do they get?'

'It depends on the rank of the demon biting them but they would at least double their normal strength and resilience. They get a little stronger each time they're bitten… stronger but more desperate for human blood and flesh to replenish their own, demon corrupted body.'

Alicia cut in. 'Once they have been bitten three times they can never recover – they have too much demon essence in them and they can't live without it.'

'But why don't the victims just escape before then?' Jason asked.

Alicia pursed her full and lovely lips. 'Even after the first bite, a Touched is filled with a craving to return to the demon for more. Also, the Touching establishes a link with the demon – it can coerce them to its will and even tune in to their senses when they're close.'

'So, in today's world, the Brethren are winning for two reasons,' Brash pulled the attention back to himself. 'Their demons touch politicians, security chiefs, business heads… anyone who will be useful to them as they slowly spread out over Europe.

At the same time, the Watch has diminished - entire Gifted families have been hunted down and wiped out and others have left us - sick of the slaughter like your father or fearful of their entire family line being destroyed. We call them the Lost. Sometimes they come back to us or we find the descendents of Lost families from centuries ago but it doesn't happen enough and the Brethren sometimes get there before us.'

'So,' Brash smiled, 'you can see why I am so desperate to bring you into the fight.'

Jason nodded. 'That's another thing I don't really understand – what difference could I make? What exactly will I be able to do when I'm trained?'

Brash shook his head. 'Now the answer to that will come clear as soon as you begin to learn your Gift,' he pushed his chair back, slapping Jason on the shoulder as he stood up.

'Still, it may turn out that you're totally rubbish and no use to us after all.'

'Somehow, I don't think that will be the case,' Alicia purred, winking at Jason as she dabbed at the corner of her mouth with her napkin.

Jason stood up as Brash eased Alicia's chair backwards to allow her to stand. She smoothed down her bodice and skirts although there wasn't a crumb on her.

'Now, we need someone to show you to your rooms so you can change for a little Jakra assessment...' Brash said, drawing Jason's attention back to him.

Alicia looked heavenwards. 'Oh now, I think I might be able to manage that.' She smiled at Jason and raised both eyebrows a fraction. Jason's cheeks caught fire.

At that moment, Myers, who had faded away after serving lunch, re-appeared at the bottom of the stairs. 'Master Jason's rooms are prepared, sir. Shall I take him down?'

'That's all right, Myers, I'll take him.' Alicia said, stepping forward and slipping one cool hand into Jason's.

'I don't think so,' Brash said, his gaze flitting to their held hands. 'Jason doesn't need any distraction from his training. Myers can take him.'

Alicia made a disappointed face then gave Jason's hand a secret squeeze before she letting go.

'This way, Jason, if you please.' Myers said.

Jason walked down the steps to join the butler. 'Spoil-sport,' he heard Alicia petulantly whisper to Brash.

'You're not free to "sport" with anybody,' Brash replied, his voice sharper than normal.

Jason suppressed a grin and glanced back up the stairs. *Surely Alicia wasn't doing anything more than teasing him but Brash did seem perturbed by it all.*

Alicia smiled at him and Brash raised a hand. Jason gave a short wave back and turned to watch where he was going.

They were walking between the gothic bays and now he could see that in each bay, perfectly lit by gentle hues of natural and artificial light, were the most wonderful works of art.

Jason gaped at the treasures as Myers led him quickly clicking over the black marble floor. There were oil paintings in heavy, gilded frames; statues in all conceivable materials; sculptures; bejewelled relic caskets; cases of ancient jewellery and crowns; gilded and precious stone studded weapons and armour, all of it backed by ancient, golden threaded tapestries.

They stopped in front of the overwhelming black mahogany doors at the entrance to the church. Jason took the opportunity to look back down the aisle. Brash and Alicia had disappeared but from this distance he could make out the design on the stunning stained glass window behind the dining table - some holy man blessing the spirit of a deceased woman as it rose to heaven while his hooded disciples calmed the wild beasts of the forest... mainly wolves.

Myers slid aside a marble panel and tapped some lengthy number combination into a concealed keypad then pressed his thumb onto a small squared section.

There was a soft whirring and clicking and the doors opened effortlessly outwards. Myers led Jason onto the steps and twisted a golden ring on the outside of the still opening doors. They eased to a halt and began to close again.

Myers waited until the doors clicked shut. 'A word of warning,' he said, '- no one can enter or leave the church unless Mr Brash has released the master lock – do ensure you're not left in there when the master leaves the grounds or no one will be able to get you out until his return.'

'You could smash a window,' Jason joked.

'All bullet proof glass, I'm afraid, my young heathen,' Myers smiled and led the way down the dozen steps splaying out from the church doors.

They crunched across the gravel, hot and glaring white in the afternoon sun, passed the many arched doors of the garage and arrived at the sprawling three storey manor house on the south side.

The house was faced not in black marble, but in grey stone blocks laced with pale ivy.

'The Guest House,' Myers announced. 'It is a great deal more homely than the abbey, you'll be glad to hear.'

Jason smiled but then a movement caught his eye through a gap between the guest house and the end of the garages. A footbridge crossed the Darkston River and beyond that, two men stood half hidden, just at the edge of the valley tree line. They wore Brash Security blue with a holster openly strapped to their right legs and a rifle barrel rising over each of their shoulders.

Myers followed Jason's stare.

'Clumsy.' he tutted and pointed two fingers at the men like a gun. They sank back into the trees. 'They're meant to be discrete so as not to perturb guests and business associates.'

He led Jason up one of the twin bank of steps curving gently around a stone bench up to the doorway. To either side, two huge matching windows stared darkly out at them.

Myers lifted a cover to one side of the door and again tapped in a series of numbers and pressed his thumb onto a small pad. There was a tiny click as the door swung open and he led Jason inside.

They were in an entrance hall. A large fireplace, cold and dead now, dominated the far wall with a dozen white draped armchairs scattered around it. Statues leapt out at him from alcoves all around the wall – skeletal horrors, gargoyles and the odd knight in armour.

'I thought you said this place was homely,' Jason said.

'It softens somewhat with the fire lit and you students lounging around moaning about the Jakra masters.' Myers said, smiling. 'Come on, we had better get a move on. You don't want to be late for training, take my word for it.'

Myers quickly led Jason through a door on the left and along a corridor passed identical panelled oak doors, each with a tiny gold number in the centre and a gold rimmed keypad to the right. Then it was up a narrow stone spiral stairway to a second floor which was the same as the first.

Myers stopped outside door number twenty six and reached for the keypad.

'Three – Zero – three – two,' he said aloud as he typed in the numbers, 'and don't forget the thumb pad.' The door clicked open. 'Will you remember that?'

'You haven't got my prints on your system yet, though,' Jason said, glancing at the pad.

Myers just smiled and eased the door wide open.

Jason hesitated for a moment but it was obvious he wasn't going to get an explanation. He shrugged and stepped a little way into the room.

Inside, there was a carved mahogany single bed, a small wardrobe, one chair and a table with a small plasma screen television on it. A bay window stood open on the far side of the room letting in light and warmth from the afternoon sun. It had a seat built into the bay which would be perfect for flopping out on and reading. Another door led off to the right.

'The staff have placed some of our delightful training kit in the wardrobe for you. Don't be long... I'll wait for you in the entrance hall.'

'Okay,' Jason said.

Myers nodded and turned to go. 'Oh – press the gold button to get out. The red one is for reception.' Myers pointed to a couple of buttons on the left of the door then disappeared back down the corridor. The door silently closed by itself.

Jason walked over to the larger window in the bedroom. A slight breeze greeted him and he sat down on the red

248

cushioned bay seat. His room overlooked a small courtyard with an ancient tree growing out of the flag-stoned centre.

Three floors of windows identical to his stared back at him from all sides – each of them dark and closed.

There was a small gold button buried in the stone frame of his window. Jason pressed it and the window began to shut. He pressed it again and the window opened again letting the breeze and a soft rustle of leaves back in. Jason smiled. He liked this room already. Perhaps he'd stay in the abbey for a while especially if Dad gave him a hard time when he confessed he was going to learn his Gift with Brash.

Jason opened the wardrobe and found his training kit – close fitting but stretchy dark blue trousers, matching T-shirt and black trainers. He changed, pressed the gold button next to the door and dashed down the corridor to the spiral steps. Myers was just starting to come up.

'Ah there you are – I thought perhaps you had lost your way?' he said, turning around and leading him quickly back to the entrance room.

'Uhh, no, sorry… just playing with the window. Nice room.'

'I'm glad you like it,' Myers said, opening the front door using another gold-rimmed keypad. 'It is the same number as your room code to get in and out – in fact that personal number matched with your thumbprint will get you in and out of any of the permitted areas in the abbey.'

They didn't go back through the church but retraced Jason's first tour of the abbey by cutting through the garages, brushing passed a spectacular silver Aston Martin on the way, out across the still baking cloister, in through the office-filled chapter house where the pretty blonde woman smiled at him again, across the cool small garden and then away from the church door and into white corridor he'd seen earlier.

'Now, this is the infirmary corridor,' Myers explained, 'for the sick and injured to take their constitutional walks. The monks showed a little softness here as you can see – white and warm to help the healing. Come on, I'll show you the training rooms.'

They turned left towards a small door some fifty metres away. This one was inlaid with a small red cross. Jason felt chilled despite the bright sunlight. It was as if he was trapped in a labyrinthine mausoleum.

'I'll leave you here, Jason,' Myers said, 'I find all that sweating and exertion somewhat unpalatable. Just knock twice, open the door and wait to be invited in by the master in charge. Have fun,' he winked, turned on his heel and strode back down the corridor. In his black coat-tails he was like a bat trying to escape the shafts of sunlight.

And then Jason was alone, in front of the dark door with the white marble corridor blazing brightly all around him.

Chapter 16

Jason did what Myers had told him to do - knocked twice, opened the door and waited.

He was staring between two pillars into a huge white marble hall brightly sun lit through long, narrow windows stretching up into gothic arches high above.

Two pairs of blue clad students were sparring in half time on thin floor mats. They didn't break their concentration to even glance at the new arrival.

Suddenly Cadaveril strode into his restricted view from between the pillars. The chauffer was wearing black sparring trousers and jacket tied with a white sash cord. He totally ignored Jason and paced around the students, taking in every strike and block and hissing curt instructions and corrections. Every so often Cadaveril threw in a punch or kick of his own which the student had to fend off as well as defend against their opponent.

Great, Jason thought, *Skeletor also just happens to be some sort of Jakra master.*

Accepting that he was going to be kept waiting, Jason focussed on the students' techniques and the hints Cadaveril was giving them. The four students all looked a little older than him, perhaps in their late teens or early twenties. There were three boys and a girl.

The girl, perhaps about nineteen or twenty, was stocky and had brown hair tied back in a bun. She was fighting a spikey haired youth of perhaps eighteen. They were both very good but she seemed to be controlling the sparring.

The other pair looked like brothers with the same thin noses and lank, straw coloured hair although one was clearly a couple of years older than the other. Jason thought he could give all of them a run for their money but the girl and boy pair would be especially tough despite all the progress he'd made with Eddie's training.

Suddenly he noticed Cadaveril staring at him. He straightened up and gave the respect sign - right fist enclosed in left hand with a slight bow, eyes up.

Cadaveril returned it, his fist flashing into the open palm and leaving it just as quickly. Then he stopped the sparring with a word and beckoned Jason into the hall.

Jason stepped out from between the two columns and the huge training hall opened up around him bringing with it the smell of fresh sweat.

The room stretched for perhaps fifty metres to either side. Three large squares were marked out on the matted floor and all around the room hung the usual dojo paraphernalia of punch bags and balls, blocking posts and climbing ropes. However, there were also racks of wooden weapons – staffs, bo-sticks, wide bladed Chinese swords, Katannas, long-knives and even shurikens.

More intriguing than all of this were two mock buildings - one at either end of the hall.

'Hurry it up, lad – from all we've 'erd about you, you must've seen a training 'all before,' Cadaveril said, his London East-End accent echoing around the vast spaces.

'Sorry,' Jason said, stooping down to take off his trainers.

'Leave 'em on – ain't you got eyes? We've all got shoes on'

'Right,' Jason said, re-tying his laces and jogging over to Cadaveril.

'When you're being attacked by an 'undred bloodthirsty Brevren you aint got no time to take your shoes off, 'ave you? You've got to get used to the weight of 'em and know how much they hurt if you let a kick through.'

'Of course,' Jason agreed. He noticed the spikey haired student sneering at him.

'And you call us instructors – Master,' Cadaveril added.

'Of course, Master,' Jason said, keeping his voice level.

Cadaveril stared at Jason for a few moments, a slight smile jerking one corner of his thin lips into his pale, parchment-like skin.

Finally he turned to the others. 'This is Jason Willow – 'e'll be joining us... for a bit. I'm sure you've all 'erd the gossip – Mr Brash 'as big plans for him if we can train 'im up right.'

The students all turned to face Jason. The young woman smiled, the brothers nodded and spikey-hair just stared at him with an impassive expression.

'Hello.' said Jason, immediately feeling stupid for opening his mouth.

'Friendly, ain't ya?' Cadaveril's one sided smile twitched tighter still. Jason thought his face might tear. 'These will be your little playmates for this afternoon - Anna Smith, Carl Slattery, Marshal and Mark Martin. Marshal's the older one but just as fick.'

Jason nodded to them but stayed quiet this time.

'Just two rules here, Willow,' Cadaveril continued, still with his lop-sided smile. 'Do everything a master tells you and be ready for anything. You got it?'

'Yes, Master,' Jason answered.

'Are you warmed up?'

'No Master, not yet.'

'Good.' Cadaveril half smiled again. 'You won't get time to stretch out when they jump you in the alleyways or mountains of Romania. Learn to stretch out while you fight. Now, we'll start you at half speed with the younger Martin boy - the rest of you watch and learn Willow's weaknesses and strengths. Positions - go.'

Mark Martin trotted to the centre of the mat while the other three darted off to kneel at the edges. Jason quickly joined his opponent. Mark's face was unreadable but his eyes stared into Jason's. Jason raised his eyebrows once then dropped his gaze to focus on Mark's chest where his peripheral vision could detect every movement of legs, arms and head. His heart began to beat faster and he rolled his shoulders and flexed his fingers to loosen up.

'Half speed sparring - go'

Mark launched into a fairly fluid attack sequence of low kicks, punches and knife-hand strikes. Jason defended against them comfortably. He'd been doing this since he was four years old. He quickly picked up on Mark's tells – the tiny physical hints of an opponent's next move. One of the most obvious was that Mark always tilted his head slightly before side kicking.

Mark picked up the speed a little but Jason still blocked every strike easily then started some basic attacks of his own. Mark began to tense up and his defence started to rely on moving slightly faster than Jason's half speed attacks.

Jason stepped back, intending to draw Mark in then counter when suddenly his back leg was kicked from under him and he sank to the ground.

'Full speed - go' Cadaveril shouted, stepping back from sweeping Jason's leg from behind. Mark leapt forward lifting one leg high to smash down on Jason's stomach.

Jason deflected Mark's foot to the side of his body, rolled into the back of his knee and brought him crashing forward onto the mat. In an instant, Jason was on Mark's back holding one ankle in a painful lock.

'Lock on,' Jason said, calming his breathing.

'Marshal, full contact - Go,' Cadaveril shouted.

The older Martin brother sprang up and sprinted at Jason from the edge of the mat. Jason rolled away from Mark and flipped to his feet - only to have his legs swept from under him again by Cadaveril.

254

'Constant vigilance, boy – ready for anything I said,' Cadaveril sneered over him as Marshal arrived and stamped at his knee cap.

Jason only just twisted in time to avoid the full weight of Marshal's stamp but it still caught him a glancing blow.

Jason rolled and twisted around the mat trying to get to his feet but Marshal kept up with him, kicking at his legs and torso. Jason's movements absorbed the force of the blows but he couldn't gain enough distance to stand up.

He changed tactics, blocked a stamp with one leg and kicked the back of Marshal's knee with his other. Marshal went down and instantly Jason was on his back and locking up his right arm.

'Lock o…' Jason began, breathing hard.

'Smith, full contact. Go,' Cadaveril cut across him.

Anna Smith rose from the mat-side and trotted calmly in to the centre. Jason stood up, stepped backwards and blocked a trip kick from Cadaveril. It was like stopping a demolition ball but at least he was on his feet when Anna licked out her first half dozen punches.

She was fast, strong and very well coordinated, easily sequencing full speed flat-hand strikes, low kicks and elbow and knee attacks into her fluid fighting rhythm. Jason blocked most of it, but caught a numbing jab to his right shoulder and a couple of only half-turned kicks to his legs.

It was hard to focus completely on Anna knowing Cadaveril was dogging his every step and likely to kick, trip or pull him at any moment. She was too good for half his concentration however, and Jason put more strength and speed into his counter attacks desperately trying to find a weak spot. She was slightly slower moving than he was and he managed to slip three body punches through in a couple of minutes by blocking and side-stepping. They were solid hits but her counter attacks came on instantly and caught him twice.

Jason was breathing hard now. He'd been fighting solidly for perhaps five minutes. His guard dropped for just a moment and Anna snaked through a palm strike to his forehead.

Jason reeled backwards but as Anna stepped in to finish him he lashed out a basic front kick into her stomach. She doubled over and Jason chopped her neck at quarter strength.

As she dropped to her knees a hammer blow from Cadaveril hit him in the small of his back and he flew over her and fell sprawling onto the floor, winded.

'Slattery, full contact. Go' Cadaveril shouted, stepping away from Jason.

Instantly, fourteen stone of muscle and bone sprinted towards Jason as he scrabbled to his feet, trying hard to take in a full breath. Carl kicked him straight through his hasty block and Jason staggered backwards. Somehow he stayed on his feet to defend against a storm of rock-hard, relentless kicks and punches, giving him no chance to counter.

He survived for perhaps half a minute before some of the blows started getting through. Cadaveril kept stepping in from behind and slapping the side of his head as he desperately tried to avoid everything being thrown at him.

Carl managed to catch his nose and Jason's vision split into a million speckles of light. Through the starry veil he could just make out Carl taking the opportunity to pull his arm back for the finishing blow. Jason lashed out a snap-kick at Carl's knee cap.

Carl jerked down as his knee buckled and an instant later Cadaveril slipped in between them to simultaneously kick Carl and flat palm Jason's chest. Both students flew away from each other and sprawled out flat on the wooden floor.

'Time.' Cadaveril spat out. Jason heaved himself to his knees and faced the master. He glanced across at Carl who knelt facing Cadaveril, heavily favouring the knee Jason had just kicked.

'Aghh,' Jason suddenly clasped his arm. A four-inch dart stuck out from his right sleeve, its point embedded in his flesh. A burning sensation flared out from the shining steel.

'Constant vigilance, Willow.' Cadaveril said, his half-smile jerking back again. 'Now pull out the dart before the irritant spreads up to your empty head.'

Jason sucked in air through clenched teeth as he tugged out the dart and felt warm blood trickle down his arm. He stared at the reddened inch of steel that had been deep in his flesh.

'Both the Brethren and the Watch use poison darts,' Cadaveril explained, 'they're silent and poisons are more difficult to deal with than a bullet wound. These little trainers are nothin' the burnin' will ease off in a bit. P'raps it'll remind you to keep your eyes on me.'

Jason stared at him. Half his arm was roasting from the inside and it kindled a hot anger in him. He wanted more than anything to hurl the dart back at the sadistic git. Cadaveril just looked back at him, holding his half smile.

'We've got the antidotes to all the poisons they use but they do keep coming up with new ones. Best not to get hit in the first place.'

Cadaveril dropped his smile and nodded once. 'Now, you try to 'it me with it – go o...'

Jason flicked the dart straight at the man before he'd finished giving the order. Cadaveril sidestepped and caught it crisply between his index finger and thumb and replaced it in the folds of his sash.

A door opened behind Jason – the door to the white corridor he'd come in by. He just stopped himself in time from turning to look and kept his eyes firmly on Cadaveril. After a few moments Cadaveril glanced towards the door, straightened slightly and began to walk over to it, reaching to remove the white sash around his waist.

Carl stared across at Jason, eyes narrowed and slowly shaking his head. Glancing to make sure Cadaveril wasn't looking, he drew his finger across his throat and mouthed 'Next time...' at Jason. Jason winked and mouthed 'How's your knee?' back at him.

'No, no, Cadaveril, old boy, keep it on,' came a familiar, rich voice. 'Just popped in to see how young Jason is doing before we pack him off home.'

'Mat side - go,' Cadaveril barked. Carl rose painfully and hurriedly limped his way over to join the other students.

257

Jason followed him but knelt next to Anna. Alan Brash stood next to his chauffer-cum-Jakra master, smiling broadly.

'Done some damage, has he?' Brash asked, glancing at Carl.

'The boy needs a lot of work.' said Cadaveril. 'He tires quick and aint aware of nothing but his prime target.'

Brash's white-toothed smile broadened. 'Oh, I'm sure a couple more sessions with you will straighten that out. Now, Jason, time to get you cleaned up and back home. I dare say your father will be interested in where you have been all afternoon. I am sure Miss Smith can be excused long enough to take you back to the guest houses.'

Jason bit back a question. He thought he was going to start learning to use his Gift today. Now however, wasn't the time to ask.

'Willow, Smith - dismissed.' Cadaveril said.

Immediately, Anna stood, made her respect to Cadaveril and Brash and trotted towards the white corridor. As Jason followed her Brash nodded down at his bleeding arm. 'Hard lessons, Jason but they will keep you alive out there,' he said and slapped him on the shoulder.

Jason nodded and forced a thin smile. Brash winked and closed the door behind them.

Jason squinted in the still sun-bright marble corridor. Anna breathed out heavily and her shoulders sank as she relaxed. She stepped closer and looked at Jason's arm then shook her head.

'Cadaveril's such a... sadistic freak,' she whispered, glaring back at the door.

Jason smiled at her, rubbing several aching ribs. He didn't know whether to trust her or not – what if she went running back to Cadaveril with every bad word he was tempted to spit out about the man. He decided to play safe.

'He's only doing it to keep me alive, right?'

Anna raised her eyes and started to jog down the corridor. 'Maybe, but he enjoys his job too much. We'd better run – Bonehead will expect me back in a couple of minutes.'

Jason smiled – "Bonehead" was a great name for the skeletal Cadaveril. He followed Anna at a gentle run. Each step jarred in about a hundred places but at least his arm had stopped bleeding.

At the very end of the white corridor, Anna stopped and unlocked a door out into a rose garden in full bloom. It was enclosed on three sides by the abbey buildings but opened out onto the meandering river on the fourth.

'Pretty isn't it?' Anna asked, breathing in the sweet, heady fragrances.

Without waiting for an answer, she led him down a well worn stone path which wound through the garden and down to the river bank.

'What I said about Cadaveril, back there…' Anna said quietly, '…it's okay to bad mouth the trainers outside the training halls, you know…'. She glanced across at him with a wink, 'although there are cameras and microphones everywhere, so don't go too wild.'

Jason grunted again. He tried to loosen his aching shoulders and neck as they walked but that only made them tighten up further. Anna seemed annoyingly recovered from the sparring, however. She looked across appraisingly at him as they walked.

'So you're the "great hope" Eddie's been hot-housing are you?'

'The "great hope"?' Willow half laughed, trying to rub both his sets of ribs at once. 'I don't think so.'

'Oh you did pretty well, I thought,' Anna smiled – she had a big smile just like Alan Brash. 'Anyway, you must be pretty special because a tiddler like you should still be playing gangs and Pit-fighting at Silent Hill for another couple of years yet.'

Jason really didn't feel like chatting right now. He hurt all over and half his arm was burning and to top it all, he hadn't learned a thing about his Gift. Fortunately, they were approaching the south end of Brash's enormous garage block. The guesthouse and his quiet room lay just on the other side.

Anna turned to him, waiting for an answer.

'I am in the gang at Silent Hill but... um... I've sort of been suspended for a while, I think. Mr Brash said I should come to train here while I'm off school.'

Anna nodded. The path narrowed between the garage and the river as the guesthouse came into sight. Anna wasn't finished chatting yet though, 'I used to be in the Brash when I was there – a fighter of course, not a moll.'

'What's a moll?' Jason asked.

Anna raised her eyes. 'Duh... the pretties that swoon around the gang boys... the carrots to join and win fights.'

Jason stared blankly at her. Then as the word 'pretties' sank in he inadvertently flicked his eyes over Anna's well muscled but somewhat masculine frame and face.

She caught his glance and laughed, a little too harshly. 'Yeah, I know... good job I didn't want to be a moll, eh? Believe it or not, I do scrub up fairly well out of this training gear though.'

Jason felt his face redden. 'Sorry, I didn't mean...'

'Don't worry about it... I don't fancy you either – junior,' Anna grinned.

Jason relaxed a little. 'How long have you been training here – are you like a particular belt or something?'

'Oh I've been in this place forever and I'm really senior and important but we don't have belts - just students in blue, masters in black. In the real world you won't have any clues about how good your opponent is and if any Brethren actually got through to us we don't want to set out their targets for them. You don't even get to wear anything special if someone's Gifted like you.'

Jason stared at her. 'How do you know I'm Gifted?'

Anna gave her Brash-like grin again. 'You're the great hope, remember?'

They came to a stop at the foot of the split steps up to the guesthouse. Anna did some stretches to loosen up, chatting all the while. 'Now, do you remember your code to get in? Do you need your aunty Anna to help you in the shower?'

'No... I mean yes... I remember the code and...' Jason saw her smiling and calmed down. '... and I'll be fine getting into the shower on my own, thanks.'

'Excellent – are you back with us tomorrow?'

'Uhh – I'm not sure. I think so.'

'Good – I'll kick your butt properly then.'

Anna slapped him on his good arm and jogged back the way they'd come. He watched her run – strong and relaxed. He supposed that she might scrub up well after all but she was a bit old for him, of course.

And then he thought of what Anna had said – molls... carrots to lure in recruits... rewards for doing well. Was that really all Tanya had been – a bit of temptation to pull him in to the Brash? Had she just been doing her job?

He ran up the steps, punched in his code and thumbprint and shoved the door open. To hell with them all. He was always going to be rubbish with girls. He'd wanted to join the Brash anyway, push his Jakra, learn what his Gift can do... having a "pretty" to pull him in was just a bonus.

Jason stormed through the corridors and up the stairs. He'd show them - he'd go way beyond the pathetic Brash gang here. He'd be the fastest, strongest, most Gifted fighter they'd ever seen. Then Tanya would be begging to go out with him... instead of doing it because she was told to.

He'd showered and dressed within ten minutes and was on his way back across the entrance hall when he wondered where he was supposed to go now. It was getting on for five o'clock. Brash had said something about getting him home but how was he meant to get back there?

He opened the doors and his answer awaited him... in the shape of the silver Aston Martin Vanquish he'd squeezed passed on his way to training. A tall, sandy haired, young man in chinos and blue sweatshirt leant against one side of the gleaming bonnet.

'Hi Jason – want a ride home? Say yeah, because then we get to borrow this beauty.'

The man had a soft, southern American accent. He smiled, crinkling his lightly freckled cheeks and spread one hand over the stunning Aston.

'Sure.' said Jason, fitting in with the man's easy manner and trotted down the steps.

'I'm Lance Van Garde, a student of Mr Brash's.'

Lance stuck out his hand and Jason shook it. He'd a firm, enthusiastic shake.

'Uh… Jason Willow… school boy,' Jason smiled back.

'Well jump in, school boy.' Lance said as he strode around to the driver's side. Jason climbed inside to be gripped by the calf-hide seats. He felt like he was about two inches off the ground. Lance jumped in the other side and slipped a credit card-type key into a discreet slot. A red "START" button glowed on the centre of the dashboard. Lance winked at him and pressed the button.

The Aston roared into life then quickly settled to a purr of anticipation. The air conditioning kicked in, lights and dials flashed up green, Lance's thumb touched a small silver paddle on the steering wheel and they were off. Jason frantically tried to clip his seat belt as the Aston shot up the drive and pinned him back against the leather.

Small, green statistics and pulsing bar charts had flashed up in the bottom right of Lance's windscreen and the Americn kept glancing at these as the drive sped beneath the bonnet. Steering with just one hand, Lance ran his thumb over a tiny gold button on the steering wheel and the cab filled with Queen – "Don't Stop Me Now".

'You've driven this before then?' Jason said, forcing himself to relax and stretch out his legs into the cavernous foot well.

'Oh sure, dozens of times. Mr Brash is pretty generous with his toys… particularly if there's a lady I need to impress.'

'Mmm,' Jason swallowed awkwardly. 'Are you learning Jakra with Cadaveril?'

'Sure am, and the rest of the package – guns, explosives, swords.' Lance glanced across at Jason. 'And I get one-on-one with Master Schmidt… you know what that means, right?'

'Uhh – no.'

Lance looked back at the road just in time to avoid a tree. 'Gifted, am I,' he explained, in about the worst imitation of Yoda from Star Wars Jason had ever heard.

They skidded to a halt before the Abbey's gatehouse. Two security guards, each wearing a holster, stepped out from the guardhouse. One stood just to the side and front of the Aston, the other came to Lance's window which hissed down. The bass speakers thumped Queen out into the evening air.

'Van Garde, running Jason Willow home. Exit code GVL459' Lance said, not bothering to turn the music down.

The security guard unclipped some sort of palm top computer from his belt and thumbed a couple of keys.

'Have a safe journey,' he said, after a few seconds and nodded back to the guard box. The cross bolts slid back and the massive gates whirred open.

Lance hit the accelerator and the Aston wheel span under the arch and almost took off down the hill to Darkston Village.

'So what do you think of the old place?' Lance asked, swinging the car around a corner at eighty miles an hour. The tyres squealed but held steady.

'Umm, amazing… huge… black,' Jason ventured, not quite able to focus on conversation.

Lance glanced across and grinned massively, then looked ahead to take the next bend between the first set of cottages at the base of the hill.

'Oh yeah… all of that and more.' he nodded. 'Aint it just another world… so glad Mr Brash found me or else I'd still be festering in Hicksville, Alabama.'

'Mr Brash found you?' Jason asked, tensing as the windscreen display plummeted from ninety to sixty to take a particularly sharp corner. The engine roared in protest as Lance dropped a gear to give him more control.

'Yeah – a couple of stories in the local paper about… some weird stuff I did back home got picked up by his people and they brought a team over. There they found me – a barn blasting freak to my friends and neighbours but a World saving Gifted to Brash Industries.'

'Didn't your dad explain anything to you?'

Lance slowed down a little and his smile faded. 'My pa was killed when I was a baby – "family gunned down by drive-by punks" was the story. They tried for the buggy too but ma jumped in the way and lost half a hip for her trouble. We moved out of state and no one talked about it much after that.'

'That's horrible…' Jason began.

'Others have had it worse. Mr Brash reckons those punks were probably agents who'd tracked us down. He looked up the press stories – no one else on the street was shot and the papers said Pa had a reputation for doing weird tricks – smashing bricks and running his arm through fire – stuff like that.'

Jason didn't know what to say. Lance shook himself and hit the accelerator again. 'I sure as Hell am going to return the favour some day soon.'

'Are you going to join the Watch then, go over to Romania?' Jason asked.

'You need to ask?' Lance said, incredulous. 'Jesus, Jason, there are filthy, blood-sucking demons out there that nobody knows about and I have the power to take them out. Hell, yeah, I'm going to join up – maybe with the Watch or maybe I'll just hang with Mr Brash. He kicks demon ass his own way. Whatever,' Lance tapped the Aston's steering wheel and grinned, 'the payback is pretty good.'

Jason smiled back and looked through the Aston's steeply sloping windscreen. They were speeding past the pizza place where he and Tanya had eaten. Had she really just been his "payback" – was all the laughing and kissing just following orders?

Lance suddenly swung a left and roared off down a side street. Jason decided not to think of Tanya. 'How long have you been over here, Lance, in the abbey I mean?'

'About a year and a half. You wouldn't believe the stuff I've learned… Mr Brash and the other masters – hell - they pull it out of you. Back home I levelled a couple of chicken coops and stuff when I got mad but I didn't know how the hell

I did it. I sure ain't the most powerful guy here but Schmidt and Cadaveril together are using what I've got to turn me into somethin' pretty special.'

Lance revved to a halt at the main gate out to Drunken Abbot. Once again, two security guards approached the car but they'd no weapons showing. Lance gave them the same information and "exit code" and after checking a palm-top they were waved through.

'You know,' Lance began, wheel spinning the Aston through the gates so the back end whipped from side to side, 'the word is that you're something special yourself... Third Order even?'

Jason shrugged. 'What's Third Order?'

'You know – 6-6- something... Now I know we are not meant to talk about it but... Jesus, aren't you excited? With that sort of power you'd be treated like a god over in the Carpathians.'

'I haven't decided to join up yet. My dad used to be in the Watch but he doesn't want me to get involved with it all.'

'Oh, right... he's one of the quitters, huh?'

'I suppose so.' Jason said flatly.

They were silent for a time. The Aston roared through Drunken Abbot, past pubs just beginning to fill up for the evening. Angry, hate-filled glares followed but they were travelling in one of Alan Brash's personal cars and it seemed no one was stupid enough to attack it. Besides, Lance drove too fast for any bottle to have a chance of reaching them

Jason thought back to that night with Fast Eddie – fighting for their lives in the Abbot and Lashing and running from a beer crazed mob that would have surely ripped them to pieces.

In no time they were out of the town and speeding towards the Darkston Wick turning. Lance suddenly pulled hard left on the wheel and they slid onto the forest road to Darkston Wick. A moment later he skidded to a halt. Without saying a word, he lowered his window.

Lance breathed in deeply, drew his right hand in tight to his chest then with a huge exhalation thrust his palm through the open window. A spruce convulsed and the top half ripped away from its trunk and crashed into the trees behind then dropped to the ground in a hail of branches and leaves.

Lance turned to Jason, his eyes bright. 'You'll be able to do a hell of a lot more than that.'

'I quite like my trees in one piece, actually,' was all Jason could manage to say.

Lance grinned then his smile faded. 'Seriously - even if you don't join up, you need to be able to look after yourself - don't let anyone stop you learning, Jase, not even your pa.'

He held Jason's gaze and hit the accelerator. The Aston took off along the road and Lance finally looked where he was going. He pushed the technological dream machine ever faster through the trees. Trunks and branches whipped past them in a blur and in just under two minutes they burst out of the tree line to fly down the hill and slide to a halt in a spray of the Old Mill's driveway gravel.

'Dad will be out raking the drive smooth for hours tomorrow because of you,' Jason said, a half smile playing on his lips.

'You, Jase, have more important things to think about than raking the yard. Pick you up at seven sharp, right?'

Jason held Lance's gaze. 'In the Aston?'

'Or something better.'

'I'll be here,' Jason said and climbed out. He turned to thank Lance for the lift but the Aston was already speeding away, Aerosmith's "Love in an Elevator" blaring out of the open windows.

Jason turned back to the Mill House. Now it was time to really face the music.

Chapter 17

There were voices from the kitchen when Jason opened the front door – Dad, Miranda, Marakoff's vaguely Russian tones and Ilena Russof's calm, measured voice. Jason was tempted to go straight up to his room but decided against it. He might as well face them all now.

The talking stopped immediately when Jason strode into the kitchen. They were all sitting around the big farmhouse breakfast table with mugs of tea in front of them. Dad and Ilena were sitting very close together. Jason nodded a hello and headed straight for the fridge to dig out a can of Coke.

'Your taxis are getting classier,' Miranda said, breaking the silence.

Jason leant against one of the stone topped work surfaces and opened his can. He wasn't going to lie to them. 'I got a lift back from Darkston Abbey – I started training there today.'

Ilena and Marakoff glanced at each other and visibly sank back into their chairs as if to say "this is family stuff".

'And what about school?' Dad asked.

'Things are a bit… unsettled there. Mr Brash said I should stay away for these last few days of term... we wouldn't be doing much work anyway and…'

Dad cut him short. 'Is he intending to teach the Gift to you?'

Jason didn't hesitate. 'I think so, yeah.'

Dad was nodded, staring at him with steady eyes and his mouth in a tight line.

Jason dropped his gaze to take a drink from his Coke. No one said anything. Even Miranda kept her mouth shut for once.

Jason swallowed and carried on. *They weren't going to stop him doing this.* 'We've flogged this argument to death, Dad. I'm going to learn what I can do… Mum was murdered in front of me and Miranda was seconds away from being killed in Mawn. Whether I end up joining the Watch or not I'm never going to feel that useless again. If any of them come for us again I'm going to be ready.'

Dad shook his head slowly. 'It won't stop at that. If you learn your Gifts then, one way or another, you'll be drawn in to their world. You'll be too powerful to ever be left alone by either side.'

'They'll never leave us alone anyway, will they? One day they could find us here and a few Jakra kicks and punches won't be enough to keep us alive.'

'You can't fight them all, Jason – even if you had the very best trainers and the years it would take to learn everything. All of us only ever have a chance of survival by working in a team, a really close team, or by being totally hidden. Look at your grandfather – even with all his… fight, he set up home in the remotest place he could find.'

Jason bit back a reply and just grunted. He hated arguing with Dad. 'We've run away and tried to hide for the whole of my life and Miranda's – it doesn't work – they always find us,' he said finally. 'Why don't you teach me my Gifts so we can stand and fight?'

'No, Jason. I won't be the one to push you into that… that sick world.'

'Just because you quit, it doesn't mean I won't be able to handle it!' Jason snapped.

Dad's mouth shut.

'You're such a prat, Jason,' Miranda spat out, leaping to her feet. Dad instantly caught her wrist then gently pulled her back down into her chair. When she looked back up at Jason her eyes were shining but there were no tears. She took a slow breath and continued calmly. 'You can't even see when people are watching out for you, can you? Trying to stop you making huge great f...' she glanced at Dad, '... flipping mistakes.'

Jason put down his can and chewed his lip. Miranda was right - he was a prat. Why the hell had he said that about Dad?

'If I may say something?' Marakoff looked at Dad who shrugged an assent.

'I understand your wishes Jason,' Marakoff said, 'and your father knows that I would have you learn your Gift and join the Watch but my concern is Alan Brash. He is not the right person to train you. We have warned you already – he has no limits, no boundaries and everyone is a tool to be used by him.'

Ilena spoke up for the first time. 'You won't see this at first - he covers his tracks very well, as you say in English. In the Carpathians, all most of us outside his enclave only ever heard rumours of his... methods... there was never any proof.'

'Tell my dense brother what you told us about Brash.' Miranda said.

'One of the rumours,' Ilena said, 'was that Brash wasn't just killing the demons he hunted... he was trying to find a way to control them.'

'Redeem the possessed person, right?' Jason asked. 'Isn't that what we're supposed to do only it's too dangerous for most people?'

'No, you have not understood,' Ilena said, dropping her voice. 'Brash wasn't trying to remove the demon from the possessed person, he was trying to control the demon inside... just like the Brethren Summoners do.'

'And you're sure that's true,' Jason asked, 'that's definitely the reason they stopped him hunting?'

'As I said, all we have is rumour.' Ilena said, calmly.

'But they kicked him out for something.' Miranda added.

'Well I've got no choice have I?' Jason shot back. 'I'm going to learn my Gift and nobody else here will teach me anything,' Jason stared at Dad for a moment then shook his head. He reached for his Coke to take another drink.

'All right, enough discussion,' Dad said, his voice resigned. 'We knew this might happen and as I've said before, I can't stop you forever.'

He took a sip of tea, seeming to gather himself. 'I won't stand in the way of you training but there's just one condition – we keep talking. I want to know exactly what Brash or anybody else is teaching you at the abbey each and every day.'

Jason sat down at the table. 'Okay, Dad. I'll let you know everything and... well, thanks. And I won't decide about joining the Watch and everything without talking to you first.'

'Or me,' Miranda said.

'Naturally, Sis,' Jason said, 'when have I ever been able to leave you out of anything?'

'That's because you need my superior intelligence.'

Jason nodded – no point in arguing. 'Oh, one other thing. Brash mentioned sleeping over there, to really focus on my training... perhaps over half term?'

'Let's see how your first few days go first,' Dad said. 'It could actually work out if you do stay there as I'm thinking of travelling up to Mawn if I don't hear from your grandfather in the next few days.'

'I thought everything was okay up there.' Jason said.

'Well, that's what he said in that letter at the beginning of term,' Dad answered, 'but I've sent two back to him since and no reply.'

'That's not unusual,' Miranda mumbled.

'True, but he hasn't left it quite this long before. If that agent – Black - did let other Brethren know where he was going when he followed us…maybe a time-delayed email or 2nd class snail-mail to give him a head start at glory-hunting…'

'It's sounding a bit far-fetched, Dad,' Miranda said, topping up everyone's tea from the pot.

'Perhaps,' Ilena said quietly, 'but agents are always trying to impress their demon masters and obey the Brethren's strict rules.'

'I just want to be certain everything's all right up there.' Dad said.

'We'll come with you,' Jason said. *If Grandfather was in trouble then his training would have to wait.*

'Not this time,' Dad said, 'just in case anything really is wrong. Miranda will stay with Ilena and you'll be safe behind the abbey's ridiculously high security.'

'You don't really think anything's happened to the old git, do you?' Miranda asked.

Dad shrugged. 'Not really – most likely he's trying to get me worried because I didn't spot Black following us.'

Jason looked up at Dad who didn't meet his eyes. He was concerned after all, but obviously didn't want to talk about it now.

'It'll be weird you not being around the place.' Jason said, quietly.

'Tell me about it,' Dad answered. 'However, Marakoff will follow through on his retirement cover story and arrive at the abbey this weekend so he can keep an eye on your… indoctrination.'

Jason gave a tight smile. It felt as if he was pulling away slightly from Dad and Miranda and they were agreeing to let him go.

'Thanks, Dad,' he said, '… for letting me do this. I'll keep out of trouble.'

'Yeah, right,' Miranda said, looking pointedly at his various cuts and bruises, 'you're good at that.'

***

Lance van Garde picked Jason up at seven o'clock next morning, this time in a silver Jaguar XK8 convertible. Lance started off chatty, asking Jason how it had gone with his father last night but soon let the conversation drop, after getting little more than one word answers.

Jason stared out of the smoked-glass windows. Last night, worries about going head to head with Dad had been more or less sorted but that had just left more room for another one - *What if something had happened to grandfather?* As much as they didn't get on, Dad and Grandfather had always kept in touch with a fairly regular exchange of letters – basically to say they were both still alive.

As they passed through Darkston Abbey gates, Lance tried to make conversation again.

'You've been real quiet, Jase – you're not changing your mind are ya? You've a real chance here, buddy... I mean, maybe your pa gave you a rough time last night but... well, he'll get over it. Remember what I said - don't let anyone stand in your way.'

Jason took a slow breath and turned to face his driver. 'Don't worry – it's becoming clearer all the time how much I need to do this.'

***

'Go on, boy – finish him.' Cadaveril hissed.

Jason side kicked his staggering opponent and sent him crashing to the floor.

Cadaveril had matched him against two older and bigger students. Now they both lay flat out on the mat.

Jason made his respect to Cadaveril – his right fist of martial combat hitting the open left hand of rule-book and respect a little harder than was strictly necessary. His defeated opponents struggled to their feet and did the same.

'Not bad at all,' an unfamiliar voice pronounced from behind Jason. It was a powerful voice, clipped in Germanic tones and full of authority.

Willow kept his attention firmly on Cadaveril – remembering only too well the dart in his arm yesterday.

Cadaveril looked a little disappointed but after a moment said, 'Make your respect to Master Schmidt, Willow.'

Willow turned around to make the sign to this new master.

It was as if the man had just stepped out of some clichéd spy film – he was the archetypal villain's chief henchman. Tall, muscular, clean cut, chiselled good looks, piercing blue eyes and short, spikey blonde hair. He wore the same black, sleeveless T-shirt and trousers as Cadaveril.

Schmidt strode through the ten students kneeling around the edge of the mat and looked down at Jason, quickly appraising his body and then holding his gaze. Jason dropped his eyes. This man had a huge sense of presence, giving off an almost irresistible urge to do whatever he said, very quickly.

To Jason's surprise, Cadaveril handed over the white sash that had been tied around his waist. Schmidt nodded and put it on. Obviously relieved of command for now, Cadaveril made his respect to Schmidt and strode off the mat.

'Ready,' Schmidt snapped without warning and every student, even Jason's two battered opponents, sprang to their feet into Jakra's First Stance – left leg in front of right, knees slightly bent and fists up.

Twelve of them surrounded Jason, all older, all stronger.

Jason breathed in deeply and readied himself. He didn't have a hope against a dozen opponents of course but he'd go down fighting. Perhaps he could even up the odds if he drew the fight in to one of the mock buildings at either end of the hall - they wouldn't all be able to surround him in there. Scanning each of the fighters to cover any clue to his intentions, he judged the distance. Three, maybe four opponents at most would reach him before he made it to the door.

Everyone waited for Schmidt's command.

'You would have to be very good to make that run to the pub,' Schmidt said in his clipped tones. Jason didn't look at the Jakra Master – he was in the ready stance and now was expected to keep his attention on his opponents. *How had he known the plan?*

'Still, it was not a bad idea... far better than deciding to go down in open ground like some heroic English knight of centuries ago.' Jason kept scanning the students surrounding him. At any second, Schmidt could snap "Begin".

'Are you a coward, Jason... that you would run and hide in a pretend building rather than stand and fight honourably? Master Brash tells me your father was a great hunter... in his time. He would be ashamed to see you running away from a few miserable opponents.'

Jason would not be drawn. Insults had never had the slightest effect on him. 'There are too many to fight in the open, Master.'

'You think so? Would Master Cadaveril run and hide do you think?'

Schmidt started to walk around him now. Jason tried to stay relaxed and keep his vision wide to cover as many of the surrounding students as possible as well as waiting for an attack from Schmidt.

'Master Cadaveril is far more highly skilled than I am, Master – he'd have no need to take cover against this number.'

Leaning against one wall, Cadaveril snorted.

'Is Master Cadaveril stupid, Jason?' Schmidt asked.

'No, Master.'

'How many of these fit, well trained students would it take to hold one of Master Cadaveril' arms do you think, or pin one of his legs?'

'One... two perhaps.'

'I see twelve students about me, Jason. Two for each limb leaves four to break his ribs, crush his face, rip out his eyes and smash his wind pipe.'

Jason swallowed. All around him, the students waited. He didn't know any of the group and he'd hurt two of them.

Those two wanted revenge and every eye was fixed on him, every fist angled towards the new golden-boy's face.

Schmidt moved away to stalk around behind the students. He made small adjustments to their ready positions – a fist higher here, an arm slightly more bent there, right leg in a touch. 'I ask you again - would Master Cadaveril run into the pub?'

Jason resisted the temptation to twist a little to glance at Cadaveril. 'Perhaps he'd look for a better position, to limit the number of attackers.'

Suddenly Schmidt flipped himself right over one of the boys, twisted in mid air and landed directly in front of Jason.

He's Gifted then.

Schmidt stared at him. 'And me, Jason? Would I need to seek a "better position to limit the number of attackers" ?'

Jason didn't know how to answer. If he said no it might imply Schmidt was stupid, if he said yes, it would mean he thought Schmidt was no more powerful than Cadaveril.

Schmidt ended his dilemma. 'All on me, full contact – go,' he snapped.

Every eye widened in surprise momentarily then, an instant later, twelve well trained students swarmed forward to attack the master as Jason leapt out of the way.

It was like a whirlwind in reverse. Schmidt whipped his hands through the air in pushes, punches, side-swipes and sweeps and all around him students, still feet away, flew backwards, flipped sideways through the air and sank, pole-axed to the ground.

Three of the twelve actually managed to make contact with Schmidt. He blocked two in a flash of limbs, wrist locked one over and flick-kicked the other away. The third flashed a lightening punch only to connect with an invisible shield two inches in front of Schmidt's staring eyes and then suddenly flew backwards at a swat of the Master's hand.

Others scrambled to their feet for another attack. Schmidt actually smiled and held up his hands.

'Stop,' he said. His breathing had hardly quickened.

The students made their respect and sank to their knees.

Schmidt turned to face Jason. 'So - you have an answer. Sometimes there is nowhere to run and sometimes running blindly into unknown territory will lead you into much worse danger. With our Gift, we have a choice. It is time you learned what power you have. Come with me.'

Schmidt tossed Cadaveril the white cord from around his waist before walking over to one of the side doors. Jason jogged to catch up whilst, behind him, Cadaveril called the class to order.

'On your feet,' Cadaveril began, 'You were pathetic – the lot of you. You all know Master Schmidt's wonderful powers, yet you all ran at him like sheep. What if you did that against a turned Gifted or a puppeteer? You'd get more than a little bruise or bloody lip – they'd give your soul to their master and then I'd 'ave to kill you myself.'

Schmidt led Jason through one of two side doors on the east wall of the training hall and cut off Cadaveril's voice by closing the door behind them. They were in a narrow corridor with five small archways leading from it.

'The bars to begin with, I think,' Schmidt said and stepped through the an arch directly in front of them. The room beyond was perhaps twenty metres square with no windows and lit by small lights sunk into the high ceiling. A full length punch bag hung in the middle of the room but that was where training room normality ended.

At ground level it was like a silver jungle. Twenty or more shining rods rose up from the floor in pairs, each supporting horizontal bars at different heights. Stranger than that were another couple of dozen single rods, each ending in a flat disk to form stepping stones almost up to the ceiling. Finally, three thin metal beams stretched horizontally through the air, again supported by the metal rods rising straight out of the floor.

'What is this place?' Jason asked.

'These are for another day.' Schmidt replied, flicking one of a number of switches by the door. All the rods sank silently down and small covers slid back in the floor to reveal depressions the exact size and shape of the descending trapeze

276

bar, stepping stone or beam. In ten seconds, the incredible metal jungle had disappeared beneath a, once again, smooth floor.

Only the punch bag remained, heavy and black in the centre of the room.

Schmidt pointed to one side of the room and Jason crossed quickly over to kneel there.

'So. 'Schmidt said. 'Today we will try to bring out a small part of your Gift. It is not hard to do. Now you are of age you would begin to do some small things without any training at all, perhaps when you are angry or afraid... you may have already experienced this?'

'I think so,' Jason said, thinking back to the Pit and knocking Baldwin's legs out from under him.

'I and others will teach you many things here - how to control your powers, focus and strengthen them and reliably call on them whenever you wish. You must devote yourself entirely to the mastery of your Gift – learn quickly and well for the Brethren may find us at any time.'

'Yes, Master,' Jason said, wondering if Schmidt would ever get on with teaching him something.

'So – first you must understand that all of the Gifted's power comes from drawing in energy from around him. As you pull in the energy from the air, it hardens to become a solid of whatever basic shape you desire and you take its energy inside you to channel in many ways.'

Jason frowned. 'I'm sorry, Master, I really don't understand.'

'Of course,' Schmidt nodded, 'this is something unfamiliar. Let me try another way... do you make tea?'

'Yes.'

'Think if you filled an electric kettle with ice and switched it on. You understand that the curling metal element would become hot and pass its energy into the ice, which then turns to water and then to steam?'

Jason nodded.

'Good, imagine this backwards now. The element sucks in energy from the steamy air which turns first back into boiling water. It becomes colder and colder as more energy is pulled out of it and finally it turns back into a block of ice freezing around the element. Can you imagine that?'

'Yes, Master – I think so.'

'Good. Then see the hand of a Gifted as the element of the kettle. It draws in the energy from the air around it which turns instantly through a liquid and into a solid around his fist. Do you understand?'

Jason nodded again. 'Yes, I think so, but how do we... pull the energy out of the air and into us?'

'Ah, now if we knew that we could make machines to do it for us.' Schmidt shrugged – too human a gesture for the almost henchman stereotype. 'Now then, we will begin with the fist.'

Schmidt brought one hand slowly up and drew it back as if to strike, closing his fingers into a tight fist and breathing in slowly. The air shimmered around his hand, like a heat-haze in the desert. Schmidt held for a moment then punched forward into thin air.

Five feet away, the heavy punch bag creased double and flew back as if hit by a sledgehammer.

'So.' Schmidt said, looking at Jason, 'copy my movements to begin.'

Jason moved to stand by the master. For ten minutes they ran through the punch move, becoming perfectly synchronised as the punch bag swung slower and slower until at last it settled still.

They continued raising their hands, pulling back slowly, closing into a fist and punching. Schmidt talked slowly as they moved. 'Now – imagine your fist is a freezing rod being dipped into water – some of the water freezes all around your fist, taking on its shape like a cast around a broken arm. Breathe in slowly, deep into your stomach, hold and push out.'

Jason sank deeper into the rhythm. The physical movements were part of the Jakra training he'd been doing with Dad all his life. Oxygen filled his head, making him feel like he was floating.

'Watch just in front of my fist this time,' Schmidt said, still keeping their synchronised movements going.

As Schmidt slowly pulled his hand back into a fist, the space around his closing fingers shimmered again, becoming opaque, as if turning into a solid cast of his fist. Schmidt punched forward and the opaque air-fist hurtled into the punch bag, sending it swinging high again.

Schmidt carried on, his voice almost hypnotic now. 'I draw the energy deep inside me; the air hardens around my hand like a glove; I throw the energy back into the punch to propel the air-fist forward.'

Schmidt kept the practise going, with Jason following him in perfect time. It was almost as if one brain were controlling the two bodies.

'Concentrate on the air around your closing hand; imagine you're pulling a heavy weight towards you as you draw back your fist, your fingers closing. You're pulling the energy from it... draw it deep inside you, deep into your stomach.'

They continued the movement, flawlessly, breathing as one person now. Jason started to feel a tingling filling his fist and arm each time he drew it back, becoming stronger each time. In his stomach, it felt like a small sphere began to spin, sucking in energy along his arm.

'This time you pull the energy from the air. This time...'

Their fists began pulling back together for the hundredth time.

'... slowly pull now... pull the energy into your stomach... feel it being drawn through your arm...'

Jason pulled his hand back, closing his fingers into a fist. He imagined easing a hand full of clinging seaweed strands from a rock.

The sphere in his stomach whirled like a turbine firing up. A single pulse of heat surged up through his arm and was sucked into the sphere. All around his fist, the air shimmered in a solid cast.

'Punch,' Schmidt barked and Jason snapped his fist forward. The energy surged back out along his arm and the air-fist shot forward. A blink later, the punch bag creased in its exact centre and flew back, almost swinging to the ceiling.

Jason dropped his hands and stared, open mouthed, at the wildly swinging punch bag. He glanced at Schmidt and for the first time saw a look of surprise, almost uncertainty, crease those chiselled features.

Their eyes met and Schmidt's surprise vanished. 'We have not finished yet - keep with me,' he barked and Jason snapped back around to face the punch bag. Schmidt began to repeat the punch and Jason came back in synch with the master.

For the next half hour they did it over and over again, speeding up the move until Jason could draw back and throw the 'fist' as fast as he could punch with his own hands. This impossible power came easily now, as if he'd been doing it all his life… as if he'd been born to it.

Schmidt never praised him but pushed him to move faster and hit harder with the flying opaque air. Then they moved on – changing hands, punching with two fists, then on to chops, slaps, finger and thumb jabs, all with hardened, sculpted air, all with tremendous power that battered time and again into the punch bag. Each new move came more and more quickly to Jason. His head swam and his arms pulsed with the energy sucked in and pumped out by the flaring Catherine Wheel in his stomach.

Finally they stopped.

Jason knelt at Schmidt's signal. 'Thank you, Master – I… I can't believe I can do all that… after just an hour.'

'Your training is overdue and this is natural for us, a part of who we are. We are loosely linked when close to another Gifted - you would have learned even more quickly had your father consented to teach you – the link is many times stronger between family members.'

Schmidt's mouth tightened a fraction as if he was deciding on something. 'However, you should know that you have mastered the fist much quicker than anyone I have ever taught and your strength at this early stage is almost unprecedented. We do not discuss our generation so the

Brethren have no clue who to target but you must be highly Gifted... you should keep your development secret.'

Jason dropped his eyes. Such power... Dad could have taught him this weeks, months ago. If he could have done this when the agent attacked in Mawn or when Mum was killed...

Schmidt's voice cut into his thoughts. 'This rapid progress is, of course, good for us but it is also very dangerous. You have not had the months of struggle to become used to your power, to develop slowly and control your actions. You could kill the moment you leave this room today.'

Jason let Schmidt's words sink in as his energy-fuelled elation drained away. *How would it feel if he did actually kill someone, took their life, stared down at their dead face, no breath in their body? Had he been able to do this that night in Abbeywell Park when the Skins ambushed him... it could easily have happened.*

'So,' Schmidt said, 'you have much to learn yet – we have just scratched the surface. We will begin with control.'

And so they continued for the rest of the day, with a short break for a lunch of pesto pasta and bacon brought in to them by a smiling Myers. The butler ordered Jason to eat the energy boosting pasta if he wanted to survive the afternoon session with Master Schmidt.

Jason's appetite to learn was insatiable however, and he didn't seem to tire. Schmidt told him that was because he was using outside energy for his punches and blows and very little of his own – it was, he said, very unusual to do this so efficiently for an experienced Gift wielder let alone for someone so early in their training. The exertion would, however, catch up with him soon.

By the end of that first day, Jason had indeed learned some control. All the energy drawn in for a punch didn't have to be used in a single blow, it could be stored in what Schmidt called chi – the Catherine Wheel-like ball of energy Jason both imagined and felt whirling in his stomach. In fact, lots of energy could be built up for a massive attack or for astounding physical feats but, Schmidt said, they were weeks away from that yet. Learning to save some of the drawn-in energy at this stage did mean that Jason could tone down his air-punches to a light tap... sometimes.

As well as gaining a measure of control and practicing how to air-strike in every conceivable fashion, Jason also began to block with his Gift – forming the solid air not around his fist but stretching out his fingers to form a plate sized shield before his open hand.

'Adequate - that shield could perhaps stop a knife blade.' Schmidt told him after hurling air-strike after strike at Jason who stopped every one with shields in both hands. 'When you improve, you will be able to tighten the shield enough to stop a bullet and expand it to cover your whole body or even more.'

When they finally stopped it was early evening. Jason had been training for almost the whole day but was eager to carry on. Schmidt however, began warm down stretches and motioned for Jason to do the same.

'Thank you, Master,' Jason began, sinking into the splits, 'I can't believe what you've taught me to do... I feel invincible.'

Schmidt glanced up from his own full splits and flicked out one hand to the side. Jason's right leg flew out from under him and he fell flat on his face.

A memory from the fight in the Abbot and Lashing flashed through Jason's mind - something unseen had sent him sprawling that night as well, just as he was rushing to save Erin Brock from having her head bashed in. He shook his head and climbed back into the splits position. That was stupid - one of the semi-conscious bodies on the floor must have just managed to catch him.

'No one is invincible, Jason – never think that you are. You will face highly trained agents with the latest weaponry, invisible assassins, turned Gifted, Touched and worst of all, their possessed masters with the strength to crush your skull between their hands. The weakest Brethren informant can still kill you with a single bullet through the back of your head.'

Jason bowed his head and changed to side splits. 'Of course, Master – it was a stupid thing to say. I'm just so stunned by all of this. What will I learn tomorrow?'

'We have planned your training very carefully to produce the maximum results. Each day will bring something new for you as well as improving the things you have learned already. In two weeks, perhaps less, you should be able to confidently survive against any normal agent the Brethren send after you.'

Jason allowed himself a small smile. He'd never be as defenceless as that day on Mawn ever again.

Schmidt straightened up from his cool down. 'You would develop even faster if you were staying in the abbey – we could start earlier, finish later and you would not lose your focus.'

Jason dropped his eyes. Dad had said see how the first few days go before staying over. Besides, he wanted to get home to see if there was any news from Mawn. 'I should be allowed to stay over the half-term holiday.'

Schmidt was as impassive as always. 'That is something, I suppose. Go to shower in the student house now - someone will meet you there to take you home to your father.'

'Yes, Master,' Jason said. He made a deep respect and left quickly.

The student quarters were deserted when he eased open the huge door into the entrance hall. Jason wasn't surprised as there had been plenty of chat and crockery clashing in the refectory as he'd followed the river back from the training hall. Schmidt had not suggested he go in there to eat with the other trainees – perhaps he was making a point about Jason choosing not to fully integrate with abbey life yet.

Once back in his room, Jason quickly showered and changed back into the jeans and black tee shirt he'd taken off that morning. Was it really only a few hours ago that he didn't have the first clue how to use his Gift?

Lance Van Garde was waiting for him in front of the guest house when he stepped outside.

'I can do it, I can use my Gift,' Jason shouted, jumping down the steps.

Lance smiled. 'My, it sounds like someone has had fun today.'

Jason leapt inside the car, a black Porsche 911 this evening, and began telling Lance all about his training from the first punch to the last double shield block against Schmidt's storm of air-strikes. He didn't draw breath until they were heading out of Drunken Abbot.

'You've learned a hell of a lot in just a day.' Lance whistled. 'I don't recall any novice here taking to it so fast. You should stay over - the things you learn when you're a real part of this place – training from dawn 'til dusk, then chewing it over with your buddies half the night.'

Jason shot a look across at Lance. *Had Schmidt put him up to this? What was it with these people, what was the rush for him to progress so quickly? Surely they could see how keen he was – he was going to keep on coming back. What difference would a few nights break from training make?*

Lance glanced back at him good naturedly. It hadn't seemed like a loaded statement.

'I promised my dad that I'd come home each night until the holidays.'

'D'ya think he'll really let you stay over the vacation – he isn't just trying to put this off?' Lance asked, raising one eyebrow. He turned back to his driving – already flying along a main street out Drunken Abbot.

'No – Dad isn't like that. Another three nights and then I'll be staying over for a week.'

Lance shrugged. 'If that's how it's gotta be, I guess I'll have to keep fetchin' and carryin' ya 'till then. Still, not such a bad deal if we get to play in these little beauties,' he stroked the Porsche's black leather steering wheel and swung a left into the little forest road to Darkston Wick.

Several heart-stopping minutes of forest road driving later, Lance skidded the Porsche to a halt in the Old Mill's driveway.

'I guess I'll be seeing ya in the morning then, huh?' Lance asked.

'Early as you like,' Jason said, grinning, 'I'll probably learn to fly tomorrow.'

He climbed out of the car and leaping up the steps into the porch.

It was only when he turned to watch Lance speed away that he remembered Schmidt had told him to keep quiet about his rapid progress.

Chapter 18

Dinner wasn't as awkward as Jason had expected. Dad chatted easily enough over his speciality meal of shepherd's pie with double cheese topping and Miranda must have had special instructions not to pester him about what had happened at the abbey.

Jason was desperate to talk about learning his Gift however - what sort of things he'd learned to do already and ask Dad just how powerful did it get. It was obvious after only a few minutes, however, that although Miranda was fascinated, Dad was finding it difficult, so Jason played down his excitement as much as he could and reluctantly moved on to other things.

They discussed going back to school after half term and how Jason was going to keep out of trouble and stop fighting for the Brash in the Pit now he'd moved on to proper training in the abbey. Although the majority of the Skins held no fear for him now, Jason still balked at the thought of leaving the magnificent abbey for the grey granite menace of Silent Hill.

'Any letter from Grandfather yet?' Jason asked over the washing up.

Dad shook his head and the conversation stopped there. It looked like Dad was going to make the trip up to Mawn after all. For the first time, Jason started to worry about what Dad would find up there.

Finally Jason said goodnight and went for a soak in the bath. Just as Schmidt had warned, the hours of training finally caught up with him. Exhaustion washed over him with the hot water and he had to virtually crawl into bed.

The next morning, the Wednesday before half term, Lance picked him up at about seven and he was back under the scornful eye of Cadaveril in the main training hall by eight. There must have been fifty or more students training that morning, ranging in age from late teens to perhaps early forties. They were spread out across the three training squares, along the wall bags and blockers and in both the building simulations at either end of the hall.

Jason was grouped with the students he'd fought on his first day at the abbey – Anna Smith; the lanky, thin-nosed Marshall brothers and Carl Slattery, the heavily muscled, black spikey-haired, twenty year old.

Cadaveril worked them all hard for two hours before Schmidt emerged from the 'training pub' and signalled for Jason to follow him into the side training rooms. Anna winked at him as he turned to follow Schmidt although she was careful that Cadaveril didn't see her momentary lack of attention. Carl, who had beaten him in two out of their three non-Gift Jakra bouts that morning, sneered with a particularly effective curled lip. Cadaveril, for once, seemed to ignore one of his students being distracted.

Once in the side room with Schmidt, however, everything but the Gift was swept from his mind. He learned to strike with fist, chop and finger from point blank range up to six or seven metres away and with more power than any punch or kick he could deliver physically.

It all came so easily to him – he just modelled Schmidt's actions, working in perfect time with him and almost always, he succeeded the first time he called on his Gift. The energy ball he'd felt in his stomach yesterday - his chi - felt larger somehow, sucking in the air's energy quicker, rotating faster and pulsing out power more easily than ever. Schmidt told him that the more he practised, the more power he could pull in, store and push out up to a maximum that his level allowed. Without practise, that capacity shrunk. Just like a muscle – use it or lose it.

Striking wasn't all Jason worked on. He improved his shielding, using both hands to spar with Schmidt with ten feet between them. The shimmering air fists and fingers that punched, chopped and jabbed at him were now as clear as flesh to Jason's eyes and he found it natural to block the casts of solid air with his own hazy hand-shields.

Schmidt must have been satisfied with his sparring as, after another private lunch taken in the training room, they moved on to something very different.

Schmidt pressed some of the buttons by the door and the metal disks Jason had seen when first entering the room hissed up from the floor on their thin silver rods.

The master didn't explain why, but simply told Jason to walk a particular route over the stepping stones. Luckily, with a lifetime of Dad's balance "games" behind him, he stepped and jumped along the half-metre disks confidently, even five and six metres up.

Schmidt made him repeat the route again and again, faster each time. Then he had do it while dodging air-strikes from Schmidt. After half an hour, Schmidt hit more of the switches and the thin beams and trapeze bars hissed up all around Jason and they were added to his route.

After perhaps an hour, just as Jason leapt for a bar, twisting to avoid an air-jab from Schmidt, he glimpsed Alan Brash standing at the open door.

Jason flipped off the bar and landed on one of the disks. He wobbled slightly, six feet up, but then stabilised himself.

'Enough. Come down now,' Schmidt said and turned to make his respect to Brash. Jason dropped to the floor and did the same.

'I hear it's going extremely well, my boy, faster than any of us had expected,' Brash said, stepping into the room.

'Thank you,' Jason said, glancing around the jungle of metal rods. 'The Gift is amazing although I'm not sure what all this has to do with it,'

'Oh, you'll find out tomorrow if I'm not very much mistaken.' Brash answered. 'There are so many things you can learn to do – it's not all smash and block. The power must become second nature to you, like using your own hands or feet – just a thought and it happens. There is no time to prepare and concentrate when a demon is intent on ripping your throat out.'

Brash pulled the door closed behind him and flashed his big generous grin. 'Still, that will come in time. Now let's see what you have picked up so far, shall we? Attack me from there.'

The gleaming apparatus whispered back down into the floor and the covers slid into place.

Jason swallowed hard and made his respect. He was desperate to show what he could do. Without warning he threw three rapid air-punches at Brash, instantly followed by flick kicks and chops. Brash easily blocked them all with Gift-shielded hands but that only made Jason try harder. He threw out more and more attacks, each one faster and harder than the one before. The ball of energy in his stomach span wildly, pulsing out energy quicker than ever.

Brash blocked or dodged every attack but his easy smile hardened in concentration. Jason tried something else – an air sweep to Brash's lower leg and ankle, one way then the other. Brash leapt over both sweeps but Jason threw pinpoint-accurate finger flicks to the knees and temples, simultaneous double punches and snap-kicks to three separate body areas. Brash's smile dropped away but he blocked, side stepped and twisted his way out of each attack like a grand master half his age. The dodged and deflected air-strikes battered into the walls to hammer out stone chips and dust clouds.

'Time.' Brash said at last.

Jason stopped immediately, made his respect and stood at rest, trying to calm his breathing. He felt drained. His attacks had been so intense that he'd used up more energy than he'd been able to pull in from the air. Also, all the air-strikes still required hard, fast movement and massive concentration – a little like shadow boxing. His legs began to tremble slightly and sweat trickled down his face and back.

Mr Brash ignored Jason's exhaustion and looked around at the minor damage to his training room.

'Amazing Jason, absolutely amazing - especially for only two days training. I know only too well the skills of my most senior master,' he nodded to Schmidt respectfully, 'but this progress… this is also down to you, to your generation. It is as I suspected - only a triple six could possibly learn this quickly and draw such power so early on.'

Jason nodded, a grin spreading across his own face. Triple six – Louisa had mentioned that before but he still didn't really understand what it meant. Before he could ask, Brash walked over to him and clapped him on the back so heartily he nearly fell over.

'You're going to be our greatest asset, Jason – but we need you strong very quickly and you need to learn not to drain your energy so. You must keep a balance between what you draw in and what you push out.'

'You're telling me,' Jason panted.

Brash smiled. 'These are dangerous times – at some point the Brethren are bound to discover us here and the residue of your powerful Gift…' he shivered in the cool, energy drained air, 'will draw them straight to you. Your father has explained about the signs left by using the Gift, I hope?'

'A bit, yeah,' Jason said, 'the wind… zephyr thing?'

'Exactly – the air is pulled in towards you when you draw power and with the strength of your Gift those ripples of could run out for miles. Then there is this chill, of course – it takes several minutes or more for the air to warm up again after you have sucked the energy from it.'

'Dad said that's why it's dangerous to learn this stuff.'

'Indeed,' Brash nodded, 'a Catch 22 situation – don't practise and be defenceless, do practise and risk drawing in the Brethren. Still, we are shielded here to some degree - no zephyr, not even yours, can ripple out through the solid rock of the valley sides.'

'So we're safe to practise here?' Jason asked.

'Nowhere's safe, dear boy – they could stumble across us at any time. You need intensive training so you're ready for them – I want you to be here at the abbey full time.'

Jason dropped his eyes. He could understand the argument but he was beginning to get sick of the pressure to draw him in to Brash's little empire full time.

'I'm really keen to learn, Mr Brash, but Dad's finding all this hard enough – I promised I'd go home for the first few nights so he knows what's going on.'

Something flashed across Brash's face, almost a spasm, pulling his usual toothy smile into a snarl. The expression was gone in an instant, happening so fast that Jason wondered if he'd just imagined it. When Brash spoke, his voice was calm, if cool. 'And if he then decides he doesn't want you to stay over at all?'

'He won't. He's happy that I'll be safe surrounded by abbey security while he's away...' Jason let his voice trail off. He didn't want Brash wandering where Dad was going.'

'I see,' Brash said, visibly relaxing. He paused for a moment. 'Your sister could, of course, stay here with us as well... if your father is going to be away for some time?'

Jason swallowed. It was phrased as a question but Jason had no intention of telling Brash where Dad was going or for how long. 'Oh, I think she'll be fine, thanks. I don't think Dad would...'

'... like Miranda staying here?' Brash finished for him. 'Your father doesn't really trust my intentions at all, does he? He stared at Jason without saying anything for a while longer.

Finally he nodded. 'As you wish, Jason. Work hard – half term will be a big week for us all,' he turned and walked to the door which flew open before he reached it. Both Jason and Schmidt made their respects to his back, only straightening up when the door slammed shut again at the twitch of Brash's finger behind his back.

Schmidt looked at Jason with an unreadable expression. 'So... we will continue. We have much to do.'

✳✳✳

The next two days training at the abbey were even more intense. Jason learned very quickly why he'd been drilled on the silver disks and bars for hours on Wednesday – it was because on Thursday he learned to replicate the apparatus from thin air.

Schmidt taught him how to form the small stepping stone disks, the trapeze bars and the thin beams, all supported by air-rods dropping down to merge with the floor below. It was difficult at first, very difficult. Jason kept losing concentration and the half formed shapes under his feet would shimmer and disperse back into air as they drew back energy from around them. By the end of Thursday however, as well as having sparred with Anna, Carl and the Marshals for two hours and air-fought with Schmidt on and off the steel apparatus for half a day, Jason had mastered forming the stepping stones long enough for him to walk up three of them and back down again.

Schmidt had grudgingly admitted that it took most Gifted weeks to gain that level of control.

More of the same followed on Friday but a long run all through the abbey's magnificent grounds was thrown in to the schedule. Schmidt made Jason form low air-stones to cross the Darkston River which meandered through the length of the abbey's grounds. Drawing the energy from the water to form the base of the supporting rods was harder than pulling it in from air but Jason managed it after three dunkings.

The last session on Friday was a fight against four adult students. All of them were helmeted, heavily padded and armed with wooden batons. For the first time, Jason was allowed to use his Gift in sparing. It took him two heart pounding minutes and three whacks with the batons before all the men stayed down and Schmidt called a halt.

Then he'd been told to shower, go home and say goodbye to his family for a week.

And that was it. No 'well done' or 'looking forward to you staying with us over the holiday'. Just a range of surprised to envious looks from his beaten opponents and Schmidt impassive dismissal.

Jason felt that tomorrow he'd be walking into a den of lions and asking for a sleepover.

***

The following morning, the first Saturday of half-term, Jason woke up aching and bruised. His alarm showed it was six a.m.

Groaning, he crawled out of bed and headed for the shower. Last night Miranda had been waiting for him with Dad and they'd all eaten a late supper together. Over one of Dad's dodgy chicken curries, the three of them had eased closer again now the arguing about Jason's training was over. They'd agreed to get up early for a last breakfast before Jason went to the abbey for a week and Dad drove up to Mawn.

When Jason came downstairs, dumping his small backpack of clothes in the hall, Dad was just finishing a pile of bacon sandwiches. Miranda was slumped over a cup of tea at the table – she wasn't always at her sparkling best in the morning.

'Just in time,' Dad said, dumping the plates and a steaming fresh pot of tea on the table. 'Tuck in before Brash sends his henchman to kidnap you the moment my back is turned.'

Jason sat down and grabbed a sandwich. 'Dad – I forgot to tell you... I let it slip to him that you were going away.'

'Oops,' Dad said as he shoved a sandwich under Miranda's bowed head. He was obviously in his "keep everyone cheerful" mode. 'Oh well – I'll just have to do some fabulous driving to lose anyone he sends to spy on me. I'll set off later in the day and disguise it as a trip to Morrisons.'

Jason nodded. 'Sorry about that.'

'It happens when you have no brain,' Miranda mumbled, as she sniffed at her bacon.

'Morning Sis,' Jason said and messed up her hair. 'Looking good today.'

'Now before you two start cuddling because you're going to miss each other so much,' Dad cut in, 'I want to make sure you've got things straight in your heads.'

Jason grunted. 'We went over this last night.'

'Go on then – tell me what you've managed to remember,' Dad said.

Jason raised his eyes – his father was such a teacher. 'You're not using the motorways, stopping over somewhere this evening and should be in Mawn by late tomorrow night where you'll argue with Grandfather then be back down here by Tuesday afternoon.'

Miranda took over. 'You'll phone me at Ilena's at eight o'clock, morning and night, from a payphone.'

'And Marakoff will be coming into the abbey sometime over the weekend under his cover story of
relocating here to retire,' Jason finished.

'Excellent,' Dad beamed, 'you two do occasionally listen to your wise old pop after...'

The crunch of a car skidding on gravel cut Dad short and a horn blared.

Dad sipped at his tea. 'One day I'll make that boy rake the drive back into shape himself.'

Jason glanced at his watch – Lance was ten minutes early.

Suddenly Miranda threw her arms around his neck in a death grip and cuddled him. Wisps of her less-than-perfect bed-hair tickled his nose but he put up with it.

'Be careful and don't get too beaten up every day.' She mumbled into his neck.

'Thanks for the vote of confidence,' Jason said, gave her a quick squeeze and tried to stand. After a moment she let him go.

Before he could manoeuvre away from the table, Dad snaked an arm around his shoulders and pulled him into a bear-hug.

'Dad!' Jason complained but gave him a quick arm-around before weaselling away.

The horn blared again.

Dad walked him out to the hall. 'Try to phone Miranda from the abbey – the call will almost certainly be recorded so be careful what you say. Marakoff will contact you once he's in the abbey – but remember to act like you don't know him.'

'Yes, Dad, I'm not stupid,' Jason said, picking up his backpack.

'Duh!' Miranda said, making a stupid face.

'Still looking good, Sis,' Jason grinned.

'Be careful, Son,' Dad said and the pretence of light hearted banter faded.

'I'll be fine,' Jason said. His face must have shown how uncertain he was feeling and Dad grabbed him in for another hug. It was useless to fight it – his father was very strong.

'You'll both be safe as houses, Son – I wouldn't leave you otherwise. You just stay in the abbey grounds.'

Jason nodded into Dad's shoulder and a moment later was released.

Lance sounded his horn for a third time and Jason grabbed his backpack in the hallway.

This was it – he would be sleeping apart from his family for the first time, would come back to them with the devil-knows-what abilities and might have decided to join the demon hunting Watch by the end of it all.

The next seven days could change his whole life.

Stopping himself from chewing his bottom lip, he opened the door.

Chapter 19

'You're going to have a hell of a time, Jase.'

Jason sat in the superb Aston Martin Vanquish with Lance Van Garde. He stared at the long, low block of arched doors which stabled the rest of Alan Brash's collection of fabulous cars and nodded.

Lance slapped him on the shoulder. 'Don't sweat it – we'll be nice to you... for a while. Now – orders are for you to get changed in your room then follow the river to the refectory back door, okay - your training buddies will be just finishing up with their morning run and you're supposed to go in to breakfast with them.'

'Right,' Jason said. 'Thanks for the lift – last one for a while.'

'About time,' Lance said.

Jason nodded and got out. He jogged into the silent guesthouse, typed in his code and pressed his thumb to the pad. Inside, the place was deserted. He hurried up to his room and found three new training kits hanging in his wardrobe.

He quickly changed and left the silent building. Glad to be outside again, Jason walked between the guesthouse and the end of the garage building down to the river. A group of Jakra students were spread out on the grass – some stretching, some flat on their backs.

He spotted Anna Smith straight away, then the Marshal brothers and Carl. It felt strange – were these to be his friends now – replacing Louisa and Mouse... at least for the next week? He took in a slow breath and started forward.

Carl, stretching in a full splits, saw him first and his lip sneered up to one side.

'Nice of you to turn up, hot shot. Too good for the morning run, are you?' he shouted over the burble of the river. The rest of the students all fell silent and turned to look at him.

Carl straightened up. He wasn't finished yet. 'Suppose you think you're the big hero now Schmidt has taught you some magic tricks?'

'I sort of thought that we're all meant to be on the same side,' Jason said, his voice calm as he joined the students, '...that the Gifted, big heroes or not, were part of a team all trying to keep each other alive.'

Carl took a step closer to Jason. 'The trouble is that it's two way – us lowly shields have to depend on you magic boys as well. I don't want to trust my life to some jumped up kid who thinks he knows it all.'

'As if I think I know it all...' Jason began but Carl was already turning away and sinking into another stretch.

'Carl, darling smiling one...' Anna sat up from being flat out on the river bank. She smiled broadly at Jason, her slightly crooked teeth glinting in the morning sun and then turned back to Carl. '... a little grumpy after our trot around the grounds, are we?'

Carl totally ignored her and made for a small wooden door into the abbey.

'I'm not sure you're helping, Anna.' Marshal Martin, the older of the two brothers, said as he rolled out of his stretch and began to follow Carl. 'Wait until he's had something to eat.'

Anna blew Marshal a kiss and moved over to Jason. 'You're not a grouch in the mornings as well, are you?'

'No – I'm all sweetness and light.'

'Good. How are you feeling about moving in for a while?'

'Really welcome.' Jason said, watching Carl disappear through the small door.

'Oh don't mind Carl, he's like that with everyone. Now, that is the refectory,' she said, '– where you eat with us low-lives if you're not being served exclusive little lunches in your private magic training rooms.' She lowered her voice a little as the rest of the students started drifting away into the refectory. 'A word of warning – don't go telling people like Lance how well you're doing. It gets around and makes people like Carl… even less happy.'

'Okay,' Jason said.

'Come on, lets eat before security scoff it all.'

The refectory was a huge eating hall. Three trestle tables, each able to seat perhaps forty people, stretched the length of a sunken floor and an impressive set of steps led back up to a grand double door at the far end of the room. The sun streamed down in dusty rays through arched windows high on the east wall to shine on a fourth table draped in white linen and laden with all the ingredients for a full English breakfast – bacon, eggs, mushrooms, sausages, tomatoes, black pudding, fried bread, toast, jams, juices and pots of tea and coffee. The room hummed with the soft talk of perhaps sixty people – mainly Jakra students, but with some dark blue uniformed security guards scattered amongst them in groups of three or four. The guards all had some sort of machine gun leaning against their benches.

'Real food,' Anna said and skipped down the few steps to the sunken floor and over to snatch up a wooden tray. Jason, his stomach rumbling despite Dad's bacon sandwiches earlier, followed her.

The two of them joined Carl and the Martin brothers after loading their trays with breakfast. No one chatted very much as they all seemed intent on wolfing down their food. A large, roman-numeralled clock ate away the minutes.

'Time to get hurt,' Anna announced at 8:25 precisely. The five of them dumped their dishes in bowls of water in one corner and left through the small door with a stream of other students. They turned left and followed the river until they reached the door into the long, white marble infirmary corridor which led to the training hall.

'You know,' Anna said, as the sound of chatter echoed around the brilliant, sun-glared walls, 'this bit used to be the monk's infirmary - the hospital. Not very encouraging is it – training in a hospital? Sort of gives you a bad feeling about where you're going to end up.'

Master Schmidt was waiting for them in the centre of the mat. He quickly distributed groups of students with other masters into the mock buildings and smaller rooms where Jason had been learning his Gift. Finally there were just about a dozen of them left.

Jason waited, glancing at the other students kneeling around the mat. None of them looked back at him. Their eyes were all fixed on Schmidt. Remembering Cadaveril's harsh lessons, Jason quickly returned his full attention to the master.

'Jason in the centre. The rest of you – full body armour and one weapon of your choice. Go.'

Jason stepped on to the thin mat and walked to the centre to stand next to Schmidt. The other students trotted to different places on the walls and chose from various wooden swords, staffs, shuriken packs and knives. Then they quickly grabbed thin flack jackets, shin pads and helmets from racks and returned to the mat edge where they began to suit up.

Jason began to have a bad feeling about this.

Schmidt glanced around at the array of weapons chosen as the students strapped on their armour and helmets. He spoke to Jason, in the quiet teaching tones of their sessions the previous week.

'To survive this you must negate each opponent in one or two blows only – there will be no time to play at fancy sparring.'

Jason looked at the dozen young adults adjusting their body armour straps and testing the weight of their weapons. He was going to be a slaughtered.

Schmidt continued his instruction. 'In the field, your life will depend on fast, accurate and devastating attacks. Your shields will do their best to protect your back and sides but it will be up to you to push forward and destroy the target'

'Wouldn't I be facing guns in the real world, Master, rather than swords and things?' Jason asked.

'Not if they knew who you were – they would want you alive so you could be possessed. Also, much of our war remains silent. Guns and explosives are used, of course, but these ancient weapons still have their place. Remember, both sides want our war to be kept secret. With the sword, shuriken and bow a battle can be fought half a mile a outside a city and no one would know.'

Jason looked up at him and nodded his understanding.

'Finally, of course,' Schmidt smiled tightly, 'the possessed and even the Touched are not easily stopped with bullets. You slow them down by taking their limbs and finish them by removing their heads.'

Jason's mouth fell open.

Schmidt nodded at four students in different positions around the mat.

'Martinez, Slattery, Martin senior, Harrison.'

The other students backed away to kneel off the mat as the four chosen stepped forward.

Martinez was a Mediterranean looking young woman, olive skinned with long dark hair scraped back into a tight bun. Harrison was a short but muscular youth of perhaps nineteen who reminded Jason of Mouse, apart from the fact Harrison had over-large, staring eyes. Martinez had chosen a body belt full of blunted wooden shurikens and Harrison had a quarterstaff tipped with a slim, wooden blade at each end. Jason glanced over at Carl Slattery and Marshal Martin. They both held wooden swords with wickedly curved blades. Carl's eyes were glinting slits of malicious intent.

Schmidt faced Jason, again talking loudly in his clipped, Germanic tones. 'You have been taught the basics of your Gift. You need to practice these until they're second nature, until you no longer have to think what you are doing, just as you don't think of how your fist is formed, or how your arm extends when you punch. You will face multiple opponents when hunting the Brethren so we begin practicing now against their stealth weapons. Later you will learn to deal with guns and explosives.'

Jason nodded, forcing himself not to swallow loudly. Schmidt hadn't finished though.

'This is no game. These students will try to hurt you, if their weapons hit, you will be injured. You must use your Gift to neutralise them before they reach you and to protect yourself against their weapons. Jakra alone will not save you here. Do not hold back – they are also learning to survive against the powerful blows of the Touched and perhaps even a possessed. You will not help them learn by trying to be gentle. Understood?'

'Yes, Master.'

'Full contact - understood?' Schmidt said to the students, waiting all around him, tense and ready just fifteen feet away.

'Yes, Master,' they snapped back as one.

Carl slowly lowered his sword tip towards Jason's throat and smiled.

Jason's heart was pounding but he winked back at Carl.

'Prepare,' Schmidt said, backing away from Jason to the mat edge.

This must be serious – the masters didn't usually give any warnings. Jason raised his hands, breathing deeply and pulling in energy. The energy ball deep in his stomach began spinning and the air around his white knuckles shimmered.

'Full contact – go.' yelled Schmidt and a wooden shuriken streaked towards Jason from Martinez.

He blocked it, with his air-gloved hand then sent an air-fist to smash Martinez off the mat. The three men raced towards him, weapons raised. Jason air-punched towards Carl who double arm blocked but Jason's blow sent him sprawling backwards off the mat anyway. He air-sliced Marshal's legs from underneath him and then leapt out of the way as Harrison jumped at him from a couple of metres away with his blade scything down.

Jason landed in a roll and pushed back an open hand. Harrison was launched off the ground to land metres away. A slight scrape warned Jason and he span around to air-chop Carl's wrist and send his sword spinning to the ground. Jason air-jabbed him in the stomach and as Carl bent over double, Jason surged into a flying kick towards him.

Smack. A wooden shuriken slapped into Jason's thigh as Carl dived away from his kick. Jason's leg buckled as he landed and he sank to his knees. Instantly he air-chopped Martinez who was about to launch another flying star at him. She cart wheeled over the matting and stayed down this time.

'Stop,' Schmidt called and everyone froze. Carl and Marshal were back on their feet, Harrison was sitting up and Martinez managed to raise her head.

'You would be dead now, Jason,' Schmidt said, walking around the five of them. 'When the Brethren use these weapons, they are poisoned. You are Gifted – your purpose is to destroy quickly, efficiently, ruthlessly using your powers. You do not have the luxury of physical attack to make you feel like a real man. You win in the shortest possible time or else you will die and your team will die with you.'

Without warning, Schmidt's open hands flashed out four times, once at each of Jason's opponents. All four students flew off the mat, rolling and sliding straight into the white marble walls.

'That is all it takes. Am I a coward for using powers they do not have, for not allowing them in close enough to use their weapons? No - this is not a competition with rules and prizes. Out there...' Schmidt threw one hand at one of the high, arched windows, '... you kill or be killed and you do it quickly. Understood?'

'Understood, Master.' replied Jason. From the edges of his vision, Jason saw Carl and the others struggling back to kneel at the mat edge.

Schmidt turned to them, his voice icily measured. 'Each one of you could be fighting for your lives tomorrow. Treat each training session as your last,' he pointed one ram-rod of a finger around all the students. 'Do you understand?'

'Yes, Master.' They all shouted back as loud as they could. Jason knew Schmidt's finger could send an air-dart to break any of their ribs if he wasn't convinced of their comprehension.

'Then why have you all forgotten your training?' Schmidt shot dark looks at each of Jason's opponents: Marshal had spots of coughed-up blood over his body armour. 'You will face blows harder than this from the Touched and a possessed will rip off your limbs two at a time. Do not hope your armour will absorb all the blows, do not be so stupid as to try to block them – push the attack to one side or get out of the way. Duck, dive, roll, twist, dodge.'

Schmidt focussed on Carl. 'When should any Jakra block ever meet force head-on?'

'Never, master.' Carl replied.

Schmidt crossed his arms in front of him, imitating Carl's earlier block, and strode forwards. 'And yet you chose to defend an air-strike like this. Perhaps you thought Jason is only a boy, his attacks are nothing? Perhaps you wished to be macho, prove yourself against the powers of a Gifted?'

'I messed up, Master.' Carl said, shooting a baleful glance at Jason. This drubbing wasn't going to help their relationship.

Schmidt stopped five feet away from Carl and pointed a finger at him. 'You wish to be a shield, to protect the Gifted... do not "mess up" again.' Without warning, Schmidt shot out a finger of hardened air. Carl twisted and snapped his hand up to knock the shimmering air-dart to one side where it smashed over a heavy weapons rack.

'Better,' Schmidt said, then turned his back on Carl to glare at the other students. He pointed at Jason, kneeling in the centre of the mat. 'Only when you reach this Gifted boy, will he stop hurting you.'

Jason looked around the twelve pairs of eyes, staring at him from behind the face protecting bars of their helmets. All of them, even Anna, stared back at him with grim determination. He guessed it could start to get a little rough from now on.

'Now, we will try again – try as if your lives depend on it.' said Schmidt.

And try again they did – many times over. Jason faced four, five and even six attackers at a time, all armed and all determined to take him out. He threw out air strikes, kicks and blocks without thinking and flipped, rolled and ran around the mat like a cat on speed. Despite his Gift coming to him ever more naturally, out of seven further bouts, Jason was still hit five times – twice by Anna.

She was a superb Jakra gymnast. Her body, although heavier set than perhaps would be deemed lithe, was strong, fast and supple. She seemed to be able to see Jason's air-attacks more clearly than any of the other students and instantly read his intended moves. She knocked aside his air-strikes, leapt, ducked and weaved her way across the mat towards him and too often got close enough to strike with her slim wooden katana.

Carl got to him once, on the very last bout.

Jason was facing six of them, including Anna and the shuriken wielding Martinez. He took them all down at least once but Anna and Carl avoided most of the force of his blows and Martinez kept up a distracting storm of missiles despite Jason knocking her back into the wall as Schmidt had done. Anna almost reached him. He swept her legs away at the last moment, leaping over her whistling Katana but as he landed, Carl rolled forward from where Jason had felled him earlier to whirl his sword at Jason's ribs.

Jason leapt away in time to miss most of the force but the wooden tip sliced through his tee-shirt and opened up his side in a stinging but shallow line.

Schmidt had ordered a break at that point, telling Jason to stay.

As the others filed out of the training hall and into the white corridor, Jason sank to the floor, bleeding and exhausted. He just caught Anna's concerned face glancing back as she closed the door.

Crashes and bangs of smashing furniture from both mock buildings resounded around the hall and drowned out Jason's ragged panting. During one of his bouts, a shaven-headed man had come flying out of the pub window. He'd leapt up, shaken himself off and dived back in through the same opening. Jason had taken a shuriken hit from Martinez for glancing at that.

Schmidt looked down at him. 'A good thing that was only a wooden Katana – a real one would have sliced through your ribs like paper. You would be trying to push your heart back inside at this moment.'

He lifted his hand indicating Jason should get up and led him to a small room off the main hall. As they walked, Jason pressed his sliced T-shirt to his chest to slow the bleeding

'Sit,' Schmidt said as they entered the room. It was a small, first aid centre – a chair and stretcher in on corner, a bed and sink along one wall and cupboards filling in the gaps.

Schmidt took off Jason's tee shirt, sized up his wound and reached for some ointment, liniment and tape from one of the cupboards. 'You will live,' he said as he bandaged Jason up.

'You must be harder in your attacks – you do not help them by holding back. If they do not learn to defend against full power then they will all die the moment they face any of the Touched. And if your team dies, then so will you. Once they recognise who and what you are, you will be a magnet, a target for every attack. Any Brethren, from the lowest agent to the most powerful Touched and Glimmerman will be desperate to take you for possession by their demon master. You understand this?'

'Yes, Master,' Jason said, automatically.

Schmidt looked at him for a moment, his strong-jawed visage unreadable. 'Still, you have progressed faster than any of us could have imagined. It would be a great loss to see you slaughtered.'

'Uhh, thanks,' Jason said.

A hint of a smile flickered over Schmidt's lips. 'Go. Clean up. Have lunch. There is more to come this afternoon.'

'Yes, Master,' Jason said and with a groan that he only allowed in his mind, he stood up and left the sick room.

***

Freed from training, Jason flopped down on the riverbank close to the guesthouse. It was Saturday lunchtime and he should have been looking forward to lunch on the sun-soaked lawn at the Old Mill, bantering with Miranda and groaning at Dad's supremely un-funny jokes.

Those days were gone... long gone. The world of demons and Brethren had opened up all around him and nothing would ever be the same again. He'd never felt so alone. It would be so good to talk to Dad right now, to touch base with something familiar, even if it meant a row. Miranda – he even wanted to talk to Miranda.

'You okay, how's your cut?' Anna stood over him, silhouetted against the sun and brilliant blue sky above.

Jason sat up, stifling a groan. 'I'll live... so Schmidt says.'

Anna glanced down at his bloodstained T-shirt and sat down next to him.

'You did really well in there, you know? Everyone is talking about how quickly you have come into your Gift, how natural it seems to you. We've been up against a lot more experienced Gifted and they've not done half as well. You just need to be harder – make sure that once we're hit, we don't get up again. Leaving someone like Carl still mobile and that close to you was a big mistake.'

'It won't happen again,' Jason said, touching his bandage gingerly.

Anna stared at him for a long moment. She'd quite small eyes but they were just as startling a blue colour as Alan Brash's big, film star ones.

'Just don't do too much damage – you may need him to be in one piece fairly soon... that goes for me as well.'

'What are you on about?' Jason asked, easing back down to lie on the grass and stare at the blue of the sky.

'Oh, nothing...'

'Apart from...?'

'... you're going to need a couple of shields to train with soon...'.

Jason took a moment to realise where Anna was going with this, then groaned. He closed his eyes in resignation. 'And I'm going to get you two?'

'There's no need to sound so happy about it.'

Jason's lips slipped in to a smile despite himself. 'Well I'd want you watching my back... when you're not flying fifteen feet into the nearest wall anyway...'

'I was just trying to make you look good.' Anna said, poking him in the good ribs.

'Yeah, right... but Carl? We've not exactly... clicked have we?'

'Carl's a prat a lot of the time but I've team-trained with him for a couple of years now and we are the next two to be assigned as shields. We're the best of what's left, I'm afraid. We actually work pretty well together – work with each other's strengths and weaknesses, read intentions... all that stuff. He only got to you with his blade because I took the fall to distract you at exactly the right time.'

'Can't I just have you?'

'Afraid not – we come as a package.'

'And Brash will agree to this even if I say that Carl would rather stab my back than watch it?'

Anna hesitated and Jason turned his head to look at her. A smile pulled at her lips. 'Oh Brash will absolutely insist upon me being with the most powerfully Gifted student in the abbey.'

Jason stared back at her. 'Why?'

Anna glanced around. 'Well,' her voice dropped to almost a whisper, 'it's the worst kept secret in the abbey but no one is supposed to mention it…'

'… yeah… but you're going to.'

Anna grinned. 'My name isn't really Smith, that's just a name anybody takes here if they want to hide their past…'

Jason's forehead wrinkled before he puzzled it out.

'Your surname's Brash, isn't it - you're Alan Brash's daughter?'

Anna nodded. 'And darling daddy who barely acknowledges me in public, "for my own protection", of course, wants me teamed up with the Gifted "Golden Boy".'

'Great,' Jason sighed and flopped down onto his back again. *How tightly was he being reeled in to Brash's empire - now he and Brash's daughter were going to be responsible for keeping each other alive?*

'Hey,' Anna said, flicking his ear, 'you should be honoured – you're getting to hang out with Darkston Abbey royalty.'

Jason raised an eyebrow. 'Lucky me. Are there any more of you "royalty" around that I should know about – brothers or sisters?'

Anna looked down. 'No… just me. My mum died when I was about one.'

'Oh hell,' Jason said, 'sorry. I didn't mean to…'

'Don't worry about it – you didn't know.' Anna looked back up and forced a smile. 'Come on, lets get some food inside us – we're off to the pub this afternoon.'

'What?'

Anna started to stand. 'You may have noticed the rather large buildings at either end of the training hall?'

'Oh,' Jason said, groaning to his feet and following her to the refectory door, 'that pub.'

***

That afternoon, after lunch, Jason glimpsed Eddie, Erin and Oliver in the training hall for the first time. Eddie grinned at him but there was no time to speak as his group were led outside into the grounds by a female Master Jason had not seen before.

Cadaveril took Jason's group back from Schmidt and led the thirteen students to the simulated pub. For the next three hours Jason faced a constant hail of shurikens and throwing knives as blade wielding assailants leaped at him over and under tables, burst in through doorways, windows and out of wardrobes.

He did well. His reactions and awareness had been trained since he could toddle and were now becoming even sharper. As using his Gift became more and more automatic he was also being more inventive. He flipped up tables to block shurikens, pushed furniture over to block doors and span chairs into charging, body-armoured attackers.

He didn't survive unscathed however, not by a long way. Martinez was so quick and deadly with her unending supply of missiles and she never stayed still long enough for him to take her out completely. She hit him a half dozen times, each strike accompanied by Cadaveril appearing from nowhere and hissing "poison – dead.'

Anna and Carl got him again, too. Anna hadn't been boasting before lunch. She and Carl did work well together, seeming to read each other's minds in attack and defence. They saved each other from Jason's air strikes and Gift-hurled debris countless times and one would distract him with efficient, vicious attacks while the other edged ever closer. Each of them reached him once. Carl's curved blade took a chunk of flesh out of his arm and Anna's weapons, a pair of long-knives this time, somehow flashed across his throat and abdomen simultaneously as he was sending Carl through a window.

Cadaveril was everywhere and nowhere throughout the afternoon. Jason would suddenly half-glimpse him in a corner and then he'd be gone. Nothing touched the master, no flying body, no shattered furniture or shard of sugar-glass. You didn't even know he was there most of the time yet under his all-seeing eye, every student fought harder than ever to reach their target. By Jason's reckoning he'd 'died' about twenty times by the end of the afternoon.

Even given this high mortality rate, when at last Cadaveril called a halt to the maiming and destruction, Jason decided that he'd done well. When he'd hit any attacker out of cover, without exception, they stayed down for the rest of that bout. A steady stream of wounded had limped and crawled out of the pub only to return for the next round after patching themselves up.

They all knelt facing a sour-faced Cadaveril in front of the seemingly bomb-struck pub.

'Crude and obvious most of the time,' Cadaveril said, his hawkish eyes slashing across the kneeling students, 'but some of you are startin' to fight like you mean it at last. Now, warm down, sort your wounds out, eat a belly-full and sleep – tomorrow we'll do some real work.'

He motioned for the students to leave. As they stood and sank into the respect, Cadaveril waved Jason over to him. Jason limped across the mat – in the very last bout, Marshal Martin had managed to clip his knee with a bo-stick a split second before Jason had air-pushed him over the bar.

Cadaveril's eyes, set deep in his bone white face, swept over the walking wounded filing out of the training hall. Then he surveyed the half-demolished pub with its sugar glass windows and decimated furniture scattered out on the mat behind Jason. The last student closed the door quietly behind him. Cadaveril's voice, when he finally spoke, was just a whisper.

'You learn quickly, boy – you're a natural. Even for the most powerful Gifted, this amount of control and power so early on is unusual.'

'Thank you, Master,' Jason said, bowing his head. *What was this about - Cadaveril never praised him?*

'You will be a great loss to the Watch.'

Jason snapped his head up and Cadaveril's black eyes bored into him. 'Twenty two times dead.'

'I…' Jason began but Cadaveril stopped him with the slightest narrowing of his eyes.

'There's a hell of a lot more you need to learn if you're going to survive out there in our world. We do our work in pubs like that one where you've just been slaughtered. Flats, offices, restaurants, slums – you name it, we hunt there. Stealth, the unseen blow, the whispered death… sometimes, boy, these will be the only things that can save your supposedly valuable skin.'

'I understand…' Jason began but Cadaveril cut him off.

'No you don't, not yet. Demon huntin' with Mr Brash all over Europe I've seen too many Gifted who think they can take on anythin' with their powers - most of them are dead now, their teams slaughtered with them.'

'Yes, Master. I know I've got a long way to go,' Jason said, 'but I want to learn everything there is to know about my Gift.'

Cadaveril continued to stare at him. Jason felt as if the man was burning into his head with twin laser beams. He dropped his gaze. 'Then you'll 'ave to bloody well commit to it, boy, commit to us… work out who can learn you to stay alive and do what they say.'

Jason glanced up – Cadaveril didn't scare him any more. 'I will.'

The master gave thin smile. 'We'll see. Go and rest up – using your wonderful magic makes you superheroes a little bit tired I believe. You'll need to be in full working order to get through tomorrow.'

Jason nodded and sank into his respect. 'Yes, Master,' he said and limped out of the training hall.

Chapter 20

The bedside alarm woke Jason up at five-thirty and it didn't have a snooze button. Jason sat on the edge of his bed trying to work out what happened. He'd sank into the bath after leaving Cadaveril yesterday and he just thought he'd close his eyes for a few minutes on the bed before dinner…

'Bugger.' He ached all over and had significantly added to his collection of cuts and bruises.

He struggled to get out of bed into the half-dark, cheerless room. There would be no Dad and Miranda waiting for him with a massive, Sunday morning breakfast today. Maybe he could try to call Miranda at Ilena Russof's this evening to touch base. The trouble was there didn't appear to be any telephones in the guesthouse.

'Food,' he muttered to himself. After missing dinner last night he was starving. He stood up and groaned as muscles twinged and tensed all over.

A hot power-shower loosened him up somewhat and soon he was tapping in his number on the inside door lock and pressing his thumb to the pad. The door clicked open and he trotted out along the corridor ignoring the last of his aches and pains.

Anna was waiting in one of the big white chairs in the entrance hall.

'About time too – I was just about to come up there and knock you up. We'll miss first breakfast if we don't hurry.'

By the time they reached the refectory it was almost full of students and security guards. "First breakfast" consisted of bowls of muesli and cut fruit of all descriptions. Jason wasn't a big fan of muesli but he piled in lots of strawberries, bananas and apple at the self-service breakfast bar after Anna warned him he was going to need it. They squeezed onto a bench and ate quickly. Students were already beginning to leave.

Anna glanced at the big clock above the grand steps and doors out to the cloister. 'Time to run,' she said and got up with her bowl only half emptied.

They dumped their dishes in a pile at one end of the serving table and went out into the cloister. Six-thirty in the morning and it was already warm on the perfect square of pristine grass. The central cross almost seemed to pulse with the sun's heat as its iron manacles hung down in the stillness. Jakra students were spread all over the grass and under the shaded colonnades, stretching out and loosening up.

'Our day begins with a gentle jog,' Anna explained, '– about five miles or so around our pretty grounds to warm us up. Such a shame you missed it yesterday morning.' She moved on to the grass and began reaching for her toes. Jason followed her and began his usual series of warm ups.

Suddenly, the low talk and groans of stretching students stopped and everyone turned to face the northern edge of the cloister where the church rose up high into the perfect blue sky.

Jason eased up from touching his toes. Below one of the church's towering, sun-shining windows stood Master Schmidt.

'So – we begin now,' he said and led them through the garages and out onto the large gravelled area. Then they began to run.

Twenty minutes in, Jason dropped behind the pack of sweating students for the third time. He'd never been much of a distance runner - he could hold a steady jog for a while but the pack were maintaining a leg-jellying pace.

Schmidt who had been regularly dropping back from the lead to yell at any of them who fell behind, fell back with Jason.

'Breathe in, push out.' the master intoned. 'Just like the punching but send your energy into your legs... small pumpings of force with each push away. Feel the rhythm of your heart, the throb of each of your steps.'

Jason imagined a whirling, sparking ball in his stomach pulsing energy along the arteries in his legs with each stride, a force throbbing through him, pushing his feet hard away from the ground.

It worked. Suddenly he surged ahead as his strides lengthened into fast, low leaps. The grass flashed under him in measures of two or more metres. The ball of energy inside sparked and roiled, beats of force pulsated through him and he flew past the others.

Just how fast could he go. This power, this Gift he had – was there nothing he couldn't do with it?

Schmidt caught up with him, matching his leaps exactly. 'Slow down. Put less force into each step... you will be spent before you finish the course.'

Reluctantly, Jason toned it down. He slowed the ball of energy inside him, letting it fire down as he envisaged the surges of energy pulsing slower and slower through his arteries. His strides shortened, taking him down to a more normal cross-country pace.

'Now – keep using your Gift until the end of the run,' Schmidt said, '... for the practice.' Without looking at Jason, he joined the front of the pack as they caught up with them.

Jason nodded.

He easily stayed with the leaders for another mile to the finish point – the small stone bridge outside the refectory. However, when he finally let his Gift go, a wave of exhaustion swept over him. He sank to the grass and tugged off his trainers and socks before dousing his burning feet deep into the river and flopping back on the grass.

'Come on fit-meister general – we get a second breakfast now.'

Jason forced open his eyes, blinking away slug trails of sweat. Anna stood or rather bobbed over him as she loosened up. 'A little more sustenance to see us through the halls of pain. Come on.'

'I'm dying,' Jason moaned, closing his eyes again. Distance running was definitely not his thing – with or without his *super powers*.

Anna kicked him in the ribs – gently. 'Rubbish. Schmidt let you use your Gift most of the way – he's never let any of the other Gifted do that.'

Jason groaned and sat up. Carl walked past him, his lip-curl already in place. 'Pathetic – you can't even run without using your "magic". Enjoy showing off, did you?' He spat in the grass a foot from Jason's head and walked away.

Jason got to his feet. Tomorrow he'd run the entire course without his Gift.

Inside the refectory, students were all hurriedly tucking in to 'second breakfast', as Anna called it, which consisted of more fruit, bacon and eggs, toast and water. Jason had just twenty minutes to snack it down before following the rest of the students out of the small refectory door, along the river and into the cool of the long, white corridor that led to the training halls.

Everyone was worked harder than ever during the morning session. After non-Gift sparring for an hour or so, Jason was taken off into the "steel jungle" room again by Schmidt where he practiced Gift strikes and blocks endlessly whilst dodging between and over the gleaming apparatus. For the last hour, he was back in the halls for two-on-two sparring where you worked with a partner to defeat another pair. When Jason joined with Anna they were almost unbeatable and he even worked well with Carl – the two of them winning three out of four bouts.

At last they were allowed out for lunch.

'Is it always this bad?' Jason groaned as Anna led him over to sit with Carl and the Martin brothers in the refectory.

'They're just getting us psyched for the invasion exercise in a couple of days.' Mark Martin said through half a mouthful of food.

'Invasion exercise?' Jason asked.

'It's where we get invaded.' Carl said.

'Really?' Jason said.

'Now, now you two,' Anna cut in, 'don't start arguing. You played really nicely together in training.'

Carl grunted then, amazingly, began to explain. 'Half of Security and some of the Masters and students act as Brethren forces breaking into the abbey. We have to try to stay alive and clear the place of the baddies.'

'Sounds great,' Jason said. This was the most civilised Carl had ever been to him.

'We practice it all the time in small teams,' Mark Martin added, 'just defending a small area. But this time the whole abbey's involved – they've been buying in extra weapons and vehicles and stuff for weeks...'

'Even a couple of little choppers,' Marshall cut in. 'It's going to be amazing.'

'And,' Anna added, lowering her voice, 'rumour has it that Brash has even flown back a few of his most trusted teams for the occasion.'

They chatted on about the forthcoming exercise, Carl continuing to be almost human, until it was time for the afternoon session.

The improvement in relations between Jason and Carl had come at just the right time because for most of that afternoon, Carl and Anna acted as Jason's bodyguards or shields as Cadaveril put it. Gifted students and their team of two or three shields alternately defended a room in one of the mock buildings and then tried to clear a floor. Their opponents were the other students, all armoured and armed with an array of wooden weapons.

The students were kept at it for three solid hours. Finally they were allowed a water break and finished off with weapons practice. Mark Martin was assigned to Jason to show him some very basic attacks and blocks with wooden Katannas. Jason was shattered but thought he picked up the sword-work fairly well – Mark was a very patient teacher.

Finally the session was over and the students were dismissed. Jason hung back and approached Cadaveril and made his respect.

'Master… is it possible for me to telephone my sister from somewhere this evening? There don't seem to be any phones in the guesthouse.'

Cadaveril shrugged. 'I'll check with Mr. Brash,' he said.

'Thank you,' Jason said, sinking into the respect position and turning to leave.

'Don't hold your breath, though,' Cadaveril added. 'Comms in and out of the abbey is limited… for security purposes.'

'I understand, Master,' Jason said. *Perhaps he should have asked Schmidt.*

Cadaveril watched him leave in silence.

***

Jason made it to the refectory this time. He had just sat down next to Anna with a steaming plate of coq au vin when the refectory's main doors opened wide and Schmidt and Cadaveril entered. They took positions on either side of the second step down as Brash appeared with the sunlit shining in behind him.

The chatter and clatter of the refectory immediately stilled.

'Good evening to you all – I hope you're enjoying your dinner,' Brash started, beaming down benevolently on his assembled students and security. 'I just wanted to wish you all well in the forthcoming training exercise – the "not-very" surprise attack on the abbey will kick off within the next few days.'

'Now - I'd like to introduce you to a minor legend from the Watch who has literally just arrived on our doorstep.'

Brash moved a little to one side and Marakoff joined him with a curt nod to the captive audience. His limp was much more pronounced than Jason remembered and he noticed something like a sneer flash across Cadaveril's face although the Jakra Master hardly glanced at Marakoff.

'This is Sergei Marakoff, one of our most highly regarded ghosts before his injury. The Watch Council asked me to help Sergei retire to Britain several weeks ago and now he has finally arrived...' Brash grinned at Marakoff who gave a tight smile and shuffled awkwardly. 'It'll be no gentle retirement here though,' Brash said, slapping Marakoff on the back, 'we'll put you straight to good use in training all the little ghostlets out there.'

Cadaveril started to examine his nails – obviously bored with the introductions.

'Now,' Brash said, beaming his smile back across the audience like some dental lighthouse, 'don't let me hold you up any further – eat, drink and be merry for tomorrow we... work even harder.'

Brash, Marakoff, Cadaveril and Schmidt all left and noise returned to the refectory.

'I'm not sure that Marakoff bloke is very "highly regarded",' Mark Martin said, 'did you see Bone Head's face?'

'We might get some first hand news of what's happening in the Carpathians though,' his brother said.

'Yeah, right,' Anna grinned, ''cos ghosts are always so chatty, aren't they?'

'Mr Brash said something about him training us - surely they're not going to make him a master?' Carl said. 'The guy could hardly walk.'

Jason stayed out of the following discussion and soon after made his excuses and left for an early night.

Marakoff turning up like that had unsettled him. Jason had known he'd be coming into the abbey to keep an eye on him while Dad was checking on Mawn. However, now he was here, it made Jason realise how much he was actually missing his family.

Despite the full-on day and the exhaustion from using his Gift catching up with him, it took Jason a long time to get to sleep.

***

Jason woke up in the dark.

It took him a moment to shake the strips of his familiar nightmare from his mind – the multi-storey murder, the agents' shots echoing all through his head; mum's warm blood soaking through her new blouse. How still everything seemed for a moment after her death, how frozen – no sound, not a breath of concrete-dusted air; Miranda and him petrified, staring at her twisted body on the ground. Dad's whisper – 'Say goodbye to your mother.' And then sound bursting in again – their car roaring down the ramps, crunching away out onto the road – all far too loud.

Jason sat up, reaching for his watch – the face just visible in his room half lit by moonlight – 3:20am.

The traffic sounds from his dream were still there.

Jason kicked away the duvet that clung to his feet and reached for the button to open the window. It slid silently outwards but stopped with just a twenty centimetre gap. He pressed the button again, twice, but the window wouldn't open any further. Was that to keep danger out or him in at night?

The cars noises were real. He couldn't see anything apart from the dark silhouette of the oak tree rising from the courtyard below but there was plenty of noise. Smooth car motors, rough, throaty jeep engines and the odd growl of perhaps a small lorry all reverberated around the inner courtyard. All the vehicles were coming closer, parking up, he guessed, in the large gravelled area in front of the garages and guesthouse.

What was going on? Was this part of the invasion exercise – starting already. Jason went over to press the door release but nothing happened. *No one had said anything about being prisoners in their own rooms.*

He went over to the window again and tested the frame. It was well made but he was sure he could break through it using his Gift. Still, what would Brash or Cadaveril say in the morning when they discovered part of the wall and an expensive, motorised window casement in pieces on the courtyard floor?

More vehicles kept on coming, intermittently now, parking up and engines dying away only to be replaced by others drawing in. Doors slammed and the odd shout reached him. Then he heard half-hushed voices in the corridor outside. He rushed back to the door and pressed his ear against it. People were being shown to rooms not many doors away. Jason wondered if they would be locked in as well.

Surely if the invasion exercise was beginning, they should all be rushing to "battle stations" or something... not that he knew where he was supposed to go of course.

He went into the bathroom – not switching on the light. The window there was wide but only about half a metre high.

He climbed up on the stool and opened the window. Steel bars were fixed to both lower corners. They slid out of the wall then stopped the frame from opening more than thirty centimetres. He could break out here – use a small air-strike from his finger to smash the wooden window frame away from where the bar was fixed in to it. They might not discover the minor damage for some time.

He thought for a moment. Outside, the noises had subsided. Just one or two engines still sounded in the darkness.

Slowly he closed the window and sat down on the edge of the bath. He'd see what was going on outside soon enough anyway – their alarms went off at five thirty every morning.

He climbed back into bed and dozed fitfully for an hour before giving up. There was still the odd vehicle noise from outside but he ignored it and began a long session of limbering up, Jakra and Gift practice. By the time the alarm went off, he was showered, dressed and ready to take on the world. He pressed the door release and this time the latch clicked open obediently.

He wasn't the only one shooting out of the stalls. Half the other doors popped open just as he stepped into the corridor. Everyone turned to everyone else.

'What was going on last night? Did you hear it – cars and stuff?' It was Martinez, the Mediterranean looking student who took delight in peppering Jason with shurikens. Jason had no idea that her room was only four doors to his left.

There were various grunts and shrugs from the students then they all had the same thought – the stairs. More doors opened and the corridor filled with eager, chatting students. En masse, they bundled down the stairs, along the lower corridor and burst into the entrance hall where others were just coming out of the opposite corridor.

Anna was standing at the double entrance doors, holding one half open and looking out.

Jason frowned. *She must have got out of her room before everyone else? Perhaps Alan Brash's secret daughter did get some extra privileges after all.*

'We've got company,' Anna announced and pulled both doors wide open to let the surging mass of students see outside.

Vehicles filled the gravel approach – perhaps fifty or more: cars, 4x4s, military jeeps and three small lorries.

'It must be part of the invasion exercise?' someone mumbled.

'I'm not so sure.' Anna said, stepping out on to the little walled terrace that topped the double steps. 'I think we're going need a good breakfast.'

Anna trotted down the right hand steps and headed for the refectory. Bursting into excited chatter, everyone followed her, their eyes scanning the vehicles massed before them. The cars and lorries were all empty – not a soul to be seen apart from a pair of security guards watching them from the tree line beyond the church.

Jason caught Carl's eye as the students filed across the bridge to the refectory. Carl nodded and edged passed him. At least he hadn't scowled.

In the refectory the buffet tables were laden with hot full English breakfasts instead of the pre-run fruit and cereal. There was also an entire bench full of newcomers eating the student's food.

'This isn't good.' Carl mumbled, looking over the new people. 'Looks like we're going to have to baby-sit you a little earlier than expected, doesn't it Hot Shot?' He turned to stare at Jason.

Anna placed herself between them. 'It's not a question of babysitting – we watch each others' backs. Now get some bacon before these new buggers finish it all off.'

Carl wasn't finished however. 'When the time comes, just make sure you do your bit, Golden Boy, or we're all dead.'

'No pressure then,' Jason said.

Carl shook his head and pushed past Anna, swinging a cuff at Jason's temple as he went.

Jason blocked the swipe easily then bit down a yelp as Carl's foot flicked into his shin. Anna shot out her hand but Carl had made his point. He dodged away from her and headed for the buffet table.

Jason forced a smile and rubbed his shin. 'You know, I get the feeling Carl doesn't really want to be on my side.'

'You don't do a lot to help the situation, do you?' Anna replied. 'Don't worry – he'll do the right thing when he has to. A lot of shields get annoyed at the glorifying you high and mighty Gifted get treated to.'

'But we deserve it.' Jason said.

Anna flicked a cuff at him just like Carl. He dodged it and foot-blocked her snap kick to his shin as well.

'You're learning, junior,' she said, grinning.

Jason smiled back then turned to scan the newcomers. 'Do you know any of these people?'

'A few.' Anna said, shuffling along with the queue to get some breakfast. 'They're all our top managers and scientists, security guards' families, that sort of thing.'

Jason allowed his plate to be piled high as he looked over the strangers. There were around forty adults – men and women from perhaps eighteen to fifty or so, dressed in everything from hoodies to suits. They sat along the benches at the far side of the refectory and each of them looked as if they'd been up half the night. Tired, dark-shadowed eyes had watched the students enter over the rims of coffee cups but the majority of them were returning their attention to breakfast.

Jason's eyes suddenly widened. Sitting at one end of the bench were Fast Eddie, Erin Brock and Oliver Stone. Eddie caught Jason watching him and nodded. Jason nodded back.

'Anna, I've just seen some friends from Silent Hill. I'm just going to go over and find out what's happening?'

Anna glanced over where Jason had been looking. 'Ah, the illustrious Fast Eddie, your gang leader. Carl and I were down to be his shields when he left Silent Hill but then we got an upgrade when you came along. I'm afraid Carl would still prefer Eddie though, what with him being a couple of years older and rather experienced…'

'And who do you prefer?'

'With another couple of month's training I'd probably go for you... maybe.'

'Cheers,' Jason said.

'You're welcome,' Anna said, finishing loading her tray. 'Say hello to Eddie for me.'

'Sure,' Jason said and worked his way passed the rapidly filling benches.

'Jason, old boy – how the devil are you?' Eddie grinned as Jason squeezed into a space opposite him. 'Good to see you getting on so well with my mate Carl over there.'

Not for the first time, it struck Jason how much Eddie sounded like Brash… or perhaps how much he wanted to sound like the Master of Darkston Abbey.

'He loves me really,' Jason smiled. It flitted across his mind that the balance of power between them had shifted. Now he'd mastered some of his Gift and had been training directly under Schmidt and Cadaveril, perhaps he was in some way superior to Eddie. He realized he was holding Eddie's eye and quickly looked away.

'Erin, Oliver – good to see you again,' Jason said, glancing at the shoulder Erin's had injured during their Drunken Abbot raid – at least there wasn't a sling or anything on it. 'Can anyone tell me what the hell's going on?'

Eddie shrugged. 'Not one hundred percent sure there, old boy – it seems we were all woken up by security at about one this morning, told to pack a bag and get ourselves over here. After the usual security checks most of us were shown to a room full of camp beds and sleeping bags. Then they called us for breakfast.'

'No one told you why?' Jason asked.

'Nope,' Erin answered, sipping at a glass of fresh orange juice. Her red hair framed a face that wasn't happy. 'I dare say they'll get around to letting us know what's going on when they feel like it. Then maybe I can phone my parents to stop them both worrying themselves sick.'

'Is anyone else from school here?' Jason asked.

'A few – most of them are still flaked out in the dorms.' Eddie said. 'All our Gifted are here, of course and some of the older, more competent members of our happy little gang. In short - everyone Mr Brash considers worth saving has been brought in.'

Jason caught Erin's eye. *Obviously, Brash didn't consider her parents "worth saving".*

'I don't suppose…' Jason hesitated. 'I don't suppose Tanya is here…'

Eddie raised an eyebrow. 'You really liked her didn't you, old boy? No she's not here, I'm afraid, and my sage advice would be to forget her.'

'None of the Skins are here, of course,' Oliver scoffed, shoving in half a sausage and speaking for the first time, 'not even Callum – I hope he's the first to go.'

'The first to go?' Jason said. 'This is just part of the invasion exercise, isn't it?' He chewed his lip –Miranda were out there.

Eddie answered. 'Probably – it would be just like Brash to practice shipping us vitally important folk into the abbey in the middle of the night. But then again, this might be the real thing.'

He looked across at Erin. 'Of course, if the Brethren have finally found us they'll most likely know there's nothing of much interest to them in Drunken Abbot or Darkston. They'll just power on through and head straight for us here in the abbey. Ironically, those on the outside will be the safest.'

The small, riverside entrance opened before Jason could question Eddie any further. Two large security guards entered and stationed themselves on either side of the door. One of the guards had a quiet word with a couple of students who were just about to leave and a moment later, they shrugged and went to get another coffee.

'They're not letting people leave,' Jason said.

'Perhaps they're just going to gas us all and get it over with.' Oliver said grinning with a bit of bacon stuck in his teeth.

'I don't think so.' Erin said. Her eyes were fixed on the main doors that led out to the cloister.

They followed her gaze. The doors were being held open by four more security guards, all with machine guns slung over their shoulders.

A moment later, Brash walked in with Alicia Sirensong a pace behind his right shoulder. A shadow peeled away from Brash as he took centre-stage on the top step and Cadaveril materialized on his left. Finally, Marakoff limped in, immediately shrinking back against the wall behind the three of them.

Security closed the doors and all talk in the refectory died away. Brash stepped further into the light and opened his hands like some benevolent saint.

'Good morning to you all – staff, students and to our esteemed guests from Darkston village.' Brash's handsome face beamed over his minions seated below him.

'No doubt you're all wondering what on earth is going on. Why, for goodness sake, have all the great and the good been herded into the abbey at such a ridiculous hour this morning?'

He surveyed the room – a showman building the tension, drawing in everybody's full attention.

'Well, at the risk of sounding like I'm in a bad war movie... this is not an exercise.'

Whispers rose up from around the floor but died the instant Brash spoke again.

'The Brethren have found us. Just before midnight our infra-red sweep caught two agents dug into the valley side with high powered surveillance equipment. They could have been watching the abbey grounds for hours, the whole day even. Heaven knows who and what they saw.' Brash paused, his gaze sweeping over the room and resting for just a second on Jason.

'One problem of course, is that they usually come in threes and we only got the two of them. A second... concern is that they were both equipped with a satellite navigation tracking device. When they don't report back, more will come and if we catch them, more still. We have to assume the Brethren know we're here and that they'll throw everything they have at us before we have a chance to get out.'

Brash paused for a moment, letting the news sink in and the whispers start. Finally he spoke again, his rich, powerful voice commanding the room's focus to return to him.

'Fortunately, evacuation has never been the plan. We have all trained countless times for just such an attack as it was always going to happen at some point – and this will be our best chance of finally drawing out the Brethren worms from their burrowings into British government, business and security services. To be honest, I couldn't have planned it any better.'

Brash smiled again, searching faces, judging reactions. 'Over the next couple of hours, you will be reminded of your duties and your stations. I don't know how long we will have before the Brethren come for us – a few hours or a few days – who can say? But when they do come, by hell we'll be ready for them.'

Brash took a long slow breath in. He seemed to be expanding, growing in height and presence. 'This my friends, is what we have been preparing for –'

Brash suddenly leapt from the steps, forming an air bar three metres above the nearest table as he flew. He grabbed and somersaulted around the shimmering air to catapult himself further into the refectory and landed deftly on the centre bench.

He punched one fist into the air, his eyes blazing. '-bring them on!'

The room erupted into cheers and applause. Students stood up, clapping and pressing in on Brash to shake his hand, touch his leg, anything to partake of his magnificence. For a few short moments he indulged the throng then without warning, he sprinted through mid air - forming air-steps faster than Jason thought possible - over their heads and dropped back down next to Alicia. Security swung open the double doors and Brash swept out of view.

Cadaveril and Marakoff quickly disappeared but Alicia Sirensong hesitated. She caught Jason's anxious stare and raised her eyes in exasperation before smiling wickedly and gliding out into the sun-bright cloister.

Excited conversation quickly built to a roar as the doors closed and students, guests and security began milling around the packed refectory.

Jason needed to get out – Miranda was out there and the Brethren were coming. Louisa and Mouse as well... and Dad would be hundreds of miles away in the north of Scotland by now.

With the zephyr from Brash's Gift use still squalling around him, Jason sidled away from Eddie and the others to slip out of the now unguarded riverside door.

Alan Brash was standing not ten feet away. He was talking to several security guards but ushered them away as he caught sight of Jason.

'Hoped I might catch you getting some air, Jason, old boy,' he smiled. 'Let's take a walk, shall we?'

Jason nodded and Brash led him left, along the river towards the huge open lawns at the rear of the abbey.

'Mr Brash,' Jason began, 'my sister's out in Darkston Wick, staying with Ilena Russof while Dad's...away. I can't leave her there on her own.'

'Ahh – well actually we tried to bring Miranda, the Russofs and even that little Mouse character in last night but Ilena point blank refused, I'm afraid.'

'Then I'll go and stay with them...'

'Jason, Jason,' Brash said, holding up a placating hand, 'hold on a minute. You do realise how indescribably vital to our cause you are, don't you and how much the Brethren desperately want someone of your power?'

'I don't see what that's got to do with making sure Miranda's safe.'

Brash stopped and looked directly at him. 'I know we are not supposed to talk about this but there is no time for the niceties of Watch tradition now – you are a triple six, Jason, I'm sure of it. Eighteen generations of slowly increasing power to produce you – the Gift does not get any more potent. There are only three other Triples in the World that we know of and one of them is over seventy.'

'Fine, but the Brethren don't know I'm here so...'

'I understand you used your Gift in the open grounds yesterday – on the morning run?'

'What?' Jason asked. 'Yes, Master Schmidt told me to but I don't see what that has to do with...'

'If those Brethren agents saw you,' Brash cut in, 'if they recognised you as Richard Darillian's son, they will have already called their entire UK forces down on us. They know how powerful your father was and will be absolutely frantic to capture you even on the sniff of a chance that you're a triple six.'

'You're exaggerating, I'm not all that…' Jason began.

Brash cut in. 'A triple six is the only one of us capable of defeating a demon prince should any Brethren Summoner be powerful and crazed enough to ever bring one through. Ironically, Triples are probably the only ones powerful enough to summon a prince from the lowest layer of the demons' prison - the Abyss.'

'What – the Gift isn't used for summoning demons is it?.'

'We believe it might be… something to do with forcing open a hole in the walls of the Abyss.'

'But they could never force me to do that - I wouldn't have a clue how, anyway.'

'If you were possessed, you would.'

Brash let his words hang in the air until Jason worked out where this was leading.

'So you're not going to let me leave the abbey, are you.'

'I couldn't take the risk.'

'What happens when Dad gets back?'

Brash took in a slow breath and started them walking along the river again. 'He will understand what I'm doing – he knows the abbey is the only safe place until this threat is over.'

'So you're just going to leave Miranda and the Russofs out there?'

'They can drive here any time they like, day or night, and we've asked your sister to tell your father what's happening – maybe he can talk some sense into Ilena. Apart from forcing them to come in at gunpoint, there's nothing more we can do.'

'Let me speak to Miranda – phone her or something.'

Brash shook his head. 'I'd love to but…'

'… but nothing, let me phone her.' Jason almost shouted.

Brash carried on, visibly forcing his voice to stay calm. '… but we don't know how far the Brethren are into us. They're extremely sophisticated and may well have phone taps already in place. One call from an abbey phone to Miranda could lead their agents straight to her and almost all my security has been brought back into the abbey grounds – I can't defend the whole valley. If you phone her, you could be signing her death warrant.'

'So I can't see or contact my own sister in any way?'

Brash shook his head. 'I'm sorry. I daren't even send any more of my men there to try to persuade Ilena. If more Brethren are already in the valley, then a succession of abbey cars to Darkston Wick would lead them straight to her.'

Jason drew a breath for his next argument but then let it slowly out. There was no point – Brash obviously wasn't going to let him go.

Brash gripped one hand on Jason's shoulder. 'Come now – we may have a day or more before anything happens by which time your father will be back and bring them all in to safety.'

'I suppose so…' Jason said, hesitantly. He had to feign grudging agreement now or Brash would probably lock him up or something. He needed to talk to Marakoff – either that or he'd get out by himself tonight.

'Good lad,' Brash said, shaking his shoulder and letting him go. 'Now, the very best thing you can do is to push on with your training. When the attack comes, you will be in the safest place with my other V.I.P.'

Jason looked up at him inquisitively.

Brash smiled. 'I'm sure you've cracked the abbey's worst kept secret… the real identity of Anna Smith?'

Jason nodded.

'I thought so,' Brash said. 'Well you just make sure you look after each other.'

'Of course, Anna's been really good to me – I like her a lot,' Jason said. 'Someone else I need to ask you about – Violet – will she be with us "V.I.P.s"?'

Brash's smile faltered just for a second and he looked away to turn them back towards the abbey. 'My ward is not combat trained – she'll be perfectly safe elsewhere.'

'But I thought you said Anna and I will be in the safest place.'

'Indeed I did but I'm not burying you two totally out of the action – you need to have some exposure to what a real

330

fight is like… to give you half a chance of surviving when you become hunters yourselves.'

'Perhaps I could help out.' Jason said.

Brash glanced down at him, frowning. 'Not yet. There must be no heroics from you, no trying to prove yourself. You do understand this, don't you?'

'Yes,' Jason said.

'Are you sure?'

Jason nodded. 'I'm really not planning on dying any time soon.'

'Glad to hear it,' Brash said and stopped again. They'd walked into the middle of the lawns at the back of the abbey and stood facing the magnificent church tower with its giant gothic windows and graceful flying buttresses. 'Beautiful, isn't it? Who would guess it will become a slaughter house for the Brethren scum?'

Jason didn't answer. Unless Miranda came into the abbey in the next few hours, he wouldn't be here to see any slaughtering of Brethren. He'd get out and leave the valley with her tonight.

'Now, before I send you back, I was curious about one thing,' Brash said in a light, casual tone that didn't quite ring true to Jason. 'The man who I introduced to everyone yesterday, Sergei Marakoff, retiring here from the Watch – have you ever seen him before?'

Jason shook his head. 'The one with the limp? No – why should I?'

Brash smiled thinly, his gaze fixed on Jason's face. 'Well, it's just that he was a good friend of your grandfather's you see - they worked closely together for a time. Did he or your father ever mention him?'

Jason snorted. 'Yeah, like Dad loves chatting about his past… and Grandfather for that matter.'

Brash continued to watch him for a moment longer then smiled. 'Of course, I'm sorry. I know things were difficult when Richard decided to… retire early. Your grandfather was still hunting and made no secret of his disapproval. Terrible thing – rifts in a family, especially in our world.' Brash patted him on the arm. 'I only mentioned it because Marakoff shared your grandfather's somewhat hard-line views and may be a little… disdainful about your father if you come across each other.'

'Then I'll break his other leg,' Jason said, defiantly.

Brash nodded, dropping his searching gaze. 'Good – I'm glad you're still willing to defend your father's good name, despite everything.'

Jason nodded but didn't reply. *I'm not getting in to this.*

They were almost back at the abbey buildings and Brash stopped walking.

'Now above all, remember to keep yourself safe, Jason, for all our sakes. There is absolutely no way we can have you falling into Brethren hands. Keep out of sight, all right?'

'Yes, I understand, Mr Brash.'

Brash searched his eyes again, looking for something – a hint of suspicion or mistrust perhaps. Jason returned a level gaze and forced a tight smile.

'I'll be fine Mr. Brash, don't worry. I understand what's at stake.'

Finally, Brash nodded and slapped him on the shoulder. 'Good. Now – time for you to meet the man who is going to babysit you through this little fracas. Run off to the cloister – your battle group will be there already.'

Chapter 21

Anna met Jason at the river by the refectory door. 'Come on – I've just been sent to find you. All the other groups have set off for their battle-stations already.'

'Sorry,' Jason said, 'Mr Brash…'

'Yeah, yeah – we got a message. It doesn't stop Sergeant Smith getting narked though.'

'Great - another anonymous "Smith",' Jason mumbled.

Anna ignored him and hurried through the refectory and out the other side into the sun-bright cloister.

A small group was waiting in the shade - Carl, Fast Eddie, Erin Brock and Oliver Stone. Jason smiled to himself - *So these are the V.I.P.s* Brash was talking about.

A man in the dark blue uniform of Brash Security stepped out of a small doorway just next to the chapter house and closed it behind him. Judging by the three small stripes on his right arm, the man was a sergeant. He was tall, well built and perhaps thirty years old.

'About time, lad, we've got us work to do, you know?' The sergeant had a hard vowelled, Yorkshire accent

'Yes – sorry. Mr Brash wanted…'

'A chat with you - aye, we were told as much. We could have done with you 'ere half an 'our ago though. You've got some quick learnin' to do - I've been training these sad-cases in battle stations for the past six months so they already know the drill.'

'Right,' Jason said, 'sorry – I'll do my best to catch up.'

The security guard nodded. 'My name is Sergeant Smith by the way, and you're lucky enough to be in Cloister 5 group.'

Jason nodded. He wondered if Smith's accent meant he was local, perhaps schooled in Silent Hill and groomed in the Brash gang to work in abbey security.

'Right – let's get to it.' Smith said and turned back towards the small wooden door he'd just come through.

There was one narrow window to either side of the door. To Jason it looked like Brash had decided to hide them in a cupboard.

Smith tapped a code and pressed his thumb onto a concealed pad and the door swung open on well-oiled hinges. What looked like an insignificant old door actually had a steel core, five centimetres thick. Sunlight spilled into the room to reveal that the cupboard was, in fact, an armoury.

Jason whistled softly as he stepped inside. Only perhaps four metres wide, the room was made even narrower by weapon racks and shelves bolted floor-to-wall on either side. Kalashnikov machine guns, rifles, pistols and cases of ammunition were stacked neatly along the length of the room. There were also crates labelled "grenades", a rack of combat knives and, oddly out of place, four slim long swords hanging in their scabbards.

Smith switched on a light and the harsh, bare-bulb glare was thrown back at them by the walls, floor and ceiling – all cased in steel.

'Shut the door, New-lad,' Smith said to Jason who was standing at the back.

The bulb light shone off the sergeant's number-one cropped hair. 'Now, to fill you in, Jason. Our main task is to guard the armoury and supply runners with any arms they might need. Our best Kalashnikov users will be stationed at the windows and the rest of you will act as "gofers".'

''Scuse me sergeant,' Oliver grunted from the front, 'Are you reckoning on the attack going on for a while then... if people are going to have to run back here to re-stock with ammo?'

'I doubt that, Stone. The whole abbey will be a death-trap for whatever the Brethren chuck at us. It should all be over right quickly but, we have to make sure we're set for the worst case scenario, as them on high would put it.'

'Sergeant,' Eddie said, 'might I ask a question?'

Smith turned his steel grey eyes on Eddie and a crooked smile bent his lips. 'You usually do, Eddie, lad. Get on with it.'

'Despite all our training, we are in a sort of crèche here, aren't we? The Brethren are never going to reach us.'

Smith smiled. 'Aye, this is one of the safest places you can be during an attack. Mr Brash has a hell of a lot of folk in the likely break-through areas – he's not risking you youngsters on the front line. The idea is you'll be right safe here but a bit useful as well.'

'And if the Brethren parachute straight in to the Cloister?' Jason asked, peering through one narrow window onto the cross-shadowed grass. 'Won't we be in the front line then?'

'If they get past our surface-to-air missiles and armed choppers, you mean, lad?' Smith answered. 'Even if they do get themselves into the cloister, they'll be caught in an almighty crossfire that will rip them to shreds. Nothing will survive out there.'

Jason nodded.

'Now then, lads and lasses,' Smith said, 'I know you've heard this a hundred times or more but I want you all, not just the new boy, to listen up to your procedures and escape routes.'

Smith was a good instructor – clear, concise and graphic. He quickly covered the essentials. Anyone approaching the armoury was to be ordered to halt, scanned with their walkie-talkies which apparently had a detector to pick up signals from identity pin transmitters all abbey personnel were going to be wearing. If cleared, they were to be given the ammunition they needed and sent on their way.

In the unlikely event the cloister was overrun, they would fall back through a small door at the rear of the armoury which opened into the chapter house. From there they were to make their way into the church itself.

Smith didn't stop with just explaining things however. Cloister 5 group then spent the next two hours practicing and re-practicing each routine - everything from checking an approaching guard with the radio pin-detector and scurrying for specific ammunition to laying down a cross-fire of blanks across the cloister and running through the fallback routes to the church doors.

Jason tried to take a measure of solace from the fact that most of the procedures seemed well thought out and everyone else seemed to know what they were doing. However, the deafening crack and echo of the blank fire around the cloister called up memories of his mother's murder and his stomach filled with moths whenever he imagined agents landing in on the grass and swarming towards their armoury door.

The fallback plan worried him as well. To reach the supposedly safe church, the members of Cloister Five group had to get into the chapter house through the rear of the armoury, run along a corridor past all the offices and out across the small rose garden, dash in through another door and turn left for the high security entrance into the church.

If, Jason wondered, the abbey was overrun with heavily armed Brethren agents and demon-possessed killers, that escape route was hardly secure. The chapter house had its own group of defenders – Cloister 4 – but what happens if they were also overrun and the building was crawling with Brethren? Also, even though the rose garden was completely enclosed by buildings, the Brethren could parachute in there as well and be waiting for them.

They practised the route nonetheless and after three attempts, the whole team were evacuating the armoury and slamming in to the locked church door in under a minute. Perhaps the route was a good one after all. In any case, there was no other way out from the armoury.

Finally, Smith stopped the rehearsing. 'Right my little soldiers, I think you've got the procedures fairly straight in your heads at last and mayhap you're getting' a bit bored now. Still - the next time we do it we'll have a few score Brethren at our heels to liven things up a mite, eh?'

He glanced at his watch. 'Now then, before you all run off for a quick lunch, I'm to give you these.'

Smith pulled out a small, slim case from his pocket and opened it. Inside was a row of pin transmitters. They were no bigger than a penny coin, completely black and each had a printed name tag tied to it.

'Here,' he said, handing them out and tearing off the name tag as he did so, 'pin these to the inside of your clothes and don't go anywhere without them from now on.'

The students each carefully pinned the small transmitters to the inside of their T-shirts.

'Now remember, these little pins are your best hope of not being shot by 'friendly fire'. Control can tell exactly who and where you are and they can be scanned by our walkie talkies to call up your photo id.'

'What happens if we lose it?' Jason asked.

Sergeant Smith shook his head. 'If you have no pin, lad or even if your face doesn't fit the photo, you'll likely get yourself shot.'

'Excellent,' Jason mumbled and double checked his transmitter.

'Now then,' Smith said, 'off you go to feed your faces before it's time for a spell of shooting things with that nice Mr Mann.'

Groaning, Anna led the team out across the cloister towards the refectory.

***

Lunch consisted of ham and cheese sandwiches, salad, fruit and cereal bars. Anna piled up a plate full and dragged Jason and his food outside.

'Come on, we need to chat a bit.'

Most of the students had also decided to eat outside and they were flaked out all along the river bank and onto the huge lawns at the rear of the abbey.

Anna found a quiet spot and plonked herself down. 'Now then, youngster, something's bothering you, isn't it?' she said quietly'

'What – apart from the fact that we're going to be attacked by murdering, Brethren agents at any minute?'

Anna smiled. 'Yeah, I can see how that might be a little unsettling but you're worried about something else. We need to clear out whatever is clouding that tiny little adolescent brain of yours before they put a gun in your hand.'

Jason couldn't help it, he grinned back at her. *How could she be so calm about it all*

'My sister, Miranda, is staying with some friends in Darkston Wick – they won't to come into the abbey because they don't trust your... Mr Brash.'

'Can't say I blame them – he can be a bit of a git at times. Still, to be honest, they're probably safer staying put – the Brethren won't waste time or manpower scouring the valley if they've worked out all you juicy Gifted are here in the abbey.' Anna shrugged and took a bite out of her pile of sandwiches.

'Maybe,' Jason said, 'Mr Brash said the same sort of thing.'

'There you are then – it must be true,' Anna said. 'Now, any other worries Aunty Anna needs to hear about?'

Jason bought himself some time by shoving some banana into his mouth. Even if Anna was right, he still couldn't risk leaving Miranda out there, especially if Dad wasn't back. He felt torn however – if he sneaked out of the abbey tonight, he'd be abandoning Anna and the others.

'Everyone seems pretty sure that they can take on whatever the Brethren throw at us.'

'That's because we can.' Anna said.

'What if there are some Touched agents or a demon itself?'

'Security and the Gifted teams have trained against the Touched – they can cope.'

'What, really?' Jason asked. 'How can they do that?'

'Captured spies and agents of course. When the hunter teams bring them in, we can't ever let them go again. Until a couple of years ago we'd hardly ever seen any Touched. Transporting any of the captured ones over from Europe by land and sea is really dangerous and takes so long they're half degenerated before they get here but now our teams are capturing more and more of them in Britain – half a dozen this year alone…'

'Hold on – are you saying you bring Touched Brethren agents here to, what, kill in training?'

Anna held his eyes. 'A few, yeah.'

'But… but that's disgusting,' Jason said, searching her face to see if she was trying to pull off some sick joke. 'You can't kill humans for practice…'

'Oh don't be so righteous, Jason,' Anna snapped, 'they'd do worse to us. Do you even have half a clue what goes on in the Carpathian Mountains if any of us are captured? We need to be as well prepared as humanly possible before we go out into the field and that includes having seen and maybe done some killing.'

Jason stared at her then looked away across the grass to let things cool down for a moment. He chewed his bottom lip. So Anna shared some of her father's ideas then – use anybody in any way necessary to achieve the goal.

'Do Touched agents get… used like that all through the Watch?' he asked.

Anna narrowed her eyes at him, perhaps assessing if he was on side with her father's training methods or not. 'Not exactly – over there, advanced student teams pair up with experienced hunters on real missions deep in the mountains. That won't work in Britain – most of the Brethren we've managed to find here have been in cities and towns so we can't... practise hunting them in front of half the UK population.'

'So you ship them back to the abbey where your murdering them won't be seen?'

'Yes, Jason, that's right,' Anna said. 'If they're Touched, they're as good as dead already and the alternative is we send out untried teams to be slaughtered or Touched themselves.'

Jason dropped his eyes from Anna's stare. *This was all part of what Dad had tried to protect him from. He needed to face it, learn about it all.*

'You said there's more Touched agents over here now. That must mean...'

'... there are demons in Britain. Well done, Lightning,' Anna said, visibly trying to lighten the mood.

Jason chewed his lip. 'I guess I sort of imagined all the demons were in Eastern Europe somewhere.'

'Now wouldn't that be nice and neat? Unfortunately for us, the demons go wherever their summoners go and that means most of Europe.'

'Only Europe? What about America, Australia and so on?'

'Demons have problems crossing over water, even high up in planes. They're really weak when surrounded by any water, especially seawater. However, it seems they've found a way of coping with crossing over to us - maybe the channel tunnel makes things easier for them.'

Dozens more questions bubbled up in Jason's brain but Anna put a finger to her lips. 'Enough talking for now – it's time to shoot stuff. You're going to just love Joshua Mann.'

They put the remains of their lunch on a trolley that had been wheeled outside and followed a meandering line of other students across the lawns and into the trees. A minute later they arrived at the firing ranges.

Half the students from the refectory including Fast Eddie, Oliver and Erin were grouped in a large clearing between three buildings. The largest structure was low-roofed, thick walled, triple glazed and perhaps forty metres wide and over a hundred long. The other two buildings were smaller - one low and flat and the other thin and two storeys high.

'Those two are for simulations – like the pub and hotel in the training halls.' Anna explained, nodding at the smaller buildings. 'They've got pop up targets and all sorts - just like in the movies.'

The door to the main building opened and the students filed inside. The place was huge and housed perhaps thirty shooting lanes which were dark for their entire length but with a spot-lit, man-size target at their far end. The shooting gallery end was dimly lit in red light and, despite the size of the place, it was almost claustrophobic.

'Welcome to my playground.' said a computer-geek type voice rising up from the front of the small crowd of students. 'Of course, it is quite a dangerous playground… one where you will probably get killed if you don't follow my rules.'

Jason stood on tip-toe to get a glimpse of the instructor. He'd bushy brown hair, small pig eyes and was short and scrawny.

'For those unfortunates who do not yet know me, my name is Joshua Mann – I am Mr Brash's chief fire-arms instructor here at Darkston Abbey.'

Mann paused for a moment. He'd three assistant instructors standing behind him all cradling machine guns.

'As most of you know, we train in two basic weapons – the Kalashnikov AK47 machine gun, and the Heckler and Koch MK23 pistol. Most students cannot handle a Kalashnikov well enough to be considered safe; however, we will allow you to try. Today's trials will confirm which weapon you are allocated for our forthcoming showdown with the Brethren. Now, choose a lane and don't touch anything.'

Eddie and co. were at the front of the group and eagerly dashed off to secure three lanes together. Jason followed Anna somewhat less enthusiastically.

For the next five minutes he tried to concentrate as Joshua Mann belaboured basic safe-firing instructions for both weapons in his derisive tones. Finally he gave them all ear defenders, which pleased Jason no end until he realised they were fitted with a tiny internal speaker so they could still hear their instructor's learned voice.

Finally, Joshua Mann ordered everyone to take a pistol to the lanes and begin shooting at the targets.

The kick-back from the first four or five shots took some getting used to but then, to Jason's immense surprise, using the hand gun - the MK23, Mann had called it - began to feel natural to him. He could judge the aim quickly and accurately and the weight of the cold steel seemed to fade away. When he pressed the switch to zip the target back Anna whistled in admiration from the next lane.

Next up was the Kalashnikov and within a minute Jason proved to be a disaster with it. Even trying to stick to short bursts, the butt hammer-drilled into his shoulder and the muzzle seemed to jerk everywhere. He hit his own target with about ten percent of the rounds, the rest decimating the targets to either side or thudding into the concrete roof and floor. Joshua Mann took the Kalashnikov away and gave him back the pistol with a patronising shake of his head.

They stuck at it for over an hour. Motorised belts whipped the targets to different distances and back to the shooter to check their score. Jason quickly became consistently accurate with the pistol, grouping most the magazine's eleven rounds closely together even on a thirty metre target. His success even brought a pursed-lipped nod from Joshua Mann before he took the gun off Jason, reloaded it in a flash and grouped all eleven bullets in the target's forehead after increasing the range by 10 metres.

'Still some way to go, sonny,' Mann said, handing back the pistol and turning on to stroll down the gallery.

'Silly man,' Jason mumbled, staring at a spot just between Joshua's shoulder blades, 'turning his back on a boy with a gun.' Reluctantly he returned to shooting down the range at the cardboard targets.

Halfway though the session, Marakoff joined them in the firing range. He took both a pistol and a Kalashnikov and found an empty lane about five stations away from Jason without even glancing in his direction.

Jason did his best to watch the former ghost surreptitiously between shots. Marakoff was deadly, particularly with the pistol. Target after target was burst apart through the forehead or heart. Joshua Mann kept stopping to watch the former ghost's prowess and seemed to shout a lot more at the students.

At last they were ordered to stop and make safe. As they gathered by the door, Marakoff strolled over to Jason.

'You are Jason Willow, yes?'

Jason nodded. 'Mr Brash said you used to work with my grandfather.'

'Yes indeed – a fine man. He would have liked to see your shooting today. I am pleased to meet you.' Marakoff held out his hand.

Jason shook hands. Something hard pressed into his palm.

'A pity your father didn't continue to show such... dedication to the fight,' Marakoff said.

Jason gripped whatever Marakoff was passing to him with his thumb and pulled his hand away, angrily. 'I don't want to hear this – my father risked his life countless times for the Watch.'

'This is true, but there are few of his power left to us – he should have stayed hunting until he could do it no more,' Marakoff said, rubbing his injured leg. 'I hope you will be more loyal.'

Jason turned away, mumbling under his breath. Joshua Mann stood by the door, watching them with the hint of a smug grin on his face. 'Come on, hot-shots,' the instructor said as Marakoff shrugged and returned to his practise, 'time to feed your ugly faces.'

Jason handed back the pistol and was the first one out. He shivered despite the early evening sunshine streaming into the clearing. The next time he shot a pistol it might be at Brethren agents swarming out of those trees.

In his pocket he closed his fingers around the thing Marakoff had passed to him. It felt like a small piece of paper, tightly rolled up. He skirted around the simulation building and ducked into the trees. No one seemed to take any notice of him but who knew how many cameras were covering the area? He found a particularly large trunk and sank down behind it.

It was a note. Jason opened it and frowned at the rounded, girlish writing style:

> *Dear Jase,*
> *I haven't had a chance to catch you on your own for ages. Please meet me in the trees behind the guesthouse tonight at eleven o'clock. Don't go out through the front door or cross any light as there are cameras everywhere and they're bound to ruin things for us. I can't wait to go out with you.*
>
> *Love... you know who xxxx*
>
> *P.S. It is probably best to destroy this note because they don't like students getting together. x*

Jason shook his head. *Really subtle! Either Marakoff had hidden his real feelings for him very well or he was trying to disguise the note as a love letter in case it was found.*

He quickly ripped the note into shreds and buried the pieces in three different places. Then he walked back into the clearing.

'Why were you skulking off into the trees?'

Jason jumped. Anna was watching him as she stretched out her arms and shoulders. Most of the others had already gone.

'You're not upset about what that ex-ghost prat said about your dad are you?' Anna asked, straightening up.

'What? Oh, no – your... Mr. Brash warned me that he might say something like that.'

'Fair enough. So you were wandering around in the trees because...?'

'Uh... you know... too much water at lunch.' Jason said.

Anna started working out her neck, rolling her head slowly back and forth. 'There's a toilet block just there – see?' She pointed without looking to a small, wooden annexe with clear male and female toilet signs fixed over the door.

Jason shrugged.

'Honestly, boys and peeing up against trees. Do you ever grow out of it?'

Jason grinned sheepishly. 'Just our way of marking our territory.'

'Lovely – well no holding hands with Aunty Anna before you've washed them.' She stopped stretching and straightened up, groaning like a granny. 'I hate shooting, it makes me so bloody tense.'

'I know what you mean,' Jason said, doing a few half hearted stretches of his own.

'You were pretty good with the Heckler though,' Anna said, 'it might just be worth having you around after all'.

'I aim to please.' Jason said.

'Such a wag,' Anna grinned. 'Come on, let's clean up and eat something.'

'Sure,' Jason said, looking away. If he left the abbey with Marakoff tonight, this might be the last meal he ever had with Anna.

***

Finally it was dark.

Eddie and the others had joined them at dinner but the mood in the refectory had changed from excited to sombre. They'd all been told to return to the guesthouse as soon as they'd finished their meal and at eight o'clock a young, spikey-haired, security guard began knocking on each room to click the students off an electronic register. The guard had been in a hurry – his face was all tight lines and his voice a little too high. After the visual check, the doors were locked.

It was a good job Jason had been planning a different exit to meet Marakoff.

Now Jason checked his watch for what must have been the hundredth time that evening – half past ten.

'Time to go,' he said to himself and stuck the pin transmitter Sergeant Smith had given him on the underside of his pillow. If anyone was bothering to monitor the student pin transmissions tonight they would think he was still safe and sound, tucked up in his room. The downside was if he was caught outside without it, Smith had told them they could be shot on sight.

Jason stopped chewing his lip and focussed on the positive – he was meeting with Marakoff the ex-ghost, they wouldn't get caught.

He'd been going over his plan for this escape for the last two hours. He couldn't just walk out the front door. As Marakoff had warned, the area was heavily covered by image-enhancing cameras and he was locked in his room now anyway. It would have to be the windows.

For the twelfth time, Jason touched the open button to his large bedroom window and, as before, it opened to about ten centimetres then stopped. He nodded, turned his small television on and flicked to MTV. 'Love In An Elevator' by Aerosmith rattled out of the small speakers. Perfect. Jason increased the volume a little and went in to the bathroom.

The long, narrow window was already open. He drew in breath, concentrated on one of the steel bars fixing the bottom corner of the window to the wall and jabbed his right index finger straight at it. A pencil thin bolt of solidified air thudded into the wall and small chunks of plaster and brick burst into the bathroom. He tugged the bar free of the debris. He did the same to the bar on the other side and pushed the window open.

The way was clear. Coughing a little at the brick dust floating in the still night air, he went to turn down the music in case anyone came knocking to complain and then hoisted himself half out of the narrow window.

The central courtyard below was as still and dark as a mass grave. The yew tree, which was usually spot-lit, was

346

now only a dark silhouette against the lighter walls. Heavy cloud which had been building slowly all evening obscured any moonlight. Everything seemed to be on his side apart from the fact that he was hanging out of a window two floors above some very hard paving slabs.

Jason reached out a hand and formed a large air block in front of him and dropped the needle-thin support column to merge with the slabs below. He pulled himself out on to the shimmering platform of air and scanned the windows around the court. Most were locked shut and all were curtained with the odd chink of light escaping from a few. The spikey haired guard taking the register had told them to keep their lights low and curtains closed.

Quickly Jason formed block after block to step up and onto the roof edge.

Now he couldn't use the air steps any more. The support columns needed somewhere stable to merge with and slanted, crackable roof tiles weren't a good option. However, he'd already thought of the solution.

Silently, he formed an air plank which rested on the tiles and butted up against one of the stone gargoyles. He scuttled up his air-beam to the top of the roof and then used the same trick to get down to the gutters on the other side.

There he waited, studying the ground below. A few drops of light rain began to fall, icing down his neck and back. He smiled tightly to himself. The conditions were perfect for his escape – cloud-darkened sky and now rain to cover any noise.

The hundred metres of lawn between the guesthouse and the wooded valley side was brightly lit by floodlights and covered by CCTV. Everywhere would be closely monitored tonight and there were bound to be guards patrolling in the woods.

Taking a deep, calming breath Jason formed his first air block a foot out from where he crouched. The support column dropped twenty metres to the grass below and sank deep into the ground.

He stepped off the roof. The block wavered on its super-thin support and then steadied. Quickly Jason formed the next one and the next. Even at this height, forming the blocks and supports was almost second nature to him after the hours of practice with Schmidt. He just tried not to think of the drop below.

When he reached the tree line, his nose almost touching the outer branches of a huge pine, he stopped and crouched down on his small platform of air. For a count of sixty he stared into the tree shadows below, listening and waiting. Then, daring to feel pleased with himself, he began to slowly "melt" the base of the air-column under his block. It was jerky at first as he hadn't practised this one much with Schmidt, but ever more quickly, he descended from the tree tops down to perhaps three metres. Although he was half hidden in branches, floodlight still dappled over him but he forced himself to stop again and listen. All he could hear was the soft hiss and spatter of drizzle.

Jason lowered himself to the ground and stepped silently into the woods.

Hands locked around his mouth and throat and he was dragged backwards into the tree-dark.

***

'It is me, Marakoff.'

Jason breathed out slowly and let his Gift fade – Marakoff had been a second away from having two elbow blasts to the stomach. The hands slipped away and Jason turned around. He could just make out half a silhouette.

'Nicely done, Jason.' Marakoff whispered, 'You left your pin in your room, yes? I forgot to remind you in the note.'

'Yes,' Jason said, rubbing his throat. He'd no idea the rangy Marakoff had such strength. 'Nice note, by the way – I didn't know you cared so much.'

'Perhaps it is that I am shy, yes?'

Jason grinned, despite their situation.

'Now,' said Marakoff, 'we need to move quickly – there are guard-teams everywhere but fortunately the ghosts are not patrolling – they are on stand-by with their teams.'

Marakoff kept turning his head slowly this way and that as he whispered. He seemed to be using his ears, more than his eyes to search in all directions.

'Is Miranda okay?' Jason whispered. 'Is Dad back yet?'

Marakoff began to answer then put a hand over Jason's mouth and froze. After a minute he spoke again. 'A patrols is close by. Yes to both questions but we need to get out now or your father may get himself killed coming into the abbey to fetch you.'

'What? Why?'

'We are not sure how far Alan Brash will go to keep you here.'

'He wouldn't touch Dad, though.'

'I hope not. Now - enough explanations. No more speaking and follow exactly in my footsteps.'

Before Jason could ask anything else, Marakoff was fading into the night and all he could do was try to follow. The man was nearly invisible in the dark woods and silent, even over the fallen twigs. In less than a minute Jason had lost him.

Then Marakoff was suddenly beside him, one hand clamping over his mouth and easing them both down into a low crouch.

'Patrol,' Marakoff whispered in Jason's ear and slowly released his hand.

Jason slowed his breathing and peered into the darkness between the trees. He couldn't see any movement at all but a faint rustling of branches reached him over the gentle leaf-drip of drizzle.

'Lie flat. Ease down onto every twig beneath you,' Marakoff whispered in his ear again and they both slowly stretched out onto the damp, rich loam of the forest floor.

A moment later, perhaps twenty feet away, two large figures stepped quickly through a slash of cloud-busting moonlight then disappeared again.

Jason raised his head to make sure they'd gone but Marakoff pushed it down. 'Wait for their tail.'

Wondering what Marakoff was talking about, Jason kept his head down. They waited for another thirty seconds or so before Jason heard a rustle slightly out of time with the wind-stirred branches but he couldn't see anything. The waiting made his blood freeze and he tried to keep his breathing calm. The smell of earth filled his nostrils while its cool dampness soaked into the bone of his half buried chin.

Still Marakoff made them wait. One, two more minutes passed.

At last he tapped Jason's forearm and they eased themselves to their feet. 'Cadaveril has trained the guards well, I think.'

'What were you talking about just then – wait for their tail?' Jason whispered, still unnerved by the guard's passing.

'The tail is a third guard, often trained by a ghost. He parallels the more obvious patrol a little way behind… to catch the unwary or add surprise crossfire should they find trouble.'

'I didn't see a third man,' Jason said,. All this invisible ninja stuff made his own powers seem useless.

'I am not surprised, she was very good and passed only ten metres behind us. Now stay close to me this time.'

Marakoff seemed to almost ice-skate up the wooded valley side while Jason struggled after him feeling like a ballet dancing rhinoceros. Finally they reached the top of the slope where the trees abruptly stopped. Marakoff signalled and they crawled on their bellies to the very edge of the tree line where they could study Darkston Abbey's defences starting just ten metres down the far slope.

It was like a Russian border crossing from the Cold War days. Anyone looking up from outside the abbey grounds would only see an ancient, fifteen foot high, dry-stone wall, albeit topped with razor wire and punctuated every hundred metres with stone watchtowers mounted with spotlights.

The wall, however, was only the start of the defences.

Should anyone manage to get over the wall and wire, they would find themselves in six or seven metres of no-man's land between the back of the wall and a second perimeter – a steel posted fence, three metres high and overhung with more razor wire – this time electrified, judging by the warning signs. Incredibly, other little red-on-white signs warned of landmines between the fence and the wall.

Marakoff touched Jason's shoulder and slowly pointed out cameras in the wall and in the trees to either side of them.

He whispered in Jason's ear. 'Heat and movement detectors scan most of the no-man's land. The moment anything is detected the whole section is floodlit. The watchtowers are each manned twenty four hours a day by one guard equipped with a heavy machine gun and a laser-sighted sniper rifle. There are also, I believe, some small rocket launchers hidden inside.'

'Great. So how do we get out – air steps?' Jason whispered.

'A good thought. At perhaps ten feet above the ground we could avoid the heat sensors but the movement detectors would very much like your support columns. Also the watchtower guards would enjoy the show I think – until they shot us down. If we were unlucky, perhaps we'd also explode a land mine, yes?'

Jason scowled. The rain was getting heavier now, dripping on to his neck and trickling down his back like someone else's cold sweat. This was looking hopeless.

'What then – air-blast the fence, the towers, the wall and set off a path through the mines?'

'Possible – with a few weeks' more training for you – but still a little noisy, I think. I suspect we'd have a small army and a number of Gifted teams joining us before we were very far beyond the wall.'

'Okay…' Jason mused, staring up and down the barrier to freedom. 'but there aren't that many Gifted here, so perhaps…'.

'Ah – I am afraid that is no longer true. Brash has trained many teams over all the years he has been here in the abbey. Perhaps it is just a lucky coincidence that a number of them were here for the training exercise. Then again, perhaps this emergency was a little more planned than it would at first appear.'

Jason stared at him for a moment more then went back to examining the no-man's land. 'So how are we going to get across?'

'Well, somehow the guards have to walk into their watchtowers, yes?'

'And you know how?'

'It is, as you would say, my job to know such things.'

'So tell me,' Jason said. He was getting cramp, lying flat out on the damp ground.

Marakoff held up a pacifying hand. 'All in good time, yes? First we must tell your father we are about to leave.'

'Dad? Is he out there? How are you going to reach him - mobiles don't work in the valley do they?' Jason asked.

'Your father is hiding in the village and I will use this,' Marakoff answered, pulling out a radio no bigger than a flip phone.

Jason felt a tug in his stomach. Somewhere on the other side of the wall, Dad was waiting for him. He swallowed a lump in his throat and concentrated on Marakoff. 'Hey – isn't that one of the walkie-talkies we used to play spies with?' Jason asked.

'Indeed – old technology now but they are still very sophisticated toys. The messages are scrambled on alternating frequencies as they are transmitted.'

'Won't security pick up anything?'

'Without a computer decoder and several hours all they would hear is interference… I hope.' Marakoff winked at him and pressed the transmit button.

'Hello, Richard…' he began.

And then all hell broke lose.

Chapter 22

Instantly Marakoff pulled Jason down and they squirmed further back into the trees.

Then they froze, each lying flat with their heads pressed against a tree trunk to break any silhouette. Slowly Marakoff allowed Jason to raise his head and squint out at the wall's defences.

Sirens wailed, piercing through Jason's head and making it impossible to think clearly. Searchlights from the towers burst in to life, sweeping the ground outside the walls.

Why were the lights focused outside the walls?

'It was not my radio,' Marakoff whispered right in his ear so as to be heard through the sirens, 'they are not searching for us. The Brethren must be here.'

Jason turned to face Marakoff whose features were no more than a slightly less dark shadow under the trees. 'If they attack now it might give us the cover we need to get out.'

'That would be too high a risk to take, I am afraid. We do not know how many Brethren are out there or where they are.'

'So what do we do – stay in the woods and wait to see who wins?' Jason hissed through the noise wailing through his head.

Marakoff pushed him down low again. A moment later a covered truck thundered in from their right. It barely slowed down in front of the nearest watchtower before a guard leapt out and the truck accelerated away again.

The guard rushed over to stand by the fence. There was no visible gate but suddenly a three foot section of the wire pulled out of the ground and concertinaed itself up to create a door-sized hole. Bright red lights burned into life just below the soil to show a zigzag path across the minefield to the base of the watch tower.

The guard stepped through the gap and carefully followed the light path to the tower. The wire section whirred down, the path lights winked out and the man disappeared inside a steel door.

'Reinforcements for the tower - the attack will be heavy, I think,' Marakoff said.

As if to back up his judgement, two small explosions sounded in the middle distance - perhaps only a mile away. Three more followed. The guard manning the tower-top searchlight in front of them swung the beam quickly to the right and it bounced back from a billowing cloud of white smoke.

'The Brethren are using smoke grenades to cover their assault,' Marakoff explained quietly. 'We will have to return to the abbey. We are too exposed out here. Back to your room, I am afraid.'

'What? We can't go back. What about Dad? He's waiting out there for us…'

'Your father can look after himself very well indeed. We agreed, should an attack happen before you and I escaped, we'd stay inside the abbey grounds.'

'So what's Dad going to do?'

'If the Brethren break into the abbey, he will follow them through and find us. Otherwise we will try to leave at the same time tomorrow night.'

A dozen or more small explosions burst out of bright flashes on the other side of the wall. They were getting closer. The sirens finally faded out and Jason heard the rattle of machine gun fire from the towers some way along the wall.

'Jesus – they're almost here.'

'Put this in your shoe.' Marakoff pulled out a piece of plastic a quarter of the size of a credit card. 'It will help your father to find you if you have to leave your Cloister 5 position. I will be close by.'

'Aren't you staying with me?' Jason asked.

'No. I am not sure Brash believes my story - I think perhaps my identity pin will be sending an… unfriendly signal. I will have to leave it behind and stay out of sight.'

Jason flinched as more explosions echoed through the night. The searchlights blazing down from the tower tops now lit up a solid bank of smoke rising above the walls. wire-thin red lasers pierced the smoke and the powerful crack of a sniper rifles spat out their first shots.

'We have to be quick now,' Marakoff whispered. 'Back to your room for your pin first – otherwise they will shoot you before ever you get near to your little hiding place in the cloister.'

Quickly Marakoff backed them deeper into the dark of the wood where they got to their feet and dashed down the valley side. Marakoff must have been depending on the patrols all being either at the walls or taking positions around the abbey. Jason hoped he was right. Although Marakoff was still almost undetectable at this speed, Jason's legs and arms seemed to rustle and crack against every branch and fallen twig in existence.

They made it to the forest edge and stopped to stare across the floodlit lawn to the dark bulk of the guest house. Rain still drizzled down, glistening silver in the bright lights.

Marakoff grasped Jason by the shoulders. 'Only use your Gift if your life depends on it – Touched and demons can sense the zephyr just as Gifted can – the strength of your powers will lead them straight to you. Now – back to your room the same way as you got out.'

'You just said don't use my Gift.'

'They are not close enough yet to feel the small uses of your Gift. Now go – you may have already been called to the cloister.'

'Right... uhh, thanks and, you know, be careful.'

Marakoff nodded and turned him around to face the guesthouse. 'Go. I will always be near you.'

Jason formed his first air-step in the shadows of the tree line. He felt numb - none of this seemed to be really happening. Some time tonight the abbey might be filled with men and monsters intent on destroying everyone and possessing him. He turned back to Marakoff, but the ghost had already disappeared.

Chewing his lip, Jason stepped on to his air-platform and rose up through the trees.

At the roof top Jason caught a glimpse of security guards and vehicles milling around in front of the garages. A couple of jeeps, headlights flaring, sped off up the drive towards the gatehouse but all the other vehicles kept their lights off as they moved. In the darkness, men and machines seemed to be ebbing away into the trees beyond the church.

Jason quickly moved down the inner roof on an air-beam and stopped at the edge. Lights were flicking off behind curtained windows – the students must be leaving for their attack stations.

Jason quickly formed another air stepping stone, the support column dropping silently down onto the dark slabs three floors below and started crossing to his broken bathroom window.

His room was silent and dark when he crawled back in. He quickly pulled on some dry training trousers and T-shirt and clipped on the identification pin from under his pillow. Finally, he slipped Marakoff's thin plastic transmitter in one trainer – *would Dad be tuned in to it already, following it in right now to find him?*

Taking a moment to calm himself, breathing deeply, slowly he walked to the door and rested his forehead against it. It was quiet here in his little room, quiet and safe.

Bang, bang, bang.

'Jason – get up now.'

He heard the tiny tones of his key pad being pressed. He rushed back to sit on his bed, flicked on the low table light and tore off a trainer.

Sergeant Smith burst in, two guards in the hall behind. 'What the bloody 'ell have you been up to lad?'

Jason laced his trainer back on. 'Sorry... I only woke up a couple of minutes ago. What's happening? Is this a practise?'

Smith looked around the room then stared at the half open bathroom door for a moment. If he went in there and saw the window...

'No, it's bloody well not,' Smith said, checking the corridor outside. Four guards with Kalashnikovs scuttled passed. 'The Brethren are almost at the walls and the tannoys called everyone to attack stations five minutes ago.

'Sorry. I sleep through anything... always have,' Jason said and crossed the room to Smith.

Smith stared at him for a moment then reached for his walkie-talkie. 'Smith – found him and returning to Cloister 5.'

'Come on, then,' Smith said and turned to leave. The two guards darted ahead and Jason dashed out after him. The corridor lights had been dimmed to almost nothing and dark shapes with rifles crouched next to every third window on both floors as the four of them raced by.

Outside, the gravelled approach Jason had watched from the roof top was almost deserted now. He scanned the windows and tree line but there wasn't anything to see through the curtain of drizzle.

'Come on lad, this isn't a sight seeing tour.' Smith fiddled with something in his ear – a small, blue earphone - and they leapt down the stone steps and ran around towards the little stone bridge that led to the refectory back entrance.

Jason caught up with Smith. 'Will they be able to get through the walls?'

Jason could have sworn a smile flickered across Smiths rugged face. 'It's possible lad, more than possible, you might say.'

Suddenly a tiny red dot appeared on Smith's forehead – a laser sight. A second beam lanced out at one of the other guards from behind the bridge's low wall.

'Freeze. Check in.'

All four of them skidded to a halt.

'Sergeant Smith, Jason Willow, Alexor and Ludovich.'

Two bright torch beams flared in their faces for a couple of seconds. 'Pass.'

The laser dots disappeared and Jason breathed again. The pin system worked then: their identification and photos beamed to the guard's walkie-talkie monitors and Smith confirming their names.

They reached the small riverside refectory door just as two explosions sounded from the hill-top gatehouse.

'Inside, Jason – quickly,' Smith said and shoved him into the refectory. The normally bright and cheerful room was now only dimly illuminated in red light. The door closed itself behind them and silence fell.

They dashed between the long benches, their footsteps echoing in the deserted hall.

'Why isn't there a team stationed in here?' Jason whispered.

'We don't want any of our lot in 'ere if the enemy break in,' Smith said, jerking his head up towards one corner of the refectory.

Jason looked up. Half hidden in the shadows was a camera and beneath it, something that looked like the barrel of a gun – a big gun. Next to it was the dark open end of some sort of tube. Jason checked the other corners – all the same. The entire refectory could become a killing-ground of cross-fired bullets and whatever was going to hiss out of those pipes.

Smith reached the main door out to the cloister then stopped, tapping his earpiece. 'Sergeant Smith entering cloister from the refectory.'

He nodded once and opened the door.

'Bloody hell,' Smith spat as two red laser dots appeared on his forehead. Distant gunfire rattled in sporadic bursts now, echoing dully around the cloister. There were three explosions and this time the sky over the gatehouse flashed bright white.

'Check in' two voices called, almost simultaneously. One of them sounded like Oliver Stone's powerful bass rumble.

'Sergeant Smith, Jason Willow, Alexor and Ludovich.' Smith yelled.

'Pass,' Both voices shouted back over the gunfire and the dots winked out.

The armoury door flew open and Anna appeared. 'Jason - where the hell have you been?'

'I was asleep. I didn't hear…'

'Shut up,' Smith said. 'Get inside. Alexor, Ludovich – thanks for your company.'

The two guards nodded and hurried into the chapter house next door as Jason and Sergeant Smith stepped passed Anna into the armoury. She slammed the heavy, steel-cored door behind them and hastily bolted it top and bottom. The sharp crackle of gunfire dulled a little.

As Jason's eyes adjusted to the dust-dimmed red lighting, four white faces emerged from the gloom around him.

Oliver Stone was at one of the small windows, his big frame cramped into the corner on top of two boxes of ammunition. He held a Kalashnikov pointing out into the cloister and a walkie-talkie lay on the windowsill.

Carl was at the other window, sitting more easily with his Kalashnikov propped against the wall next to him. He stared back at Jason for a moment then turned to open the window's steel shutters. Still distant gunfire spattered in with the drizzle.

Erin and Eddie sat together on boxes further back into the room where it narrowed to the claustrophobic aisle between stacks of wooden cases and weapon racks. They both wore an earphone like Sergeant Smith's and kept glancing at their walkie-talkie readout screens. Eddie gave Jason a casual wink that convinced no one.

Anna coughed behind him.

Jason turned around. She stood, hands on hips facing him from the closed door.

'You slept through the alarms and the screeching bloody tannoys?' She said, incredulously. 'We thought…'

Smith nudged past Jason and reached for something lying on one of the packed shelves. 'Tellin' offs can wait, Anna. Here, put this on lad.'

Smith handed Jason a gun belt – an MK23 pistol was fastened into a holster on the right, a radio clipped on the left and ammunition pouches ran around the front and back. It was cold and heavy – much heavier than Jason remembered from training. He strapped on the hard leather, his fingers fumbling with the buckle. The holster pressed against his thigh – awkward and distracting.

Jason took in a slow breath. *I might have to kill someone with this tonight – just point, squeeze the trigger and take a life.*

Smith looked at him, shook his head and unclipped an earphone attachment from Jason's radio. 'Put it in your ear and press this button if you've something important to say. Otherwise just listen to what's going on. Now sit down over there with your friends out of the way.'

Jason nodded and moved to take a box next to Eddie. It was getting hot in the packed room, hot and stuffy. His head was mugging up.

'Right,' said Smith, moving over to check the locks on the cloister door, 'now listen in. We're as safe as houses in here. It's my job to baby-sit you youngsters and it's your job to pass the ammo forward if need be. You know where everything is from this afternoon but chances are this will all be over before anyone comes knocking for some more bullets.'

Four more explosions rattled in through the windows but were quickly deadened by the heavy boxes and thick walls. Jason switched on his walkie-talkie and earphone.

Immediately gunfire filled his head but a digital clear voice shouted above the zing of bullets.

'... breached – repeat, main gate breached. Estimate thirty vehicles approaching at high speed.'

Jason glanced down at the readout window – the speaker was someone called "Eldridge". Jason's head filled with images of the massive gatehouse, its grand gates blasted from their hinges and twisting in the mud as enemy tanks rolled over them.

'Good,' Smith mumbled to no one in particular, 'come and get it you buggers.'

The sergeant absently touched the Kalashnikov slung over his back and ambled over to join Carl at the window.

Anna, her hand to her own earphone, slipped over to Jason and leant back against a set of shelves. A faint trace of some spicy body spray reached Jason through the musty, metallic air.

'Enemy coming through – can't hold them,' Eldridge shouted, breathless, his voice breathless.

Another voice, stronger and calmer oozed over the airwaves.

'Captain Eldridge – hold the Main Gates unless they take you down to fifty percent - then fall back to secondary positions. You're doing just fine.'

It was Brash.

'Yes sir - understood, Mr Brash. We'll hold as long as we can.' Gunfire filled the speaker and it went dead.

It sounded like Brash was in a helicopter. Jason had heard the rotor blades throbbing through the radio. Was he going to run the defences from a few hundred feet up?

Jason forced himself to breathe in slowly – it must have felt like this in the Blitz air raid shelters – helplessly waiting for a direct hit while outside, destruction reigned all around.

'Thirty percent casualties – defensive line buckling,' Eldridge's strained voice informed the rest of the abbey.

Jason brushed his fingers back through his hair – people were dying only a few hundred metres from where he sat - actually dying. Why had Brash told Eldridge to hold the gate area until half of the security guards were killed? All those men and machines disappearing into the woods around the gravel approach surely meant the ambush was set for there. Even Sergeant Smith had just mumbled "come and get it" or something. Did Eldridge have to stay there just to make the defence seem convincing... sacrifice lives so the Brethren didn't suspect a trap?

'Scared?' Anna asked, cutting into Jason's thoughts. Her tone was serious, stern almost. Jason guessed a pep-talk was on its way.

'Realistically aware of the dangers,' Jason said.

A tiny smile pulled at one corner of Anna's lips and she nodded. 'Good. Remember though - just treat this as more training. Sadly, we're all too precious to be risked anywhere near the action... like Smith said, nothing is likely to get anywhere near us cooped up here...'

Eldridge's voice flared back onto the open channel. He panted his report between running breaths: 'Main Gate team falling back – sixty percent casualties... Brethren pushing through... heading for the approach at high speed... numbers higher than expected, perhaps one hundred and fifty.'

'They're in.' whispered Jason. His heart began to thump.

'Ready, Green Force. Seal the drive once they're all through.' This time it was Schmidt giving the orders.

'Roger, Captain.'

Jason looked up at Anna. 'This is all planned, isn't it – let them break through and ambush them in front of the garages?'

Anna just winked at him.

Schmidt's voice burst into life again. 'Garage – quarter fire on first sight. Woods and guesthouse - hold fire. Make them think we are weak.'

Jason could see it all in his mind – guns pointing out of the small windows between the garage's arched doors, the guards crouching in the guesthouse and the forces he'd seen disappearing into the trees edging closer for the order to begin their devastating cross fire.

'Enemy sighted.' This was a new voice, a woman – someone called "Celestine" according to Jason's read-out screen. Her accent hinted at France.

The trap was working. The Brethren were racing down the main drive into a huge open bowl surrounded on three sides by solid walls or thick tree cover. There was only one way in and out for vehicles and it was about to be sealed behind them.

'Quarter fire - commence.' Celestine announced and intermittent rifle and Kalashnikov fire crackled then disappeared from Jason's earphone as Celestine must have released her transmission button. The muted rattle of gunfire still reached him though. Jason shivered. A hundred and fifty Brethren were coming for him and they were only forty steps away.

'All ambush forces...' Schmidt's voice was measured, unhurried. 'Full fire – go.'

Lights blazed into life through the armoury's two small windows and a storm of gunfire and explosions ripped through the night air.

And it didn't stop. There must have been human sounds as well - screaming, men being riddled with bullets and torn apart by grenades, desperate orders being shouted - but no voices could be heard above the relentless outpouring of blazing lead, bursting shrapnel and exploding vehicles.

For minute after minute the slaughter went on.

Jason glanced at Anna, then across to Eddie and Erin. Their eyes were hard, their faces fixed. Jason stared down at the floor, trying to block out the noise. He could almost feel the lives being ripped out of the bodies just one building away.

'When will it stop... ?' Jason began, getting to his feet, '... surely they must all be dead by...'

'There's someone in the main firing range.' "Joshua Mann" flashed up on the id screen. 'We can't pin-point the intruder but the alarms have...' The transmission stopped dead – there had been no hint of a struggle, not a single shot by the expert marksman.

'They're coming in from behind,' Anna said, standing and snatching up a Kalashnikov. 'How the hell did they get in without any warning?'

Orders filled their earphones - Schmidt's voice again, a lot faster yet still clear and in control.   'Code Red for Glimmermen inside perimeter One. Rear defences breached. Expect attacks from any direction.   Green, blue and black teams cover the training halls. All patrols to your tree line and close positions. Snipers to infra-red. All entrances at amber seal. Full open area lighting.'

'Sit down, Anna.' Sergeant Smith said, glancing back from the window where he stood next to Carl. She ignored him.

Schmidt's voice came through again.   'Repeat – all entrances at amber – shoot to kill any visual i.d. not matching pin transmission.'

Jason chewed his bottom lip. Marakoff was out there somewhere. He'd said he'd be safer without his pin. Jason edged forward to look out of Carl's window.

Smith leant across Carl and slammed a steel shutter across one half of the small window. Oliver quickly did the same on the other side of the door just as the cloister outside burst into light. The night air was immediately filled with drizzle, sparkling slashes of silver against the glistening black stone. Not a soul moved across the floodlit grass. The shooting had even died away from the ambush.

Smith left the window and stared at Jason and Anna. 'Keep back and sit down.'

Reluctantly they both returned to their ammunition boxes.

Smith nodded and strode down the aisle to the door at the back of the armoury - their escape door. He checked it was locked then turned back to his charges.

'We don't want any uninvited guests coming in our back door now, do we?' he said, then attempted a smile. 'Now don't go all worried on me lads and lasses. We half expected something like this – the whole point was to bring the Brethren in to us, as many as we can. We've reeled in a few more agents than expected at the front and maybe some nice glimmermen at the back if they've managed to get past without a twitch from the surveillance equipment or the teams. It's nothing we can't handle...'

'Brethren helicopters – three choppers, four troop carriers – approaching west wall.' Celestine's voice shouted over intermittent gunfire.

'Two choppers, four carriers – North Wall – five hundred metres and closing fast' That was from someone called Captain Norris.

'Six choppers, three carriers – South Wall. Seven hundred metres and closing.' This from a Captain Sarandon.

Smith's mouth tightened. 'Now how did they get that lot here without anyone noticing?'

'We have the surface-to-air missiles.' Anna said, slowly standing up again.

'Not enough of them, lass... we didn't expect quite this many birds...' Smith turned towards the cloister windows. 'Keep an eye to the sky, lads. That amount of air transport means they have another hundred or more agents to drop wherever they like.'

'Approach cleared of ground forces.' Celestine's soft French accent gave some good news. A moment later she spoke again. 'Birds hovering at two hundred metres.'

Smith cocked his Kalashnikov, making Jason jump at the loud click-clack right by his ear. 'Get yourselves set Stone, Slattery. It's show time' He glanced back at Anna.

'Sit down, lass,' he said, then rejoined Carl at the half shuttered window to stare up at black skies.

Anna stayed on her feet. Jason pulled out his pistol, flipped out the magazine and checked it was full. He'd at least another dozen in his belt pouches. His hands were damp around the knurled cold steel and he quickly put it back in his holster.

Outside the gunfire and explosions had all but disappeared. For a precious few moments it was almost peaceful.

Then the drone of rotor blades reached them.

Missiles screamed upwards to meet the invaders and moments later, three... four... five explosions shook the abbey.

Schmidt sent out his orders. 'Surface to air missile stocks exhausted – five birds down. Remaining airborne are targeting the rear training halls and south side. Patrols hold close and tree line positions – we'll catch them between us the moment they land.'

Jason edged further forward to peer out of Oliver's half shuttered window and stubbed his toe against a box. Smith whipped around and opened his mouth to speak but Schmidt cut in across the radio. 'Code Red – cloister. Chopper attack.'

Like two giant, bulbous flies buzzing up from hell, a matched pair of Brethren helicopters rose over the roof of the church and hovered over the floodlit green of the cloister.

A firestorm of bullets rattled up from all around the cloister. Carl and Oliver emptied their magazines in seconds and scrabbled for new ones. The noise was deafening, crashing through Jason's head and fragmenting all sensible thought. Then one of the choppers exploded and a fire-filled torrent of shrapnel burst down over the cloister.

Oliver slammed his second shutter closed and jumped back from the window as whizzing edges of burning metal thudded into the shutters and door and screeched along the marble walls outside.

Carl hadn't been quick enough. He yelped and threw himself to the floor as fragments of blazing metal and plastic burst in through his half open window.

Smith had flattened himself against the wall. 'Slattery – are you hurt?'

In the red light, Carl got to his knees and pulled a four inch sliver of metal from his left shoulder.

'Not enough,' he said and staggered back towards the window.

'Don't be a hero, lad - get yourself bandaged up. Anna – sort his shoulder out.'

Smith steered Carl back down into the depths of the room then edged back towards the window from the side. Jason moved out of the way to let Carl reach Anna and peered out of the window from two metres back.

Small fires guttered around chunks of helicopter debris in an otherwise black night. The second helicopter had pulled back out of sight.

'They've shot out the cloister lights but have flown higher.' Smith said, peering up into the night sky. 'Looks like things were a little too hot for them down here.'

Jason exhaled slowly. Behind him, Carl sank to the floor in front of Anna, with his right hand pressed to his left shoulder. Blood soaked his shirt, seeping thick and dark through his fingers.

'Fancy trying to catch bits of an exploding helicopter,' Anna muttered, pulling out a length of bandage from a pile of first-aid boxes.

'Oliver' Smith hissed across the door. 'd'you see something against the far wall?'

Oliver slipped the safety catch off his Kalashnikov. 'Where…'

Suddenly, both windows completely blacked out with a metallic "clang".

'What the…' Oliver shouted and levelled his weapon at the window.

'Hold fire.' Smith yelled. 'The ricochet will take your head off,' he reversed his machine gun and hammered the butt into whatever was blocking the windows.

'Steel shields. They must've come in under cover of the blast.' There was no gunfire from outside. 'Sounds like they've got us all blocked in.'

Smith tapped his ear phone and reported. 'Enemy in the cloister – windows all blocked with steel shields, unable to counter attack,' he tapped the transmitter off and spoke to his wards.

'Anna – cover the door. Eddie, Erin, you cover the windows. Oliver, try to knock the plate away and dive out of the way if you manage it.'

Eddie and Erin scrambled over to stand just back from the windows with their pistols levelled. As soon as they were in position, Oliver and Smith hammered at the plates with the butts of their rifles. Oliver quickly gave up and tried pushing with both hands through the small window arch. The plates didn't budge.

'They could be landing half an army out there, right in the middle of the abbey,' Smith panted between hammerings. 'Clever little buggers.'

Distant, muffled gunfire and explosions reached them in-between the hammering. Curt orders and reports burst across the open channel, the names of their transmitters flashed across the radio readout screens too quickly to take in. Battles were raging all around the abbey.

Suddenly three quick shots rang out from the cloister and Smith's steel barrier started to slip away. Instantly it was slammed back in place however and a hail of gunfire rang out.

'Damn it – should have been faster. Someone's on our side out there,' Smith cursed and hammered at the steel again.

Jason swallowed. Was that Marakoff who had tried to clear Smith's window? Had the Brethren killed him?

'Troop carrier approaching the cloister,' someone reported over the radio, 'lines dropping.'

'This is useless.' Oliver said. 'We're sitting ducks.'

Something smashed hard against their door.

'Keep at it lad.' Smith shouted. 'It only takes one of us to get through then we can clear half the other windows and wipe the buggers out. Hit harder.'

Jason moved forward. Something crashed against the door again and this time the hinge bolts screeched a fraction out of the wall.

'What the hell have they got out there?' Oliver shouted in frustration, '…a bloody battering ram?' He snatched up a sniper rifles from a rack to his side and hammered its heavier, longer butt against the steel. No effect.

'Sergeant – I can do it,' Jason said, just as the door was pounded another half inch inwards.

Smith stared at Jason for a moment then it clicked. 'Of course, lad, use your Gift.'

Smith pulled back from the window and stood next to Jason. He snatched up a second Kalashnikov and cocked it.

'As soon as you blast the shield away get right to the back – d'you understand me? The very second it's clear. No bloody heroics – people are dying all over the abbey just to keep you safe.'

Jason stared at him. *What did he say?*

The door shuddered again.

'Oliver – cover the window when I reload. Right lad, do it now.'

Jason took in a slow breath, pulled back his hands and then threw both his palms forward at the blocked window.

Twin air-strikes smashed the steel clean away and noise and light blasted in. Helicopter searchlights whipped around the cloister and in one of the beams, a twisted, brutish face span around to stare directly at Jason.

A Touched - massive, male and it had sensed Jason's Gift.

Anna pulled Jason out of the way and Smith let loose with both his Kalashnikovs. They clicked empty after a few seconds and immediately a face and gun muzzle reared up outside the window. Oliver stepped up, his weapon already shooting and the face flew backwards in an explosion of blood and bone. The Touched male had disappeared.

Oliver stepped further forward, spraying the cloister outside. Smith, reloaded and joined him, again using both Kalashnikovs.

It worked. Gunfire from other windows opened up and in seconds a deadly storm of cross-fire swept around the cloister. The steel in front of Oliver's original window slipped down and Eddie and Erin dashed over to take a side each, picking targets carefully with their pistols.

Suddenly the helicopter lights snapped off and blackness filled the window frames.

Sergeant Smith fumbled at his belt for a torch.

Crash. Their door burst inwards and the Touched hurtled into the red-lit room. He was huge. His clothes were ripped to shreds and his flesh ran with blood but he didn't seem to notice. He fixed burning red eyes on Jason and leapt for him.

Somehow, Anna was there. She barged Jason to one side and locked down the Kalashnikov's trigger. Bullets tore into the Touched from point blank range and he was pummelled backwards. Her gun clicked empty as the man sank face down onto the stone at her feet. Carl leapt on its back and shot it through the head half a dozen times.

An instant later Smith was there, backing into the room while covering the door with his Kalashnikovs.

He needn't have bothered. The Touched was dead – there wasn't anything left of its head.

'Oliver, Eddie, jam that door back in place, Erin shoot anything that moves out there.'

Jason just stared at the hulking, shaggy-haired man who had smashed through a steel door to reach him.

'Confirm target identified in cloister south east room,' Jason jumped. A refined English voice crackled out of a black walkie talkie hung on the dead man's belt. "Sections four to nine, converge on target…"

The rest faded out to meaningless noise for Jason. He was the target for the entire attack. Somehow they'd known he was here and now every single Brethren knew exactly where he was.

'Sections twenty to twenty three, move to area "F",' the Brethren radio crackled through Jason's swirling mind again.

'Bloody hell,' he swore and stamped down on the radio and it burst apart.

Smith grabbed Jason and pulled him into the light. 'Hold it together, lad – we could've done with listening in on that.'

'Sorry,' Jason managed.

'Never mind – control will be picking it all up. We're safest here for now. You and your two shields get to the back and bloody well stay there.'

'Come on boys,' Anna said, pulling Carl up by his good arm. He had started to bleed through the bandages. Pushing

Jason ahead, she ushered Carl into the narrower back section of the room.

Outside the cloister was quiet. It seemed the deadly crossfire had slaughtered everyone and even the fires were dying out in the incessant drizzle. Oliver and Eddie heaved the steel reinforced door up and jammed it back into its shattered frame then tipped over a metal shelf to prop it in place.

'I can't see a thing out here,' Erin reported, peering into the dark from the side of the window.

Jason tried to focus back in on the radio reports in his right ear.

'One troop carrier still high over the cloister.'

'Approach still clear of ground troops.'

'Training halls close positions holding.'

Jason shivered. *How many Brethren were there?*

'Heavy attack on the church east face – targeting the windows.'

Anna scoffed as she checked her pistol magazine for the fourth time. 'They won't get in that way. Those windows are bulletproof stained glass set in steel mesh. They're stronger than your average house wall.'

'They'd need a mortar to even make a dent...' Carl agreed. He was looking pale but alert.

Four explosions reverberated through the walls from the east side, the rear of the abbey.

'Mmm, mortars like those might do the trick,' Anna said.

The wry smile Jason was so fond of flashed over her mouth. Despite everything he smiled back – it helped fight the fear.

'Anna,' Jason began, '... just then you saved... I don't know what to say. Thank you.'

Anna held his eye for a moment and then shrugged into a smile again. 'Someone has to keep you alive and it would have really upset Carl if he'd been forced to do it.'

Jason glanced at Carl propped up against the wall. Carl raised an eyebrow. Notwithstanding Anna's comment, his rival had made sure the Touched didn't come for him again.

'Carl…' Jason began.

'Oh hell,' Erin's voice cut through the quiet armoury, 'they're dropping something into the cloister.'

'Get down.' Smith yelled and dropped behind a pile of steel boxes. Anna grabbed Jason's head and pulled them both down to the floor with Carl.

A single explosion ripped through the cloister and blew the wedged door back into the room and smashed the window shutters wide open on their hinges. Smoke and heat billowed in and set them all coughing for breath.

A hand gripped Jason around the back of his neck and pulled his head down further. There was air here. Anna's face was next to his.

'Stay down – breathe slow.'

'I'm fine,' Jason coughed and peered up from the floor. The whole room was a roiling mass of choking black and grey smoke but there was no sound. No sound at all he realised. His earphone had been knocked out when Anna pulled him down. He tried sweeping his hand over the cold flagstones to find it but it was gone.

Smith's shout shattered the silence. 'You're leaving lads and lasses – escape route, now.'

Jason looked up. Just visible as a crouching silhouette six feet away, Smith began to edge forward towards the cloister door.

'Jason, Anna, Carl – unlock the back door. Eddie, Erin, Oliver – get back there with them. Anything comes past me – you kill it. Move.'

'Come on, keep low.' Anna coughed in Jason's ear and shoved him backwards.

They shuffled towards the small door, Jason fumbling to pull his pistol out of its holster at the same time. His mind reeled. *They were supposed to be safe here.*

Just beyond Carl, three smoke-shrouded silhouettes scuttled back to form a defensive line. Smith was lost to sight in the swirling red-lit haze.

Outside, the heavy drone of rotor blades pulsed around the cloister. This time however, only a few scattered bursts of gunfire were raised against them and the deafening rotor noise closed in.

'Quickly,' Anna hissed as they felt their way blindly through the trapped smoke at the back of the armoury.

The helicopter downdraft blasted into the armoury and whipped the smoke into a red-hazed tornado just as half a dozen dark figures burst in through the door.

Instantly Smith's two Kalashnikovs battered the shadows back against the wall and ripped them apart. All six were slaughtered in seconds.

A metallic bouncing clinked against one wall.

'Grenade,' Oliver yelped. He leapt out of cover, stooped to snatch something up from the floor and threw it back out into the cloister. As he turned to dash back behind his boxes, machine gun fire crackled outside.

Bullets ripped into Oliver and he crashed headlong into the piled boxes.

'Olly.' Eddie yelled. He and Erin crawled forward to pull Oliver into what was left of their cover.

'Keep your heads down' Smith ordered as he raked the window and door openings with bullets.

Jason peered back through the roiling murk, the smoke burning his eyes. Oliver wasn't moving.

Three more grenades clattered in, Carl snatched one up and threw it out but the others were out of reach.

'Down,' Smith yelled but there were no deafening explosions. Instead, more smoke streamed into the room from the still spinning grenade cases.

Smoke bombs. No shrapnel. No deaths.

'Get out, now.' Smith screamed, shooting burst after burst blindly into the smoke. Jason couldn't even see him.

'Go.' Anna spluttered and pushed Jason in front of her. Desperate, half-blind and coughing, Jason scrabbled along the wall and found the door handle.

Smith's guns stopped shooting.

'Sergeant?' Carl yelled, stepping in front of the distraught Eddie and Erin. There was no answer. He clicked a magazine home and started shooting into the smoke.

'Open it.' Anna hissed. She was right by Jason now, her pistol pointing uselessly forward. Just two metres away, Erin and Eddie had stood up shoulder to shoulder behind Carl blocking the narrow aisle. Jason swore under his breath - they were lining up to die for him.

None of this should be happening. He forced his stinging eyes wide open and leant close to the keypad.

No one was firing back at them - only Carl's Kalashnikov rattled out. He sent burst after burst into the red-lit, impenetrable smoke, trying to make sure nothing came near.

'Reload...' Carl yelled, 'cover m...' his voice died in a thick gurgle.

Erin caught his body as he slumped back, his hands grasping at his neck.

Eddie pulled them both behind him and pumped twin pistol bullets into the room. Jason couldn't stop staring at Carl's fingers clutching at his bleeding throat as Erin lowered him to the ground.

'Open the door or we're all dead.' Anna hissed, putting her whole body in front of Jason now. He tore his eyes away and punched his door code into the pad.

Nothing happened.

Jason glanced back.

Erin had dragged Carl right over to them. His hands twitched against his neck now, blood covering both arms.

Anna sank down next to him and tore at her tee shirt trying to rip a bandage strip from it.

Carl's hands slipped away from his throat and flopped to the floor.

Jason frantically punched in his code again. 'It's not working,' he hissed. His head was clogging up, his brain freezing to useless.

Eddie's gun stopped firing.

Jason twisted around. No, not Eddie. He couldn't be...

'Re-load.' Eddie snapped. 'Erin cover me.'

Erin flowed to her feet and weaved in front of Eddie, shooting as she moved.

She barely had time to scream as a knife punched up out of the smoke and into her heart.

Like lightening, Eddie air-punched past her head. Something crashed back into the smoky haze of boxes and gun racks but it was too late. Erin crumpled, lifeless to the floor.

'Glimmerman.' Eddie gasped, backing up into Anna but unable to tear his eyes from Erin's body.

Jason hammered his code in again. *They were all going to die here.*

'Thumb pad,' Anna shouted over his shoulder as she and Eddie shot a matrix pattern of flying lead against the invisible attacker. Wood and metal ricocheted off the floor, ammunition boxes and ceiling.

Cursing himself for being so stupid, Jason pressed his thumb to the reader and the door inched open.

'We're through,' Jason croaked through a throat like sandpaper. He slammed the door back into the corridor beyond and the three of them stumbled out of the red-hazed killing ground.

Chapter 23

Jason, Anna and Eddie stumbled into the reception area of the chapter house and fell against the far wall, smoke swirling out after them.

'Freeze.' shouted a harsh voice and a single bullet thudded into the wall just above Jason's head.

All three of them froze. The air was clearer here, the smoke was being sucked out by air conditioning. To their left, a security guard was shooting through his smashed window into the cloister. Three other guards lay sprawled on the ground and a fifth held his Kalashnikov pointing at the new-comers. Jason recognised the last one as Ludovich – one of his escorts from the guesthouse.

'Don't shoot,' Jason shouted. 'I'm Jason, Jason Willow. I need to shut the door.'

'Don't move.' Ludovich almost screamed and shot one more round over their heads. He pointed his walkie-talkie at them with a trembling hand.

'Anna Smith and Eddie Braithwaite.' Anna snapped. 'For God's sake, you brought Jason from the guest house half an hour ago – we need to shut the door… there a glimmerman in...'

Ludovich's eyes flicked to his walkie-talkie then over to wide open door. 'Cleared - seal the bloody door.' he yelled.

Anna leapt passed Jason and reached into the smoke to grab the door. A split second before reaching the handle she was yanked inside.

Jason saw it – just for a moment – an almost transparent, shimmering silhouette in the smoke. Anna shot out an arm towards him. He snatched hold with one hand and threw an air punch past her ear with the other.

The silhouette span away into the smoke and Eddie yanked the two of them back into the chapter house. Instantly Jason leapt up for the door, shooting his pistol into the red-lit haze beyond. As he grabbed the door handle and jerked it shut something brushed past his knee.

'It's in here.' Anna yelled. 'A glimmerman.'

The three of them backed against one wall, pistols wavering. Ludovich backed up against his partner who was torn between the gun battle outside and the facing the invisible assassin behind him. No one moved.

Suddenly someone pounded at the armoury door from the far side followed by gunfire.

'Jason, it's me – Marakoff. Let me in – you have a glimmerman in there with…' A furious burst of automatic fire cut him off.

'Marakoff?' Jason hissed, turning to Anna and Eddie. 'What shall I…' he began but was drowned out by a hail of bullets tearing into the chapter house main door. One guard returned fire while Ludovich moved back to back with him and scanned the shadows with his Kalashnikov for any sign of the glimmerman.

Marakoff – if it really was Marakoff - hammered on the armoury door again. Jason bit at his lip. "Demons are faultless mimics." Marakoff had once told him.

'Jason – ' more gunfire, 'my code and print have been blocked and I have no pin transmitter as I told you earlier…' more fire. Burst after burst now. 'If you're alive, let me in…'

'Bloody hell,' Anna yelled. Ludovich and the other guard stood rigid for a moment then slumped to the floor without a shot being fired.

Jason took his chance. He threw up an air wall across the corridor cutting the three of them off from the dead guards and hopefully the glimmerman. One hand feeding his barrier, he stepped over to the door, punched in the code and pressed his thumb to the reader.

Marakoff burst in under a hail of bullets and slammed the door behind him. He backed hard into Jason, flattening him against the wall and swept the Kalashnikov he was carrying across the whole scene in an instant. Winded and with Marakoff's iron hard body pressing him against the wall, Jason somehow still managed to maintain his air barrier.

'It's over there...' Jason began.

'Drop your wall.' Marakoff whispered. 'Pretend you're exhausted,' he was aiming through the shimmering air wall just above the dead Ludovich.

Jason hesitated. The thing on the other side had effortlessly killed everyone around him.

'Quickly, Jason,' Marakoff said.

Jason sagged and closed his hand. Marakoff flicked the Kalashnikov's muzzle over to the receptionist's desk.

Blood and bone splattered the wall as a bald man materialised and juddered backwards with Marakoff's bullets hammering into him. He crashed over the desk and slid to the floor riddled with bullets.

'How... how did you see him?' Anna asked, flicking her eyes from the dead glimmerman to Marakoff.

'Footsteps in the carpet.' Marakoff said, snapping in a new magazine.

Jason glanced down at his feet which sank deep into the luxury shag pile carpet. Marakoff gripped his shoulder and pulled his attention back. 'I am so sorry about your friends. I was driven from the roof tops and without my code and pin it took too long to get back into the cloister.'

A hail of bullets flew through the shattered windows and something hard battered against the front door.

Marakoff pushed them away down the corridor. 'Come – we must follow your escape route. I will lead – stop and crouch on my signal. Watch all sides, behind and above as we move.'

Behind them, the door was hammered again and the hinges shrieked loose from the wall. They sprinted for the exit at the far end of the corridor and Anna tapped in her code.

'It is clear.' Marakoff said peering out through a tiny window to one side of the door.

They burst out into the rose garden and cool, clear air washed over them. Sporadic gunfire and droning rotor blades were muffled by the abbey buildings on all sides.

Marakoff slammed the door shut. 'Quickly.' he hissed and they dashed across the grass to the church corridor. They were almost safe. Anna punched in her code.

'We're in,' she said just as the tiny window behind them smashed outwards.

Eddie snapped his pistol around and fired at the jagged black hole.

Marakoff however remained unperturbed.

'Do not waste your bullets. It is too small to climb through and they will not risk shooting in the dark when a stray bullet might hit Jason – that is why they sent the glimmerman.'

Eddie stopped shooting but kept aiming at the window as they piled into the church corridor and locked the door.

Jason collapsed back against one wall. Lit in low level red, the corridor was quiet and calm. To the right, thirty metres away was the white infirmary corridor leading to the training rooms but the three of them turned left towards the stairs rising to the church doors. They were ten steps away from sanctuary.

The stairs and arch alcoves were in deep shadow however. Even the red emergency lights were out.

'Shouldn't there be security here?' Anna whispered. 'And other people escaping from the garages and cloister?'

Marakoff almost imperceptibly nodded towards the base of the stairs, pretending to adjust his radio. Jason saw it at once - two small dark stains on the flagstones.

Blood.

'On my command – run for the training rooms.' Marakoff whispered, tapping his earphone angrily as if it weren't working.

'Run!' he shouted, and snapped up his Kalashnikov to send bullets ricocheting beneath the dark arches.

Jason, Eddie and Anna leapt into a sprint along the corridor and Marakoff backed down after them, still peppering the shadowed stairway with burst after burst. If a glimmerman was hidden in there, Marakoff had no tell-tale carpet to help him find it this time.

They skidded to a halt just before the white corridor and span around. 'Cover him,' Anna said, obviously not trusting her Kalashnikov to fire past Marakoff.

Jason and Eddie took a side each and shot into the stairway with their pistols.

Marakoff turned and sprinted towards them in a dead straight line, snapping in another magazine as their bullets flew past either side of his head.

Marakoff skidded to a crouching halt next to them and shot his head out into the white corridor.

'Clear,' Marakoff said and all four of them scrambled around the corner.

Eddie came last. The instant Jason was out of the sightline bullets thudded into the wall centimetres from Eddie's head as he dived around the corner.

They dashed for the training room door passed bodies that had been hidden in this corridor – security guards and a couple of students.

Jason dropped to the back as they ran, Marakoff's words playing in his head – "They won't risk shooting when a stray bullet might hit Jason."

Marakoff slowed down with him but Jason shook his head. 'It won't shoot me – let me cover and you get the door open.'

Marakoff took half a second then nodded. 'Walk backwards – be ready to shoot. If it moves too quickly there will be a slight blurring of walls or floor.'

As Marakoff and the others sprinted away, Jason walked backwards after them as quickly as he could, his pistol covering the corridor. A misty hint of a hand and pistol appeared around the corner but before Jason could shoot there was a muffled pop and a red light exploded into darkness at the corridor intersection. Whatever was in the shadow was using a silenced pistol.

Jason shot into the darkness as he backed quickly away but another light shattered and then another. With each shot, the dark leapt towards him five feet at a time and with it would come the glimmerman.

'Jason, run. It's open,' Anna yelled from close behind.

Jason span around and sprinted for her just as the light exploded over his head. He leapt out of the darkness and Anna propelled him through the door as Marakoff backed in shooting down the corridor with his Kalashnikov.

Eddie slammed the door and the lock clicked into place a split second before whatever was on the other side smashed into it.

Anna pulled Jason down into a crouch behind one pillar and the four of them scanned the hall. The lights were all off but floodlights, explosive flashes and helicopter search beams dazzled in through the high window arches and threw jerking shadows across the walls. It sounded as if a war was going on outside.

The door shuddered once, then again. Single shot pistol bullets.

'It will not get through with just a pistol.' Marakoff said, almost absently, as he continued to scan the room.

'What if there are more glimmermen in here already – waiting like that one was?' Jason whispered.

'I think perhaps, we would be dead already…' Marakoff whispered back, '… apart from you, of course.'

The bullets stopped thudding into the door. The Glimmerman had given up – for now.

'Why is there no security here?' Eddie whispered.

'A dead area,' Anna answered, each hushed word quickly lost in the vast space. 'The windows are too high to shoot out from and the small training rooms have no outside openings at all. It was an infirmary remember – stop the spread of disease – one way in, one way out.'

'So what do we do now?' Jason whispered

'We find a good place to defend and wait to be rescued, I think,' Marakoff said. 'The control room will know where you all are from your pins. Unfortunately all the Brethren will also have the same information by now,' he grinned. 'It will be something of a race to reach us, yes?'

'Great,' Jason whispered.

'Come.' Marakoff said and led them towards the mock hotel.

Suddenly Anna reached for her ear phone. 'Did you hear that?' she asked. 'They've sighted a possessed – a demon.'

Marakoff kept on walking. 'Not really a surprise I am afraid.'

Jason went cold. A demon – here and hunting for him. 'Where is it?' he asked. 'I've lost my ear phone.'

Anna glanced back at him but Eddie answered as the reports came through. 'It's in the woods… just north of us… but there's one of our teams on it already.'

Marakoff picked up the pace towards the hotel door. A few moments later Eddie swore under his breath. 'It's killed them – all of them, the Gifted as well. It's coming this way.'

Suddenly, bursts of machine gun bullets hammered into the door behind them.

Marakoff stopped in front of the silent hotel. All its windows were dark, staring blankly down at the four hunted humans. A single beam of light swept across the façade from outside then disappeared.

'Go to bedroom three,' Marakoff said. 'Pile furniture against the door and keep watch from the corners of the window. The Brethren will come in through the high windows on the outside walls – the shooting at the door is just to draw our attention.'

'Aren't you staying with us?' Jason asked. It felt as if he'd ribbons of ice in his stomach, pulling themselves into painful knots.

Marakoff smiled thinly. 'I will be far more effective out here, Jason. Do not worry, I will not be far away.'

'You said that last time,' Jason grumbled but forced a smile back. Marakoff would do his best to keep him alive – they all would.

'The demon's coming straight at the east wall,' Eddie said, holding his earphone and turning to stare at the wall with the small training rooms off it.

Marakoff handed Eddie the Kalashnikov and his belt of ammunition pouches. 'Short bursts – control.'

'Come on.' Anna ordered and stepped into the hotel.

Jason and Eddie followed her and Marakoff disappeared into the shadows of the hall. In the near dark, they felt their way up the stairs to the landing. Four doors stretched away from them. They went into the third and closed it.

'They're laying another trap for them,' Eddie said, a smile shining through his voice. 'We've got about fifty men closing in to pin the demon against the wall outside.'

Right on cue, an explosion of gunfire resonated through the thick stone walls and high windows but it was answered by a helicopter's rotor-whine swooping in over the roof, massive machine guns churning out hundreds of bullets from on high.

'That's one of theirs' Anna half whispered.

Something exploded above them and a moment later the centre of the roof burst inwards as the blazing husk of half a chopper crashed through.

It seemed to fall in slow motion then crashed onto the training mats in an explosion of burning metal. Roof tiles, shattered beams and glass rained down all around the flaming steel carcass and a dozens of small fires flickered up through the dust cloud ballooning through the entire hall.

'Oops,' Jason said, his voice cracking. He glanced at the other two. They were staring out, fire flickering in their eyes and their faces frozen.

Anna turned to him, slowly pulling her fingers away from her headphone. 'They got the chopper but the demon's too powerful – it's just shrugging off our bullets. It's coming for us.'

The three of them turned to the east wall.

'D'you think we should run…' Jason began but before he could finish the wall exploded inwards.

***

Chunks of stone and black marble flew over the matting and floodlights flared in through the wall. Even before the debris settled, dark-robed Brethren were leaping silently through the gaping hole – black shadows, machine guns and swords in hand, hooded cloaks fluttering out behind them like bat wings.

Jason took aim and squeezed the trigger of his MK23.

That single shot rang through his head, even drowning out the hammering of Eddie's Kalashnikov kicking into life to the side of him. On the matting below a faceless Brethren shadow spun around in slow motion as Jason's bullet punched through his heart and he crashed to the floor.

He'd just killed a man.

Sound and speed rushed back to Jason as more Brethren swarmed through the wall. Mind numb, Jason's finger squeezed the trigger again and again, faster and faster, flicking the muzzle to target after target.

The black mass of Brethren flowed apart and rushed for the darkened walls and doorways.

The three students kept on shooting and the Brethren left a trail of twisted silhouettes on the floor behind them as they flitted towards the hotel façade. Jason's feelings had frozen - he was numb now to the killing but his every sense was sharp and aware of every movement before him. His aim was unfalteringly good and he sent a second and third round into each body to make sure it was dead.

Two thoughts hammered at his ice-cold focus – where was the demon and what would it do to him?

The Brethren agents kept on coming through the wall - black shapes darting between fire and shadow. Some found cover and set up a counter fire to the students' defence. Their bullets decimated the breezeblock some metres above the student's window sending chippings of concrete and dust into their faces. It was quickly apparent they weren't aiming to kill, but distract and confuse.

'They're inside the hotel.' Eddie coughed, pulling back to reload.

'Block the door some more,' Anna ordered.

Jason and Eddie toppled another wardrobe and shoved it against the door, then piled a set of drawers on top of that.

Anna scanned the room, planning their defence. 'Jason - watch the window in case they try climbing in – shut what's left of it so a glimmermen will have to knock out the glass if they come for us. Eddie we'll cover the door and walls.'

Anna's voice wavered, a touch higher than normal but her face was set, her eyes determined. 'Keep calm, alright - we only need to hold on for a few minutes until D… Mr Brash breaks through to us.'

Jason nodded. His mind flicked to the transmitter in his shoe – was his father coming to save the day as well? With no identity pin, Dad would be targeted by both security - he might already be dead.

'Focus, Jason,' Anna hissed, 'shut the window!'

Jason reached to pull the glass frame back down into place. Bullets tore into the block above and half the frame split as he tugged it down in a crash of glass shards. Anna hauled over the bed to cover them both and crouched down next to him. Eddie took a position in one corner to provide crossfire.

Jason peered out of one corner of the window. The Brethren had stopped shooting at them now. Dark shapes flitted unhindered from cover to cover towards the hotel. Every one of them seemed to be looking straight up at him.

Outside the training hall, the battle raged. Through the blast-hole it appeared the Brethren were defending the training halls – their territory now, with their prize neatly trapped inside.

A twitch of movement at the back of the hall caught Jason's eye. One of the Brethren sank silently to the floor and a darker shadow slipped away from the body: Marakoff.

The ghost worked quickly. All down the west wall, Brethren intent on covering Jason's window silently died one by one. Three, four, five bodies. *Was Marakoff clearing an escape route for them – back into the infirmary corridor – the way they'd come in?*

A radio crackled just outside the bedroom door and was quickly silenced. Jason flicked his pistol towards the sound.

'Watch the window.' Anna hissed. 'That sort of mistake might be a diversion.'

'Sorry,' Jason mumbled and turned back to watch outside. Shadow after shadow was slipping along the hotel façade and into the building now. He shot twice but the angle was too tight and sniper bullets hammered into the brickwork outside to shower him with stone chippings.

'Here they come,' Anna whispered. Despite his orders, Jason turned to follow her gaze.

The door handle, with the furniture wedged beneath it was turning.

'So many of you are going to die trying to get in here,' Anna said to no one but herself.

Jason frowned. The Brethren must be suicidal – especially if they were going to burst in through the door without shooting for fear of harming him.

What did Anna say about distractions? This might be one, carefully timed to stop them seeing the real danger which could only come in… through the window.

A single shard of glass clinked to the floor behind him and without thinking, Jason lashed out a spread hand. The whole window frame exploded out from the wall and a skeletal man all in black shimmered into existence as he arced down to the matting below. The glimmerman landed in a tight roll and immediately started to disappear again.

Jason smashed the shimmering silhouette flat with an air-punch and peppered it with pistol shots. Blood spattered over the mat and the body wavered back into sight – dead.

An axe head splintered through the top of the bedroom door and Anna and Eddie opened fire. Jason glanced turned back to see.

'Watch outside,' Anna shouted over her own gunfire.

Jason turned back and there, the demon waited.

Chapter 24

It was just a man but Jason knew it for demon-kind instantly. The body it possessed was a massive, shaggy haired male with impossible muscles rippling beneath a ragged lumberjack shirt. For a moment it stood within the blasted wall, silhouetted against searchlights and explosions outside. It seemed to suck in the light around it and take everything back to the dark.

Then it looked directly up at Jason. The long, matted hair fell away and out of the depths of its shadowed face, two eyes flamed crimson around pit-black pupils.

It had come for him - the demon inside that man ached to possess him and claim his Gift for its own. Jason knew it, he knew it for certain. He also knew he'd die before he ever let it happen.

With Eddie's Kalashnikov filling the hotel room with flying lead, Jason took slow, careful aim at the demon outside. Its lips split across white fangs in some parody of a smile and the demon opened its arms in invitation. Casually it took a single step into the training hall.

Jason fired.

The bullet thudded into its shoulder – just high and right of the heart. Blood and flesh splattered through the light but the demon didn't even flinch. It just came on through the fire and smoke – a dark nimbus deepening all around it now to cloak its body in night and its eyes burning hungrily up at its prey.

Jason shot again and again but now the bullets didn't even reach the demon's flesh. They sank into the ink-black nimbus and were gone. The magazine emptied and Jason didn't bother to reload.

It was coming for him and nothing could stop it. Where was Brash's army of security, his highly trained teams of Gifted? Where was Brash? Where, for pity's sake, was his father?

Jason stared at the demon, forcing himself to fight down his rising panic. The fiery eyes pulled at him, lulling his mind with warmth. His shoulders relaxed, his gun arm lowered and he let the weapon clunk forgotten to the floor. There was such power in the man below, such commanding grace to every measured step. Here was a man born to rule. He'd a right to absolute dominion over life and death, pleasure and pain...

'Jason – snap out of it.' Jason's whole head was twisted to one side and Anna's face swam into view.

'The demon's here,' Jason managed.

'No shit, Sherlock?' Anna swore. 'Now don't look into its bloody eyes and keep shooting at it.'

'Re-load. Anna, cover the door,' Eddie hissed, flipping out his Kalashnikov's magazine.

With the machine gun momentarily silenced, the axe returned. It hacked through twice more until Anna shot at shadows through the decimated wood.

Jason snatched up his pistol and banged in another magazine.

Outside the demon strode around the cooling helicopter husk. Two Brethren walked a step behind it – each armed with a machine-pistol in one hand and a wide-bladed scimitar in the other. Through the hole in the wall, ragged lines of Brethren were still keeping out all attempts at rescue.

Without warning, one of the Brethren walking behind the demon had his head jerked back and a Katanna blade slid across his throat. He dropped silently to the floor.

An instant later, Marakoff sliced the sword arm from the second Brethren and slipped back behind the helicopter as the man dropped to his knees screaming.

The demon, its eyes fixed on Jason's window stopped and slowly looked down on its writhing Brethren escort. Marakoff leapt silently out of the dark on the other side, his blade a streak of silver arcing towards the demon's neck. At the last instant something jerked him backwards and the blade whipped through the dark nimbus to slice through the demon's shoulder.

The demon roared and one shadowed hand clutched high up its arm. Marakoff slammed down at its feet, kicking hard at apparently thin air.

The demon pulled its bloodied hand away from its wound and pointed a single finger at the struggling Marakoff.

'No!' Jason screamed and leapt out of the window.

In a hail of glass and wood shards, he dropped six feet on to the air step he'd formed and slammed both hands forward.

An air strike shot out and the demon flew back with the crimson fire meant for Marakoff, crackling in a great arc from its finger.

'Jason,' Anna yelled, reaching out of the window for him.

Jason ignored her and leapt down, throwing an air-punch over the floor-pinned Marakoff. The glimmerman on top of him, nothing more than a vague shimmer in the gloom, was smashed away and disappeared into shadows.

Marakoff flipped to his feet in an instant but his bad leg almost buckled beneath him.

Nothing moved for a moment. Jason could have sworn he somehow 'felt' Dad in the back of his head.

Then the shooting started.

Machine fire from a dozen positions ripped into the hotel and Anna disappeared from the window. Jason swore. Without him being there the Brethren were free to blast the two other students to shreds.

Jason stepped in so close to Marakoff that they were touching, hopefully shielding him from any similar attack. He needn't have bothered. No gunfire came their way; in fact they were all but ignored. Obviously Jason was to be left untouched.

He snapped his head around to where the demon had landed. It lay back, relaxing against a still smouldering corpse thrown from the helicopter. Slowly, red lips pulled back over dazzling white fangs.

'Do not look into its eyes. Do not let it touch you.' Marakoff whispered in Jason's ear. 'It is playing with you.'

Marakoff began edging them both back towards the west wall – lined now with the crumpled bodies of the Brethren he'd silently killed. The door to the infirmary corridor was their only way out.

Sporadic gun fire still came from the hotel. Eddie and Anna were still alive and Jason wouldn't leave without them.

The demon almost floated to its feet, the dark nimbus shimmering tight around it's whole body and its red eyes burning brighter than ever.

'It wants to fight,' Marakoff whispered as they stepped carefully across the mat, 'it wants to exhaust you physically and mentally – fear and despair are his key to possessing you.'

Jason flicked his eyes to the gap in the outside wall. The black-clad Brethren lines were holding fast. No rescue was coming any time soon.

'Our only hope is to reach the door,' Marakoff said.

Jason stared at the demon. It was waiting for him to decide – fight or flight.

Behind him Anna and Eddie were trapped and fighting for their lives. Somewhere in the shadows a bruised glimmerman was waiting for them and the demon would be on them before they could get within ten metres of the door.

Fight it was then.

Jason pulled away from Marakoff and stepped towards the demon.

'An unusual choice,' Marakoff whispered in his ear but followed him anyway.

'Excellent, boy-child.' The demon spoke. It's voice was deep, resonating with power and its grin grew to almost split its host's face. 'Let me introduce myself before I take your soul. I am Nazarhirim.'

Jason centred his gaze on the demon's chest to avoid its eyes and keep all its limbs in view. He forced down his fluttering stomach and stilled his thoughts to cold, unassailable determination. This was it. He would win here, win or die. He'd never allow himself to be possessed.

The demon took a couple of exaggerated, gunslinger paces forward, obviously revelling in its game.

'It will stop only if you cut off its head or remove its limbs. Almost everything else it can heal in moments. You may need this.'

His mind now ice cold, Jason's fingers closed around the warm leather grip of the Katanna Marakoff pressed into his right hand. It was weighted perfectly, the blade felt as light as air.

The demon, Nazahirim's eyes flicked to the blade then it laughed, scorn dripping from the base rumble.

Doubt wormed into Jason's icy resolve. 'I've hardly used a…' he began but Marakoff was gone.

Jason took a step forward, then another. *He would win here.*

Nazahirim shrugged and strode towards him, matching him stride for stride.

At six steps apart Jason suddenly punched out. The demon was like quicksilver. It twisted in a blur and the air strike smashed into the smouldering chopper shell in an explosion of sparks and metal.

The fire-burst lit up the hall for a moment and Jason struck at the demon again and again as he walked - jab, punch, flick kick, faster and faster as the two of them drew closer.

Every strike missed, blasting weapon racks apart and whole chunks out of the walls. Nazahirim's movements were impossibly slick as it twisted, ducked and span around each attack. Twice it turned aside the shimmering air-strikes with one hand cloaked in that dark nimbus.

Jason redoubled his efforts, effortlessly drawing energy in and sending it searing back out through each attacking limb in shimmering blows almost too fast to see.

Nazarhirim was forced to block more and more. Jason pressed forward.

When they were just three steps apart, a blow landed.

The demon flew backwards, doubling up in mid-air. It smashed into the flaming chopper and its nimbus dissolved.

Jason sprinted forward raising his Katanna but something swept his legs from under him.

His blade went flying as he fought to break his fall but he managed to twist back onto his knees. The barely visible outline of a man, nothing more than a heat-haze, kicked him down again.

Jason rolled passed a lump of fuselage. The glimmerman ran for him but suddenly Marakoff was there, leaping out of the wreckage and slicing with another Katanna.

He took off the glimmerman's head with one cut. The body fazed back into sight even as it dropped down in a spray of blood with the head rolling away over the matting.

Marakoff reached down to pull Jason up but flame licked over his outstretched hand and seared across his chest. Nazahirim was back in action.

Marakoff stumbled backwards ripping off his burning top. The demon leapt right over Jason and slapped Marakoff away with one hand. Marakoff flew up off the mat and smacked into the wall. He slid down and lay still, the remnants of his sweater still smouldering around him.

Jason leapt for his fallen Katanna and rolled to his feet. His legs almost buckled from the glimmerman's earlier attack but he leapt towards Nazahirim and sliced at its neck.

Like a striking cobra, the demon snapped back to avoid the blade and then whipped forward. Its hand licked out and caught Jason's sword-wrist in a grip of searing hot agony.

Jason cried out. Nazahirim's fingers were burning into his skin. He desperately twisted against the demon's thumb and lashed out with his free hand. The demon caught his blow easily and with unbelievable strength, forced Jason down to his knees, its fingers blackening his flesh. Jason could smell his own skin burning.

He was trapped. He couldn't punch, kick or twist away. The demon had the strength of five men, ten even. It brought its face inches in front of his. This close, its skin seemed alive with pulsing red veins and its breath was a harsh rattle that stank of decay.

Jason slammed his head forward, smashing the demon's nose.

The grin curled back even further and it started to get inside his head.

Jason twisted his head from side to side but it clamped both his wrists in one huge hand and grabbed his chin with the other. Jason squeezed his eyes shut but Nazahirim's blazing crimson slits still filled his vision. A red mist began to lace through his mind, cloying his thoughts, sapping his will.

No.

Jason focussed on the word, imagined it frosting over in the centre of his mind, pushing tendrils of ice out through his brain and freezing the red mist, destroying it.

The contact broke. Jason's vision began to clear. The demon stared at him, its eyes burning still. Suddenly it snapped its head to one side.

Marakoff was pulling himself towards them, his face drenched in sweat and his bad leg dragging behind him.

Nazahirim's eyes narrowed to slits. 'Your resistance forces me to harm your devoted protector.'

The demon snapped Jason down flat on the floor and pinned him down with one hand burning at the back of his neck. Jason's mind was still numb. He couldn't think clearly, only stare at Marakoff, stare into his eyes.

The demon pointed one finger at Marakoff and a ribbon of fire leapt out. Marakoff screamed as the flame laced itself all around him, crackling across his body as he wrenched himself back up to his knees. It wrapped around his legs, head and arms in searing coils as he tried desperately to roll back into the shadows. His flesh smoked and blackened everywhere the fire touched him.

'Nooooo,' Jason screamed, writhing and twisting to break the hot iron grip on his neck. The demon pinned him down harder with one knee on his back and continued to burn the screaming Marakoff.

Despair flooded through Jason and instantly the red mist streamed deep into his mind.

An ice-white image suddenly blazed through the swirling mist in Jason's head - Dad.

The infirmary door exploded into the room. The demon whipped its fire-hand around even as Jason's eyes found his father stepping into the light.

Red fire crackled out at Dad but he had already begun. A scalpel-sharp air-disk silently sliced away the arm holding Jason's neck an instant before the demon was blasted across the room, it's fire lashing harmlessly over what was left of the ceiling and into the night sky.

Nazahirim bounced over the mat and tried to roll to its feet but Dad sent it smashing into the wall with a mighty double push. Marble and bones cracked with the impact and Nazahirim slid to the ground.

The dozen or so Brethren agents scattered around the room who had been watching Jason's struggle realized what was happening and turned their weapons on Dad. Ilena Russof stepped out from behind him with a Kalashnikov in each hand and gunned down half of them as Dad threw out his fingers to send a storm of nail-thin shafts of solid air piercing through the rest.

Ten metres away, Nazahirim jerked up from the floor and roared with a multi-voiced scream of tormented souls as its bones crunched and snapped back into line

It was the last sound that body ever made.

Dad literally flew at it, launching himself over half the burning helicopter with one hand snapping forward. This time, the demon slammed so hard against the wall that its spine burst apart and ribs splintered through its skin. As he landed, Dad whipped out a Katanna strapped to his back and in the same motion, sliced off Nazahirim's head.

Even as the body dropped away from blood spattered wall, a black mist hissed out from the headless neck.

The Katanna already sheathed, Dad's flashed his hands around in a gesture like smoothing wrapping paper around a large football. Instantly the demon spirit was trapped in a shimmering sphere of solid air, supported by a pencil thin shaft.

The gunfire outside faltered and moments later, began to draw away in sporadic bursts. A Brethren retreat?

Ilena dashed over to Marakoff and Jason stumbled towards his father. 'Dad, I...'

Schmidt burst in through the hole in the wall with a score of security guards leaping in after him. He sent half of them to check the dead Brethren while the other half joined him to form a wide circle around Dad, Jason, Ilena and Marakoff.

'Please – no one move.' Schmidt said. For some reason they held their weapons trained on the four of them.

Dad ignored Schmidt's team. He kept his hands cupped, a double, shimmering stream drawing in energy from the sphere to keep the air solid. Inside, Nazahirim's demon spirit was roiling black mist, vaguely human shaped and still with those red eye-slits burning in the darkness.

Dad backed over to Jason, 'Are you hurt, son?' His voice cracked a little as he glanced at him but his face was calm, composed. His eyes darted around the silent room.

'I'm okay but Marakoff...' Jason stopped talking and glanced over at the fallen ghost. Ilena crouched over him now, her eyes and guns covering Brash's men. He was still alive... somehow.

'We have to get him some help,' Jason said, staring down, not knowing what to do with his hands.

'I will live.' Marakoff opened his eyes, took in a deep breath and struggled to sit up. 'The demon was planning to play with me for quite some time to break your will, I think. He did not want me to die too quickly.'

A door creaked open at one end of the halls. Ilena whipped one Kalashnikov over to the hotel and a dozen more flicked around as half of Schmidt's men followed Ilena's lead.

'Don't shoot.' Anna's voice came out of the darkened lobby and a moment later she and Eddie stepped outside with their hands up.

They both had pistols pressed against the back of their heads.

Four Brethren men held them captive. Instantly, Jason knew they were all Touched. They didn't have the wild look of the super-strong beast in the cloister but their eyes burned with fierce life and each one carried itself as if it could rule the world. Two held the guns to Anna and Eddie's head and the other two swung wide bladed swords and had bandanas of glinting shurikens strapped across their chests.

Six black cowled Brethren appeared at the hotel windows, each snapping a rifle out. The instant the rifles appeared, Dad flipped up an air shield between them and the hotel with one hand while the other hand maintained the demon cage. Schmidt and his men all dived for cover and snapped up their weapons.

A half dozen more security appeared at the hole in the wall. Schmidt flashed a hand signal and they sank down into the rubble.

Stalemate.

The Touched pointing a gun at Anna's head smiled. He was tall and thin with long blonde hair tied back in a ponytail.

'This will happen quickly or not at all,' he said, his baritone voice rich with confidence. 'These two will walk five paces towards you and stop. Then you release our glorious master, Nazahirim. If you do not, we kill them and then you.'

Dad, his outstretched hands imprisoning a demon in one and a wall of shimmering air in the other, glanced at Jason.

'We can't let them die, Dad,' Jason said, '– they've kept me alive all through this.'

Dad hesitated for only a moment then turned to the Touched. 'Fine – start them walking. Slowly.'

Schmidt glanced across at Dad but didn't countermand his orders. Alan Brash's daughter had a gun to her head.

The pony tailed Touched smiled wider and pushed Anna forward. Eddie followed her.

One step.

'You know they will kill them anyway?' Marakoff whispered to Dad.

Three steps.

Dad nodded. 'I'm on it.'

Four steps.

Almost faster than Jason could see, Dad released the demon and the wall and swung both hands over to slam down a massive air-shield just beyond Anna, Eddie – shielding them all from the Brethren.

Instantly the demon spirit whipped through the air and flowed down the throat of the pony-tailed Touched. Both sides opened fire and Anna and Eddie sprinted towards Jason protected by Dad's wall.

'Fool!' cried Nazahirim, the human voice magnified a hundred times. Fire arced around the room and half of Schmidt's men burst into flame.

Suddenly a second, much larger air-wall crystallised into existence across the whole hall from floor to ceiling and sealed off the demon and Brethren. Bullets ricocheted off the solid air and Nazahirim's fire writhed along its length but nothing got through. The fighting stopped as quickly as it had begun.

Willow followed the narrow stream of air shimmering back from the new barrier to its source.

Alan Brash stood in the broken outer wall, a searchlight flaring into life behind him to light the hall but throw his shadow across the walls.

Brash drew energy from the immense wall with one finger, while the other hand smoothed back his golden hair.

'Heavens, what a mess,' he said, surveying the burned and twisted chopper, the rubble from roof and walls and the bullet-ripped hotel beyond his barrier.

And then Violet Gray moved slowly out from behind him, her shadow creeping out towards Jason.

Her eyes burned demon red.

Chapter 25

'Go get the nasty demon, sweetie.' Brash said and dropped his wall.

Violet flew straight for Nazahirim. Fire burst from her outstretched fingers and incinerated two of the Touched beside him an instant before she closed with the other demon.

With the wall gone, the hall burst into gunfire again. Alicia Sirensong appeared next to Brash with bullets already blazing from a machine-pistol in each hand. Thirty or forty Brash security stormed in around her to join Schmidt and what was left of his men in a devastating crossfire against the Brethren attempting to shoot from the hotel windows.

As the hotel was ripped apart in a hailstorm of bullets, Dad whipped up a shield wall again to protect his little group of Marakoff, Jason, Ilena, Eddie and Anna.

'What the hell has he done?' Dad hissed. 'We need to get out of here - now.'

Jason couldn't answer. His friend Violet and Nazahirim were wrapped in flame and ripping at each other with teeth and claws. Brash had somehow let a demon possess his ward.

'The door,' Marakoff said. He was using his Katanna to take the weight off his bad leg but before anyone moved, a bazooka rocket streaked towards the hotel and blew half of it to smithereens.

The shooting died out – there wasn't a Brethren left alive. The battle outside seemed over as well. A dozen more Brash security ran in through the blasted wall, mouths opening silently as they followed everybody else's gazes to the one remaining fight.

Violet broke Nazahirim's grip and threw him from her. Even as he span through the air, she pummelled him with air punches.

'The girl is Gifted.' Marakoff hissed. 'This is madness.'

Nazahirim crashed through the charred skeleton of the hotel and smashed into the wall beyond. Violet sent an inferno to engulf him and the flesh charred instantly from the ponytailed host's body. Violet fed the inferno with both hands and her face contorted in manic laugher from a dozen discordant voices screaming from her mouth.

Nazahirim's blackened-husk of a body sank to it's knees. Violet cut the fire and leapt on him. Her mouth frothing with red-flecked foam she tore the head from its shoulders with one sickening yank. The body spasmed and Nazahirim's black spirit burst out through the neck and streamed for the broken wall, gathering the darkness to it.

In a heartbeat, Dad dropped his wall and air-caged the demon once more.

Jason whipped back around to Violet. *What if she attacked them now? Dad couldn't hold off two demons.*

However, it seemed there were other things on Violet's mind. She knelt by the still smouldering body, its head in her hands and with one long, filthy fingernail she scooped out an eye. Jason turned away before she ate it.

The training hall stilled. The searchlight behind Brash snapped off and red emergency lights flickered on. Low fires from the helicopter continued to burn everywhere, casting shadows over the spherical prison of air where Nazahirim silently writhed against the surface, his eyes flaring a furious red.

'Good catch, Richard,' Brash said, glancing at Nazahirim.

Schmidt and Alicia moved to flank him, their weapons still out. Security guards moved to space themselves all around the hall now but their attention was torn between watching the black spirit squirm in its prison and staring at Violet playing with her victim's head.

'Tell me you haven't done this willingly,' Dad said. His shoulders were slightly hunched with the effort of keeping Nazahirim contained again.

'Oh don't sound so sanctimonious, Richard – Violet just saved your lives. And she's so tame,' Brash snapped his fingers once without taking his eyes from Dad's.

Violet's head snapped around, her eyes narrowing to slits of burning hatred. A flash of tension in Brash's face betrayed the struggle of wills between the summoner and demon, then Violet stamped to her feet and sauntered over to Brash like a petulant child. She held on to the severed head by the remains of its ponytail and dragged it, bumping along, behind her.

It made Jason feel sick. Violet was his friend, not some nameless soul that had been possessed by a demon. *Somewhere, deep in her mind, did Violet know what she was doing?*

Brash took a step or two further into the room, his demon and shields walking in with him. Around the walls the guards shifted nervously, readying themselves for action. Violet was now looking curiously at Nazahirim struggling in Dad's sphere.

'You're not going to make this difficult are you, Richard?' Brash said. 'This is the way forward - the key to finally cleansing the Brethren from the face of the Earth.'

Dad shook his head, a bead of sweat running down his temple. He stared at Violet. 'You've become the very thing we are fighting against…'

'Don't lecture me,' Brash cut in, his rich voice thinning in anger. 'The girl wasn't anything before this and now she could live forever simply by... feeding. I have given her the knowledge of the ancients, the strength and powers to rule nations...'

'She was your ward,' Jason shouted, glaring at his mentor. 'You were supposed to look after her, protect her. How could you...'

'Don't get upset, Jason,' Brash's cut in, a patronising smile playing on his lips. 'I can get her back. I can redeem her - truly redeem her, not kill her. I've been able to summon for two years now although Violet is my first stab at joining a demon with a Gifted. I can make my friendly little demon hop out whenever I wish and young Violet can go back to being her boring, insignificant self.'

'She will never be back to normal and you know it,' Dad said, his voice hardly raised above a murmur.

As Brash's attention turned back to Dad, Marakoff whispered in Jason's ear from his position just behind him.

'We will need a hostage to get out. Anna is Brash's daughter, yes?'

'What?' Jason whispered, hardly moving his mouth. 'Yes she is but...' Jason stopped to think. *Was Brash such a danger now that he wouldn't let them go?*

'Perhaps she won't be without... memories,' Brash said, his smile fading. 'but a few need to be sacrificed to save the many. We're losing the war, Richard – you'd know just how bad things are if you hadn't been hiding for the last twenty years. We have to fight fire with fire to stop the Brethren spreading – set demon against demon.'

'On three,' Marakoff whispered, 'when my foot touches yours, grab Anna and point your pistol to her head. I'll cover the boy.'

Dad seemed to know what was going on. He edged slightly away from Jason, drawing Brash's attention. ' "Win at any cost." That was always your way, Alan... but this time... you've gone too far.'

Brash glanced down at Violet who was now pulling the tongue out from her prize head and his mouth thinned to a determined line. 'Nothing can be "too far" if it means we win.

I've simply joined Violet, a quiet, weakly Gifted girl, with Xaphan - a lowly second order demon, with a moderate penchant for fire...'

Violet snapped her head up, eyes narrowed. Flame played around her fingertips but Brash ignored her and made a grand gesture towards the writhing black spirit Dad held captive. 'and by combining their powers they defeated a lieutenant of the abyss. Nazahirim is an old adversary of yours I believe, Richard – one you failed to destroy on a number of occasions despite your much lauded power all those years ago.'

'One...' Marakoff whispered, shaking his head and putting a conciliatory hand on Jason's shoulder.

Dad took a half step forward, keeping everyone's attention on him. 'The Watch will never allow this.'

Brash laughed. 'The Watch are desperate and I still have many friends there. When the Council see how my methods have wiped out everything the Brethren in Britain could throw at us they will welcome me back with open arms.'

'Two...' Marakoff whispered.

'You planned all of this, didn't you, you manipulative bastard?' Dad said, edging closer to Brash and bringing Nazahirim's air-cage with him. The security guards focussed on him and the demon spirit. 'This whole bloody charade - luring Jason into the abbey as bait for the Brethren.'

Brash shrugged. 'Of course. I have to admit we were a little... taken aback by the number of agents and the level of equipment they could muster so quickly but that was kind of the point - to pull them all in.'

Nazahirim's prison sphere faltered momentarily as the demon threw itself against the walls. Brash snapped up one hand defensively but Dad gritted his teeth and the air shimmered solid again.

Brash lowered his hand. 'You are weak, Richard. Twenty years of hardly using your Gift will have taken you down to what... a quarter-strength... less?'

Dad ignored the question. 'You risked Jason's life.'

'Oh come now,' Brash said, his hands opening wide in front of him, 'there was no real risk. The Brethren wanted him alive.'

Dad kept his voice very level. 'Nazahirim was moments from possessing him…'

Brash shook his head, his normally bouncy blonde hair, now heavy with dust. 'Fair point,' Brash said, nodding, 'but we had contingency plans in place…'

Brash's eyes flicked to Jason's transmitter pin. Puzzled, Jason looked down at the small, smiling monk's face and yelped as a streak of silver blurred across his chest, flicking the transmitter away.

Dad sheathed his katanna in the same motion.

'Well done - you always were fairly handy with a blade, weren't you Richard?' Brash said. 'The badge was only loaded with a paralysis drug, very low risk of any permanent damage.'

'You are out of control, Alan,' Dad began.

'Three,' Marakoff hissed and his foot flicked into Jason's.

Jason had no choice. He leapt behind Anna, grabbed her around the throat and put his pistol to her head. She tensed for a moment then, with visible effort, forced herself to relax.

Eddie – confused, stepped towards them, but Marakoff drew a pistol from nowhere and he froze.

Ilena was already in front of Dad, both her guns trained on Brash's head.

Like a delayed, knee jerk reaction, the guards around the walls snapped up their weapons.

Stalemate again.

Violet lazily raised her eyes up to Brash as she pulled out the tongue from her victim and began to chew on it. Her red eyes oozed contempt.

Brash carefully raised one hand. He was staring directly at Jason who held his daughter's life within a quarter inch of trigger movement. 'Disarm, Mr Schmidt.' Brash said, calmly, as if he were announcing a break in cricket for tea. 'Everyone will lay all their weapons on the floor and take four steps away from them.'

Schmidt and his men followed Brash's orders without hesitation. Brash turned to Dad. 'There really is no need for this, Richard.'

'We're leaving,' Dad said. 'You'll give us a vehicle and safe passage out of here.'

'You're making a mistake, Richard.' Brash said, the smile slipping from his lips. 'You're dragging Jason back into a life of running, hiding - denying him his birthright to eradicate demons from our world. Together, the three of us would be unstoppable - we can turn the whole war around – take the fight back to the Brethren. We could scour the Carpathians, find the Rift and seal it off once and for all.'

Brash stepped forward, a hopeful smile softening his face, his hands stretching out imploringly. 'I can teach both of you to summon massively powerful demons from the very depths of the abyss, use them to hunt down...'

'I am going to pass Nazahirim over to you now,' Dad interrupted, not even looking at Brash but scanning the room, checking their exit route. Marakoff too, was searching along the walls, his brow slightly furrowed.

Brash dropped his smile. 'I already have a demon.'

'Nazahirim is far too dangerous to be set free and you're the only other one here strong enough to hold him,' Dad said. 'It's just under two hours until dawn – holding Nazahirim will keep you occupied until the sun can do its work.'

Inside his prison of solid air, the demon re-doubled its efforts to break free.

'On three…' Dad said, raising his half-cupped left hand. 'One, two…'

'Wait,' Brash said.

'… three,' Dad opened his fingers and Brash's hand shot out. Dad's sphere disappeared and was instantly replaced by Brash's.

Dad slowly straightened up as if a mountain had been lifted from his shoulders. Nazahirim struggled violently in his sphere, eyes blazing and his body of black mist whipping around and around leaving trails of fire in its wake.

Violet edged closer to Brash and stared up at her master like a cat waiting to sink its claws into an injured bird. Brash held a smile too set to be genuine. 'Think, Richard.' he paused for breath, glancing down at Violet and shaking his head. His lips thinned further as he fought to contain Nazahirim and retain mastery over Xaphan, the name he'd called the demon possessing Violet. 'You will have nowhere to hide and no one to help you if you turn your back on me. Join us, this is the only way to win.'

Dad ignored him. 'Your men leave without their weapons. You radio ahead for a clear passage into the garages and...'

Brash's head dropped a fraction. His voice cracked just a little. 'Richard, I'm not sure I can hold Nazahirim and control Xaphan.'

Violet started plucking at his trouser leg with one razor sharp, elongated nail.

Dad smiled coldly. 'You'll manage. Now tell your men to leave.'

Brash held his pose for just a moment then straightened up. His voice returned to somewhere near its normal strength despite the sweat beginning to form on his forehead. He held Dad's eye.

'I may have to call your bluff here, old boy. Have you any idea how many armed men I have, how many of my own Gifted teams I've brought back in for this? You wouldn't get half way up the drive if I didn't want you to.'

Dad's voice came back, steady and cold. 'We have your daughter at gun point.'

Brash gave a short, harsh laugh and glanced at Jason and Anna. 'Jason has my daughter at gun point. Anna is his friend and he owes her his life. Most importantly, he suffers from the same affliction of scruples as do you. Neither of you would harm a hair of her innocent head.'

Marakoff suddenly slammed the butt of his pistol into Eddie's temple, pushed Jason aside and locked one arm around Anna's throat.

Then he shot her.

The bullet skimmed her forehead, burning a two inch welt across it. He moved the smoking muzzle to her temple. 'The Willows are valuable to you, Brash and so enjoy some hope of safety. I however, was to be eliminated during this attack, yes? I need to leave and your daughter is my best hope of doing so. Tell your men to go.'

Jason couldn't believe it. Eddie lay unconscious and bleeding at his feet and Anna stood stock still with a gun to her head and blood dripping all down her face. Marakoff couldn't kill her, he wouldn't let him. Jason moved towards Marakoff but Dad stepped between them.

'Enough,' Brash said. Jason could have sworn a smile flashed across his lips. 'Have it your way,' he turned to Jason. 'You see, Jason, I am not the only one who breaks the rules but at least I'm honest about it. There will always be a place for you with me, my boy, when you finally tire of your father's hypocrisy and turning your back on those who need you.'

'Save the speeches, Alan,' Dad said, 'you're convincing no one,'

'We'll see,' Brash said. He held Jason's eye for a moment then simply said 'Everyone out.'

Schmidt led the security out through the wall at a jog as Brash tapped an ear piece that lay hidden beneath his now sweat-slick hair.

'Jason Willow is to be allowed free passage out of the abbey – extend his access code. No one is to approach him or his party - two men, a woman and Anna Smith. Ready a Land Rover in front of the garages.'

Brash touched his ear piece again to end the transmission. His sweating and just the merest twitch at the corner of his mouth, were all that showed he was under any strain at all.

Violet still watched him whilst absently playing with her prize - this time stripping flesh off the skull and flicking it at Nahazarim's prison.

Alicia Sirensong stood quietly behind Violet, her face serene. Her twin machine pistols lay just a couple of steps from her black booted feet.

'Don't try to stop us,' Dad said, 'See Nazahirim burned, redeem this girl and give yourself up to the Council before...'

'Before what, Richard?' Brash snapped. 'Before the Brethren manage to bring through a prince and the World ends? The Watch will stand with me and it will be you who has to "give himself up". You can't just wander around with someone as valuable as Jason in tow. After tonight, you will have the every low-life Brethren agent in the World desperate to be the one who brings in such a prize.'

We're leaving,' Dad said.

Jason took a last look at the demon that used to be Violet. Somewhere in there was the girl he knew. The demon raised one eyebrow back at him and winked.

Brash breathed out deeply. 'One day, Jason, you will understand why I have to do what I do. When that happens, join me – for the sake of all humanity, join me.'

Jason didn't even look at him but turned to follow Dad towards the blasted out doorway to the infirmary corridor. Marakoff and Ilena trailed behind, Marakoff limping backwards with Anna between him and Brash.

'Release my daughter before you leave the village, Richard – it's not safe in Drunken Abbot... the Brethren survivors are trying to escape through there and the gentle townsfolk are hunting down anything that moves.'

'As long as your men are nowhere in sight,' Dad said.

'Oh they won't be.' Brash said. 'Let her go at the pizza parlour – Jason knows where it is.'

Jason gritted his teeth. *How did Brash know that? So Tanya really had been part of the plan to draw him into the abbey. How far back did Brash's planning go?*

'Concentrate Jason,' Dad said and then they were out of the training halls and edging along the corridor illuminated only by faint, pre-dawn light.

Ilena took over the lead. They saw no one, no one alive anyway. Jason tried not to look at the bodies pushed against the wall, there had been so much killing – Erin, Oliver, Carl and Sergeant Smith were all lying dead just a few rooms away. They'd all died to keep him alive and now he was turning his back on the war against the Brethren.

Ilena made for the outside door at the far end but Marakoff called her back. 'Wait, Ilena - we should try through the church. They will be less prepared for that.'

Ilena nodded and ran up the shadowed steps to the church door. Jason caught his breath. A glimmerman had been waiting for him there less than an hour ago.

'Clear' Ilena called and they followed her up. Jason tapped in his code and pressed his thumb to the plate. The door clicked unlocked and Ilena edged it open with her foot, twin Kalashnikovs at the ready.

Myers was waiting for them. He held a long barrelled pistol in one hand and a walkie talkie in the other. Two of the magnificent windows lay shattered over the floor and fresh air breathed through. Five black hooded bodies lay crumpled across the dais.

Myers slowly holstered his pistol and stepped back, hands in the air. His eyes flicked over to Anna, still held by Marakoff, then back to Ilena who had him in her sights. 'Good morning. Please come in, there is no one else here.'

They stepped in carefully. The place did seem deserted and strangely peaceful - almost as if the night-long battle had never even happened. The church was even display-lit to best show off its stunning architecture and treasure-filled alcoves.

'Please wait in the corridor,' Dad said.

Myers looked a little hurt but nodded genially. 'As you wish, Mr Willow.'

As he passed them he smiled sadly at Jason. 'Look after yourself, Jason – I do hope to see you again.'

And then he was out in the corridor and Dad closed the door. Jason wondered if he would ever see Myers again, or Eddie, Lance, Brash and Alicia or any of the others. Was this life, like all his others, to be totally left behind.

'Stay focussed, Jason,' Dad said, touching his shoulder. 'We're not out of here yet.'

They dashed through the massive nave, their footsteps echoing back at them from each alcove and ceiling arch. There was no one to be seen, nothing else to be heard. Jason unlocked the massive entrance doors and Ilena eased them open a little way to reveal the abbey's gravelled approach.

Brash's trap for the initial Brethren attack had been devastatingly effective. Outside, bright floodlights glared and silvered the drizzle that drifted silently over dozens of Brethren bodies. The corpses lay sprawled in tight groups around their burning and blasted vehicles, slaughtered, it seemed, the moment they'd tried to run. Some of them were even half naked. Perhaps they'd ripped off their black hooded robes because they were on fire or maybe they were trying to surrender. In any case, they'd all ended up dead.

The tree line that had hidden the ambushers showed no sign of life now and the garage and guesthouse windows lay dark and empty.

In the centre of the gravel a single Land Rover Discovery waited for them, its headlights on and engine running.

'There are, of course, many of Brash's men still in the trees and just back from the windows,' Marakoff said as they peered out around the half-open doors.

'Anything on the radio?' Dad asked. He'd taken out a machine pistol from somewhere - it looked similar to Jason's MK23 but had a long magazine snapped into the butt.

Marakoff had Anna's walkie talkie and ear piece. 'They have cut it off.' he shrugged.

Jason glanced at the pistol Marakoff still held to Anna's head. *Would he really shoot her if Brash tried to stop them.*

Anna caught him watching her and gave him a tight smile. He looked away, stopping himself from chewing his lip. *Was she in on this set-up from the start? Had she known her father had learned to summon demons, had put one inside Violet. Of course she had. She was the enemy as well now ... just like Alan Brash... and Fast Eddie and... just about everybody he'd met here who hadn't been killed in front of his eyes trying to keep him alive.*

'Stay close together, move quickly,' Dad said and stepped out through the doors.

They dashed out, taking the massive stone steps two at a time. Dad went first and Marakoff hobbled along behind him with his gun at Anna's back. Jason ran next and Ilena brought up the rear with her twin Kalashnikovs sweeping across every window, door and dead body they passed.

Nothing happened. Fifteen feet from the idling Land Rover, Dad held up his hand and they skidded to a halt between the burnt out husks of two jeeps which shielded them from most angles. Two Brethren had tried to find cover here as well. They both stared up at Jason with eyes pulled wide open.

Jason tore his gaze from the bodies and stared at his father's back. Dad was totally calm, totally focussed on the mission. He'd barely said a word to Jason since finding him fighting for his life against a demon. This must be the Dad of twenty years ago - Richard Darillian, the demon hunter.

Jason wasn't sure he liked it. The father he knew was gone... replaced by someone powerful, cold and ruthless. Was this how he, Jason, would become if he ever joined the Watch?

'Ilena,' was all Dad said and Ilena sprinted across to the Land Rover. Dad covered her dash with his machine pistol and Marakoff edged Anna back to watch their rear. The three of them were like some sort of machine, each part shifting and adjusting to support the others. Jason felt like spare baggage.

Ilena checked the vehicle doors, inside, underneath and then jumped in.

'Get ready,' Dad said.

Ilena slammed the Land Rover into reverse and roared back to them. The moment she skidded to a halt they scrambled inside. Ilena rolled over the seat into the back and

Dad took the wheel. Marakoff urged Anna into the back seats next to Ilena and Jason followed her in. Then Marakoff scrambled around to ride shotgun with Dad and they roared off.

Jason stared out of the back windows as they tore over the gravel and rounded onto the driveway. Slick from the rain, the black marble monolith of Darkston Abbey gleamed back at him under it's floodlights.

Another life lost to him.

The Land Rover tyres gripped firm tarmac and they shot up the drive. There was no one living to be seen. Dad ripped through the gears and the gatehouse loomed into view. Blasted, fire-gutted vehicles and scattered bodies forced them to slow down but in moments they were roaring beneath the massive arch and rattling over the fallen gates.

They were out. The thatched cottages of Darkston Village waited for them at the bottom of the Abbey hill, with the soft yellow of the old fashioned street lamps lighting their way.

As they closed in on the houses, Jason's eyes widened. Every window and door had was sealed with steel shutters.

'This whole village is a training ground, I think?' Marakoff said. 'Am I not correct, Miss Brash?'

Anna ignored his question. 'Are you going to let me go at the pizzeria as you agreed?'

Jason looked across at her but she stared straight ahead through the front window, not meeting his gaze. Blood was smeared over her face and an angry red welt from Marakoff's bullet seared across her forehead.

Dad switched his headlights to full beam as they roared between the first houses. There was no damage or debris to slow them down – the Brethren must have simply raced through the streets on their way to the abbey. It was clear no resistance had been offered – Brash had wanted them inside his trap as quickly as possible.

Finally Dad answered Anna's question. 'I'm sorry, Anna but we need to get further away from your father. I'm not convinced he's happy about letting us go. I'm afraid we'll have to hold on to you until we're clear of Drunken Abbot.'

Jason couldn't believe it. Dad always kept to his word. 'Let her go where we said, Dad. We'll be fine.'

Dad's voice was flat as he hurtled along the narrow streets. 'We need to get out, son – and we can't trust Brash. Anna will be safe enough where we drop her at the edge of town.'

'No, she won't. You heard what Brash said – the Brethren are escaping through the town and I know what the bloody lunatics who live there are like. No way are we leaving her there.'

'Brash's security will find her quickly enough – they won't be that far behind us.'

Jason chewed at his lip. They would be in the High Street in a moment and passing the pizzeria. He glanced at Anna. For the first time since they'd kidnapped her, she looked worried.

'We stop at the pizzeria or I'll blow the back end off the car,' Jason said resolutely.

'Enough theatrics, Jason – this isn't a game,' Dad said, his voice still level. 'We drop her as we leave Drunken Abbot.'

Jason breathed in deeply, drawing in the air's energy and forming an iron-hard glove around one fist.

Marakoff looked back at him from the front seat and held his eyes for a moment. Then he turned back to scanning the road ahead. 'I think he means it, Richard.'

'I know he does,' Dad said and hit the brakes. The Land Rover skidded to a halt despite its ABS system hammering madly.

'For God's sake, Jason, you'll get us all killed,' Dad swore but Jason was already getting out of the back door.

Despite his injuries, Marakoff was out next to him in an instant, cocking his pistol and scanning the rooftops. 'Please, no long goodbyes.'

Anna jumped down next to Jason. 'Thank you,' she said and, after a moment's hesitation, flung her arms around him and pulled him close.

'Did you know?' Jason said into her ear. 'Did you know what your dad was doing... to Violet?'

Anna stiffened and slowly pulled away. 'Yes,' she said. 'Jason... you don't know how many of our people are getting slaughtered out there. This is the only...'

'We have to go,' Jason said. 'Make him take the demon out of my friend.'

Anna just held his eyes. He knew she couldn't make her father do anything. She turned to jog towards the nearest house, quickly building up speed. The steel shutter hissed down from the main door as she approached.

'Get in – quick,' Dad shouted from the driver's seat. 'We'll talk about this later.'

Jason jumped back into the Land Rover and Marakoff took up shotgun again. Jason stared out of the window.

The cottage door swung open and Anna dashed inside.

Then the sirens sounded.

Anna's walkie-talkie burst back into life on Marakoff's belt. Schmidt's voice rang out. 'Brethren counter attack in the village. Secure abbey perimeter.'

'What is this?' Ilena said. 'Brash said that the Brethren were retreating through Drunken Abbot.'

Dad slammed the gearstick into first and floored the accelerator.

'Armed – seven o'clock,' Ilena shouted.

Three black cloaked soldiers burst out from the side of the pizzeria and skidded into firing positions behind its low terrace wall.

Ilena smashed the fixed bench-seat windows and let off three Kalashnikov bursts to keep their heads down just as Dad pushed his right hand out through his open window.

The wall and half the terrace burst apart and the three gunmen smashed back against the steel shutters of the pizzeria.

Marakoff suddenly started shooting from his side. He'd whipped out a second MK 23 pistol from somewhere and was emptying both magazines into a single black hooded figure sprinting towards them.

The figure stormed down on them despite Marakoff's bullets thudding into its body. It had to be Touched.

Dad floored the accelerator and sped away but the Touched dived for the back doors. The thin steel buckled with the impact but held shut as Dad swerved from side to side trying to dislodge the assailant. A second later the Touched ripped one of the twin doors right off its hinges.

Ilena pushed Jason's head down with one hand and fired her Kalashnikov with the other as Marakoff shot his twin pistols through the space where Jason's head had been.

The Touched roared and heaved itself into the Land Rover's rear section but bullets pounded into its face and body. It slumped to the metal floor – dead.

Ilena whipped out a bowie knife from her belt and hacked the head off before kicking the body out through the ripped-open doorway. She threw the head out after it.

'Bugger,' Dad said and pulled the Land Rover around in a tight arc.

They'd reached the perimeter fence but rifle shots rang out from a dozen black hooded Brethren crouching on the far side of a small pair of gates.

Ilena snatched up her Kalashnikov and returned fire through the open back as Dad screeched around a corner.

Dad slowed down. 'I'm guessing all the gates will be covered. We can't run through the perimeter fence, as it's reinforced and electrified. Any ideas how we get out?'

The sirens had stopped and it was now deathly quiet in the village. The Brethren counter attack seemed to be very "low key" and why were they trying to keep people from leaving the village?

'It's not the Brethren hunting us, is it?' Jason said.

Dad glanced at him in the rear-view mirror. 'I don't think so, Son - it's Brash's people.'

Jason's mind flicked back to the killing field in front of the abbey... some of the dead Brethren had been stripped of their clothes. Brash must have ordered his men to grab their Brethren disguises and get into the village the moment he realised he'd have to let Jason out of the abbey. The question was – were their orders just to stop them leaving or to kill them?

'Why bother with the disguises?' Jason asked.

'To confuse our decisions,' Ilena said as Dad pulled in to a small alleyway. 'Perhaps we would not leave the village if we thought the Brethren were...'

'However,' Dad cut in as he stopped the Land Rover, 'leaving the village is what we need to do. Again... anyone got any ideas?'

'I know a way out,' Jason said, '– two minutes from here. It's a break in the fence where the Skins sneak in to fight with the Brash. It's in the park where I got beaten up.'

Marakoff shook his head. 'Brash controls all the gang fighting, Jason. It is just another form of training for his... apprentices at the school. The way will be closed to us.'

'Maybe,' Jason said, 'but Eddie told me that it's always left open so they never know when the Skins are coming ... like a constant test for Brash Security. I don't think it's meant for cars though.'

'That is not a problem – we have made back-up arrangements on that side of the fence,' Ilena said.

Dad nodded. 'Two minutes – it's worth a go. It'll be a weak spot at the very least, even if it is sealed now. If we can get through the fence before they realise what we're doing we'll have half a chance...'

Dad hit the accelerator and they roared towards the end of the alleyway. 'Which way, son?'

***

In under a minute Dad was crashing the Land Rover through the main gates into Abbeywell Park.

'I think the gap's on the far side of those trees,' Jason said.

Wisps of morning mist rose from the branches. Dawn was coming, splitting the dark cloud cover with ragged cracks of lighter grey.

Accelerating hard, Dad slid them around the well on the damp grass and raced for the trees.

Suddenly tyres screeched behind them and two cars hand-braked into the road running past the park and waited, engines revving.

'It appears Brash has worked out our cunning plan, yes?' Marakoff said

'As soon as we stop, everyone out on the tree side. The three of you find the way out and I'll slow down our friends back there.'

More cars and Land Rovers joined the others and then, as one they surged forward and smashed straight through the fence after them.

Dad yanked the wheel and they slid broadside almost into the tree line. 'Go!' he shouted and they all clambered out into the trees using the Land Rover as cover.

Dad slipped out after them then punched out with both fists over the bonnet.

Two cars thirty feet away crumpled as if they'd hit the side of a house.

'Subtle, yes?' Marakoff coughed as he, Jason and Ilena scuttled into the trees.

'Move it,' Dad barked and turned back to the remaining vehicles skidding to a halt on the grass.

Ilena closed with the limping Marakoff and he threw one arm around her shoulders. They picked up speed as he took huge hops with his good leg. Jason took a last glance at Dad as gunfire and explosions began and then he was lost beyond the trees.

Thirty seconds later they skidded to a halt before the fence - electrified, fifteen feet high and topped with razor wire.

Marakoff immediately spotted the Skins' secret entryway - four square feet of wire was electrically isolated from the rest. It had been clipped and then hinged with clear plastic fastenings to make it almost indiscernible.

'I'm not leaving without Dad,' Jason said and pulled out his pistol.

'Glad to hear it,' Dad's voice called out of the trees a moment before he appeared. 'Now get going.'

Marakoff pulled open the isolated fence section and scrambled through into the garden of a derelict terraced house. Rubbish and nettles were everywhere and smashed windows stared out of the cracked wall in front of them.

'Wake up.' Dad hissed and pushed Jason through the gap.

Gunfire erupted behind them as Ilena sprayed her Kalashnikov into the trees. Dad dived through the gap then took over the covering fire through the fence as Ilena leapt through.

Marakoff stumbled over to them with an old metal bin held on a wooden plank. The moment Ilena was clear he jammed the bin sideways into the gap with the wood. Sparks flew from the fence as the bin ripped through the insulation and electricity leapt through the metal.

Dad threw up a shield wall and he and Marakoff backed through the garden whilst Ilena pulled Jason after her to the house, kicked in the back door and dragged him inside. Dad and Marakoff tumbled in and slammed the door as the first bullets thudded into the walls.

They were in a tiny kitchen that stank of something dead. Marakoff knocked out the remaining glass from its single window and shot at shadows flitting through the trees beyond the fence.

Dad tapped Jason's shoulder and the two of them scurried after Ilena into a narrow corridor running passed a rotting staircase. Ilena burst into a front room and raced to one side of a jagged window pane.

Jason and Dad followed her in. The street outside was empty, leached of all colour by the pre-dawn grey.

418

Ilena pulled out a small walkie-talkie like the one Marakoff had used in the abbey hours ago.

More shots sounded from the kitchen and Jason glanced back down the hall. Marakoff had his Kalashnikov trained on the dustbin-filled breach in the fence, waiting for anyone foolish enough to try to remove it.

'Louisa – thank God.' Ilena's cracking voice brought Jason's attention back into the living room. 'Are you all right? Brash said the Brethren were escaping through the town...'

Jason stared at her. Was Louisa in Drunken Abbot? He'd assumed she and Mouse would be safe in their cottage... but that wouldn't be safe now, of course - not if Brash was hunting for them. Was Miranda with her?

'Yes, yes, we have Jason safely with us,' Ilena said. 'We are just inside the town. We will meet you as arranged but you need to know – something has happened – Brash has summoned a demon and he does not want any of us to leave.'

A hail of bullets hammered through the window into the kitchen wall. Marakoff returned fire as best he could from below the window frame.

'I suspect that they have decided to... make their move, now.' he shouted above the gunfire.

'Or distracting us while others come around the front,' Dad said. 'We need to leave Ilena.'

She nodded and shouted into the walkie-talkie. 'I will call when we are closer to you for the pick up. Keep hidden my darling... we will be with you very soon.'

Marakoff crawled through from the kitchen, keeping his head down as lead ricocheted all around the room.

'Their guns are bigger than mine,' he said.

'Clear outside.' Ilena reported and Dad led them to the front door and out into Drunken Abbot.

Ilena raced into the lead again and they began to run. She seemed to know exactly where she was going through the warren of dark alleyways stinking of old urine.

She kept them to the most deserted rat-runs but even so they had to dive into rubbish-tip gardens or behind wrecked cars three times as huge-wheeled trucks roared past with men hanging out of the back. They were all armed with baseball bats, chains and machetes. A chopper droned over the town at one point but no searchlight from above sought them out.

Then they were forced to stop a fourth time when they heard the chanting of a crowd around a corner directly ahead.

'Here.' Ilena hissed and they dived for cover behind a rusting old Ford Transit van. A moment later a mob of twenty or more drunken Skinheads marched into sight parading their prize on a squealing-wheeled supermarket cart – a beaten and bloodied, half naked Brethren soldier with his hood tied tightly over his head.

'Doing just what Brash has conditioned them to do,' Dad whispered as they watched the pitiless parade stomp by. The men were jumping on each other and fighting for a chance to spit and punch at their victim.

Jason, pistol in hand, edged one eye around the van for a better look. He thought he recognized one of the Skins closest to them – a shaven headed girl with a thin ponytail…

Ilena's walkie-talkie burst into life. She instantly knocked the volume off but it was too late – the girl turned her head towards them and looked straight at Jason.

It was Rat-Tail – Lindsey Davenport, from Jason's bus. Her mouth dropped open and she stopped. A hugely muscled Skin immediately behind stumbled into her and swore. As he turned to follow her stare down the alley, Dad pulled Jason back behind the van and onto the floor. Jason gripped his pistol and they both watched from under the chassis.

Lindsey hesitated for one more moment, then slapped the Skin hard around the face. He bellowed a string of obscenities but she was already running after the rest of the mob. With a last glance down the alley, the Skin lumbered after her and the street was clear again.

'Get out of there … now.' Ilena was gripping her walkie-talkie tightly to her ear, her eyes and mind somewhere else. Jason focussed in. Despite the low volume he could just hear Mouse's voice.

Louisa's voice crackled back up over the radio '… they have definitely spotted us.'

Ilena's eyes were wide. She hissed to Dad. 'They've found them, they're coming to check the car... Lou...'

Dad snapped his fingers and Ilena passed him the walkie-talkie. 'Mouse - tell Louisa to start my car and run them down – this is not a game... do it now!'

A moment passed then Mouse's voice came back. 'She's turning the key but it is dead. It won't start. They're coming.'

Dad stayed calm, his voice strong and clear. 'The immobiliser has timed in. Press the padlock button on the key.'

A thumping and smashing came across the tinny speaker like the sound of bricks and bottles pummelling a car.

'Nothing's happening,' Mouse almost shouted.

'Oh my god.' Ilena scrambled to her feet and started around the van. Dad raced after her, still talking into the radio. 'The key battery's low. Hold the key next to the little black receiver by the rear view mirror.'

Jason helped Marakoff up and they chased after Dad and Ilena.

Seconds later, the engine over-revved massively through the speaker. Tyres screeched and the thump of bodies bouncing off the bonnet came through loud and clear. Glass smashing was the last sounds before Mouse cut in. 'We are away from them – Louisa ran over... oh hell– now a truck... a pick-up truck has found us.'

'Keep Louisa calm,' Dad said, as he slowed down to let Jason and Marakoff catch up with him. 'Tell her to ignore everything except driving to the back-up meeting point.'

Ilena was already at the end of the alley checking out the next street. She waved them on then sprinted out of sight. Dad carried on talking calmly into the radio. 'We're two minutes from the 'Abbot & Flagon. Get there and we'll deal with the truck.'

'Two trucks, now,' Mouse corrected through the screech of cornering tyres and thud of bricks on bodywork. 'Watch out for that post, Louisa!'

'Keep her calm,' Dad said. They caught up with Ilena and he gripped her free hand for a moment. 'Don't worry -

they're moving,' he took Marakoff's arm from Jason and flung it over his shoulder. 'Keep point, Ilena – the 'Abbot & Flagon'.'

Ilena nodded, glancing once at the walkie-talkie. Her daughter was driving for her life on the other end of that transmission. She dashed out into the next street.

It was one of the main thoroughfares through Drunken Abbot – Distillery Road - but it was like something out of war-torn Baghdad. Three cars were on fire, jagged glass clung to countless smashed window frames and a couple of telephone boxes lay ripped from their foundations. From somewhere further down the street a stereo blared from an upper window. Jason didn't recognize the thumping rock song... something about 'eating rifles' by the sound of it.

But for now, there was no one to be seen.

They raced along the street, leaping over the razor shards of windows and smashed bottles of Drunken Abbot Ale, thrown bricks and still-burning petrol bombs. They were no longer worried about stealth – they had to reach Louisa and Mouse.

Dad was back on the radio. 'Mouse – under your seat – a pistol. Flick off the safety catch and use it on the trucks – don't put your head out of the window to aim.'

Ilena glanced back at Dad, her face ashen, then flew into a sprint. Jason lengthened his stride to keep up with her but Dad and Marakoff fell behind despite Marakoff having one arm locked around Dad's shoulders and taking great hopping leaps in time with Dad's running steps. The ghost looked pale, sweating and desperately trying to keep his injured leg from being jolted.

Jason dropped back. 'Are you all right?' he asked stupidly.

Marakoff raised one eyebrow at him and hopped on.

'Sorry,' Jason panted, 'stupid question.'

Twenty metres ahead now, Ilena ran passed a pub just as the front door burst open. She skidded to a stop flat against the pub wall and span around as two burly drunks stumbled out.

The men froze. With their cropped hair, bright white football shirts and fingers studded with heavy gold rings, they looked like hardened pub brawlers. However, a beautiful woman dressed in a black cat-suit and carrying a Kalashnikov was evidently too much for them to take on alone.

The biggest one reached back for the slowly closing door, his mouth opening to shout.

Ilena was on him instantly and knocked him out with a fist to the temple. His mate swore and pulled out a cosh from his jeans back pocket. Ilena simultaneously stamped her foot into the side of his knee and pulled the door shut. The drunk crumpled to the floor.

Jason, sprinting to help, threw an air punch at the sinking man's head just as Ilena hit him from the other side. His eyes bulged and he was out cold before he hit the pavement.

Dad and Marakoff had used the time to catch up and they all raced away together without saying a word.

They ran passed the stereo-booming window. The music had changed, it was pounding out something about 'going underground' now. Ilena led them across the road and down a side street. Jason swallowed hard – it was very similar to the alleyway where Eddie had hidden the van during their mission into the 'Abbot and Lashing'. Oliver and Erin were lying dead in the armoury now and Eddie was probably hunting him down.

The roar of engines and two gunshots echoed down the alley to meet them.

'We are too late,' Ilena shouted back, slipping one of her Kalashnikovs from her back and sprinting ahead.

Dad's Renault estate roared passed the end of the alley. Jason caught a glimpse of Louisa at the wheel.

'Down, Ilena,' Dad yelled and Ilena threw herself to the floor.

Jason felt the zephyr of powerful Gift use rush past him and a shimmering wall materialised all across the road ahead. A second later an open-backed truck smashed into Dad's wall. Three men hurtled over the cab and slammed into the solid air as the truck burst into flame and flying metal.

A second truck, brakes locked, skidded past the fireball and slammed into the air-wall. Its bonnet crumpled like a crushed can and the windscreen exploded out as the driver and passenger hurtled through the glass. Two other men flew over the cab and smacked wetly into the wall from the truck back.

Ilena rolled to her feet from under Dad's shimmering air stream sucking in energy to form the wall. She snapped up her Kalashnikov and raked the wrecked vehicles with short, controlled bursts as the four of them raced to the alley's end.

Engine running, Dad's car waited thirty feet down the road. Dad dropped the wall and they sprinted past the burning trucks and bodies towards their getaway car. Louisa slammed into an engine-whining reverse to meet them as all along the street, curtains were being pulled back and windows opened.

Jason slowed down to stay with Dad and Marakoff. The roaming mobs would surely be drawn in by the explosions and any one of those opening windows might have a maniac behind it, maybe a maniac with a gun.

Louisa, a pistol-bearing Mouse beside her, screeched the Renault to a halt a couple of metres in front of her mother. Ilena threw up the estate's hatchback door and then covered the houses and street with her Kalashnikov as the others caught up.

'Back seat – quickly,' she said.

Jason dived into the cab and helped Marakoff as Dad darted back to slam the door on Ilena who had leapt into the back of the estate.

'Go!' Dad shouted, jumping in beside Jason.

'Where's Miranda?' Jason asked.

No one answered him as Louisa floored the accelerator and they wheel-span away as the first gunshots rang out behind them.

Chapter 26

'Dad – where's Miranda?' Jason asked again.

'Hold on a minute,' Dad said as they pulled clear of the town and sped into the pre-dawn light of the valley floor.

'Pull over please, Louisa,' Dad said, 'I'll drive, now.'

Louisa slowed to a halt and pushed open her door. The cool moors air washed over Jason as she and Dad dashed around the car to switch places. Louisa looked pale and tense as she got in but she gave Jason a tight smile before twisting around to stare out of the back window.

'Right - where's Miranda?' Jason asked as Dad wheel-span back on to the road.

'She's safe - in Darkston Wick.'

'But that's the first place Brash will look for her,' Jason shouted..

'We didn't know Brash was going to be hunting us down when we left,' Dad said. 'There was no sense in her risking Drunken Abbot and besides, there wouldn't have been enough room in the car for everyone.'

'So you just left her there?' Jason said.

'It would have been the safest place - the Brethren had no interest in the village,' Dad said, driving ever faster.

'Brash may think she is with us in the car,' Louisa said, now sitting next to Jason.

Jason chewed at his lip. 'Who's house is she at – our or yours? Brash knows she was staying with you... I told him.'

'Neither,' Dad answered. 'For all we know Brash might have all the houses wired and if the Brethren had somehow taken the abbey... She's hiding in the wheelhouse – it's clear of surveillance.'

Ilena spoke, braced in the boot section of the estate, searching behind for any sign of pursuit. 'With all the doors and windows still boarded up – it should be safe.'

Jason nodded... perhaps. It was no use arguing about it now – they just needed to pick up Miranda and get the hell out of there.

Marakoff sat on his other side, silently re-bandaging his bleeding leg. He looked pale, even through his rough skin and stubble.

It was getting lighter – the sun would rise in twenty minutes or so.

Jason sank back into his seat. Finally his body had relaxed enough to ache and he felt shattered. He closed his eyes and images immediately flooded through his mind.

He'd killed people – real people, not some computer generated graphic or cardboard target. He'd shot his pistol and seen their bodies jerk back with blood splattering out of bullet wounds he'd caused. He'd nearly been killed himself, a Glimmerman had been inches from him. A demon had got inside his head.

And his friends had died trying to protect him.

Brash was a Summoner – he'd put a demon inside Violet. 'Miranda, come in.'

Jason snapped his head around. Ilena was speaking into a walkie-talkie. There was no reply.

They'd reached the turn for Darkston Wick and Dad slid the car onto the woodland road and hit the accelerator. 'She won't be in range until we're out of the trees,' he said, as calm as ever.

No one spoke any more as Dad raced through the trees, flashing through the gears and cutting corners so tight that branches lashed at the windows.

At last they burst free of the woods and Darkston Wick appeared just a mile away. Nothing moved. River-mist trailed through the entire hamlet.

'Miranda – come in.' Ilena said again.

'I… I'm here.' Miranda's voice came over the radio.

Jason breathed again but caught Dad staring back at Ilena in the rear view mirror. Marakoff had turned around to watch her as well.

Ilena kept her voice level. 'We are nearly there. Come out carefully and wait in the trees until you see our car.'

There was a hesitation then the radio crackled back into life. 'Um… no. I feel safer in here. Come inside to get me… please.'

Ilena glanced at Dad's eyes in the mirror. He nodded.

'Of course, dear. Your father will come – he will be there in a few minutes.' She switched off the radio.

'What's going on?' Jason asked

Dad took in a breath. 'Someone has Miranda.'

'What,' Jason shouted, staring out of the window. They were half a minute away from the village. 'Who's got her – the Brethren… Brash?'

Dad floored the accelerator. 'Brash's men, almost certainly. The Brethren had no reason to come through here and they wouldn't know we lived here.'

'Unfortunately, Brash does,' Marakoff said. 'and we heard that chopper fly over us in Drunken Abbot.'

Dad brushed one hand through his hair. 'Ilena – I'll drop you all off next to your car and you get them out of here – take the old road so…'

'Hold on…' Jason cut in, then faltered as they sped passed The Old Mill. It was as dark and silent as an open grave.

'We've no time to argue about this, Jason…' Dad started.

'Then don't bother,' Jason said. 'There's no way I'm leaving here without Miranda.'

They hurtled past the shadowed facade of The Highwayman and the bridge stretching over into the dark of the trees. Dad began to slow down and glanced back in the mirror at Jason.

'There's absolutely no point in risking…'

Marakoff cut Dad him off this time even as he scanned every darkened doorway and misted garden. 'You won't change Jason's mind Richard. You are almost drained – it will take the three of us to help Miranda, I think.'

Dad skidded to a halt besides a battered green Land Rover but kept the engine running.

He only hesitated for a moment then nodded. 'All right, but…thank you, my friend.'

Marakoff was already getting out of the car. He flipped open the tailgate and Ilena leapt out with her Kalashnikovs.

'Clear.' Marakoff said.

'Louisa, Mouse,' Dad said quietly, 'thank you for everything. Now get out.' He managed a ghost of a smile.

Mouse smiled back then twisted around to Jason. 'Bring that lovely sister of yours out safely, yes? We will see you soon.'

Without waiting for an answer, he stepped outside and closed the door.

A pair of arms suddenly wrapped around Jason's neck. Louisa hugged him tightly for a moment then pulled back.

'Be careful. Come back to… us,' Louisa whispered then got out.

Come back to us? Jason thought. He would have preferred *"Come back to me."*

He stopped himself. He, Dad and Miranda might all be killed or captured within the next few minutes and all he could think about was how Louisa felt about him.

'Let's go,' Dad said and hit reverse. A moment later he span the wheel and pulled the handbrake and somehow they were speeding back towards the Old Mill.

'Didn't Marakoff say "the three of us"?' Jason asked.

428

'He'll make his own way there – no sense in letting them know where we all are. Now, check your pistol's fully loaded and do exactly as I tell you, when I tell you.'

Dad slapped a fresh magazine into the Kalashnikov with one hand as they swerved into the Old Mill's gravel drive. Dad span the car again and reversed up by the side of the house.

'What do we do now?' Jason asked.

Dad scanned the garden through all of the windows. 'We just go into the wheelhouse, see who's got Miranda and get her out.'

Jason nodded. 'What if Brash gets here before we've managed that?'

Dad looked out at the brightening sky. It could only be minutes before dawn. He reached over into the back seat next to Jason for his Katana. 'He'll be weak from holding Nazarhirim for so long, drained of far more energy than I lost from holding him for those few minutes. Brash won't be a problem.'

'And Violet,' Jason asked, '– will she be a "problem"?'

Dad's eyes flicked to his katana, then up to Jason. 'I really hope not.'

Jason didn't want to think about seeing Violet again – he couldn't deal with that now. They just needed to get Miranda out.

***

They both climbed out of the car, guns at the ready. The only sound was the gently stirring leaves above them, bright in the early morning sun.

Early morning sun – it was dawn.

Dad touched Jason's arm. 'In a few moments you'll feel a surge – like you feel when someone uses the Gift close to you… but it will be…'

'Hot,' Jason gasped. It felt like a furnace door had opened and a wave of heat rolled out over him and away.

Dad breathed slowly out – he obviously had felt the heat as well. 'That was Nazahirim – when a demon that strong burns in sunlight all the Gifted within miles of it get a blast. The more powerful you are, the more you feel it.'

He smiled thinly. 'It's a lot worse if you're closer – Brash will be flat out for the next few minutes.'

'Good,' Jason said. 'I hope he fried. Let's find Miranda before he gets up again.'

Dad smiled and led the way towards the river through the trees at the side of their house. He stopped in the shadows before reaching the back lawn.

For long moments they both stared at the watermill. Nothing moved that they could see. Jason hoped Miranda really was in there somewhere.

'Right,' Dad said, finally, 'whether it's the Brethren or Brash's lot in there they know we're coming so there's no sense in trying to surprise them. As neither of them want us dead, I think we'll just walk in through the front door and see what happens. Stay close.'

Dad took a breath then stretched both hands up and brought them down in an arc, palms out. A solid air hemisphere formed around the two of them.

He glanced at Jason and winked. 'Just in case I'm wrong about the 'not wanting us dead' bit.'

'Great,' Jason said, shaking his head.

They started walking down the gently sloping lawn. A couple of metres before the wheelhouse Dad lashed out an air-kick right through their shield and blew the doors in.

At the far end of the room, slashed with rays of dawn-light cutting in through the boarded windows, Miranda waited for them.

Jason swallowed hard. Miranda's lips trembled into a tight smile as she blink away the dust from the shattered doors. She moved forward to meet them as Dad nudged in front of Jason and stepped inside.

'DAD IT'S A TRAP.' Miranda shouted and lunged forward.

From nowhere, a bone white hand lashed around her eyes, pulling her head back as a knife flashed up to her throat.

'Don't move or she's dead.'

Jason and Dad froze mid-step.

Half of Cadaveril's skeletal face peered from behind Miranda's head. 'Slowly, throw your weapons over to me,' he said, his voice hardly more than a whisper.

Dad carefully lowered the Kalashnikov, one wrist brushing the small walkie-talkie at his belt. Holding the weapon's grip between finger and thumb, he flipped on the safety catch then tossed it at Miranda's feet. She stood just four steps away from them.

Jason followed Dad's lead and threw his pistol to the ground.

'The pistol and Katana as well, if you don't mind, Rich' old son,'' Cadaveril said, his blade rock-steady against Miranda's throat but his eyes constantly flitting over the shadows.

Without a word, Dad threw his pistol down and slowly pulled out the blade from behind his head. He threw it to one side of Miranda.

Dad spoke quietly and calmly, his stare never leaving the one eye Cadaveril showed from behind Miranda's head. 'Just stay perfectly still, Miranda. This man, Cadaveril, is a Ghost – an assassin. With that knife at your throat he can kill you before any of us could move. Don't try anything.'

Miranda made a small, strangled squeak. Jason felt his stomach begin to burn. If Cadaveril so much as…

'Good advice, Rich' – let's hope everyone here follows it,' Cadaveril said, this time not in a whisper but making his voice carry through the building and outside.

Jason concentrated on not chewing his lip. Cadaveril must suspect someone else was out there, someone with his own stealth skills – Marakoff.

'Arsen, Milos,' Cadaveril shouted, 'come down 'ere and cover the door. Jonas – sit over the hatch and give Mr Brash a call – tell him it's fine to fly in now. I've got it all sorted.'

There was a scraping above them and two burly security guards appeared in the open trap door and started climbing down the ladder.

'Surely you don't need three big gunmen to look after you, Cadaveril – you're holding a knife to my daughter's throat, after all?'

Jason winced inside but kept his face calm. It seemed so obvious to him that Dad was trying to pass information out to someone. Then it clicked – perhaps Dad wanted Cadaveril unsettled - his attention divided between watching them and looking for Marakoff.

Cadaveril grinned. 'Well I did want a bit of cannon fodder in case you decided to come in through the attic like us.' He glanced at the smashed-in door. 'But then subtlety aint really what you almighty Gifted do, is it?'

Dad just stared at him.

Cadaveril seemed to relax a little as the two Kalashnikov toting guards positioned themselves to either side of the doorway and another one appeared in the hatch above.

Jason stared at the guards. The open attic and the door were both covered now and boards sealed every window but no one seemed to be interested in the small door leading to the waterwheel. Marakoff could get in that way.

'Nice try…' Cadaveril's harsh East London tones cut into his thoughts, '- nailing up your pretty daughter in here with no cameras and mics. But you really should have guessed we'd have someone watching the place.'

Dad shrugged. 'I was trying to keep her safe from the Brethren, not the abbey. I didn't know your boss had turned into a demon-summoning traitor.'

'Talk of the devil…' Cadaveril grinned and nodded towards the door.

Outside the faint drone of rotor blades reached them.

This was it. If Brash landed with more men they would never get out. Jason moved a step to the right, drawing Cadaveril's eye further away from the waterwheel door.

'If you hurt her, I swear I'll crush every bone in your body,' Jason said, taking another step forward. 'I'll give you pain like you wouldn't believe.'

Dad shot out a hand to grab his arm just as Cadaveril eased his knife into Miranda's skin. Her eyes went wide but she didn't flinch.

'Possibly, my little 'ero,' Cadaveril said, '- but your pretty sister will be dead because of you.'

Jason's eyes locked with Miranda's. *What could he do – what could anyone do?*

A spotlight swept across the lawn and blazed into the room as Brash's helicopter landed on the grass. No one moved as the rotor blades slowed then finally cut out.

A few moments later, silhouetted by the helicopter's searchlight, Alan Brash made his entrance.

'My goodness,' he said, his voice somehow thinner than usual, 'I could cut the atmosphere in here with a knife.'

He strolled passed Dad and into the centre of the room. Others passed in through the doorway still blazing bright in the helicopter searchlight – Anna, Eddie and Alicia Sirensong. Finally, clothed in a hooded black boiler-suit, Violet dashed into the shadows.

'What's this Alan, just the four of you and your pet demon,' Dad said, 'or did you bring Jason's favourite mentor, Mr Schmidt, along in your six-seater Eurocoptor as well? Left him lurking around outside, have you?'

Jason forced down a wince – more obvious information giving.

Standing half in shadow, Brash frowned. He ran his eyes over Dad and found the walkie-talkie on his belt. He shot a vicious glance at Cadaveril then flicked a single finger at Dad's waist and blasted the radio apart.

Dad didn't even flinch.

Brash turned to Jason. 'To be honest with you, Jason, Sensei Schmidt has taken quite a shine to you – I wasn't sure how reliable he would have been coming to hunt you down. So it's your friend, Lance Van Garde, who's out there. He'd rather die than let anyone… unfriendly get inside and I'm sure you don't want any more deaths on your conscience, do you?'

Jason didn't answer and Brash finally let out a slow breath and smiled briefly. He shook his head like a kind uncle about to admonish a mischievous nephew for snaffling some biscuits. 'Enough of this posturing – we're all on the same side, after all… even though you did leave me in quite a pickle at the abbey.'

He stepped a little further forward and turned his hidden cheek into a thin shaft of sunlight. Jason gasped. An angry, red slash burned across Brash's face. The wound was made even more vivid by the fact the rest of his skin was as pale as mist. He wasn't standing like he usually did either – tall and powerful. He was bent somehow, drained of vitality.

'You dissolved Nazahirim's prison too early?' Dad asked.

Brash nodded and smiled thinly. His skin crinkled into ridges along the welt and he winced.

'A slight miscalculation. Nazahirim was boiling away very nicely but I was a little tired from holding him for such a long time and Violet was… testing my control somewhat. I took a chance Nazahirim was finished but there was just enough left of him to lash out a little demon-fire before he burst into flame himself.'

Brash tentatively ran one finger along his burn. 'Still, my lovely Alicia was on hand to patch me up.' He turned to Alicia and held out a hand.

Strong, poised and confident, she stepped out of the partial shadow to join him. The sun-shaft glinted off her overly bright eyes. *Had she been Touched?*

Jason shot a look at Anna, then Eddie. The searing red bullet path across Anna's forehead had been smothered in some sort of cream and Eddie had a clot of blood where Marakoff had knocked him out but apart from that, they both looked normal. They stared back at him – their faces unreadable. Were they all his enemies now?

434

Dad broke the silence. 'There's no need for Cadaveril to keep that knife at Miranda's throat,' He glanced at Anna. 'I let your daughter go unharmed, after all.'

Brash kept his voice soft. 'Only because Jason insisted you release her, I believe. The knife stays where it is.'

Miranda's eyes, scared but in control, stayed focused on Dad who nodded calmly then turned back to Brash.

'What do you want, Alan?'

'You know what I want, Richard,' Brash replied 'I want Jason... and you as well, if possible, fighting by my side and not running from me as if I was some sort of...'

'Demon summoner?' Dad cut in.

Brash gave a tight smile. 'I will do whatever it takes to destroy the Brethren.'

'Including killing us?' Dad asked, his voice so matter of fact that he could have been asking about the weather.

'If I'd wanted you and yours dead I could have made it happen any time over the past twenty years. All I wanted throughout those years was for you and Jason to join with me... to see that my methods are the only way we are ever going to win this war.'

'Your methods have left your ward screaming inside her own body, desperate to die,' Dad pointed to the darkest corner where Violet lurked, sucking on something that looked like a bone.

'Don't start lecturing me,' Brash shouted across him. 'This is the only way.'

'The Watch will hunt you down,' Dad said.

'I hardly think so.' Brash said. 'They need me too much. I've been busy while you've been hiding yourself away. I've trained and now run a quarter of the Gifted teams operating in the world today. Drunken Abbot sales account for thirty percent of the Watch's income and thanks to Violet's predecessors, I've been slowly addicting half the North's pub-going public to my brews over the last couple of years.'

'You've mixed demon essence into your ale?' Dad said coldly.

'Only a little teeny-weeny bit,' Brash answered, squeezing his finger and thumb together. 'Just enough to give a tiny boost and build up a little yearning for the next pint.'

'You're a sick, power-crazed, control freak,' Dad said.

Brash shrugged. 'Sticks and stones...' He turned to Jason and drew in a slow breath. 'Jason – this is your last chance to join us. Think of those friends who've died to keep you alive so you can fight the Brethren. Only these two survived, and they're both still desperate for you to join us.' He lifted a hand to either side, gesturing towards Eddie and Anna. Anna dropped her eyes, looking uncomfortable but Eddie met Jason's eye, nodding.

Jason stared back. 'You think it's right, do you, Eddie - what he's done to Violet?'

'Whatever it takes to win,' Eddie said. 'Your mate, Marakoff, knocked me out and shot Anna to get his way or had you forgotten that? Those Brethren bastards slaughtered Ollie, Erin... everyone in that armoury and we would have been next.'

'But it was Brash who brought the Brethren down on us,' Jason began, '- he's the reason Oliver and Erin are dead...'

'They'd have found us at some point anyway and you were the perfect bait to draw them all in when we were ready for them. We just didn't realise how many...'

'Thank you, Eddie,' Brash held up one hand and Eddie stopped mid-sentence. 'Now, Jason... we have a knife at your sister's throat and half the abbey security forces are motoring their way down here as we speak. You need to save everyone a lot of pain and do your duty... help us save the World.'

Brash made one of his usual arm waving flourishes but Jason was looking at Anna – *had she really known about her father summoning demons, possessing people even before he revealed Violet to everyone?*

Anna stared back at him now with a tight, perhaps apologetic, set to her lips.

Jason turned back to Brash. 'If I join you, will you...' he struggled to remember the correct term, 'redeem Violet - kill the demon and never summon them again?'

436

Violet's head popped out from the shadows, an almost comical look of surprise on her face. Then a snarl contorted her lips and the eyes blazed red.

Brash made a shooing motion with his hand, frowned in concentration and after a moment, Violet stepped back into the dark and carried on sucking her bone.

'There aren't enough Gifted, Jason. We need to use the demons.'

'Then I can't join you,' Jason said.

Dad placed one hand on his shoulder and squeezed.

Brash sagged a little. He still looked exhausted and pale. 'Well then, that leaves me with a small problem, I'm afraid. You see, I still have many powerful friends on the Council and the rest would most likely come around to my way of thinking eventually. However, if a couple of exceedingly Gifted types decided to spearhead a little rebellion against me, things may not go so well. Also, I really need a Triple Six on my side… one way or another.'

Jason frowned. *Was that a threat to Touch or even possess him?*

Anna shot a look at her father then turned to Jason and shook her head - it seemed she hadn't known about this particular plan.

Cadaveril tightened the knife on Miranda's throat. It was clear to everyone that negotiations were coming to an end.

'So here's the choice, Richard…' Brash continued, 'you leave peacefully with Miranda and disappear – forget the Watch as you have tried to do for the past twenty years. Jason stays with me to train in his Gift and act as insurance against you stirring up opposition.'

'And the other option?' Dad said, his head lowered and his voice starting to quaver a little.

'The other option is not so nice.' Brash said, straightening up. 'Cadaveril slits Miranda's throat, we kill you and take Jason anyway.'

'Stop this,' Anna said, stepping between her father and Cadaveril. As she moved she gave the tiniest of nods to Jason. 'You can't force anyone to join us. Just let them all go – and tell Bonehead to put his bloody knife away.' As she said this she grabbed Cadaveril's knife hand.

The instant Anna's fingers closed on Cadaveril, Dad punched out faster than Jason had ever seen him move before. Cadaveril hurtled backwards just as two bullets zinged through the space where his head had been and the ghost crumpled against the wall.

Marakoff, head and shoulder appearing through the waterwheel door, shot the two guards by the door even as Dad punched both fists at Brash and felled him instantly.

As Brash fell, Alicia leapt for Miranda. Jason slammed a hand forward, Miranda dived to the ground and Alicia's Touch-hardened body smashed right through the far wall and into the river. Sunlight burst in across half the floor.

Miranda rolled for Dad's Kalashnikov, stopped on her back and pulled the trigger at the hatchway above.

Nothing happened but Marakoff was already on it. Two more shots felled the security guard and he fell across the hatch. Something silver flashed from Dad's hand and ripped through a second guard appearing over the hook-hole above.

Then Dad staggered backwards, taking three air-blows in the chest in less than a second.

Fast Eddie.

Jason lashed out with a fan of five finger-darts but Eddie leapt to one side, landing unbalanced for an instant next to Miranda who was still lying on the floor.

She smashed one foot into the side of Eddie's knee, flipped to her feet as he dropped and knocked him out with the butt off her Kalashnikov.

'Thanks, Sis,' Jason grinned, 'even easier if you could find the safety catch,'

Miranda started fiddling with the weapon but there was no one else moving.

'Where's Violet,' Dad snapped flicking up his Katana with his foot.

But Violet had disappeared.

'She shot up the ladder, away from the light,' Marakoff said. Somehow he'd moved unseen over to the main door and was stripping the security guards of their Kalashnikovs and ammunition while keeping one pistol trained on the far wall.

Anna crouched down protectively over her father with Cadaveril still unconscious behind them both. She stared at Dad. 'You all need to get out of here – he's coming round and there's loads more security on their way.'

'Too right, we're going,' Miranda said, shoving Dad's Kalashnikov in front of Jason.   'Now - how the hell do I use this?'

Jason flicked off the safety catch and pointed to the trigger. 'Point and pull. Short bursts. Press this to change the mag…'

Brash's eyes flicked open. 'Violet – take them,' he gurgled through a mouth half filled with blood from his broken nose.

Jason air punched at Brash but Anna leapt in front of her father and took the blow. She crashed to the ground, clutching her ribs.

'No,' Jason yelled and snapped a second punch at Brash.

'Don't knock him out,' Dad shouted.

Too late. Brash's head and body jolted backwards and he thudded down onto the floorboards, unconscious.

That must have been what Violet had been waiting for. Garbed from head to toe in her sun-screening, hooded black boiler suit and gloves, she dropped down through the hatch above like a screaming banshee and landed over her unconscious summoner.

Coughing up blood, Anna scrambled across the floor to protect her father but Violet slapped her into the wall with a sickening crunch.

'Security is here,' Marakoff shouted from the door and began firing outside.

'Miranda – help Marakoff,' Dad ordered and stepped over to stand next to Jason – both of them facing Violet.

She'd pulled the insensible Brash into the shadows and was squatting on his chest, holding his mouth wide open. A dark mist burst out from her hooded face and streamed towards her summoner.

Dad lashed out a double air-punch. Violet span off Brash but she rolled easily onto all fours with the dark mist broiling back down her throat.

From the depths of her hood, Violet's eyes flared red and she leapt for Dad

As fast as thought, Dad's Katana hissed out of its sheath and sang through the air for Violet's throat.

The razor-sharp blade sank deep into an air brick an inch from Violet's neck as Dad dodged to one side just in time to let Violet fly passed him. She span in mid-air and landed in a crouch, her lips snarling back over gleaming white fangs.

Jason stood with his right arm outstretched forming the air brick which still held Dad's Katanna.

'You can't kill her, Dad,' Jason shouted, 'find a way to save her.'

Miranda's Kalashnikov rattled out deadly chaos across the lawn outside while Marakoff picked off targets on single-shot mode.

Violet hadn't moved. Her whole body shook and her face contorted through a spectrum of hatred and pain.

'Violet's fighting for control,' Dad whispered, 'I'll try to help her but I'm nearly spent.'

Jason released the Katana just as the demon won back control over Violet. She threw back her head and a hundred screeching voices burst from her mouth in exultation.

Dad cupped both hands and caught her in a shimmering bubble just like he'd done with Nazahirim at the abbey. Violet screamed, twisted and writhed against the translucent wall and punched the side of her prison.

Her fist burst through the air wall. Violet froze in amazement for one moment then, with a savage yell, she started to push her head through the weakening barrier.

'I can't hold her, Jason,' Dad hissed, 'Grab my shoulders from behind and push your Gift into me.'

'What?' Jason gasped, shoving his pistol in its holster and grabbing Dad's shoulders. Violet had head and torso were out now and a grotesque grin split half her face.

'Focus on sending your Gift through me as if I was just part of your arms – I'll do the rest. Dad yelled. 'Do it now, Jason, now.'

Jason breathed in then air-pushed out through both arms.

Dad went rigid as Jason's Gift ripped through his body and out through his own hands. The torn bubble flickered out of existence but a thick, shimmering air-shroud enveloped Violet's entire body.

Dad's eyes locked with the demon's red slits. He stepped forward with Jason in tow, grabbed Violet's skinny shoulders through the chrysalis of air and sent their combined Gift deep into the girl. Jason forced himself to keep pushing out. Xaphan was fighting them, trying to force the Gift back into Dad's body. If they failed, Dad would be wide open to possession.

Dimly, Jason heard furious gunfire and Miranda's voice from what seemed a mile away shouting that they couldn't hold them off.

Unearthly screaming voices ripped through the air, surged in volume, shaking the walls then cut dead. Violet sank to the ground. Black mist streamed from her mouth and a red-eyed spectre shot for the shadows of the upper floors.

'… coming, they're coming…' Miranda's voice erupted in Jason's head, almost drowned out by the deafening crackle of her Kalashnikov. Bullets hammered like hailstones against the thick wooden walls. Two boarded windows suddenly tore away and burst inwards under the deluge of deadly lead.

Violet lay crumpled on the floor, her eyes closed. Dad sagged to his knees next to her and a wave of exhaustion sent Jason down next to him.

Miranda's Kalashnikov clicked empty. Marakoff tossed her another magazine from across the doorway and sent her to shoot from the shredded window.

'We are nearly out of ammunition,' Marakoff called back to them. 'There will be a little more with the guards upstairs but…'

'Xaphan is up there,' Dad said, scanning the wheelhouse. 'He can't do much in spirit form but we need to leave…'

'Past the waterwheel?' Jason ventured.

'Too slow, they will pick us off one by one. We could…' Marakoff began then his radio burst into faint life.

'… are… way back… Are… receiving…'

'Ilena,' Dad said. He glanced towards the front where Marakoff and Miranda, now both on single-shot fire, were sheltering from the hammering security onslaught.

'We'll have to go out through the back and across the river,' he said, looking through the ragged hole made by Alicia's flying body.

'There's the rowing boat,' Jason said.

Marakoff's radio crackled again, this time, with a much stronger signal. 'We are half a mile away, can hear gunfire. Richard, Marakoff - report… please… report.'

Dad nodded. 'Marakoff, tell Ilena we'll meet her on the far bank. Then blow up the helicopter.'

Marakoff switched to his pistol while he spoke on the radio whilst Miranda flicked her Kalashnikov back to automatic. Dad turned to Brash, still lying unconscious. He drew out his own pistol.

'No.' Anna scrabbled over from the wall Xaphan had slapped her into and put herself in front of her father.

'He's unconscious, Anna,' Dad said. 'The second we leave, Xaphan will possess him. We will have an uncontrolled demon in the body of a massively Gifted host.'

Anna got up and started dragging Brash towards the door. 'The second you leave I'll have him out in the sunlight amongst dozens of security.'

Dad hesitated.

'You can't shoot him in cold blood,' Jason said, moving over to stand by Anna.

Then a single shot rang out from Marakoff's gun and the helicopter on the lawn exploded.

'Time to go,' Marakoff shouted, grabbing Miranda and rushing over to the hole in the back wall.

Dad took a second then holstered his pistol. 'Get him out of here, Anna, then blow up the wheelhouse… you might just get Xaphan. Jason come on.'

442

'Thank you,' Anna mouthed to Jason as she slowly dragged her father towards the door.

'Quick, son,' Dad said, his Kalashnikov trained on the front door. Marakoff and Miranda were already outside on the narrow wharf that ran river-side of the wheelhouse.

Jason ran across to Violet. 'We're not leaving her here,' he said and hoisted her thin frame over his shoulder.

'Of course not – silly me,' Dad sighed, 'now if there's no one else you want to save, let's get the hell out of here.'

As Jason climbed out he glanced back at Anna dragging her father to the door and Eddie stirring in the shadows. Would they still come after him?

Outside, Marakoff and Miranda were already in the rowing boat Jason had used that first day when arriving at the Mill.

'Look,' said Miranda, pointing across the river.

A battered green Land Rover was hurtling off the Old Road and onto the far river bank – Ilena.

'Into the boat,' Dad ordered. Jason still carrying Violet, clambered into the dinghy with Dad a step behind. Miranda and Marakoff pulled on the oars as Dad sent them cutting across the river with a Gift-powered shoved off.

'They're coming,' Marakoff said calmly, heaving on his oar.

'Shield wall, Jason, quickly.' Dad ordered.

As the first of the security guards appeared at smashed wheelhouse wall, Jason dropped Violet in the bottom of the boat and slapped up an air wall with both hands. More guards ran along the side wharf.

Dad breathed in and formed an air-stepping stone in his hands. He turned it horizontal, held it against his chest and shot the air support out horizontally to the wharf.

The boat surged towards the far bank, ripping the oars from Miranda's hands. The wake broke against the watermill and disturbed a body tied under the walkway.

Jason bit down on his bottom lip - it was Lance. Marakoff must have had to deal with him to get into the wheelhouse.

Bullets rattled into Jason's air-wall, hammering away any chance to mourn yet another death. Feeling sick and exhausted, he struggled to push more energy into their only defence. A few seconds later they grounded on the far bank with a jolt.

Ilena's Jeep roared over and skidded to a halt a couple of metres away just in front of the tree line. Ilena, Louisa and Mouse all leapt out on the far side and began shooting across the river.

'Out,' Dad said. 'Keep behind Jason's wall.'

Marakoff picked up the still unconscious Violet and struggled out first. Jason waited until last, shielding everyone with his wall and then edged off the boat backwards.

'Hurry,' Ilena said, 'their bullets are to slow us down – they will try to flank us.'

Marakoff's bad leg almost buckled as he tried to balance with Violet and negotiate the bank. Miranda and Dad both stooped to help him and that's when Alicia Sirensong dropped out of the trees.

She landed almost on top of Dad and pummelled him to the ground with two massive blows.

Miranda whipped up her Kalashnikov and shot Alicia at point blank range but the Touched slammed her away even as the bullets ripped through her flesh.

Even as Marakoff struggled to his feet and Jason pulled one hand from making his wall, Mouse rolled over the Land Rover bonnet, flipping out twin bo-sticks. He smashed them both into the back of Alicia's skull.

She stumbled back then whirled around to attack Mouse but he double-struck again just as Louisa stepped up beside him and shot her in the head.

Alicia span away in an explosion of blood and bone.

'Come on,' Ilena shouted, as she decimated what was left of Alicia's skull with her two machine pistols. Satisfied the Touched wasn't going to get up, she returned to shooting across the river.

'We have come to rescue you,' Mouse grinned, taking Violet from Marakoff and throwing her over his shoulder.

444

Jason widened his air-wall as Dad got to his feet and helped Miranda up. The wall flickered uncertainly now and the odd bullet was getting through at the edges.

'Mouse, get them inside,' Ilena ordered as they finally reached the Land Rover.

'After you,' Mouse said, dropping the tailgate for Miranda.

'I can't keep this up much longer,' Jason shouted, desperately trying to maintain his failing shield wall across the Land Rover's bonnet.

Ilena leapt into the driving seat, Mouse passed Violet into Miranda then he and Louisa and Marakoff scrambled into the back of the jeep.

'Right Son,' Dad said, calm as ever despite blood dripping from his nose, 'you can drop the wall – they won't risk shooting you.'

Jason let the wall drop and Dad pulled him into the cab.

The hailstorm of bullets switched to single shots, thudding into the mud by the tyres. Ilena threw them into reverse, hand-braked around and sped back towards the old road.

'Destroy the bridge, Jason,' Dad said as they bumped onto the cracked tarmac and skidded to a halt. He pushed open the passenger door.

'Dad, I'm drained. I don't think I…' Jason began but then the first of Brash's Jeeps skidded around the corner of The Highwayman inn.

Jason jumped out, took in a breath and pushed out with everything he had left.

A boulder of shimmering air hurtled into the middle of the bridge and blasted out half the road.

'Again,' Dad ordered, before shooting his Kalashnikov over Jason's head at the oncoming jeeps.

Gunfire rattling in his ear, his head swimming and his vision blurred, Jason moved further to the side and tried again.

A smaller bolt seared towards the bridge's keystone, smashing out great chunks of stone. The bridge shuddered and as the first of Brash's jeep attempted to cross, it began falling away into the dark waters below.

'Back inside,' Dad yelled, grabbing Jason's arm and hauling him in.

Ilena floored the accelerator and they roared up the Old Road and into the sheltering trees.

***

Deep within the shadows of the Wheelhouse attic, far from the sun's lethal touch, the demon Xaphan watched the boy escape while it finished repairing its new host. Pale skin knitted back together across a ragged wound in Alan Brash' forehead as his right hand casually wiped the dripping blood from his face. Both eyes flicked open again - malevolent slits of burning scarlet.

Xaphan pulled Brash's lips into a painful grin. It had been so easy, possessing the unconscious youth, knocking out the stupid daughter again and then possessing his summoner.

He was disappointed the Touched woman had failed his mental orders to ambush the humans once they'd revealed their escape plan. Still, she had paid the price of failing him.

Xaphan tested his control over the new body. Brash's canines mutated into fangs and back again. With all this host's Gift-power, memories and influence at his command, it would not be difficult to find the boy, Jason Darillian, once more, wherever he might choose to hide.

Of course, now he was inside his summoner's mind, he knew there was another option.

One way or another, Demon-kind would have their Triple Six very soon.

And then the Prince would rise again.

EPILOGUE

It began to rain the moment they crossed into Scotland. Heavy drops swept in dark waves across the foot hills and hammered at the camper van windows. Dad slowed down – even for him, it was treacherous driving at night on some back road as far from motorway, rail and airport cameras as they could be. To make things worse, they were hardly travelling in a rock steady, 4x4 Land Rover anymore.

Dad had bought the camper yesterday afternoon for cash in some huge Manchester vehicle lot. They needed to 'lose' Ilena's vehicle and besides, he'd explained, they might have to do quite a lot of travelling over the next few months. Dad needed to tell the Watch Council in the Carpathians the truth about what Brash had done and make sure no one argued it was acceptable.

The camper van had seven seats but only fold-down beds for four and one of those was a double. This would be a problem now Marakoff and Violet were travelling with them.

Violet. She hadn't spoken since her redemption from the demon, Xaphan. She'd barely eaten a thing and mostly just stared straight ahead, sitting and moving only when she was led. That was how she was now, belted into one of the back seats, staring out into the night without seeing a thing. *Had they really rescued her at all?*

Headlights flashed twice in Dad's mirror, the momentary change in light waking Marakoff who was riding shotgun. Ilena needed to talk.

Dad's walkie-talkie batteries had died last night and the remote, two-pump garages they stopped at didn't stock AAAs. They had to stay away from real civilisation. There were just too many police-linked CCTV cameras in high streets and the main petrol stations and what the police knew, Brash or the Brethren were likely to know as well.

Dad found a muddy lay-by and pulled over. Ilena's smaller Volkswagen dormobile, exchanged at the same Manchester mega-mart Dad had used, squelched in behind them. Like Dad's, her DVLA notification would sadly get 'lost in the post'. They didn't know how far Alan Brash's influence went.

Dad got out and cold, dark rain burst in for a second until he shut the door. His hunched silhouette brushed by Jason's window and clambered into the back of Ilena's Volkswagen.

Jason watched their shadows through the big back window. Ilena had come back for them when she'd seen the helicopter hovering over Darkston Wick. Mouse and Louisa had both insisted they couldn't leave without at least trying to help.

Now they were all on the run together, hiding from their former protector and whatever might be left of the Brethren in Britain.

Jason gave up watching Dad and Ilena's silhouettes and flopped back against the worn corduroy cushions. Miranda lay stretched out on the bench seat across from him - three quarters asleep and chewing her hair. In the front, Marakoff sat up straight – he was alert now and peering out into the dark.

Jason shook his head - it seemed their life of running away in the middle of the night wasn't over after all. Perhaps it never would be.

Miranda stirred, spitting out her hair and scowling as if it was somebody else's fault she'd the taste of conditioner in her mouth.

Despite himself, Jason smiled.

His mood quickly darkened again however as he looked over to Violet once more – her dead eyes staring into the night. More than everything he'd been through himself, it was his quiet, plucky friend from Silent Hill that had finally brought him to a decision. One way or another he'd train and grow in power until he could wipe the all demons from the face of the earth; then he'd deal with the Brethren and anyone else who would force a filthy, evil spirit into another human being. If that meant facing Alan Brash, then so be it – he just hoped Anna wouldn't be there to see it.

The driver's door banged open and Dad jumped in dripping wet. He gave a reassuring smile back to them and started the engine.

Jason's grand plan for saving humankind would have to wait for a while. For now they were heading towards Mawn. They needed to make sure grandfather was safe and warn him about Brash. Perhaps he'd travel to the Carpathians with them... just to lighten the atmosphere.

Jason forced down his dark mood. In these two battered old camper vans were the closest family and friends he could wish for – just eighteen hours ago they'd all fought to keep each other alive. Perhaps this was enough; perhaps just being surrounded by these people, wherever they ended up, was all the "home" he actually needed.

Two hundred miles to the north, another storm broke against a lightening-lit castle rising up from dark waters. The ancient stone paid the howling wind and rain no mind at all.

As it had for centuries gone by, the keep of Eila Doon silently waited for its family to return.

Want some more?

Jason Willow II
The Heart of Darkness

is on it's way.

www.jasonwillow.com

www.facebook.com/jasonwillow666